GOOD WITCHES DON'T STEAL

Academy of Shadowed Magic - Year Four

S.W. CLARKE

Cover: Covers by Juan

Proofreading: Kathy Waghorn

FREE SHORT STORY: Liara Youngblood and Lucian the demon prince clash in the prequel story *The Fae and the Demon*.

Join S.W. Clarke's reader newsletter and get *The Fae and the Demon* for FREE only at subscribepage.io/swclarke.

CHAPTER ONE

Maeve Umbra was determined to break me.

Across from me, she sat with a headmistress's patience, her fingertips touching in her lap. When I didn't speak, just held the mug of tea in my hands for a minute, her fingers rose in a staying motion. "If you aren't ready—" she began.

"No." I set the mug down on the coffee table between us—my first failure. "I just want to get it right."

She'd asked about my sister. How could I describe Tamzin Cole?

Umbra's head tilted, eyes lidded. "Tamzin was younger than you."

"By two years." My chest had heated, my hands colder. But I sustained the magic around me. "She was always sweeter, softer, easier."

"Describe her for me. I want to see her."

Damn you, Umbra. I sat back in the armchair, whose cushions had a marshmallowy give. My jaw had started an infinitesimal shaking, but I wasn't cold. Not really—just my hands felt icy.

I could do this.

My eyes closed. "Blonde hair, straight like straw. Blue eyes. Skinny as a colt. She was almost taller than me when..."

This time, Umbra didn't interject. Even though I wanted her to.

I wetted my lips, a preparation. "When she disappeared."

There it was.

In the other room, one of Umbra's grandchildren shrieked; Duck Duck Werewolf was that intense a game. Still, I sustained the magic. With the enshroudment around me, no one except Umbra—a master of the magic—could see or hear me. I was otherwise hidden from the world. One tendril of my hair kept tickling my cheek, the air cooling my heated neck.

Umbra had never asked about my sister. I didn't think she'd dare. But as she had told me on our first day here: "I will try you every day, child. And if you rise to the greatest of my trials, then and only then will you master enchantments. You'll be bombproof."

Bombproof. She knew exactly how to motivate me.

The armchair gave a creak as Umbra sat forward. "Tell me your clearest memory of her."

In the other room, both children shrieked, thumping across the rug. My hands went to the overstuffed armrests, squeezing. "I can't remember any right now."

"Tell me *a* memory, then."

She was relentless. Maybe she knew I could only think of one memory, my mind revolving on it like a spun top.

My eyes remained closed. "It was the night before." Before. That was how my life divided—not in terms of before and after I knew I was a witch, but before and after they disappeared from it.

"It was the night before," I said again. "Tamzin came to my bedroom. She knocked hard, and when I told her to go away, she said my name."

"What did she call you?"

"'Clem.' Always that."

"Go on."

The closer I got to the pain, the harder it was to sustain the magic. I could tell it had ebbed around me, my hair barely moving at all. "She said my name like she'd never said it before. Like she was indescribably sad or afraid. And..."

Umbra waited, the silence around us punctuated by a grandfather clock in the corner.

I had to do this. If I was going to be bombproof, I had to keep talking.

"She asked me if she could sleep with me," I whispered, heart galloping. "She wanted it so badly. She never asked to sleep with me, but that night she wanted it."

"Why?" Umbra asked, somehow further away.

I gave my head a shake, annoyance rising. "I didn't know. I still don't know. She just really wanted to be in my bed. Not our mother's—mine. She seemed afraid, breathless, so needy. And I…"

"And you?"

I couldn't remember anything else. My brain simply couldn't access it. My throat tightened, and I knew if I let one noise escape it, I would sob—a fact which I chalked up to frustration over Umbra's interrogation.

The magic fell away, my hair stilling around my head. When I opened my eyes, I stared at Maeve Umbra. She hadn't moved, her hands still clasped in her lap. A groove had formed between her eyebrows.

"Don't pity me," I said. "You can be disappointed in me. You can be frustrated. You can get angry. But don't pity me."

"I don't." She leaned forward, lifted her teacup. "But I do worry for you."

"Because I don't want to talk about the worst night of my life?"

"No, child." She swirled her spoon in the cup, tapped it on the rim twice. When she'd taken a sip, her eyes lifted to mine. "Because your self-loathing sits on your chest like a dark creature. And you invite it to."

I stood from the armchair, crossed my arms as I approached the fire burning in the hearth. Kept my back to Umbra. "That doesn't need to stop me from learning your magic."

"Doesn't it?" she asked. "Did you not drop the enchantment within two minutes when the shame overcame you?"

I reached toward the flame, hand diving into the heat until it licked my fingers. I encouraged it into my palm, played it over my hand like a ball trick. "No one else is going to press me about that night—about my sister—like you."

"Callum Rathmore knew about her."

I stiffened, my hand going still. "*So you're the sister*," he'd said that first night, outside the gates of Hell. And last May, he had promised me I would find her when I went after the blade in Edinburgh.

Not just her—my mother, too.

I didn't know who I would find, or in what form. Umbra was right to test my steadiness with the magic when it came to Tamzin. I just didn't *want* to be pressed. That was the truth.

But this was the path I had chosen. To reassemble the Backbiter, to descend into Hell, to defeat the Shade. And Umbra knew about the prophecy, and my involvement. When she'd offered to make me bombproof, it wasn't so I could get straight A's at Shadow's End.

She wanted me to defeat the Shade.

I turned back to her, straightening. "Try me again."

In the other room, one of the children yelled, beckoning his nana. Here in Switzerland, Maeve Umbra, the headmistress of Shadow's End Academy, was known as Nana.

She stood, swept out her robes. "The grandchildren will not be denied." When she came forward, her hand fell on my shoulder. "We'll do it again tomorrow."

I crushed out the flame in my hand. "We only have two more days here."

That familiar, sad look came over Umbra's face, and her fingers touched one of my curls. "Tonight, spend time with Loki. He understands the true meaning of restorative breaks."

"But—"

Umbra raised her hand between us. "A lesson I learned long ago: never argue with your headmistress when she's instructing you to take a rest." She winked, spun toward the doorway. "Now, which of you young kits asked for Nana?" she called out. As she disappeared into the other room, delighted shrieks followed.

Loki strolled in, tail upright, emerald eyes on me. "Don't tell me they're playing Duck Duck Werewolf again. Where does that woman find the energy?"

I stared after the headmistress. I knew she had recognized how much talking about Tamzin had affected me. She had given me space.

But all I could think of were her words as she'd held the porcelain teacup.

A dark creature sat on my chest, and I invited it to.

Umbra had enchanted the house outside Zurich. Her magic hung over the place like a gauzy curtain—which was very much how it looked, now that I had been trained to see it.

A pale blue gauzy curtain.

When I stepped outside with Loki, the sun hung over the far ridge, almost kissing it. The land sloped down to meadows, and a road pressed its way across the landscape toward us, rising up the hills until it passed under Umbra's curtain not a hundred feet from the house.

This was the magic that had protected the academy for all these years. I'd heard about it, but I hadn't properly understood until this summer. It was an enshrouding enchantment cast on a massive scale, sustained indefinitely.

I couldn't fathom the power that took. Even now, over a thousand miles away, the academy was still enchanted by her magic.

Maeve Umbra was the most powerful woman I had ever met.

Meanwhile, I couldn't even keep it steady around my own body. Press me a little, invoke my sister's name, and I'd drop the enshroudment like it was scalding.

"Gods," Loki said as we came down the front path, "you act like you've witnessed a death."

Maybe I had. I'd reopened the box of *that night*.

"I'm picking up the magic too slowly." I reached down, plucked a flower to twiddle between my fingers. "It frustrates me."

"Haven't you noticed by now?" He glanced up at me. "This is how slow you are with everything."

I pointed the flower down at him. "Eat pollen, smartass."

He was right, of course. For three years, I'd been wanting more, more, more. Always faster than I could reasonably learn, and always unreasonable in how I handled my own pace.

"But," he added, "it's kind of a beautiful curse."

We came out onto the main road. "How so?"

"You always push yourself. So you end up learning everything faster than most everyone while in a constant state of dissatisfaction."

I made a face. "Whoever that person is sounds wretched."

"Sometimes, but I don't think her wretchedness is all her fault. She did get dealt a questionable hand in life."

I scuffed my shoe over the road. "So my dissatisfaction is my beauty and my curse."

"Exactly. You'd be a great cat."

We had reached the edge of Umbra's enchantment—which, like one of her grandchildren, she'd asked me not to pass beyond. Not without her by my side. Now that the leylines were becoming corrupted, the game had changed.

According to *Witches & Wizards*, abductions had seen a huge surge over the summer. Curfews had been implemented all around the world. The Shade's army was becoming a virus. It was growing, spreading.

There had even been reports of flying creatures during the witching hour.

I'd talked to Eva, Aidan, and Liara a few times during the summer. They'd always assured me they were fine. Eva and Aidan most of all— she had guardians for parents, and Aidan *had* parents.

Liara didn't. But she was the most cunning fae I knew, and she hadn't left her sister's side since Umbra issued her warning to the academy's students early into the summer: *Stay home at night. Don't go near your windows during the witching hour. Your designated professor will come to retrieve you when the school year begins.*

When Umbra had made the warning, she had wondered aloud in the living room whether she was being too cautious, and then decided more caution was better than an academy student's abduction.

Beside me, Loki turned off onto the grass, following our usual path along the magical boundary. Meanwhile, I hesitated.

Until I was bombproof, I had to remain hidden. Curtained. Unseen by the world. Who knew how long that would be? Already I'd gotten cabin fever from a summer spent here in this house.

When Umbra took me back to the academy in two days, she advised me not to leave the grounds. Not to join the other guardians—

join Eva—on their missions until I could sustain my own enshroudment. But *they* still had to go out there. Every mage saved was one more to fight when the Shade's army arrived.

And they were coming.

We had agreed I had to master the enshroudment by the spring, but I planned to do it sooner. I wouldn't stay hidden from the world for the whole school year. Months back, I had made a secret resolution. I wouldn't let Eva go out into the world alone. Not her or the other guardians. I would push myself harder than I ever had. I would wear my dissatisfaction like a mantle. Embrace it.

By the spring, I wouldn't just be the only witch alive. I would also be the only witch who had mastered the enshroudment enchantment.

"Earth to witch," Loki called. "Did you malfunction again?"

I shot him a look, started through the grass toward him. "It's called thinking. You should try it."

"Unlike some humans, I'm capable of thinking while moving." His tail flicked as we passed through the grass. "Clem, how do you feel about all this?"

"What, Switzerland? I think it's like a picture, and Umbra's grandchildren are suspiciously well-behaved."

"The cabin fever must be bad if you're purposely misunderstanding me for your kicks and giggles."

My cat knew me too well. "Be more specific, then."

"The prophecy. Your future. A visit to Hell doesn't feel like it includes a round-trip ticket."

My heart quickened, or maybe my feet did. "What makes you think I've been feeling anything at all about it?"

"Because"—he fell into a trot to keep up with my new, brisk pace—"it's your life. The only life you have. And to sacrifice yourself..."

"I don't."

He paused to glance up at me, then rushed forward to remain by my side. "You don't what?"

"I don't feel anything about it, Loki. I don't think about it. This is my path—I accepted that when I picked up the deceiver's rod in the labyrinth."

He huffed. "You don't feel. That sounds healthy."

We didn't talk after that. Not as we walked, and not as we came back into the house to help with dinner. I spent a good five minutes scrubbing potatoes, determined to clean every groove.

Loki knew I felt. I knew I felt. But if I allowed it out in more than drips, little thoughts here and there, it would be like turning the faucet in front of me to high. Sometimes the faucet couldn't be stopped. Those times, I found a place to be alone until I could press it all back down.

Loki thought I was sacrificing myself. My only life.

The prophecy didn't mention what would happen to me once I defeated the Shade. Only that I would. But after all, how many people had ever come back from Hell?

Maybe I had already accepted the possibility that I wouldn't. Maybe I'd always felt an inevitability about my life, that it was destined to end early. Maybe...

Umbra appeared beside me, set a hand on my forearm. "Are you scrubbing, or creating art?" She gave me a small smile, pressing my hand down until the potato dropped into the colander.

Normally I'd make a joke about food art, but all I said was, "After dinner, can we continue with the training?"

"Of course." She patted my shoulder, turned away. "As we shall on the morrow, and on the way back to the academy. And we'll even begin practicing on Loki."

From a counter, Loki gave a sharp report of a meow. "'Let's practice on the cat,'" he grumbled. "Not something the cat ever wants to hear."

Umbra laughed. She'd clearly understood the feeling behind his meow, at least. "You should be glad. Imagine all the morsels a cloaked cat might steal from dinner plates."

This time, Loki's meow was far more pleasant.

CHAPTER TWO

Two mornings later, I tied my cloak at my neck. All my belongings—including the weapon—were hidden in the tangibly manipulated pocket at its hem.

I had never told Umbra where I kept the weapon. And she hadn't asked a second time. It wasn't that I didn't trust her—after a summer spent together, I did. Mostly.

But after Frostwish's betrayal, I wouldn't show the weapon to anyone else. Not unless they were Eva, Aidan, Loki, or Liara—or they were my opponent, and I was in a bind.

No, that was one secret I wouldn't share. Not even with Umbra.

We had a light breakfast with Umbra's daughter—a sweet, keen-eyed woman in her late twenties—and the daughter's husband and two children. Loki entertained the children from the edge of the table, walking lightly in circles with an arched back as they petted him.

When it was time to leave, Umbra hugged her daughter and the children with more emotion than I'd ever seen from the headmistress. Like she hadn't seen them in forever, and wouldn't see them in forever.

And yet they were maybe the safest people of all. Their home would remain under Maeve Umbra's enchantment. From what I understood, only a few mages in history had ever learned to enchant like her.

I didn't even expect to rival her—only to become good enough to do what I needed to do.

When she knelt to the little girl and boy, she pulled toys for each of them out of her robes like a magician. Two tiny walking sticks appeared, rubbed smooth like her staff. They'd been imitating her all summer with thin branches they'd plucked from the ground, in absolute adoration of the old, grand woman.

The children cried with delight. And again when they realized their grandmother was leaving.

When we came out of the house into a cloudless morning, I squinted over at her. "You sure the Shade's infecting the world?"

She drew in a deep breath, eyes drifting the length of the landscape. "It's hard to believe when you emerge into a day like this, isn't it?"

Loki appeared beside me, blinking up into the sky. He'd always hated direct sun. "Bring on the darkness."

I tsked him as we started down the path. Then, as we came through the gate and Umbra's white hair glinted into my eyes, the question I'd had since the beginning of the summer came back to me. "Umbra," I began. "How old is your daughter?"

She pressed the gate shut behind us with her staff. "Twenty-six. Where has the time gone?"

I didn't know how to be graceful about this. So I just said it. "You must have had her late."

"Yes." She pressed a little bit of mirthful air from her nostrils, as though remembering. "Quite late."

I paused, then barreled right into it. "How old are you?" She must have been in her fifties when she'd had her girl...

She glanced at me as she walked, lips curling. "How old do you think I am? If you say anything over forty, I'll fail you for the year."

She'd evaded my question. "That's fine. You aren't even one of my professors."

"Aren't I?" She tapped my ankle with her staff. "How do you expect to learn my magic without even a paltry year's worth of lessons?"

I stopped. "You're going to be my professor?"

She and Loki kept walking, her staff tapping along the road. "Keep asking like that, and I may very well change my mind."

"That's my witch," Loki added in a singsong voice. "Can't ever contain her dismay."

I caught up to them. We were about to pass through the curtain of her enshrouding enchantment on our way to the train station. "It's just me in the class, isn't it?"

"Yes." She paused at the edge of the enchantment; it shimmered in front of us as though caught in a breeze. When I'd first been trained to see Umbra's enchantment magic, I'd never expected it to be white. But not bone-white, or even antique—more like the palest shade of blue. "Come next to me. I'm going to enshroud you."

I stood next to her. "I'll enshroud myself."

"Not for this trip, child." She swung the top of her staff in a small circle, bits of electricity sparking around it. "You will have your chance. Be patient."

When she touched the top of the staff to my breastbone, electricity zinged through my body, my heart clenching and then giving a jarring, large beat in my chest. Around me, flashes of lightning peppered my vision, disappearing and reappearing as the enchantment took hold. If I had cast it on myself, I'd be seeing nearly transparent flames circling my body. The enchantment derived its power from your element, and fire worked a charm.

That was, if I could maintain it for longer than a half hour. And that was when I wasn't stressed. So for all purposes, I was invisible to the world. Except for one half-demon.

"Cute trick," I said. "I give it a B+."

Umbra snorted. "I'm not the wizard I used to be, but it'll do." She turned her gaze down to Loki. "And you, my dapper man, shall be my familiar for the day. What do you say?"

His tail flicked in the air. "My allegiances are to one witch."

Umbra reached into her robes, pulled out a small tin. When she opened it and sprinkled it over Loki's head like fairy dust, I said, "Is that catnip?"

"Yes, child, it is." She flashed me a grin. "You never know when it'll come in handy."

Loki closed his eyes, nose raising. "More."

I prickled with jealousy. "You conjured that, didn't you?"

"Certainly did." Umbra gave another sprinkle, then closed the tin back up. "Off we go, then."

Loki darted after her, eyes focused upward, already a junkie. That was all it took. Why hadn't I ever thought of conjured catnip?

We boarded our train in downtown Zurich—the same line we had taken to get here in May. It would take us just over a day to arrive in Bucharest.

Aside from her love of trains, Umbra had said she didn't trust the leylines. When I'd asked her what would happen if we parted the veil of a corrupted leyline, she'd only said, "Nothing good."

When I'd asked her why we didn't take a plane, she'd laughed. "The only thing I want carrying me through the air," she'd said, "is a litter on the shoulders of four shirtless men."

Loki and I had exchanged a look. So Umbra did have eyes.

As I'd learned over the summer, Maeve Umbra was in fact human, and an old-fashioned lady. Her sense of technology seemed to have paused around the time cars became ubiquitous, and sometimes I felt like the one guiding her.

Like, for instance, when I took her smartphone from her and brought up our ticket for the conductor. He appeared at the doorway of our roomette not long after, his eyes only on Umbra. She was the only one he could see. Well, her and the cat.

After the conductor left, Umbra stared at the phone's screen like it was itself magic. "My daughter insisted I have this. You'd think for someone who can call lightning from the sky, I could manipulate a bit of plastic and metal the size of my palm."

I sat back for the ride. "There's a learning curve to everything."

She eyed me. "That sounds familiar."

"Can't say I don't pay attention during your lessons." I nodded at her phone. "The ticket said we've got a stop in Vienna."

"Yes. No direct trains from Zurich to Bucharest, I'm afraid. And even if there were, the whole of Europe travels in August." By which she meant we'd gotten the only tickets we could get.

"Hmph." Loki licked one paw from his seat on the windowsill, the world now rolling by. "Don't suppose it had anything to do with procrastinating on booking those tickets."

I could have given her flak for waiting too long, but it was enough just to know that Umbra was human. That she had a few of my flaws.

And, more importantly: the situation this summer had been touch and go. For much of it, she'd hoped we would be able to travel by leyline on our return, that we could find a way through the veil back to the academy.

That hadn't been the case.

The Shade's army had seen to it.

"You don't think we're at risk?" I nodded out the window, visible through the skein of Umbra's enchantment magic. "When the sun goes down, that is."

"The train has one thirty-minute layover in Vienna. Outside that, we'll be in motion. And that's assuming anyone will be looking for us in the first place."

If Umbra was confident in our safety, then I couldn't ask for more.

We spent the rest of the day in the roomette, and even took meals there. Sometimes Umbra and I trained, and sometimes we read books, and sometimes we were silent, just looking out the window.

I couldn't leave our room. And while I'd thought it would be torture in such close quarters with Maeve Umbra, I found the opposite was true.

She was clever, and funny, and a fine listener when she wanted to be.

"So," she said after a time, her fingers running along the edges of her book, "Callum Rathmore. I certainly don't blame you."

I nearly inhaled the bite of rice pudding I'd just taken. When I'd finished coughing, I took a long drink of water, avoiding Umbra's eyes.

Meanwhile, Umbra smiled like a grandmother who'd just stumbled correctly onto my secrets. Thank god Loki was asleep on the windowsill, his faint reflection passing through the countryside in the dusk.

I set my spoon back in the pudding. "You could have warned me."

"I had expected feelings, but not ones that strong." Her head tilted. "If he came to help you in Siberia, I hope you know what that means."

I stared at her, waiting.

"The moment he turned his blade on Ora Frostwish, he turned against the Shade. He lost control of her army. He put himself at her mercy."

My gaze dropped. Once more, I saw a thousand of her creatures rushing toward us across the snow. Blackness on whiteness, and he was only one man.

"I left him there." I swallowed past a rock in my throat. "I left him because he told me to. I didn't think. I wasn't thinking." I paused. "Did I leave him to die?"

Umbra pressed her meal aside, leaned forward, her eyes a gravitational pull. "Tristan Rathmore would never kill his only son. I imagine he still hopes Callum will retake the mantle, and so he keeps him."

"Keeps him?"

"In Edinburgh." She lifted the latest copy of *Witches & Wizards*, passed it to me. "The Mages' Council has convened in the last week, and that's where they'll stay until the threat has been dealt with."

The threat. She meant the Shade.

I opened to the dog-eared page, skimmed the article. "Callum was on the council."

"Once. No longer."

I set the magazine on my lap. "You think he can't leave?"

"If I know the Rathmores, I know it for a certainty." She unwrapped a mint from her tray, set it on her tongue. "And that's why you're going to master enchantments, my child."

A slow-dawning understanding filtered through me. "I don't just need to enshroud myself." *I also need to enshroud him.*

She gave a single nod, her mouth working over the mint. "If you have the heart for it, Callum Rathmore deserves to be free. He's proven himself, has he not?"

"Yes," I said. "He has."

As I said it, my fingers curled, squeezing tight, the conviction like a weight settled onto my chest. I would save Callum Rathmore like he had saved me. I would get him out of Edinburgh.

"Good." Her head tilted. "Do you know why he's a half-demon, Clementine?"

"His father's a full demon?"

She waved dismissive fingers. "There hasn't been a full demon for hundreds of years. No, it's because a demon's blood is so potent, it cannot be easily diluted. So if anyone were to mate with a half-demon, their child would be no less than half of one. Something to consider for your future offspring."

This time, I nearly choked on my own mint.

Umbra set a hand over her mouth as she yawned. "Gods, I truly am old. I think I'll call for the turndown service."

When the train's attendant arrived, Umbra requested that the second bed be made specifically for her cat. Meanwhile, I tried not to snort in the corner.

When the beds had been made, Loki and I took the top one for the night. Umbra came to stand beside my bed, her hand lifting, only her thumb extended. "Just a caution, child." When she pressed it to my forehead, I felt the soft electricity of her magic.

Sleep well, Umbra said into my mind, patting the bed. *And I ask that you not leave this room tonight. Not for any reason.*

Before I could say anything, her face had already disappeared, and I was alone on the bunk with a cat curled up at my side. Umbra really knew how to tuck you in.

CHAPTER THREE

I woke to thunder, pattering on the roof. Then, Maeve Umbra's voice in my head: *Be still. Don't speak.*

When my eyes opened, the train's motion had stopped. Around me, darkness and stillness. Loki still slept by my side.

I lifted my head, glanced right. A form stood in front of the door to the roomette, where the curtains had long been drawn. Umbra's white hair was silhouetted by an ambient light from the outer window.

She pulled aside a corner of the curtain, forming a small triangle to see the hallway beyond. She listened, watched.

As though she sensed me, her head turned, eyes on mine. She gave an infinitesimal shake of her head, recognizing my body language. *Don't move, child. Someone is on the train.*

Someone.

What time was it?

My eyes moved to the digital clock across the room: 3:34 a.m.

A strange old fear gripped me. It was the same fear I'd felt the night I'd been abducted from my bedroom. It was also primal, from childhood, back when I'd been helpless. Back before I'd known I was a witch who could ignite fire from thin air, who could paralyze with a few words.

That helplessness swept over me like ice water. I had to lie here and wait on my back. I had to hide again.

A scuffing sounded on the train platform. A man's voice called two words in a language I didn't know. And far down the car, footsteps thudded inside the train.

I've placed Loki under my enshroudment with you. Keep him close, and I'll be back shortly, Umbra said to me. She grabbed her staff, unlocked the door. Just like that, she slipped out, and I couldn't even question her. Couldn't even object because I didn't have the connection to her mind like she did mine.

She'd left me alone.

She closed the door behind her, and I went on staring at it through the skein of her enshroudment. She must have masked her footsteps, because I couldn't hear her at all once she'd left the roomette.

"Loki," I whispered.

He crawled up close to my head, fur tickling my cheek. "I'm already awake. I woke when we stopped."

"Did you hear someone on the train?"

"I smelled them." He paused. "The scent is stronger now."

"Scent of what?"

His green eyes glinted in the dim light as they focused on me. "The creatures."

As he said it, a scrabbling noise sounded up the side of the car, like something was climbing it. And then, having reached the top, it began moving down the length of the roof.

"Wouldn't the conductor have noticed?" I whispered to Loki. "There are regular humans on this train, aren't there?"

"Almost all. Umbra chose this train for that reason—so we wouldn't be suspected."

Much good that did.

Then it hit me. "The humans can't see the creatures. That's why they've done nothing."

"Right. The humans think it's a regular stop in Vienna. They haven't heard or seen a thing."

The scrabbling drew near, and my eyes lifted to the ceiling. Above us, what sounded like claws scraped lightly over the metal and paused directly overtop us.

I went still. My hand automatically went up to my neck, and I found the moonstone. Even if Umbra's enchantment failed, I still had this to protect me.

And I still had my own magic.

Nothing moved on the roof, but the footsteps inside the car came nearer. They thudded down the hallway, a man's walk, and I wondered why the Shade's minions had come to this train full of humans.

All my senses were reduced to two: hearing and sight. My face turned toward the door as the footsteps came closer, closer, and I began to understand I might have to fight. Except I'd hung my cloak on the hook across the room. The weapon was inside.

Fool of a witch.

"I'll go and see." Before I could stop him, Loki leapt off the bed, landing silently atop one of the seats with his fur lifted. As he did, I watched Umbra's enshroudment slide off him.

So much for keeping him close.

From above, I began to make out the sound of sniffing. The creature on the roof above us was sniffing the air—but it couldn't have scented me. I was enchanted, which blocked all scent...

But Loki wasn't.

And now that he'd fought the Shade's creatures more than once, it was possible they had his scent.

I leaned halfway off the bed, and my hands went around Loki. I pulled him tight to my chest as the latch to the door clicked. And out of new instinct, I wrapped my own enshroudment around the two of us in case Umbra's didn't take. I did it just the way she had shown me a hundred times over the summer: closed my eyes and focused on the space around me.

Igniting a flame wasn't the issue; I could do that in a second. It was spreading the flame, directing it into a contiguous shape. In this case, it had to form around my familiar. And it had to be invisible. That part I'd yet to fully grasp, as well as sustaining it.

But the door was about to open, and I knew it wasn't Umbra. Her footsteps weren't thudding, or even audible. This was someone else—

someone who shouldn't be here at all. Who, I sensed, was working with that creature above us.

So I sent the flame out over Loki's body, enshrouding him. I didn't know if it had worked, if the guise would be complete, but it was this or fight. And in a space this enclosed, a fight wouldn't go well for me. If one of those things touched me, it would sap my fire.

The fire swept around Loki, warm under my skin—invisible, I hoped—just as the door opened slowly, creaking.

My eyes remained shut to maintain the enchantment, and for a moment I recognized this feeling as Umbra's test in the days before we'd left the house in Switzerland. She'd stressed me by asking about Tamzin, because little else could affect me more than the memory of my sister. The guilt. The grief. This was all that mattered: sustaining the magic under stress.

Distantly, I heard breathing from the doorway. It sounded human, not like a creature from Hell. But by the way Loki's claws dug into my shirt, I knew this was no regular human.

This man was with them.

All remained silent in the roomette. I could imagine him standing in the doorway, a rectangle of light cast over an unmade bottom bed. And up above, the covers had been kicked low from the top bed, as though whoever had lain in it had left. (Thank god I had been too warm to keep them on.)

But why were both beds used and empty?

Where were the passengers?

That was the question. That was why the silence persisted as I pictured him surveying the room, his eyes passing over the vague outlines of our belongings.

Finally, a footstep. Then another. He had stepped fully into the room.

I forced my eyes open, turned my head right. And then I saw him —again. The reason for my night terrors. The sole figure responsible for my fear of the dark.

He stood over six feet tall, clad in lacquered black armor that reflected the light. The plates of it were sharp-edged, knifelike in their angles. From his helmet, two horns angled toward the ceiling, whittled to points.

I had forgotten those details. But I hadn't forgotten how he'd made me feel.

Years and years ago, he was the one who'd appeared in the night. Approached my bed. Stood so close I could reach out and touch his sabatons.

And then the next morning, my family was gone.

Here on the train, the point of a sword's sheath jutted from his back, coal-dark. The crossguard and grip sat left of his head, waiting for his hand to take hold.

All at once, he came to within a foot of me, so close I could smell him. His scent hit my nostrils—a strangely familiar musk, almost over-ripe—at the same moment as my hand lifted straight out toward him, ready to blast him with flames.

My whole arm shook. I couldn't make it stop shaking.

He bent to the bottom bed, yanked away the duvet and sheets. When he straightened, I prepared myself. My palm went out, invisible to him, only a foot from his darkened face.

It was almost like he could see me. But that was impossible—I was cloaked. Protected. Invisible to everything and everyone.

When he reached out to inspect the bed, I would hex him. My lips were already parted, the words waiting on my tongue. Then I would blast his face off.

A second figure stepped inaudibly into the light from the doorway. Feminine. Long-haired.

Umbra.

It was about goddamn time.

Her staff went out, the tip pointed at his back. A pinpoint of white light appeared there, grew to blinding proportions, and then I heard the crack of lightning.

The window next to me shattered out onto the platform, and the intruder's body slammed into the beds with a grunt and the sound of plate armor shifting.

This way, Umbra barked into my head.

But I was already in motion. Half-blind, I'd swung myself off the bed with Loki still in my arms. I hit the ground with bare feet, eyes searching to make out the one thing I needed.

My cloak.

I spotted the outline of it in the corner. Umbra had already stepped forward and grabbed my arm, but I reached out, yanked it off the hook. Then we were through the doorway and into the hallway of the train.

"Maeve," a guttural man's voice called from inside our room. *Him.*

She slammed the door shut behind us, touched her staff to it. Lightning surged up and down the seam, electrifying the whole thing.

I wouldn't want to touch that, even with plate armor on.

Loki climbed up onto my shoulder as I pulled on my cloak, tying it at the throat. Umbra was already in motion, and I was close behind her.

Don't use your fire, Umbra instructed me as we started down the hallway. I noticed her enshroudment swirled around her now, too. *Whatever you do, do not reveal yourself.*

At the end of the narrow hallway, a creature appeared under the light. One of the Shade's monsters. Where the light should have hit it, it stopped at the creature's hide, repelled in other directions.

This one rose from four legs to two, red eyes appearing.

Umbra pointed her staff at it, and with a single blast of lightning, she scored a hole through its center and into the outer door. The creature dissipated into smoke, issuing through the hole.

I'd nearly forgotten Maeve Umbra could kill the creatures in one strike, like Liara. Oh, my jealous heart, be still.

Before she could keep on, I grabbed her hand, turned her to me, and pressed my thumb to her forehead. *Now*, I said into Umbra's head, *you're not the only one with the talking stick.*

She shot me a split-second glare, spun away. *Come, Clementine. We must be off this train.*

Didn't need to tell me twice.

Together, we passed down the hallway to the short staircase leading down to the entry. She went ahead, staff pointed. When we reached the door onto the platform, a single small crackle of lightning destroyed the door mechanism in an instant. Then she raised one foot under her robes and kicked the door open.

Eva was never going to believe me when I told her about that last part.

We came onto the platform, the two of us enshrouded, and found a dozen more of the creatures outside the train. Their attention had been drawn by the sound of the door opening, and by something else.

Inside, that same guttural voice yelled three words in a language I didn't know. It was sharp, rasping, angry.

It was him. The intruder who somehow knew Umbra on a first-name basis.

The creatures were in a frenzy, at least a half dozen rushing the ajar train door.

We backed away slowly. *We're enshrouded*, I said into Umbra's head. *So they can't see us, right?*

The door flew open again, slamming into the side of the car, and out stepped the intruder. He dropped onto the platform with his sword already unsheathing, his head turned in our direction. He reminded me so much of... Callum Rathmore. Of Lucian the prince.

But this man wasn't him. I didn't even know if he was a man at all.

They can't, Umbra said. *But he can. Run, child.*

CHAPTER FOUR

As one, Umbra and I turned and ran down the platform. One creature leapt off a car above us, a silent specter, and Loki's claws digging into my shoulder were all that clued me in. Even Umbra didn't notice.

My eyes lifted, the whispered words coming easily. *"Pairilis síoraí."*

The creature hit the ground in front of us in a heap, fully paralyzed. We rushed around it; Umbra didn't even pay it any mind, like she trusted I'd have taken care of it myself.

She had larger concerns.

Ahead of us, creatures rushed down the platform toward us, some atop the train, some running along its side, completely sideways in some strange defiance of gravity.

They sensed us. They couldn't see us, but I'd paralyzed one. And behind us—I took the briefest glance—the armored man or demon or wraith of the night encouraged his minions forward.

Which meant we were enclosed from both sides.

Umbra came to a halt, her hand on my arm, nails digging in to stop me.

What—, I began, but she was already lifting her staff, both hands gripping it like she held a solid weight and needed all her strength for what she was about to do.

The tip of her staff began to glow, and with gritted teeth, she drew the glowing end through the air, cutting a jagged, imperfect seam in the veil.

We weren't near a point of power. We weren't at a leyline.

And yet Maeve Umbra was parting the veil anyway.

As she went, her face was illuminated by the staff, a sudden sweat beading on her forehead. It was an awful job, like a child cutting cloth with safety scissors, but she did it as fast as I could have on a good day.

She cut four feet down to the ground as, before us and behind us, the creatures converged. And it was in that moment of absolute adrenaline a rational thought occurred to me.

Pass, child, Umbra said into my head. *The academy awaits.*

But I couldn't properly see through the part in the veil. I couldn't see the trees and the leaves and the forest.

The leyline outside the academy might be corrupted. *That* was the rational thought.

I didn't voice it, because I trusted Maeve Umbra. I trusted her more than I'd even realized, because I obeyed her at once. I didn't obey without trust, and I didn't have time to properly contemplate how she'd come to occupy that place of trust.

Maybe it was our summer in the mountains of Zurich. Maybe it was that she'd helped me more than once. Maybe it was because she was, simply, Maeve Umbra.

I stepped through the opening in the veil. And as I did, I came into a greater darkness than I'd ever experienced.

This was total darkness. This was obliterative, an absolute lack of light. Like light had never existed and would never exist.

Umbra and Loki came through after me, her shoulder touching my back.

I spun back toward the platform. The veil was already reseaming, everything disappearing. The train, the creatures, the light. "Wait," I began.

"Oh gods," Umbra said by my side, just as the veil fully closed.

And then I didn't hear her again.

When I reached out for her, I swiped through empty air. I reached again and again, turning, until I realized I was stepping on slick, marshy ground. The air had gone cold, clammy, and something brushed against my leg.

I jerked, only to hear Loki say, "It's me."

I took a breath, reached down for him. When I found his furry body, I picked him up, and he crawled onto my shoulder.

"Well," he said, his voice small in the emptiness, "this is bad."

"Where are we?" I breathed.

"I don't know."

I snapped my fingers for fire. None came. I snapped again, and still no spark. But the creature inside me had raised its head. The Spitfire had come alive, even though I hadn't called on it.

This *was* bad.

Around me, a strange, dark magic brewed, so thick I could almost swallow it like liquid. And from somewhere in the void, squelching steps sounded through the marsh. Plod-plod, plod-plod. They weren't human, but they sounded recognizable. A creature I couldn't place.

And they were nearing.

I listened, tense, the Spitfire's head raised in my chest. Loki's claws dug into my shoulder as the plodding neared.

"A horse," I whispered. "It's a horse."

The noise came closer, closer, and a great exhale sounded—a horse sending all the air from its lungs out its big nostrils. Its breath carried over my skin, and the horse's hooves went still.

I waited. No sound. The Spitfire remained in a stasis, peering out.

"Who are you?" I called, my voice at once smaller in this place and more demanding.

A pause, and then:

"Who are you?" my own voice returned. Except the words were laced with sureness and silk. It was my own voice, but with feelings I rarely felt. As though I belonged in this place. Owned it.

The Spitfire's head rose higher, intrigued. Desirous.

I knew I was being toyed with.

"Clementine," I said. "Clementine Cole."

"Clementine Cole," the voice said. "Why have you come here?"

"I'd like not to be." My fingers clenched in fear, anticipation. "I want to pass through. Where is Umbra?"

"Umbra." The voice was soft, higher. Wistful. "Maeve Umbra."

"That's right."

"She's not here. She has passed through—left you behind. Once and always a deceitful wizard." The voice paused. "You wish to pass?"

"Yes."

"So pass."

I swallowed. "I don't know how."

A soft laugh. Still my voice, but not, like my voice box had been inhabited by someone cool and coy and full of darkness. "The creature inside you knows. Allow it some agency."

The Spitfire. She meant the Spitfire.

As soon as I focused on it, its wings extended, flaring to fill the center of me. And as I had throughout my childhood, I heard its voice.

Except I had always thought it was my own voice. Just the anger in my head.

Part the veil, Clementine, the Spitfire said, easing its way into my arms, my wrists, my fingers. It wanted some control.

"Clementine," Loki whispered.

The horse stomped in the marsh. "Who is that?" the voice asked. "Is that your familiar, Clementine?"

Loki shrank against my side, and because I so much wanted out of this place—so much wanted to protect Loki—I allowed the Spitfire to have its control. At once, its impulsiveness and anger and wildness took me.

My finger lifted, the creature filling me with its fire, and as I set my fingertip to a spot in the air, a red flame appeared. With a blade's swiftness, the Spitfire parted the veil in a quick motion, head to gut, revealing the world beyond.

When I stepped through to the other side, moonlight streamed over me. The trees moved in a nighttime breeze, and the Spitfire receded.

I swayed on my feet, woozy. Feeling wet and sticky and *tainted*.

When I dropped to my knees, Loki hopped off my shoulder, turning to stare at the space behind me.

"Well," he said, deadpan. "That was bracing."

I set one hand on my thigh, glanced back. The part in the veil had closed itself up, and I could see nothing of the world I had inhabited. Not the void, not the train station. And when I looked around me, I didn't see Umbra, either.

We had made it to the academy. But not at all in the way Umbra had planned.

"Clem." Loki stepped closer. "How did you do that?"

"Do what?" I breathed.

"You parted the veil in that place." He paused. "It was the creature she mentioned, wasn't it? The thing you used to call the Spitfire before you knew I could talk."

"Yes," I said, soft. "It was the creature."

"I think"—his tail flicked—"we weren't properly in the world."

"I think I agree with you."

I couldn't bring myself to say it, but the thought came: *We were in Hell.* Or some shadow realm adjoined to it.

When I stood, my head pounded, and a strange lingering taste filled my mouth, like bile. My heart still thundered along, the adrenaline not fully receded. I only knew one thing: we had to get to the academy. It was only there, under the enchantment's protection, I could properly think.

When Loki and I had walked a couple minutes down the path, someone stepped out from behind a tree in front of us. A hunched figure with a walking staff tapping through the leaves, white-haired—

"Umbra?" I said.

Her eyes met mine, her hair half-wild around her head. She looked haggard, like she'd been in a gale storm. "You made it. Thank gods, child."

Before I could speak, she came to my side and was bringing me down the path toward the academy. She walked fast, her hand on my arm, Loki trotting alongside.

I took a glance over at her. "When you parted the veil..."

"Not now. We're vulnerable."

Her eyes held a strange, feral light like I had never seen before. The only other time I had seen this look on her face was in my first year, when she'd told me not to bring my anger into her office.

She'd looked at me like she was afraid of me then. Now, I didn't know who or what she feared.

When we finally came through her enchantment and onto the academy grounds, Umbra let go of me. She came to a stop by an old tree, leaning against it, her eyes on the ground and one hand on her thigh as though catching her breath.

I came to stand in front of her. "The leyline outside the academy is corrupted."

She gave a soft nod, not raising her gaze.

"That's what happens when you pass through a corrupted leyline," I said. "You're caught in that place."

"If you don't possess the power to escape it," she said. "Yes."

"And you escaped."

Her eyes lifted now, meeting mine. "As did you."

My fingers curled at my sides. "I met someone in there. She mocked me, mimicked my voice." I hesitated. "It was the Shade, wasn't it?"

Umbra's eyes widened. That look again. And then she covered it as quickly as it had come, as though she hadn't wanted me to see her naked emotions. "I suspect so. What did she say to you?"

"She asked me my name, and she told me to part the veil if I wanted to pass." I didn't mention the Spitfire. I didn't like talking about it.

Her throat bobbed as she swallowed, her head falling back against the tree trunk. "As I thought." She exhaled through her nose, straightened up. "What's done is done."

"What does that mean?"

"It means"—she began walking down the central path toward her office—"that the Shade now knows where we are."

I followed. "But you came through the veil outside the academy, too."

"Except I did not meet her." Her eyes met mine for a moment. "I did not meet the Shade. She did not watch me pass through. But take heart: she cannot penetrate the enchantment."

My body stiffened, and I stopped for a second before continuing beside her. "The Shade made herself sound just like me."

"She is the mistress of disguises," Umbra said. "With your voice, she could engender your trust. She could talk to you, and you would talk back. You cannot help but trust the sound of your own voice."

I shook my head, eyes on the ground. "That man on the train. Whatever he was... he led the creatures."

"Yes," Umbra said. "You encountered Tristan Rathmore."

Of course. That was why he seemed so familiar.

He was Callum Rathmore's father.

And then it clicked—for both Loki and me.

"He's retaken the mantle," Loki said by my side. "He's retaken it from Callum. He's Lucian now, isn't he?"

I glanced down at Loki, back over at Umbra. "What's happened to Callum?"

We had reached her office now, though I didn't even remember walking through the grounds. Umbra stopped, her hand on the door, and turned to me. A soft sadness entered her eyes, and the hand left the door and fell on my cheek.

"Don't tell me he's dead," I breathed.

"No," Umbra whispered. "I don't imagine he is. He is too important, too powerful to his father and the Shade be wasted so soon. But if he betrayed her on the tundra, as you said, with Ora Frostwish as witness, then his father would have hunted him down."

"And what?"

"Retaken the title and captured his son. I imagine Callum now resides in a prison cell in Edinburgh. He's likely being indoctrinated back into serving her. Maybe worse."

A band tightened around my chest. "We can't let him stay there."

Umbra sighed. "Child, I can see in your eyes there's nothing I can say to prevent you from venturing into Edinburgh after him. But I will say this: give me time. Allow me to make you into the witch who could topple that city at its foundations."

A chill went through me. "You could do that?"

She nodded at me. "*You* could do that. My only role is to guide you to your true power."

Time. She needed time.

When Umbra left me standing outside her office, she asked for my promise not to leave the grounds until the leyline was secured. She had work to do to bring the rest of the student body here safely.

And I couldn't do anything for Callum Rathmore in the meantime, except to learn. To grow in power, as I had been doing.

I turned to Loki, who stared up at me. "Way to kick off our fourth year," he said.

CHAPTER FIVE

That afternoon, the stables were empty of people and full of horses. Just the way I liked it.

When I came in through the half-door, I already knew Quartermistress Farrow was away; Umbra had told me she was retrieving students somewhere in Canada. But what Umbra hadn't told me was how Farrow could keep the stables running without anyone here to run them.

She'd only said, "I've enchanted the place a little in the quartermistress's absence."

I got a proper answer when I stepped into the aisleway.

A sturdy broom swept past me, pushing bits of hay and detritus from one end of the aisle out into the paddock. It didn't have an owner. Or, I should say, its owner wasn't anywhere nearby.

Maeve Umbra would never deign to sweep. In fairness, who would, if you could animate a broom?

A flake of alfalfa flew from the hay room and into a stall, landing with a soft thump on the bedding. A second, then a third, a fourth went out, all flying to different stalls of their own volition.

When I stepped forward, I found Siren with her head in the alfalfa, eating away. But no one was around to have fed her. Also Umbra's doing. In fact, all the horses were having their afternoon meal.

Loki slipped through the door, cat-leapt two feet in the air as the broom rushed toward him in its mindless cleaning. "Gods, you could have warned me."

I glanced over at him. "You're a cat."

"Fair." He leapt onto the half-door of Siren's stall, watching with catlike intensity as the broom moved. "A bit strange, isn't it?"

"The broom, the hay, or the fact that, all this time, I mucked stalls and cleaned horses when Umbra could have used her magic to make it happen?"

"Bitter much?"

"Only a little." I turned away from Siren's stall, approached Noir's. As I did, his head swung out over the half-door, black eyes finding mine. He was as magnificent as ever. And thoroughly my horse; his knee kicked the door just a second later, and the whole thing shuddered against its latch. "I'm guessing Farrow would say the work builds character, or that she prefers to do it herself."

Quartermistress Farrow was the only mage I'd met who used her magic so little it was easy to think she didn't have any at all. It wasn't until she'd placed the magical corks in Noir's shoes last May that I'd remembered: Yes, Farrow has magic just like the rest of them.

But she preferred calluses on her hands. And she almost never left her world here, which meant every professor was needed to escort students.

Noir nickered as my hand went up to stroke his face. Every summer I missed this horse, missed the feel of riding him. But this past summer had been exceptional, because I had never felt more vulnerable.

And I realized now, being with him again, that he brought me a sense of security. Stability. Safety. Just like Loki, he was for me, and I was for him, and now that we had ridden over a lake together, unfreezing it as one, I didn't want to go away from him for months again.

I needed—wanted—him with me in whatever I faced.

"Isn't it curious, though," Loki said, "that Umbra has never animated anything else on the grounds?"

I scratched Noir's jaw. "Maybe she does, at night or in the summertime when the students are gone, and we don't know it."

"I've prowled these entire grounds at night, and during the summer we stayed here," he said. "Trust me, nothing was animated."

He must be right; he was, after all, out every night since we'd arrived at the academy. I turned. "Loki, do you remember what happened for us to pass through the veil from that train platform?"

"Sure." His tail swished. "Umbra used her staff to part it."

"But we weren't near a point of power."

"No, we weren't."

Noir nudged me with his head, and I went on scratching under his chin. "How did she do it, then?"

"That was the exact question on my mind. Well, beneath my abject fear and active attempt not to piss myself."

The broom swept down the aisle between us, and we both watched it.

Somehow, Maeve Umbra could maintain the enchantment over miles of academy grounds, over her family's home outside Zurich, part the veil without a nearby point of power, then go on to secure the corrupted leyline, and animate the stables as she did so.

She seemed awfully powerful. Maybe she had never properly shown her hand before, or maybe...

"You know," Loki said, "the scent of her magic has changed from when we first met her."

I focused on him. "How?"

"Hard to explain. Deepened, grown more complex. Like cooking garlic on a pan."

"You're saying Maeve Umbra smells like garlic?"

"It's an analogy, pleb. She smells more like... bread. Before she was white bread, and now she's sourdough."

"Sourdough, right." I paused. "What does that mean?"

"She's grown more powerful." He gave me a slow-blink. "Just like you have."

I didn't want to know what my magic smelled like to him. He'd probably say farts, and then I'd spend the rest of my life carrying that around like a tiny, unforgettable millstone.

"Interesting," I said. When my hand lowered, Noir slung his head over my shoulder as though he was listening in on the conversation. "When Milonakis explained parting the veil in our first year, she never even said it was possible to do so without a point of power nearby. It wasn't even an option."

"It isn't supposed to be," Loki said.

"But Umbra can do it. Why?"

"That's a question for your favorite egghead."

He was right; this was the kind of puzzle Aidan North would dive into with undivided gusto.

But North wasn't here yet. It was just Umbra, me, Loki, and the horses. Which left one option.

I glanced at Noir. "It's been too long since you and I have jumped the paddock fence together."

It took Maeve Umbra three days to secure the leyline, during which our lessons together were put on hold. She wouldn't allow any of the other students to return to the grounds until the work was done. And she refused to let me outside the grounds to witness her magic, but at the end of each day, she returned haggard. Exhausted.

One night, on her way back to her home, I asked her, "What does it matter if you secure the leyline if the Shade knows where we are?"

"It matters," she said with thin patience, "because we cannot be caught in that dark place if the leyline belongs to us. You know from what you saw there that few would escape her realm."

"Could she ever take the academy now that she knows where it is?"

"She knows the academy is near, but she cannot as yet penetrate my magic. If we are careful not to travel during our nighttime, and a bit lucky, we shall evade her until the right time."

The right time.

I didn't know whether Umbra meant the second Battle of the Ages, or when I would take the Backbiter down to Hell to confront the Shade.

Maybe they were one and the same.

On the third day, when Umbra's work was finished, she allowed the other students and professors to return. Soon, the academy grounds were brimming. A large crop of first-years had arrived, at least twice the size of my class.

With the uncertainty in the world, Shadow's End Academy had become a haven for young mages. So many had wanted to enroll, some had to be turned away for lack of places to house them. Even then, some classrooms had been repurposed as dorms. It couldn't have been an easy decision for Umbra, but I found it heartening.

In the face of so much darkness, here we were.

The students arrived in groups, led by professors. Aidan traveled with Professor Goodbarrel and a gaggle of first-years, the two of them leading the group. When the group arrived, I watched them from the landing of my dorm. And seeing Aidan's brown hair, I came down and met him in the clearing.

"North," I called out, and he broke off from the group. "Good to see you with your head still attached."

A wry smile appeared. "And why wouldn't it be?"

I came up to him with folded arms. "Haven't you heard? The world's going to hell."

"I've done more than heard." The wryness disappeared. "The United Kingdom's gone into nighttime lockdown. Too many kidnappings."

My eyebrows went up. "I hadn't heard that."

"You wouldn't have. The Mages' Council didn't want it known— Edinburgh wants to give the impression of sturdiness in the face of what's happening."

"By which you mean the formalists in Scotland."

He shrugged. "They're one and the same. They remind me of my primary school maths teacher—never bowing to anyone, and never, never wrong."

My eyes trailed to the group of students Goodbarrel was now

giving an impromptu grounds tour to. "And the council allowed you to leave?"

"Most certainly not. We went carefully, using human transportation. At one point a double-decker bus was involved." He nodded at me. "What about you?"

"Oh, you know. Umbra and I were chased down a train platform by Lucian the prince and his minions, and then she managed to part the veil nowhere near a point of power, and then I got stuck inside a corrupted veil and talked to the Shade herself."

Aidan just blinked at me. Then began laughing. "And when Umbra parted the veil in the middle of nowhere, did she say any magical words?"

"Actually, Mr. North," Umbra said from behind me, jerking me out of my cross-armed casualness, "I said much in my head. Most of it involved clipped, desperate iterations of 'Godsdamn' and 'Bollocks.' Those seemed to be magical enough."

I spun. Umbra didn't stop on her course past us, sweeping toward the first-years with outstretched arms and a loud, carrying welcome.

Aidan straightened. Stepped closer to my side. "She's serious?" Then he stared at me. "You were serious?"

I patted his shoulder. "Always." Though, as I watched Umbra talk to the students, I wondered again how she'd done what she did without a point of power anywhere to be seen.

"Bloody hell," Aidan said. "What was *she* like?"

I kept my eyes on the group. "I couldn't see her in the darkness. We only talked briefly."

"What did she say?"

"She asked who I was. I told her."

"And how did you escape her—the Shade?"

I pulled in air through my nose. "She told me if I wanted to pass, I should part the veil. And so I did." No mention of the Spitfire. Even now I feared thinking of it. The way it had moved of its own volition, risen inside me, overtaken me with such ease. How different I had felt when it parted the veil on its own, full of the kind of high-octane emotions I'd only felt in moments of real anger. When I'd needed them.

Until the Spitfire had taken control, I had felt fear. Trepidation. Desperation. But not anger. And once it had, Rational Clem felt small and inconsequential. The Spitfire's emotions had overtaken me.

What was the difference this time?

The answer came at once: the Shade knew it was inside me. She knew it lived, it desired agency, and it had power.

But I didn't know how she knew. And that bothered me even more.

I pushed it to the back of my mind. Aidan North was here, and I had a puzzle for him. "Hey, North"—I nodded toward the library with a wink—"bet you've been missing our little tea-and-cookie chats."

Aidan drew a hand down his face. "Why does that make me nervous?"

"Don't worry." I hooked his arm, and we started walking. "You can trust the witch."

CHAPTER SIX

We came into the empty library, the entryway of which lit up on sensing our presence. A magical flame came to life in the lantern hanging from the ceiling, and it was strange to see Milonakis's circulation desk empty.

But it was conspicuously clean.

We pressed our way into the main room, and Aidan stopped hard when a feather duster swam by his head toward a row of books. It began a meticulous swiping at each spine.

He adjusted his glasses, staring after it. "Umbra's animated this place."

"Yeah, and basically everywhere else on the grounds while the professors and staff have been away."

"Makes sense." He stepped into the room, and two magical lanterns came to life around us. "But I do find one thing curious."

I came forward with him. "And what's that?"

"This branch of enchanting... it isn't taught here."

I swicked a finger across a table, found it clean of dust. When I raised my finger for his inspection, I said, "Why? Because all us mages would grow fat and lazy?"

He glanced at my finger, then my face. "Because it's a dead art. Few mages in history have ever been taught enchantments, and even fewer progressed to animation. So few, in fact, it hasn't been taught for decades."

"But Umbra was taught it."

"I suppose. Except there's something wrong with that."

"Which is?"

His eyes darted around the library, narrowed and thoughtful. Then he strode toward the Room of the Ancients. "Be back in a moment."

That was so like him; he always wanted to confirm his suspicions before he voiced them.

I crossed the empty library, sparing one look up at the ceiling full of wisps, then mounted the staircase to arrive at our favorite table. When I snapped my fingers, tea and steaming fae rolls appeared. I came to lean over the railing, clasping my hands as Aidan appeared from the Room of the Ancients with a big tome in hand. "So, what's up with Umbra?"

"Probably more than we'll ever know."

When he joined me at the table, sitting across from me, I could see it in his eyes: the gusto. The little machinery working in his head, click-click-clicking away. He set the book down—from the title, I could see it was a book on schools of magic—flipping it open to the table of contents and then to a specific section. Finally, he stabbed the page. "Ufeus Caligari died in 1916."

"Who's Ufeus Caligari?" I said around a mouthful of fae roll.

His eyes met mine. "The last mage to ever master animations."

I nodded at a broom sweeping over the floor on the first story. "Does it take mastery to do that?"

"Very nearly." Aidan didn't even look away from me. "Clem, to animate an object without even being in the same room... that's something you only see in ancient, eternal enchantments."

"Like at the Kowloon Library," I said, remembering the way the books had flown through the air in the Singaporean library, reshelving themselves.

"Exactly like that. You won't find one mage creating new animations like this."

"So why now?" I said. "Umbra never animated anything like this in our first three years."

"And how does she know a dead art?" he added. "She isn't old enough to have learned it from Caligari. Is she?"

We both paused. Was she?

"She'd have to be over a hundred years old," I said. "She looks old, but..."

"Not that old," Aidan finished. He sat back, hands sliding over the armrests of his chair. "I don't know. I need to think about it."

"Loki told me the smell of her magic has changed since we first met her. 'Grown more complex,' he said."

"Huh."

"Which explains what she managed to do on the platform, and the animations, and uncorrupting the leyline. Right?"

"Sure, except I don't understand why," he said. "Why more complex? Why now?"

My fingers drummed on the table. "She's teaching me one-on-one this year. Everything she knows, apparently." I half-smiled. "Which means I'll get lots of chances to fish for clues."

"Please don't tell me you'll be breaking into her office. Or her home."

I straightened, one hand at my chest. "Pardon? Such behavior is beneath a good witch."

"Yeah"—he tore off a bit of roll—"which is why I'm worried."

I snorted. "Touché. If I break into her place, I won't rope you into it."

"Maeve Umbra," he said, rolling the name over his tongue. "I'm a little jealous, you know."

"Of me, or her?"

"Of the fact that you get to learn from her. Personally. Do you know how rare that is?"

"Probably not."

He tilted his head, observing me. "I've never heard of it happening."

"I'll be sure to rub it in your face every chance I get." I winked at him. Then, after a pause, "Aidan, after what happened last May. On the tundra…"

"Yeah."

"Are you all right?"

He shook his head, eyes unfocusing. "I've thought about what happened every night this summer. With Frostwish and Liara and Eva and Rathmore. All the creatures."

"I'm sorry," I said. "For what happened to you." Frostwish had cast the pain hex on him, sending him to his knees. I could still see his agonized face behind my eyelids.

"I'm sorriest of all," he said. "Every time I thought about it, I wished I'd done more. I wish I'd known about Frostwish. I wish I'd fought. In a strange way, I wish I was more like my grandmother."

My eyebrows went up. "Farina North?"

"Yeah." His hand went to the birthmark on his neck, rubbing. "I wonder if she was right—if this gift was wasted on me. She would have done so much more with it."

I leaned forward, elbow on the table, one hand out to clasp. "Aidan."

He eyed my open hand. "Are we going to arm wrestle now?"

"Just take my hand, egghead."

He did so, leaning forward with his elbow on the table. Meeting my eyes with some discomfort.

I squeezed his hand. "This is maybe the second time in my life I've ever been sentimental, and it might be the last time. So listen up: I don't care if you never use your gift. I don't care if I have to fight every fight. Stop blaming yourself for being a fish trying to climb a tree, all right?"

His breathing was audible through his nose. "A fish?"

"Yeah. Screw the gift, Aidan. Your brains, your insight—I'd be dead without those. You've always been right here when I need you. And I'm going to need you a lot more before this is all over."

"Wow," he said. "Sincere Clem. Never thought I'd meet her."

I made a face. "Just squeeze my hand, North."

And he did.

"Now," I said. "Let's talk about this prophecy."

His eyes lit, and he slid a familiar book forward that I hadn't even noticed him grab from the Room of the Ancients. "I've already deciphered the part about the blade. There's another riddle."

I groaned. "Wonderful."

He opened the book, found the section describing the prophecy. With one finger, he read off, "'The thief's blade resides where power and pleasure cross.'"

I sat back, grimacing. I had no clue what that meant, and from the look on Aidan's face, he didn't, either.

"What do you suppose it does?" he said. "The blade."

"Obviously it *thieves* people's lives—when you cut off their heads."

His nose wrinkled. "That's crude."

"Your face is crude."

He set a hand to his cheek. "Did you seriously just use that line on me?"

"Anyway," I said. "What do you think the blade is for?"

He set both elbows on the table with a definitive lean forward. "What's the most valuable thing you can steal from a mage, Clementine?"

I stared at him a moment. "Their favorite pair of boots."

He groaned, rubbing his face. "Not all mages even wear boots."

"But if they did"—I smiled at his agony—"that would be it."

His head lifted, eyes locking on me. "*Power,* Clementine. The most valuable thing you can steal from a mage is their power."

That was a juicy theory. I didn't know if he was right, but I hoped he wasn't wrong. Still, I also wouldn't mind a good decapitator.

The next day brought a new shock.

If you'd ever told me that Evanora Whitewillow and Liara Youngblood would arrive at the academy together, by consent, I wouldn't have believed it. They felt like more than oil and water—they were of two different worlds.

Light and dark. Sweet and calculating. Sincere and sarcastic.

But the day after Aidan arrived, they came together, as part of a group of fae led by Professor Fernwhirl. And when they saw me coming out of the dining hall, they surprised me again.

Both dropped their bags, came flying toward me with such enthusiasm I didn't know whether I should put my arms out or my fists up. Eva ran into me, arms wrapping around my shoulders with relieved laughter, and Liara stopped short, landing with sharp, dancing eyes not two feet away.

"I'm so glad you're here," Eva said into my shoulder. "That we're here."

I met eyes with Liara over Eva's shoulder, through the gauze of her wings. "Sounds like you two had an eventful time."

"Oh, it was terrible." Eva pulled away. "Every leyline around Vienna is corrupted, Clem. Fernwhirl had to fly a few of us far enough away from them to avoid their corruption seeping into the points of power. We ended up high atop a mountain before we could make our way to Singapore, and then we got word from Umbra to wait for her to secure the leyline outside the academy. It took three days."

"Three days in Singapore," Liara said. "Sounds like anybody's worst nightmare, doesn't it?"

I half-smiled at her. "Only if you're trying to get into the restricted room at Kowloon Library."

"Too soon," Liara said, solemn.

"We brought Obe," Eva said, her eyes and mind elsewhere. "My parents wanted him to stay with Liara's little sister and her grandparents in Singapore."

So it wasn't the journey that had been terrible—it was what had happened with her family.

"Why?" I said.

"Eva's parents are both guardians," Liara said, and that was all she needed to—and maybe could—say in Eva's presence. They were guardians, and they were on missions. They couldn't leave their young son alone.

"Singapore's safer for him," Eva murmured. "There are fewer kidnappings."

As if she'd known I would ask why, Liara said, "We have more guardians in Singapore. The city is vigilant about protecting its young."

I nodded. All at once, Eva had gone from a kind of manic excitement to wide, distant eyes and a lowered chin. She'd had a hell of a time. My arm went around her, jarring her with a squeeze. "Hey, Guardian. We've got work to do, too."

Eva's eyes lifted. "Gods, I'm a guardian."

"That's right." I glanced at Liara. "What should we get her drunk on after initiation? Red wine, or white?"

Liara's eyes softened. She knew this was as important as acknowledging the state of the world. No human—or fae—could put a cork on that kind of stress for long. "Red," she said. "It's more potent."

"Now wait a second," Eva said.

"It's tradition," I cut in. "Isn't it, Liara?"

Liara gave a nod.

"Don't want to defy tradition, do we?" I turned Eva toward our dorm. "Tomorrow it is."

As Eva and I walked to our room, we passed a group of first-years who walked together on their way to the dining hall, eyes on us in a wary, hunch-shouldered way. Eva waved at them, said hello, and only then did they relax enough to speak.

They looked *young* to me. When the hell did that happen?

When we had passed them, she gave me a long look. "It doesn't feel the same, coming back here. Does it?"

"It's the same place, but..."

"The world's changed," she said. "Everything's changed around us." She nodded at one of the trees that used to contain a classroom. "And the feeling here has changed, too. There's fear."

She was right. Before, the enchantment around the academy had felt like a cute trick, superfluous. I hadn't understood for a long while why it even existed.

Now, it felt like a thin, invisible skein of safety from *her*.

Eva leaned against my shoulder as we walked. "For a second, when I saw your half-sullen face, I almost forgot. And then you asked how we got here, and I couldn't forget."

I nudged her. "Hence the post-initiation booze."

She scuffed the dirt with her shoe. "I've got a secret, Clem." Then, before I could ask, "I've never been drunk."

"Never? What about buzzed?"

"Not even that."

"Well, Eva, it's really not all that bad until you get to the puking—"

"I've got an even bigger secret," she said, stopping us at the steps up to the dorm. I turned to face her, and she said, "I hate that I've never been drunk. And after this summer, all I want is to stop worrying about my family for at least a few hours. A few blissful hours."

A bad taste came into the back of my mouth. I ignored it. "They're fine, Eva."

"You can't know that." She sighed. "Clem, all I ever wanted was to be a guardian. To protect the magical world." She paused, her porcelain throat bobbing. "And then all this shit happened. One of my neighbors was kidnapped in June. She was seventeen."

"I'm sorry, Eva. Was she…"

"Saved? No. She wasn't."

Silence fell between us. The happiness of seeing her again had gone as quickly as reality had rushed back. For the first time, I felt wistful for the simplicity of my first year here. My hotheaded innocence. My single-minded desire to tame a horse.

"Come on," I said. "Let's get in something comfortable and pretend for a night like the world isn't falling apart."

CHAPTER SEVEN

The next morning, Loki and I were called to the guardians' common room, nestled not far from the faculty apartments in a large tree on the grounds. When I came into the common room, the others were already gathered: Mishka, Akelan, Keene, Elijah, Isaiah, and Liara.

They'd been waiting on me. Silence fell when I entered.

I gestured back the way we'd come. "We can leave if you want to keep talking."

Elijah came forward, bear-hugged me. "Gods I missed your negative assumptions about people's behavior." A second later, Isaiah was hugging me, too.

I stood there in surprise. I hadn't been that close with the twins. Then I got it. "You found out what happened with me and Umbra."

Liara, leaning against the wall by the fireplace, gave me a look that said, *I wasn't part of any of this.*

"Story's all over the school already," Mishka said from her armchair. She lifted the latest edition of *Witches & Wizards*. "Lucian the prince was spotted at the train station in Vienna during the witching hour a few nights ago."

"The same night you and Umbra came back," Akelan said.

"Counting backward from how long she told us she'd been working on the leyline."

"Which means," Keene said, "the prince nearly got to the headmistress. And since you were with her, I suppose you would have been a casualty of war, wouldn't you?"

So they thought Tristan Rathmore had come after Umbra. And why wouldn't he? No one but Liara knew the full truth. I may have been a witch, but I was also just another student at the academy, as far as the others were concerned.

That was fine by me.

"Well, you don't have to miss my negative assumptions anymore." I crossed to the sitting table, pulled out a chair and sat. Loki hopped up on the table and sat by me. "What's on the docket this morning?"

"We're picking a new leader," Akelan said. "Now that Fi is gone."

I hated that Fi was gone. She had been the leader we'd needed: steady, calculating, rational. Now she was out in the world, graduated. I'd heard over the summer that she had joined the guardian ranks in Amsterdam, which was all the better for it.

"I vote for you," I said to Akelan. "Now can we go eat breakfast? I have to meet with Umbra in an hour, and she dislikes it when I'm hangry."

"Why me?" Akelan said.

I shrugged like it was obvious. "You've got the same qualities as Fi."

"It's true," Mishka said. "He isn't quick to anger or fear. He's deft at coordinating attacks."

"I'm not one of the candidates," Akelan said from his seat on the overstuffed arm of a chair. "Fi had two of us in mind. The outgoing leader has always picked the nominees."

I had forgotten about this.

Elijah pointed at Liara. "You"—then at me—"and you."

Beside him, Isaiah grinned. "Witch and fae. Should we have them duel it out?"

Mishka made a face at him. "Inappropriate."

Liara and I met eyes. This wasn't what I wanted for myself. I needed to spend this time focusing on finding the thief's blade, readying myself for the Shade...

"I forfeit the role to Liara," I said. "She'd be better than me."

All eyes turned to me. Even Loki's. "And why is that?" Liara said.

"You're fast. Brave. Persistent. And if I'm being real honest, guys, you're gonna hate the sound of my voice in your head by the end of this year. I get shrill when I'm annoyed."

"Except," Liara said, "you're also fast, brave, and persistent. And if I'm being real honest, the only rescues we managed last year were because of you."

"That's why Fi recommended you," Akelan said, eyes on me. "Because between you and Liara, things started happening. Good things."

I swept out my hands. It wasn't that I wasn't grateful, or didn't want to help. It was that I felt overwhelmed. "I'm disqualified, anyway. Umbra wants me to stay on the grounds for the foreseeable future."

"Actually," a voice said from behind me, "that doesn't disqualify you."

When the headmistress crossed into the center of the common room, no one looked surprised but me and Loki.

"It's tradition," Umbra explained, "for the headmistress to preside over the choosing of a new leader."

My eyebrow arched. Wonderful; she'd arrived just in time to foil my excuses.

Umbra nodded at Liara and me. "You would both be fine leaders. May I propose, given the extenuating circumstances of the world outside the academy, a dual leadership?"

Akelan's face tilted. "How would it work?"

"Yeah," I said. "How would it?"

"Clementine is correct that she should not leave the grounds." Umbra tipped her staff toward Liara. "But this one may. And given how the Shade's powers and creatures have grown more dangerous, it would behoove you all—especially the new guardians to be initiated tonight —to have one leader watching from afar, and one on the ground."

Watching from afar. I wasn't good at watching a microwave from afar, much less people.

Mishka sat forward. "Do you mean the globe?"

Umbra nodded down at her. "Yes, Ms. Reddy. I mean the globe."

Her face lifted toward the two stories above us. "From here, Clementine can apprise you of what's coming, what you face, and Liara can coordinate your forces on the ground to face it."

My eyes lifted, too. I couldn't see it from here, but I knew what Mishka and Umbra were referring to. The magical globe on the third level. I had thought it only acted as a map, a signifier of what had gone before, but maybe the magic in it was greater than that.

"No one has used the globe that way for decades," Akelan said. "Not since the eighties."

"Then it's about time it be dusted off," Umbra said. "For these are fraught times."

A sense of agreement flowed over the room. Everyone seemed to like this idea, though Liara and I still gazed at one another. I could see in her eyes that she would accept this, sharing a role with me.

But I didn't want to be here during a mission. I was meant to be *out there.*

"Ms. Youngblood, Ms. Cole," Umbra said. "Provided I can teach Clementine to use the globe, would you accept this dual leadership?"

"I would," Liara said, arms unfolding.

Finally, my eyes trailed over to Loki. The one who knew me best, who knew how much I could actually take on. *Say no. Please say no.*

He licked his paw. Lowered it, then met my eyes with his emerald ones. "Do it, Clem."

Well, I couldn't argue with my cat. Not without looking stupid.

I returned my attention to Umbra. Nodded. "All right. For now." *Until I master the enshroudment.*

"It's a brilliant idea," Keene said, eyes flicking between the two of us. "But I still want to see them duel."

"You would," Liara bit out.

The guardian initiation began at nightfall, and both Loki and I were in attendance. Two new guardians, one of them my best friend and roommate.

Evanora Whitewillow was finally becoming what she was meant to be from our first year. When she stepped before Umbra in the wisp-lit antechamber, she whispered her name through a tight throat, her wings trembling beneath her lavender hair.

This didn't just matter to her. It was her life's purpose, to guard and to protect those who needed her most.

Next came Maise Wheatless, a fifth-year from House Spark. She'd always been shrewd and witty and full of solid power, and I'd liked her from the day I met her. She was exactly who I wanted by my side in a fight.

Last to be initiated was a fourth-year I didn't really know at all. "Paxton Tarrensteam," he said with a voice as clear as a bell, his dirty-blond, short-cropped head a foot higher than Umbra's, his hands clasped behind his back. He stood with feet apart, serious and formal, and just by the look of him, I knew his house.

I leaned toward Liara before he finished introducing himself, whispered, "Twenty bucks he's Gaia."

She gave a quick exhale through her nose. "I'll take that bet."

And then, just as quickly as I'd offered it, I lost that twenty bucks. "House Crest," he said, and Liara's hand went out to me, palm flat for the receiving.

I stared at Paxton Tarrensteam as he returned to the group, a new guardian. Crest? They were soft, flowing—this guy was rigid, all angles in his walk and his stance. He was dissonant, and it bothered me.

Dissonance, I'd learned over the years, is something we explain away in ourselves. I might look like a bad witch on the outside, but in my better moments I'd convinced myself I was really just a soft marshmallow of a witch on the inside.

But dissonance in others? Unacceptable.

Which was why I approached Paxton after the initiation, when everyone was leaving for the dining hall and the ceremonial game of Duck Duck Werewolf. "Paxton," I said as we came into the night. Loki veered into the darkness after a mouse, and I walked alone alongside our newest guardian from Crest. "I'm Clem."

His green eyes narrowed as he looked over at me. His walk was formal, even. "You say that like you've never seen me before."

"Have I?"

"We're in the same year. We were in Rescue together with Milonakis, and we usually go to the dining hall around the same time, and the library..." When I didn't register any of it, he trailed off. "Okay, maybe you've really never seen me before."

"If I'm being honest," I said, "most people aren't on my radar."

He ran a hand over his hair, eyes facing ahead. "Sure."

"Listen," I said, "I'm not Eva Whitewillow. I'll probably be on your bad side before I'm on your good side. Maybe I'll always be on your bad side, but hey, one upside is that I have to stay here on the grounds while you're away. You won't have to see my mug all the time."

This brought his gaze back to me. "And you're the leader of the guardians. You and Liara."

I shrugged. "You want the job? I might be able to pull a few strings."

His eyes lit for the first time, vaguely amused. "Truth is, I always avoided you. For obvious, witchy reasons. Probably why I was never on your radar."

"Fair enough. We witches can historically be a pain in the ass." I paused. "I only have one question for you before we go in: How good are you with water, Paxton?"

He stopped, his back as straight as an exclamation point. The others had trailed into the dining hall, leaving us alone in the night. And in the cricketing summer evening, his hands went out before him, shaping an invisible ball.

I stared, squinting in the dim light, as water began to shimmer there. He was calling the moisture from the air. And just that fast, his ball had grown to the size of a watermelon.

With a lowered chin, eyes on me, he thrust his hands forward faster than I could follow. The water formed a wall, but nothing like what I'd seen any other water mage create. Where other water walls were curving and iridescent, his was perfectly flat, unforgiving, and roiling on the inside with froth.

It was dissonant. It made no sense, but there it was.

The water broke on me in the same moment I closed my eyes, and it was like hitting a river from a hundred feet up—except I wasn't falling. It was simply the force of his power rushing at me, and then over me, yanking and pulling like a gale storm, and I got the feeling he'd avoided going too hard.

Didn't want to break his leader's bones, after all.

Just as quickly, it passed, slapping the grass in a wave. And I was left drenched, hair covering my face, spitting water from my mouth and blowing it from my nose.

Paxton came forward, lifted a lock of my hair away so we could meet eyes. "Am I on your radar now?"

Now I understood. He wasn't dissonant at all—he was perfectly congruent in the way he talked, walked, and used water magic. This guy was all hard angles and unrelenting force. He and Maise would be perfect guards out there for the others.

"Paxton Tarrensteam," I said, "that was the best goddamn thing I've seen all summer."

CHAPTER EIGHT

After Eva dried me off with a strong gust of air, we played eight rounds of Duck Duck Werewolf. Or maybe it was ten, or twelve. I lost count when the grape drink began to run out, and this time I didn't hold back.

Every time it came my turn, I was a vicious, fiery werewolf. And I caught so very many drunken mages.

The night was a blur. I nursed a drink that someone would refill when it got low, and I ate the conjured foods on the table when I could get a chance to snag them. Chocolate cookies and salt and vinegar chips. Fae rolls (my doing) and Mishka's favorite, baklava. Grapes and slices of cheese. Some fae fruit that looked like a pear, but tasted like mint chocolate chip ice cream.

I'd never been so full.

Some rounds I sat out, and I found myself shoulder to shoulder with Mishka, who hugged me and forgave me for everything that had happened to her on that mission when she'd been injured last spring. Or I sat with Elijah and Isaiah on either side of me, the three of us debating whether Liara's lightning was more like Palpatine, or *X-Men*'s Storm.

They said Palpatine. I maintained Storm.

Akelan and I just stood in silence for a good ten minutes, watching the group, and when he offered to get me more drink, it wasn't an awkward way of getting away from our quietness. That was just who we were together: silent, observing. It was right for us.

I congratulated Maise, who pulled me into a hug, thumped me on the back. "I'm glad it's you leading," she said. "Ever since I first saw you, I thought you had fire. The figurative kind, too."

And at the end of the night, it was finally just me sitting the last round out, watching the others. I was tired, bleary-eyed, slumped into a chair, and happy to be with these people.

That was rare for me.

When I was younger, if I wasn't alone I itched for it. Other people felt dangerous, like they could bite without using their teeth. Or maybe it was me who was dangerous, and I didn't trust myself not to run them off.

When I was sixteen, I wouldn't have seen a difference between this academy and my group home. Stuck around other broken, problematic people my age, forced into places and conversations I'd never wanted.

Now, as Eva tripped and burst into laughter as she dropped to the floor, I realized I didn't feel unsafe. Not around these people. But maybe I was still dangerous. Not because of what was in my head, but what lay coiled in the center of me. The creature. The anger.

For the first time, I could see the distinction between me and it.

Liara helped Eva up, and I pushed all thoughts of the Spitfire aside.

This year, I understood what the ceremony was really for. It was freedom from responsibilities, letting out all that stress and anxiety for one night before the whole weight of saving people's lives descended with the same fury as one of Paxton's water walls.

Tonight, we could just be people. Regular young people with regular burdens, like drinking too much.

The game was stupid. But it was also perfect, and by the end of it, I had decided I liked Paxton. When he got inebriated enough, he got clumsy. He started to laugh, and then all his hardness fell away and he was just a guy who'd been initiated as a guardian, who didn't quite know what he was doing and wanted to impress us.

Afterward, Eva insisted on flying. But she was slow and uncertain, weaving her way off the landing from the dining hall, sometimes using only one wing, then the other.

I'd thought I had let loose. Compared to Eva, I was practically sober.

I came down the steps, crossing my arms as she made a drunken path through the air. "That's right," I said. "Keep heading due north."

"North?" One wing stopped working, and she nearly hit the ground before it did again. "I can't even tell which way is up."

I gestured up at her. "All right, get down here, lightweight."

She went into a slow spiral, finally touching the ground and nearly tipping onto her hands and knees before I caught her. "Woah," she said when I helped her straighten. "You caught me. Am I the werewolf?"

I resisted laughing. "Eva, we're outside now."

Her face lifted, eyes finding the canopy and the sky. "So we are. Gods, Clem—have you ever seen the stars?"

"Sure." I began walking her toward our dorm. "Once or twice."

She toddled along with me, eyes still heavenward. "No, I mean really seen them. They're like diamonds."

I cast a quick glance up. The stars really were brilliant tonight, the sky clear of clouds. "They are. They really are."

She grabbed my shirt with both hands as we reached the staircase up to our dorm. Turned to me. "Clem, I need to tell you something."

"Yeah?"

"Neverwink's going to make me into a real healer."

My eyebrows went up. "Neverwink is teaching a class?"

"Independent study." She paused, her throat bobbing like she might hiccup or burp. Then, once the threat had passed, "I practically had to beg her. But she said yes in the end."

"So you want to be a healer."

"I want to save people's lives if I need to."

"Well that's—"

"Clem, I've got something else to tell you." She stared at me like she couldn't quite find my face, her lidded eyes wandering. "This summer, the guardian leader in Vienna, he sent my dad to Edinburgh on a mission."

"Edinburgh? Why?"

She gave an overlarge shrug. "Top secret, you know. But do you know how much they hate mages there?"

This was her drunkenness talking. If she were sober, of course she would know I knew.

Nonetheless, I said, "A lot?"

"Oh gods, they keep it on lockdown. Only a few can have magic. Their police even specialize in 'anti-magic.'" She made uneven double-quotes with her fingers in the air.

I eyed her. "Anti-magic?"

Eva's grip on my shirt tightened, her throat convulsed, and then she keeled over and released the contents of her stomach onto the grass.

I knelt with her. "Eva?"

She groaned, eyes shut, and swayed on her knees. "That tasted like grape." And then she sighed, head lowering until her chin touched her chest.

After that, she was pretty useless to the world. Especially to me, by which I mean I had to practically carry her up the stairs and to her bed. And as I helped her in, my mind revolved on what she'd told me.

Her father. Edinburgh. Anti-magic.

If Tristan Rathmore led the Mages' Council, then I could see why he'd hoard the magic amongst himself and his councilors.

More mages meant more potential problems.

When I questioned her the next morning, Eva didn't remember saying anything about her dad or Edinburgh. And the way she acted told me it was something she wasn't supposed to have mentioned.

I left her hungover in bed because I had early morning training with Umbra in the guardians' tree. I would be back for Eva and her secrets later.

"On the train platform," I said, eyes drifting from the globe in front of me over to Umbra. "How did you part the veil?"

"Focus, child," the headmistress said, her face lit as the globe slowly spun before us. "This is critical."

I swallowed, forced my eyes back onto it. The two of us stood alone on the third floor of the guardians' tree, the massive magical globe taller than both of us and shimmering with leylines.

I had so many questions for Umbra. But ever since we'd met this morning, she'd been single-minded about teaching me to lead the guardians. Of course, she was always single-minded in her teaching.

My fingers went up to the globe, flicking outward. As they did, it zoomed in on Iceland, expanding the landmass until I could see the roads and towns and the capital city. With an upward slide of my finger, I brought the focus down to the capital, Reykjavik. And then, flicking outward again, I zoomed in until I could even see the one-lane streets.

"You know," I said, "there's this thing called Google Earth…"

Umbra ignored me. Her fingers went out beside me, creating tiny moving dots on one of the roads. Some were green, and some were red. "The rescue has failed. Now, two of your guards and two of your chasers are on Laugavegur Street. They're flanked by a dozen of the Shade's creatures, and more are moving to intercept them on their left. What do you do?"

As I watched, the four green dots—my guardians—moved down Laugavegur, and were pursued by twelve red dots, with four more moving in on their left, as Umbra had said.

These were a simulation, a trick of Umbra's magic. It would be my own magic—my connection with each of the guardians—that would ultimately allow me to follow them, to perceive where they were and what they faced.

I still didn't quite know how. But Umbra had assured me she would teach me that, too.

I pointed. "I'd have them turn off onto Reykjanesbraut at the first opportunity. I would tell them to follow it until they came alongside the Elliðaá River, where they would have to leave the road and use it as a point of power to escape."

"So be it," Umbra said. With a flick of her finger, she allowed the simulation to play out, directing the guardians in the way I had described.

The green dots took a right onto Reykjanesbraut, and the creatures followed. When the guardians came alongside the river, they passed into the snow. The two guardians on horseback slowed in the snow-pack, while the two fae kept at the same pace in the air.

The creatures, on the other hand, didn't slow. And the two guardians on horseback were quickly overtaken, while the fae escaped by the river.

"That wouldn't happen," I said when it had finished.

"Oh?" Umbra cast an imperious eye on me. "And why not?"

"One of the horseback guardians would have used their fire to clear a path through the snowpack. And even if there hadn't been a fire mage among them, the fae wouldn't have left the other two behind to be killed."

Umbra turned to me, staff tapping as she did. "What would the fae have done with fifteen of the Shade's creatures chasing them?"

"Rebuffed them, slowed them down." I threw an arm out, and it passed through the globe. "Or Liara would have made a new call. It wouldn't end like that."

"Clementine, your plan was flawed from the beginning. You sent the guardians on horseback into snowpack in Iceland during the winter."

"There was no other choice." My focus returned to the globe. "The closest leyline was corrupted, and they had to make for the river."

"Wasn't there?" With a revolving finger, Umbra returned the simulation to the start. She swiped her hand through the air, and the green dots raced down the same street they had begun on. This time, instead of turning right, they passed straight down the road. The two fae branched off, rushing back toward the creatures and passing over them.

As they did, the creatures followed them.

Meanwhile, the guardians on horseback raced down the road until they came to a farther, uncorrupted leyline. There, they just barely passed through before the creatures caught them. And then the two fae guardians, who had been safe in the air, swung back around and flew toward the leyline themselves, passing through.

When all four green dots had disappeared from the globe, I just stared, silent.

"You made your call too quickly," Umbra said, soft. "It was the wrong one."

"You have to make quick calls," I said. "It's how you survive."

She shook her head. "No, Clementine. The great boon of having you here, watching from safety, is that you don't have to make calls the way Liara will have to. You can see the whole picture. You can consider all the factors, and you *must* be sure before you give instructions, because you will supersede Liara when you do."

I turned toward her, sensing this wasn't just about steering the guardians. "And how will I observe what they're doing in the first place?"

A faint smile appeared, and she began walking us toward the stairs. "By the same means that all magic passes through this world."

Leylines.

As we came down the stairs, I said, "If the closest leyline hadn't been corrupted, this wouldn't have been a simulation at all."

She tilted her head at me. "It's a moot point. The leyline was corrupted."

"You uncorrupted the one outside the academy grounds."

"Over the course of three days, child. You wouldn't have but twenty minutes."

I twirled my fingers through the air. "How hard could it possibly be?"

"You do know how to make an old woman's day, don't you, Clementine Cole?"

We came down to the first floor. "It's one of my specialties." I grabbed my cloak from the hook as we headed out. "Another of my specialties is chasing monsters."

"I know, child. You want to be out with the others. But tell me, how many of the creatures did the Shade send over the tundra when you retrieved the chain?"

In a flash, my mind placed me there again. The white expanse, the round moon, the stream of monsters passing over the earth like a swarm. All rushing toward me. "Hundreds," I said.

"You will endanger their presence," Umbra said as we came into daylight. "Simply by being there, you will endanger the guardians."

My gaze sharpened on Umbra. "So teach me what I need to know to go unseen for as long as I need to."

"Demanding, aren't we?" Her eyes flicked to the sky. "Ah, and now I see why. It's time for lunch." She gestured for me to follow. "We should break."

I walked alongside her. "Are you trying to distract me with sandwiches?"

She glanced at me, eyes twinkling. "Never. Though you did ask me a question about the train platform. If you want the answer, you'll join me."

CHAPTER NINE

Maeve Umbra's home at Shadow's End wasn't what I'd expect from a headmistress. And in over three years, I'd had quite a bit of time to imagine.

She lived in a tree at the edge of the grounds, not far from the meadow. It wasn't a tree I'd ever really noticed, but it did have steps winding up its trunk and a door right there in the side.

As we climbed, the academy bustled with its first day of classes. Students passed along the ground, and fae through the air, and every time I caught a glimpse of it, I was struck by how different the academy was to my first year.

It had felt practically empty by comparison.

I stopped on the landing. Through the trees, I could see Professor Fernwhirl with a group of fae in the meadow. It was an introduction to flight, and the class was twice the size mine had been.

Umbra paused when she opened the door to her home, watching with me. "Fernwhirl told me she gave you a fake broom on your first day."

I snorted. "She did. I couldn't look her in the eye for months after that."

"She was testing you," Umbra said as we came into the entryway and she closed the door. "I suppose you can imagine what she reported back to me." That was followed by a wink.

I turned on Umbra just as I'd taken off my cloak and set it on a hook. "That's mature."

"She needed to gauge your temper. The woman's not properly malicious, for gods' sake." Umbra passed down the hall and disappeared around a corner. If her home was like the others I'd been in, she had two or three rooms—living room, bedroom, kitchen. "Well," Umbra's voice echoed back toward me, "not on most days of the week, at least. Never knock on her door on a Tuesday."

My temper. *Because I'm the fire witch*, I thought but didn't say.

When I came down the hallway and into the next room, I came into a high-ceilinged, airy space. A spiral staircase ran up one wall to a second story with an open side and an overlooking balcony. On the far wall, sunlight filtered through large curving windows. Built-in bookcases, packed with tomes, covered two of the walls. In one corner sat a four-seater square dining table. And in the center, two wildly comfortable leather couches were arranged at two sides of a large coffee table.

On my left, noises echoed through a curving doorway—the familiar sounds of someone in the kitchen.

"Umbra," I said, stock still. My eyes traveled around the large space. "Maybe you can clear something up for me.."

"What now, child?" Her voice carried from the kitchen.

"Well, I'm not quite sure how a home this big fits into this tree. It's kind of impossible."

Her head appeared through the doorway. "Clementine, Goodbarrel told me you were the best tangible manipulations student in his course last year. Please don't tell me he was mistaken."

Tangible manipulations? *No.*

I stared at her, open-mouthed. "I sewed a small pocket into my cloak. It took months."

Her lips curved. "One sandwich, or two?"

"One." When her head disappeared back into the kitchen, I crossed to the center of her living room. When I approached a bookcase, I surveyed the different titles. A lot of them looked ancient.

Some were falling apart. I turned back around toward the second story. Up there I spotted the edge of a bed and an armchair.

Umbra had manipulated this home into being. We were standing inside a massive pocket in the veil. This must have taken years. Decades, even.

"So"—I paused, searching for just the right words—"do you ever worry this place could become a black hole while you're sleeping and start sucking things into its massive manipulated veil-pocket?"

Umbra's laugh rang out through the doorway. "Of all the things weighing on my mind, that is not one." When she emerged, she carried a wooden tray with sandwiches carefully cut into triangles arranged on it.

I pointed. "You could have conjured those."

"Yes, but I prefer the taste of real food from time to time." She set the platter on the dining table and pulled out a chair. When she snapped her fingers, a carafe of drink appeared, flanked by two glasses. "Though I do enjoy my own conjured lemonade."

I sat down in the chair adjacent to hers as she poured lemonade for me. "How long did this take you? This place."

"Thirty years," she said without even glancing up at me. She moved the carafe over to her glass. "Thirty-two, actually."

"You've been the headmistress here for that long?"

"Feels like much longer." She sat, spreading a napkin across her lap and bringing two triangles onto her plate. "Eat. We'll make it a quick lunch, and then back to it."

I picked up a sandwich. "You told me you'd answer my question."

"Yes, how I parted the veil." She pointed toward the entryway. "My walking staff, can you guess its name?"

"Your staff has a name?"

"Does it not seem fine enough to you to merit one?" She leaned closer. "Why should your weapon have a name, and mine none?"

"I didn't name mine," I said. "Someone else did."

"Well, that's dull." She ripped off a piece of sandwich in her fingers. "Anyway, the staff is called Parity. Do you know the meaning of that word?"

I didn't. "Sure," I said.

Her eyes narrowed, half-amused. "The staff desires a balance between good and evil, light and dark. And as darkness spreads in the world, it brings light."

"So the staff is growing in power..."

She nodded, gesturing for me to go on.

"Which means it's become its own point of power," I finished.

"Good girl." She proceeded to bury her attention in her drink, downing half of it in one satisfied go.

"And one other thing." I set my sandwich down. "The animations around the grounds. You made those happen, didn't you?"

Now she did meet my eyes. "Ah, so you've grown curious about the feather dusters in the library and done a little research. I imagine Aidan North's nose was in a book or two as well."

Trust Maeve Umbra to come to all the right conclusions with hardly anything to go off of.

"Aren't animations a dead art?" I asked.

"Yes," she continued. "For all intents and purposes, animations are no more. I was taught them as a child, long before your time. If you're wondering why I don't pass on the art, it's because I never mastered it. Not like the mages of old."

"Who was your teacher?" I asked.

"A man named Caligari," she said without a moment's hesitation. And it was her lack of hesitation that told me she wasn't lying or searching out a different truth.

Ufeus Caligari had taught her the art. The only problem was that, as Aidan had discovered, Caligari had likely died before Umbra was born. Unless, of course, the headmistress was older than she looked.

Of course, it wasn't polite to ask a woman her age, and I suspected Umbra would dodge the question anyway. Whenever I plumbed her past, she grew vague.

As I watched Umbra eat, my eyes traveled over her crow's feet, the lines around her mouth, and I wondered how old her "mages of old" really were.

In the afternoon, I left Umbra's home with her thumbprint on my forehead and mine on hers. She remained in her house, and it was my job to walk the entire circumference of the grounds for the next four hours without losing my connection to her.

I had to be able to hear her voice in my head, to speak to her from anywhere I stood, though miles may separate us. And, as a new challenge, I had to sense Umbra wherever she might go. Follow her with my mind.

A half hour had always been my upper limit with this telepathic magic. Four hours was torture.

And how, I asked as I tromped along the edge of the enshrouding enchantment at the edge of the grounds, *am I supposed to maintain this from another continent?*

The leylines, came Umbra's response. *You will funnel your magic through the uncorrupted leylines. They will empower you.*

So I had to trace the leylines all the way across the world to talk to the guardians, to follow their rescues. To guide them back safely.

What I wanted was to prepare for Edinburgh. Not this. But that seemed selfish, short-sighted, because the truth was I was only thinking of what I wanted. I wasn't thinking of the guardians or the mages they would rescue.

All I wanted was to see my sister again. Just that.

When I passed the meadow, I sensed Umbra had left her house and was heading toward the dining hall.

Second lunch? I asked. *And you didn't invite me. I'm hurt.*

A lunchtime announcement, came Umbra's reply in my head, *about tonight's ceremony. Child, do not make me regret this exercise.*

Tonight's ceremony was the first-years' induction into the four houses. I had almost forgotten. I knew one person who would be there: Eva, who attended things like that religiously. Which meant I would be there, too—to fill Eva in on everything I'd learned about the Rathmores.

That night, after an agonizing day of training, I came into the dining hall with aching calves and thighs and spotted Eva's wings sticking up from one of the tables near the back. She was seated with the other guardians and a whole crop of first-years, which came as no surprise.

People liked Eva. Eva liked people.

Which was why I apologized to everyone as I dragged her away to an empty table where no one sat but us.

"Eva," I said as we sat down.

"Clem." She had carried a glass of tomato juice with her. "How good of you to isolate me from everyone."

"The witch is gonna witch." I nodded at the tomato juice. "How's the hangover?"

"Gone." She took a sip. "But the memory of the pain remains."

"Good enough." I leaned close to her. "I need to tell you something. About Lucian the prince."

She moved closer, all thoughts of socializing forgotten. "Tell me."

"Tristan Rathmore." I paused when she didn't react. "It's him. *He* is the prince. Well, now that Callum gave up the family mantle."

Her eyebrows and wings rose at the same time.

"And," I said, "he found us on our train in Vienna. Chased Umbra and me down the platform..."

Umbra came to the front of the dining hall to begin the ceremony —which would involve some talking, some walking, and lots of time in the amphitheater—Eva and I devolved to whispers.

She scooted closer to me. "And then what?"

As I whispered the rest of the story, Eva's eyes opened so wide I could see the sclera above and below her irises.

When I had finished, she let out a breath. "So all this time, my mom and dad have been spying on Lucian the prince."

"What?" I hissed.

"From the bits and pieces he's told me, he and my mom were sent to infiltrate."

"Infiltrate where?" I whispered.

"Edinburgh. The Mages' Council. And—"

Just then, everyone stood from their tables, and the first-year students filed toward the center of the dining hall. The procession had begun.

Eva and I had no choice but to stand as well, to divert our attention to getting in line with the rest of the student body and professors at the right time, in the right spot. Eyes fell on me, and some of the first-years recoiled.

I knew why: it was what Ora Frostwish had said in *Witches & Wizards*. She'd maligned me, the witch, and to anyone who read the magazine—which was most of the magical world—and didn't know me, I wasn't just the last witch.

I was a supreme bitch.

It didn't help that she'd described me to a sketch artist, and my likeness had appeared in the magazine. The big red hair and the pale skin didn't help me blend in.

That was fine. Things had come full circle from my first year, when I'd been just as outcasted; it almost felt right.

Eva and I walked as a pair from the dining hall to the amphitheater. She had gone respectfully silent. Like every other ceremony, she took this one seriously. But this year especially, now that she was a guardian, she wanted to set a good example.

I, on the other hand, kept whispering at her. When we finally sat in the amphitheater and Umbra stepped up onto the stage behind the four braziers to begin sorting the first-years, I gripped Eva's forearm and said, "You're killing me."

Her face turned slowly toward me. Her lips worked, and finally she found words. "Mama and Papa are gathering information on Tristan Rathmore."

My mind spun, reeled, sparked. I'd completely drowned out everything else now. "They must know who he really is, then."

She nodded her head, a tiny movement, worry on her brow. "Maybe. I don't know." This was dangerous for them. That was what her expression said.

Her eyes became glassy, and then they darted to the stage. "They've been away in Edinburgh for two months." She hadn't told me that part.

My grip on her arm loosened. "Have you heard from them?"

"Once," she whispered, and now I understood why she'd gotten so drunk on the night of her guardian initiation.

Her mother and father were spying on Lucian the prince.

CHAPTER TEN

This year, the quartermistress had once again asked me to teach bareback riding. Except I had not just one, but two crops of students. Each class was composed of twelve first-years, and we would meet early on alternating days, just after breakfast, before the sun blasted us in the paddock.

On the morning after the ceremony, I stood in the paddock talking about mounting a horse, and I'd hardly gotten two sentences out when one student's hand went up.

"Yes?" I said.

"Are you the witch?" she said, her voice a leaf on the breeze.

"That's one word for me," I said. "You may also call me the blaster of asses, the fomenter of failure, or Your Majesty Her Graciousness. Whichever you choose determines your grade, so choose wisely."

I let an uncomfortable silence ensue, my face serious, my eyes never leaving the girl.

Then the others began to laugh, and from then on, I had them. If I told them to mount, they tried. If I told them to mount again, they tried again. They fell in the dirt happily, and I only had to sprinkle a dark joke here and there.

It didn't seem to matter to them that someone in a magazine had called me Bad with a capital B. If I could make them laugh, didn't bore them while they were in their enforced captivity with me, that was all they needed.

When the class was finished and the students were leading their horses back to the stables, I turned to find Maeve Umbra leaning over the fence, her eyes on me.

The shimmer of her magic flowed around her. She had enchanted herself to be invisible to all but me. I knew why: wherever she went on the grounds, someone wanted her attention. The first-years would have slowed and gawked at her if they'd seen her.

I approached Umbra, balancing one foot on the bottom board of the fence. Before I could speak, she said, "You have a way with people."

I snorted. "That must explain why those foster families never kept me around for more than a week."

"You could have stayed, if you'd wanted," she said, no uncertainty in her voice. "But that wasn't what you wanted, was it?"

My arms folded. "Just so you know, I'm not paying for this therapy session."

Her lips curled, eyes crinkling. "You haven't impressed me enough yet today to merit sarcasm. Come." She turned away, her magic still swirling around her as she stepped through the grass with Parity, her staff.

We went to the Contemplator's Copse, which I had found by accident last year. There, she sat on a log facing me, and I straddled it facing her. And we continued the work we had practiced throughout the summer.

I ignited my flame, wrapped it around myself, making myself invisible to the world. She allowed us to sit in silence for fifteen, twenty minutes, a sort of meditation we often did at the start of our sessions, practicing the simple act of holding the enchantment around our bodies.

But this time, I felt the Spitfire as I held the enchantment. That had never happened. I could feel it coiled inside me, purring at my sustained use of magic. And it occurred to me that the Spitfire liked my training, my lessons, my practice. It wanted me to become more powerful. More potent. And its desires were separate from mine.

Were its intentions separate from mine, too?

When Umbra felt enough time had passed, her eyes opened and she started in on me. "Tell me your worst memory from the group home."

"Every time they served us oatmeal," I shot back. "Next."

Her eyes narrowed. She didn't speak, but her eyes said it all. My quips did nothing for me.

Then again, she kept going harder with these questions. Deeper. Last time she'd asked me about my sister. Now she wanted my worst memories.

I swallowed. I knew. I knew exactly what the worst memory was. "It was the day I turned eighteen."

"Your birthday."

The fire flowed and ebbed around me. "Yes."

"What happened on that day, Clementine?"

"I became an adult, and as I walked through the door of the house and came out into the daylight, I finally understood."

"What did you understand?" she whispered, and it was the sadness, the pity in her voice that got to me. Almost like she knew what I was going to say.

For a moment, the flames flickered, weakening. I tried to recover them, but I couldn't hold the feeling and the magic at the same time. The enchantment dropped, and I was left staring at Umbra, and her back at me, with nothing between us.

I cursed. She tilted her head and smiled.

It was the day I knew no one was going to save me but me, I thought but didn't say.

The first few days back at the academy were a cluster. Between training with Umbra to become the guardians' leader, our ongoing training sessions in enchanting, and teaching my two bareback riding classes, I hardly had time to scarf food. I didn't even have time to feel anxious—which was a good thing.

Ever since I'd become a guardian, one thought was always in the back of my mind: at any moment, the horn could sound. At any moment, we'd be responsible for other people's lives.

It hadn't sounded yet. But it would.

Umbra had forbidden anyone at the academy from leaving. We weren't to use the leyline, and no one had. Not since that day Umbra and I had passed through it. And even though she had managed to cure the corruption, the Shade had seen me part the veil. She'd seen the forest I had stepped into.

Even if she couldn't see the academy, she could leave her creatures in wait in the woods. They didn't seem to sleep or eat or want anything except to do what she commanded. And it would only take one slip for someone to be caught or killed. I had the moonstone and my enshroudment, but the other students had nothing.

Umbra didn't want to take that risk. Not when she had another option.

Parity.

When the time came, she explained, she would use her staff to part the veil from inside the academy and send the guardians through. When the mission was done, they would return the same way, fixing their focus on the staff as a point of power so that when they parted the veil, they would step through and find themselves under the enchantment's umbrella.

It sounded like a fine plan. I didn't have the bandwidth to think about it, anyway.

On the third morning, I sat in the library with Aidan studying a 1500s map of Edinburgh. We had laid it out over the entirety of the table, and our noses were only a few inches away, our fingers tracing the streets. Back then, the city had been smaller—just the central road they called the Royal Mile, and offshoot streets and alleyways, many of which the Scottish called "closes." Streets that were once open to the sky, but now lay under the city.

Most of them didn't even have names back then. At least, they weren't recorded on this map.

As an American, I'd never conceived of such a thing. Ancient streets, long buried. Long hidden. Even old homes, closed off from the world, lay in the darkness under the modern city. Somewhere in all of this, a five-hundred-year-old orichalcum blade waited for me. And once I had it, the weapon would be complete.

We'd pulled over a second table, and on that one lay a modern map of Edinburgh we sometimes referenced. The city sprawled atop an underground tangle of streets, tunnels, vaults.

Beside me, I had a notebook where I'd written down the names of every close that still existed—not demolished, just built over.

There were dozens of them.

Plague victims had died in them, sealed in. Murderers had been walled off. Ghosts were said to wander. And soon they'd have a witch down there, too.

"This one," I said to Aidan, my finger jumping between the ancient map and the modern one. "It's still there."

He had a book about Edinburgh's streets flipped open, which he consulted, turning pages. When he found what he was looking for, he read down the page. Then he shook his head. "There's no entry point."

Another one without a way to access it. That was the fourth.

I'd half-crossed that one off my list when I stopped. "Aidan, what if—"

Someone stepped into my periphery, arms folded. Above me stood Liara Youngblood with raised eyebrows on me. "Clem."

I sat back in my chair. I knew exactly why she'd come. But what I said was, "Either I've done something wrong, or Chef Vickery's coffee was lacking this morning."

Liara's eyes trailed over the spread between us. Back to me. "Did you completely forget about our leaders' training?"

I lowered my pen. "I would never."

She swept a hand out to indicate the maps and books and Aidan, her expression an obvious, *So what's this, then?*

I gathered up my things, stood. "Listen, Youngblood," I said, low, "when you're the subject of an ancient prophecy, then you'll understand the difficulty of time management."

She rolled her eyes, turning away in a swing of silky hair. "Don't make me drag you along, Cole. It's unbecoming in front of the first-years when I pull you by the ear."

My gaze snapped to Aidan. "Tomorrow, same time?"

"Until we solve this," he said. And then he tapped another book—one about the history of enchantments as a school of magic. "And this."

He was referring to the mystery of Maeve Umbra and her mastery of enchantments. I'd relayed everything she'd told me when I'd visited her home earlier in the week, and he was even more fascinated and perplexed.

My gaze also fell to his satchel, which brimmed with two more fat books from the Room of the Ancients. We weren't supposed to take them out of the library at all.

When Aidan noticed where my attention had gone, he flipped his satchel shut. And ignored my narrowed, suspicious gaze.

He was up to something.

As Liara and I left the library and started toward the meadow, she said, "What's the progress on the blade?"

"Not much. We've figured out that Edinburgh has lots of hidey holes."

She glanced at me. "Why don't you ask Umbra?" Over the summer, I had told Liara that Umbra was aware of the prophecy and everything I had done to fulfill it. She knew the headmistress was training me to find the last piece of the weapon.

"What would she know about Edinburgh?" I asked.

"It wasn't always a formalist stronghold," Liara said. "Don't you know anything about magical history?"

"My bad. I should have signed up for that class in *regular human* high school."

She made a noise that sounded like disdain. "The formalists only rose to power in the last twenty or so years. Before that, Edinburgh was liberal. Less rigid. Someone like Maeve Umbra would have traveled there regularly."

"Doesn't mean she'd know anything about the blade."

"But," Liara said, "it does mean she'd know a thing or two about its streets."

She had a point. As we arrived at the meadow, Umbra turned to face us, her head dappled by the sunlight through the leaves of the tree above her. One hand went up in greeting, and in it she held a strip of black cloth.

CHAPTER ELEVEN

We high-stepped our way through the grass out to Umbra, who stood at the edge of the meadow in the shade. As we neared, her eyes surveyed us. "Well," she said. "You're both late."

Liara and I jerked our thumbs at each other in the same moment, and before we could start in on our explanations, Umbra began laughing. "It was both of your faults and neither, is that right?"

"Something like that," Liara said.

The headmistress shook her head. "Ah, you're far too alike to co-lead easily. Why in the gods' names did the other guardians want you two?"

We exchanged a glance.

I shrugged. "They said they trusted us."

"Only the gods know why," Liara said.

Umbra smiled. "Well"—she extended the black strip of cloth toward me—"let's see what we can do with the two of you."

I accepted it, twirled it in the wind. "I don't usually wear blindfolds outside, but I'll make an exception for you, Umbra."

"Oh, just put it over your eyes," the headmistress scoffed. "And tie it tight, child. I won't have you cheating."

I set an aggrieved hand to my chest.

Liara's expression changed at once. "The enchantment magic you've taught us doesn't work that way. It's only aural."

"Is it?" Umbra reached over to lift my thumb and waited for Liara to present her forehead. "Perhaps you should tell that to Clementine."

When my thumb met Liara's forehead, I sent my magic through, into her, establishing the connection between us. If I wanted to, I could speak into her head.

"Now," Umbra said, impatiently plucking the cloth from my hand and tying it around my head herself, "Clementine, you'll sit. Liara, go where you will. Fly, if you wish. Fly far."

I sat cross-legged in the grass, the sun warming my head and shoulders through the canopy. Around me, I heard the sounds of Umbra moving, and of Liara taking off from the ground. Her wings beat so softly they melded with the swishing grass before they disappeared, and I was left alone with the headmistress.

I sensed Umbra seating herself across from me with a small grunt. "Now, tell me what Liara sees."

I sat there, staring into nothing. "Trees, probably."

"Not probably. Precisely."

"I would tell you, but there's the small problem of the cloth you put over my eyes."

I could hear Umbra's soft breathing. "Your magic gives you a connection to Liara. The training you've done with me over the summer has strengthened your ability to sustain your magic, to enshroud—and, conversely, to see." She paused. "Can you feel the thread of your magic to her?"

The thread. Was there a thread? I had never considered the idea.

"I don't feel any thread," I said.

I could hear Umbra patting the grass. "Remove the blindfold." I did so and found Umbra's fingers tented at either side of her. "Beneath us lies a leyline. Can you see it?"

I shook my head. I had never seen a leyline—not here or anywhere.

She traced her finger back toward the central grounds, beneath where we sat, and straight off through the center of the meadow. "It runs right through the center of the academy, and it glows a beautiful color." Her eyes shifted back to me. "Once you can see this leyline, you'll be able to see the thread of your magic as it connects to Liara."

That was the end of our lesson for the day. The next day, Umbra only asked me to return. I wouldn't be ready for the next step until I could see the leyline, she said. And so we sat in the grass on that day, and the next, and the next, as Umbra tried to teach me the most basic concept of seeing a leyline.

It wasn't dissimilar to seeing a magical place, as Eva had taught me years back. There was a certain amount of belief involved, of imagination. But I still couldn't see what Umbra could see. I *wanted* to see. I *wanted* to believe, but I couldn't.

Until on the third day, it finally clicked.

"Unfocus," Umbra instructed me. "You're all tensed up, wound tight. Allow your shoulders to fall, your lungs to open. Don't stare so hard at the ground, child. Allow the shifting angle of the sun to do its work. Haven't you heard the expression of a watched pot?"

"That so doesn't apply here," I said, but did as she asked, relaxing into my seat. And as the sun moved through the sky, angling differently over us as it did, I began to see it.

The sun on the grass. It shone differently where we sat. And as my lidded eyes trailed across the meadow, they followed a soft, glowing line of magic.

It was beautiful, shimmering, iridescent.

"That's how I felt the first time, too," Umbra murmured.

The next day, Liara and I returned together. We repeated the blindfold exercise, Liara disappearing through the meadow and into the trees, and Umbra once more asked me to focus on my thread of magic to her.

And as soon as I did, I sensed it. An invisible spider's thread of my flames stretched off from where I sat, weaving its way through the meadow and into the trees... and to Liara.

There, some small portion of it surrounded her.

With this realization, I straightened. "I feel it."

"You see," Umbra said, "the connection isn't you speaking into her head so much as you whispering into her ear."

Even though—or maybe because—Liara couldn't respond, I said to her, *I'm going to find you, wherever you are.* Followed by a soft, sinister laugh... right into her ear.

"Focus, child," Umbra snapped.

"What makes you think I wasn't?" I said.

"You smirked. Quit taunting the fae."

I reduced my smirk to half of one. "But she's so easily taunted."

"Coalesce your magic around her ears," Umbra said. "Hear what she hears."

I did so—well, the coalescing, at least. But I didn't hear anything through the thread of my magic. I made a face.

"You're focused on the magic," Umbra said. "Focus on her. Be her ears."

Be her ears? The concept seemed strange, but I tried, as best I could, to do what Umbra asked of me. To be Liara's ears. I focused on her. On layering my magic over her ears, both outside and inside. And as I did, the sound of water came to me with crystal clarity.

A fish had just jumped, splashed back into it.

Except in the meadow, there was no water to hear.

"She's by the pond," I whispered.

"Good," Umbra said. "Quicker than I expected. Now be her eyes, too."

She wanted me to be both at once. I was already sweating from the exertion of following the thread of magic through the meadow and into the trees, shaping it over Liara's ears. I was already struggling not just to sustain the connection, but to trace my way along the thread at all. The longer I did it, the more jumbled everything felt. Like I was becoming disconnected from my own body. My hands and feet had begun to tingle, my ears ringing.

A few seconds later, I lost it. The thread disappeared, crumbling, and my connection with Liara disappeared.

I was seated in the meadow with the blind over my eyes, sweat dripping into the cloth from my forehead.

Umbra leaned forward, pulled the blind down, revealing a stunningly brilliant sky. "Rest, child. You've overdone it."

"Overdone it? I did what you asked."

"Yes, and you so rarely do exactly what I ask." With a flick of her fingers, Umbra conjured a small picnic basket and glasses of lemonade with ice inside. She lifted one of the glasses, passed it to me. "Liara," she called across the meadow, "fly back to us."

I took a long sip from the lemonade, feeling shaky. And tingly. And unwell.

When Liara had returned, seating herself between us, Umbra passed her the second of the three glasses. "Did you feel Clementine's magic?"

Liara took a long sip from the glass. "In my ears, for a moment."

"Soon enough she'll be in your eyes." Umbra winked at her, opening the picnic basket to reveal a bunch of goodies inside.

"Should I head back out then?" Liara asked.

"Of course not." Umbra began to unpack the basket. "That's it for today."

"But"—Liara lowered her glass—"we only trained for twenty minutes."

"Look at her, child." Umbra nodded at me. "Look at her and tell me she could go another twenty minutes."

Liara did look at me. Her eyes narrowed, then softened. She sighed. "But how are we supposed to co-lead at this rate?"

"Clementine can follow your progress from the guardians' globe," Umbra said. "She can speak to you, though she won't be able to hear what you hear or see what you see. Not until she masters this. She'll still be a boon to you."

Liara didn't say any more on the subject. But as I drank and ate and began gradually to regain my strength, I wondered if what she was teaching me out here was simply to help the guardians.

This was powerful magic. It was magic linked, part and parcel, with what she had been teaching me to do all summer. Umbra was simultaneously training me to enshroud myself and to see.

<hr>

Two days later, Eva and I were seated side by side on a log near the pond just after lunch. She was tangibly manipulating a large piece of olive-green cloth with a needle and thread. The whole of it was draped over her knees, and she wouldn't tell me what it was. "Elijah and Isaiah evaluated me," she was saying, "and they recommended me as a guard."

I tossed a stone into the pond, where it skipped once before sinking. "Good call."

"You would have picked that for me?"

"Because it's what you are." My Eva was nothing if not the fae who looked out for everyone else. "And nobody can heal like you."

Earlier in the week, I had trained and evaluated the two humans—Maise and Paxton—to determine their roles. I had an idea before I'd watched them ride across the meadow, but after, I was certain. Maise rode like Fi: watchful, ready to raise the earth at the first sign of Noir and me galloping in from the side. She took point on keeping Paxton safe from the witch.

Paxton rode with his eyes ahead, rushing toward the dummy I had set up at the meadow's far end. He would spear its head off with a massive shard of ice if it was his last act.

She was a guard. He was a chaser.

"I'd kind of hoped to be a chaser," Eva said, her needle pausing in midair as her eyes lifted to the water.

I turned to her. "Really?"

"It's what my parents were."

I nudged her. "The roles aren't set, Eva."

"Aren't they?"

I swept a hand out. "We're at the academy for just a few years. It isn't forever. You want to be a chaser after we're out of here? Follow your sweet fae dreams, Evanora."

She half-smiled, resumed with the needle and thread. "If the world still exists after we graduate."

"Oh, it'll exist." I picked up another stone, tossed it. "Just maybe not in the form we've grown used to."

"Clem," she began. "About Edinburgh..."

The distant sound of the horn cut into whatever she was about to say. We had both straightened when Umbra's voice spoke into our heads. And I knew now it was her magic tickling the inside of my ear, whispering to me. *Acapulco. A boy, seventeen.* That was followed by the brief image of a nighttime street in the city, where palm trees swayed under the moon.

As we stood, I wondered for the first time at how Umbra could place an image before my eyes. It must be her magic coalescing in front of my pupils, in the same way she'd asked me to thread my magic into Liara's ears.

If we could whisper, then we could also show.

Just as quickly as the thought entered, it disappeared. I pointed toward Umbra's office. "Get to the headmistress. Elijah and Isaiah will prepare you. I'll be there in a minute."

Eva bundled up her cloth and took to the air. She flew through the trees toward the central grounds, disappearing in a wink of lavender. I ran after her, feeling slow and heavy-footed.

I had to be with the other guardians before they all went through. A shame I hadn't actually been meant to ride a broom—that would have made my life a lot easier when I had to haul ass from one end of the grounds to the other.

Meanwhile, the sound of the horn went on echoing through the forest. I had mixed feelings about it: on the one hand, I hated the thing and would be glad to never hear it again. On the other, a strange rush of dopamine and adrenaline flowed through me when it actually did sound, like I could finally act on the impulse I'd been feeling ever since I'd arrived back at the academy.

Finally, our first rescue of the year.

When I got to Umbra's tree, she stood outside the double doors, surrounded by the other guardians. The humans were already on horse-back, the fae hovering two or three feet in the air. Loki sat by Umbra.

Good. Even Maise and Paxton had gotten saddled up and mounted, which boded well. They weren't slouches.

Clusters of students had gathered, watching from a distance. Some stood on landings, some sat on tree branches, some just stood clutching their satchels. That had been me, once.

"Ah," Umbra said on spotting me. "All our guardians are present. Make your connections, Clementine, and the rest of you prepare yourselves to pass through."

I broke into the group with my thumb out like I was offering a benediction. Without a word, I stamped Liara on the forehead, creating the magical connection. She did the same with me. The humans on horseback leaned down for me to reach them, each of us touching each other's foreheads one by one. Then I moved on to the fae.

They didn't bother with their thumbs on my forehead; they couldn't talk to me from this distance like I had been trained to do with them. It only went one-way.

The moment I was done, Umbra had already raised Parity, set the tip of it at an angle in the air. The end of it glowed green as she did so, and she made a precise, slow cut through the veil.

When she parted it, I could see Mexico on the other side. Could smell the salty sea air, feel the balminess.

But I wouldn't be passing through. I only stood aside as the fae swept through first, and then the guardians on horseback. And even then I was backing away with Loki, heading toward the guardians' tree.

I caught a glimpse of the last horse's tail flicking through, and then Umbra lowered the parting, her eyes meeting mine. "Get to the globe," she called. "They need you more than ever."

When I came to the empty guardians' tree and ascended to the third floor, Loki raced ahead of me. I found him seated beneath the globe, staring back at me. "I've been waiting for ages."

"You're joining me for this, huh?" I took up my spot in front of the globe, spinning it to the western coast of Mexico and zeroing in on Acapulco. As I did, my eyes traced to the nearest leyline, glowing golden on the map.

It was uncorrupted, and it ran straight through the center of the city. That was what I would use to maintain my connection with the guardians.

"Of course I am." Loki stared up at the globe. "I'm as much a guardian as you are."

I seated myself, crossing my legs. "Then let's do this thing."

CHAPTER TWELVE

T he leylines streaked across the globe before me, some golden, some black. About half were dark—which seemed worse than when Umbra and I had sat before the globe just a few days ago.

I had to find my way through them, keeping to the uncorrupted lines and tracing that thread of magic all the way to Acapulco, where the guardians were.

My eyes closed, and I focused on the magic connecting me to them. As Umbra had trained me, I followed it through the leyline running past the academy, tracing its course through hills, valleys, over mountains, until it crossed paths with another leyline that would take me where I wanted to go.

Sometimes I had to detour around the corruption. When I encountered it, I felt it like an oppressive darkness, both terrifying and alluring—and familiar, now that I had entered a corrupted leyline. One detour took me under the Atlantic Ocean, and I came out the other side in Florida. My magic traced through the leyline, rushing toward Acapulco.

And when I arrived, I could feel them. I could feel all the guardians.

Sweat had already broken out on my forehead and my spine. My breathing had quickened. This wasn't just work—it was a combination of maintaining my connection in the midst of danger, of the adrenaline I'd been feeling since the horn had sounded.

This was grueling.

But I had managed to find my way to Acapulco. My eyes opened, and I saw the guardians on the globe before me. Nine green dots appeared at my wish, just like in the simulation. They moved down a street, small specks in the vastness of the world, and they were following three of the creatures, one of whom carried the seventeen-year-old boy.

I knew, because two of the fae had eyes on the creatures from above.

The rest of the guardians were two blocks behind, following the creatures, who were making for the ocean.

"They've got maybe five minutes," Loki said, observing the globe, "before the Shade's monsters hit the water."

I nodded. The other guardians didn't know this; they only had limited vision. Which was where I came in.

The creatures are a half mile from the ocean, I said into Liara's head. *You've got just over four minutes at best. Send the chasers left down the first cross-street, then right at the next intersection. They can cut them off.*

And though Liara couldn't respond with her own magic, I heard her voice as though it was right next to me, even though it was thousands of miles away. When she spoke, it ricocheted through the thread of my magic back to me. "Got it," she breathed.

Liara must have relayed my instructions into the others' heads, because not five seconds later, the horseback guardians broke away in the exact direction I'd told them to go. Left down the cross-street, then right at the intersection.

But the monsters went right, too, as though they'd sensed the guardians. Maybe they'd heard them.

"Shit," I whispered.

I shifted my focus to the two fae who had eyes on the creatures: Elijah and Isaiah. When I concentrated my magic on Elijah, I didn't hesitate—I went straight for his vision. I needed to see what was going on.

And for a gleaming moment, a cityscape flashed into my head, brilliant and bright and vast. I gasped, and then it was gone.

The strain was too much. Going for the eyes was on another level, as I'd learned during my training with Umbra and Liara. My magic retreated, exhausted, and I began to shake as I had out in the meadow.

I was all but useless. And I wasn't meant to sit here—I was meant to chase.

On the globe, the creatures were keeping pace ahead of the guardians. And a second group of the creatures had appeared, at least six tailing them. Giving chase. Catching up.

And here I was, functionally useless. Half-blind. I couldn't properly see them, couldn't hear them. The thread of magic had dissipated, and even if I wanted to, I didn't have the strength anymore to give Liara instructions.

Not without *its* help. I needed the Spitfire.

So be it.

Loki brushed up against me. "Clem."

I used what strength I had to push myself to my feet. "This isn't going to work." As the Spitfire uncoiled inside me, I headed down the stairs two at a time.

I needed to get to Umbra.

<hr>

I sprinted to the stables, Loki on my tail, and threw open the half-door. I ignored the quartermistress's questions and went straight for Noir's stall.

He was ready, his head high, eyes wide.

A minute later, I'd led him into the paddock and swung up onto his back. Loki leapt up to the edge of my cloak, climbing his way onto my shoulder. He knew better than to question me right now.

We galloped toward the clearing, where I had last seen Umbra—where she would be waiting for the guardians to return. When we came around the edge of the amphitheater, she stood facing me, her eyes already on us as the horse came galloping up. "Send me to them," I said, breathless, coming to a stop directly in front of her.

Her eyes tracked over the horse, then me, observing my exhaustion. "You couldn't maintain the thread with your magic, and yet... you're radiating with power."

"The thread won't work," I bit out, anger swelling in me. The Spitfire roiled. "They're being chased. Send me."

"It's not safe outside the grounds, child."

We were losing time. Noir was anxious to go, and he started into a walk. I urged him in a tight circle, keeping my eyes on Umbra. "You told me you'd never forbid me from leaving the grounds."

One eyebrow rose. "So I did." Her eyes gleamed. "You're ready, then?"

There was something odd about that twinkle in her eyes, about the tone of her voice. Like she'd expected this moment to come. Like she'd never expected me to be able to withstand sitting here alone on the grounds, away from the action.

But it was more than that. I had the distinct sense that she'd been testing my will. Because, after all, she had explicitly told me she'd never forbid me to leave the grounds. She'd only strongly advised against it.

Years ago, when Umbra and I had first met, she'd told me my magic depended on my belief in myself. And while it was dangerous for me to leave the grounds, maybe she'd been waiting for this moment. The moment when I believed I could use the enshrouding magic she'd spent three months—every damn day for a whole summer—teaching me.

The Spitfire flared inside me, thrilled. Eager. Ready to provide me with its power.

I stared down at her, setting my jaw. "I'm ready." And in the same moment, the invisible flames raced from my hands up my arms, encasing my entire body in one massive ripple of fire. Within a few seconds, it had spread to Loki and to Noir.

We were fully enshrouded. It had been so easy when I let the creature inside me have its way. Just as it had been out on that lake in Siberia.

I could use the enshroudment. I was ready, and probably had been for weeks. It just took this urgency to bring it out of me.

Umbra gave a soft, respectful nod. "Well done, child. Well done." She lifted Parity. "Very well. Keep your wits about you."

When she began to part the veil, she raised the tip of the staff high into the air, drawing it down from over seven feet up. She'd only barely finished the cut before I pressed Noir forward, ducking low to pass through the parting.

In a second, we crossed from grass to asphalt, from daytime to nighttime. From safety to the witching hour.

And all at once, I could feel them again. The guardians were half a mile away, on the move. The connection hadn't been broken after all—it had only gone fallow.

Loki perked. "I smell them. And the monsters. Lots of monsters."

"Great." I pressed my heels into Noir's side, and we broke into a gallop down the empty side street, made narrow by all the compact cars parked along it. We swerved left at the first intersection, then right at the next one, Noir navigating the streets with ease.

Meanwhile, I focused my magic on Liara. I wanted to hear what she heard—and it was so much easier now. So little distance lay between us, and it felt even shorter with the Spitfire's wildness surging through me.

As soon as my magic entered her ears, I heard a scream.

It was a horse's scream. Somewhere nearby, hooves clattered in an awkward, jarring way.

"Right at the next street," Loki said.

I swung Noir right, and two of the creatures came into view, rushing ahead of me, chasing the other guardians. They couldn't see or hear us past the enshrouding enchantment, anyway.

"*Pairilis síoraí*," I whispered, and they both went completely still at the same time, stuck in place.

We swept past them, leaving the creatures behind in their stasis.

This time, I didn't have to hear what Liara heard. In the sky above me, lightning cracked. She was in battle.

"Take a left two blocks up," Loki said.

I followed his instructions, turning Noir left. When the street came into view, I finally found the guardians.

They were surrounded at an intersection.

Dozens of the Shade's minions filled the street ahead, all of them in erratic motion. One leapt onto a car, threw itself at Paxton, who yanked up a wall of water and intercepted the creature just in time. The thing slammed into the shield of water, hit the ground... and promptly scrambled back up.

One form of magic couldn't take them out. That was a hard lesson I'd had to learn early on.

Another crackle of Liara's lightning illuminated the whole scene, driving up into the sky and revealing horses in frantic motion, water spraying, bits of earth being launched, and a tumble of wind through the street.

Liara's lightning pierced two creatures, but so many more filled in their ranks. I even spotted one flying—or maybe just leaping. *Unless the reports of flying creatures were right.*

Why were the guardians so unorganized? They shouldn't have gotten caught like this. Not after all the trouble we'd gone to to keep this from happening last spring.

Then I saw her: Liara was on her back in the middle of it all. Only one of her arms was moving, and the other one lay limp. She was injured. Badly.

"Clem," Loki said.

"I see her."

This rescue had been an absolute failure, and it needed to end. Quickly, before things got worse for them. I reached back, into the depths of my cloak, and retrieved the weapon.

The Spitfire was ecstatic with bloodlust.

CHAPTER THIRTEEN

I gripped the weapon in both hands, riding only with my thighs as the quartermistress had taught me to do through so many months of barrel and trick riding.

Bet she hadn't expected this from the witch. Or maybe she had.

The weapon's power amplified my own, singing sweetly with the Spitfire, the two of them working in a strange and perfect concert, almost like they were meant to be.

And I knew exactly what I needed to do.

Liara, I said into the fae's head. *I'm here. Keep drilling them.*

Liara's face turned, her eyes searching the darkness. When she didn't find me, she returned to attention, lightning spearing from her one good hand.

The chain hung long at Noir's side, swept back by the wind as he galloped toward the scene. I drove my magic into each guardian's head, giving them each the same instruction: *When you see the fire, kill them.*

On that lake, fire riding had been the greatest challenge of my life. I'd had to give a small piece of myself away, inhabit the old anger I'd felt for so many years.

And now that I'd given it away, it came easier. Faster.

Between the creature inside me and the metal in my hand, I craved it—the power and the fury. And so, with one quick breath and my eyes briefly closed, it only took a moment to empower the enshrouding flames, to make them burn hot and hard.

The Shade's creatures would be able to see me, but not for long.

The Spitfire enveloped me, the flames burning bright over me and the horse as we rushed in, trampling the creatures underfoot, setting them aflame.

I sent my fire down the rod and the length of the chain, swinging it at them, lancing them one and two at a time if Noir's hooves didn't get them. We made an arc around the intersection, lighting the whole place up, and around me, the other three elements surged.

And I kept riding, kept swinging, kept burning until I was certain I'd gotten every single one of the bastards.

Until Eva's voice called, "Clem, stop!"

It took gargantuan effort even to acknowledge what she'd said, to process it. And inside me, the Spitfire hissed, *More. More. More.*

But through the flames in front of me, I couldn't see them. I couldn't see any more. I only saw Maise's face appear in front of me, her eyes wide and wild with fear.

The Spitfire hissed words into my head—ones my conscious mind refused to acknowledge. They were killing words. *Make her pay for getting in your way.*

But from somewhere deep inside me, Rational Clem clawed her way toward the surface. *It's Maise*, she said. *She's human. She's your friend.*

Maise. I shouldn't hurt Maise.

I drew my grip back on Noir's mane, brought him to a skidding halt with the weapon aloft, the chain swinging with flame. My arm shook with the restraint it took to avoid slinging the chain at her, slicing her in half as I had with the Shade's minions twenty seconds ago.

Maise's horse danced away across the wreckage in the intersection, head jerking at the sight and sound of the flaming witch and her steed.

As Rational Clem came to the fore and my fire began to ebb, the real world returned to view, all the colors that weren't red and white and orange and yellow. Well, not *just* those colors. Because, as I looked around, I realized the whole intersection was on fire, a big ring of it that was starting to burn low as my magic seeped away.

Eva's lavender hair glinted in the moonlight as she landed in the street, and Siren's dappled gray coat gleamed, and the brown of the earth that Akelan had yanked up lay in a spread all around.

I half-slumped on Noir's back; I couldn't get a proper breath. With the Spitfire gone, I had no energy left.

"Clem," Loki whispered from my shoulder, "hide the weapon."

I realized with a start I was still holding it, and now I was visible to the whole world. Before I did anything else, I extinguished the flame and replaced it in the tangibly manipulated pocket inside my cloak.

Then I led Noir over to everyone else.

Eva knelt by Liara, helping her up. Paxton came around on his horse and Elijah and Isaiah helped lift her up to sit with Paxton. Liara slumped, her eyes half-shut. That was rare for her; she never showed what she considered to be weakness if she could help it.

Akelan had put his magic to work repairing the asphalt that had been displaced, fixing the street to where the humans wouldn't notice what had happened in the morning.

"We need to get back." My eyes traveled over the group. Then, eyes on Mishka—who seemed to be in the best shape of all—I said, "Part the veil. We're headed back to the academy."

Mishka nodded, got to work with an efficient cut in the center of the road. When she parted the veil, light from the academy grounds filtered through.

I ferried everyone through, and I went last of all. On the other side, Maeve Umbra stood with a glowing Parity in the clearing, her scrutinizing eyes focused on Liara, whom Paxton was already riding to the infirmary.

Good. He had initiative, too.

"If you're hurt," I said to the other guardians, "follow them to the infirmary. Otherwise, we're done. Meet me in the guardians' common room tomorrow morning at seven. We're debriefing."

"Debriefing?" Akelan said, hesitating on his horse. "We don't do that."

"We do now." I waved a hand through the air, too tired to elaborate beyond, "Shitshows need debriefs."

I slid off Noir's back as soon as the others had gone, and Loki hopped off my shoulder to the ground.

Umbra stood observing me. "You fire rode."

I didn't know how she knew, but she did. "Yeah."

"And revealed yourself in the process."

I lifted sullen eyes to her. "Not that I don't see the value in a good lecture, but... Actually, I don't see the value in it."

Umbra reached out, set a hand on my shoulder. It was only when she touched me I realized I was coated in sweat from the flames. "Lectures are for children who don't know better. You do, and I know you did what you had to."

It was the first time she had shown true esteem in me. And though I wanted to be thrilled, I couldn't help wondering what Umbra would think if she'd known how close I had come to killing Maise.

Maise, who had definitely seen the Spitfire in my eyes.

The next morning, Loki and I came into the guardians' common room early to find Maise sitting in an armchair, staring into a low-burning fire. She'd probably lit it herself.

She glanced around when I came in, her brown bob swaying. "We're the only ones here so far."

Loki and I exchanged a glance, and he made for the stairs, disappearing like a slip.

I crossed the space to the empty partner armchair. Gestured to it. "May I?"

Her eyebrows rose for a moment, coupled with a nod.

I sat. Leaned back, both hands on the armrests, and stared into the fire with her. "Nice mixture of flames you've got going there. White-hot at the center, a pretty orange at the edges. Good lick to them."

"You can thank Goodbarrel for that precision. The man loves nothing more than an exact flame."

I half-smiled. It had been months since I'd thought about the classes I'd taken with him, and yet I drew on what he'd taught me just about every day. "I think he's a little bit of what stopped me last night."

Maise's eyes met mine. She knew exactly what I was talking about—that moment I'd been about to slice her in two. "On my first rescue, I didn't expect you to be the most terrifying thing out there."

I swallowed, the sight of her frightened face as clear to me as her reserved one was now. "When I'm in a fight, I can get a bit single-minded. You remember how I was during our duels in class."

Her gaze searched me over, like she was seeking out a lie. "I remember."

"So—"

"But I wish I could show you," she continued, "how you looked last night. It was different. I wasn't exaggerating when I said you were the most terrifying thing out there."

I saved you, came a small, petulant voice in my head.

I pushed it aside. Sat forward with my elbows on my thighs. "I had to do what I had to do to keep you all safe."

She shook her head. "Did you, though?"

"You were surrounded by those creatures."

"Things were intense, but then you came in like a bat from hell and lit the whole place up and things got... chaotic. If I hadn't gotten out of the way—"

My chest caught. "I stopped myself."

"Yes," she said. "But you almost didn't."

Words flew into my head and out my mouth. "I was fire riding. It takes all my focus, and it's hard to control—but I can. I can control it." I paused. "Liara was hurt."

She drew in a long breath. "Yes, she was hurt."

I leaned closer. "I would never hurt you, Maise. Not you or any of the others."

Would I never hurt her? a tiny voice asked.

Of course not, came the instant reply.

Her eyes softened on me. "I believe you. And I won't say anything to anyone about this, but keep that flaming chain away from me, would you?"

So she sensed something was different about the weapon, but she would keep my secret—whatever it was. I'd always known I liked Maise for a reason.

I lifted my first two fingers in the air. "Promise."

Footsteps sounded at the doorway. Akelan had arrived, along with Liara. The fae looked completely healed, her arm functional; Nurse Neverwink's doing.

My attention flicked back to Maise, but she was already standing. "Let's do this," she said, and started toward the stairs. Akelan followed, and Liara stopped beside me, looking down at me.

"Neverwink's a miracle-worker," I said up to her.

She glanced down at her arm, raised it and splayed all five fingers. "Neverwink fixed the radius and ulna breaks. Eva did the fine finger work."

I stood. "Eva did?"

"Yeah, she was with me for hours last night in the infirmary. Sat by my bed like a nurse."

Other guardians began to stream in, Eva among them, and I just kept up a blank stare at Liara. I hadn't even noticed that Eva had come back to the dorm late last night; I'd just gone straight to my bed and collapsed into it, exhausted.

As Eva passed, she smiled at me—that same, sweet, unbegrudging smile. Then she disappeared in a flutter of wings, headed up.

Guilt seeded in my gut. I should have gone to the infirmary. "Liara," I began.

"I know what you're going to say," she cut in without malice. "And I don't care that you didn't visit me. Focus on yourself, Clem."

Liara didn't wait for me to say anything else; she turned away, followed Eva in a flash of wings.

My face lifted, staring after her. *Focus on yourself.* She was one of just a few people who knew the full gravity of what she was saying.

Umbra arrived a minute later, and we all migrated up to the third floor and sat down at the meeting table, Loki atop the table beside me. Umbra remained standing, pacing her way into everyone's view. Stood before us all for a moment in silence.

Finally, she said, "You all survived last night. The rescue was unsuccessful, but I'm grateful to see your faces here now." She nodded at Liara, then at me. "Leaders, I'd like to know what happened."

Liara and I looked at one another, and I nodded at her to start. She sighed. "Everything was going fine, until it wasn't. First we were chasing, and Clementine was giving instructions, and then she went silent. Not long after, we were being chased—and not just on the ground."

I straightened in my seat. So I *had* seen flying creatures.

"The Shade's minions," Liara said. "They fly now. They have wings. Two of them flew in from the sides and ambushed me while I was chasing."

So that was what had caused Liara's injuries. That explained why they'd been so disoriented.

Umbra nodded. "That was sooner than I had anticipated. Much sooner."

"You anticipated that?" I blurted.

Her eyes shifted to me. "Fae have not been exempt from the kidnappings. The Shade takes humans and fae alike."

The others looked as horrified as me.

I had always suspected, but now I had it confirmed. "So the creatures she sends out into the world during the witching hour, they were once humans. Or fae."

"Once," Umbra whispered. "Now they are but wraiths."

"And you knew," I said, unable to stop myself. "But you never told us."

"It is one thing to slay a monster," Umbra said, apology laced in her words, "but it is entirely another to slay what was once a sentient with a brain as functional as yours."

Last night, I'd demolished them. Every single one I could find, without remorse. The wraiths—the once-humans and fae.

"Now," Umbra said, "the Shade has regained the power to fly, if only through her creatures. Her power has grown hugely, which means the guardians must adapt."

CHAPTER FOURTEEN

Two hours and an intense meeting later, Eva and I emerged into the daylight, the two of us walking together as the other guardians filtered to their own dorms. Loki trotted off toward the dining hall and Vickery's post-lunch leftovers, which left us alone.

We took an aimless path through the grounds, and Eva's eyes were unfocused; she'd been fully wrecked by the knowledge that she was killing once-humans, once-fae.

Especially the fae.

When we had walked a time, she finally said, "I killed a fae last night. Me and Mishka together."

"It wasn't a fae," I said. "Not anymore."

She shook her head. "I thought the outline of its wings looked familiar. Just like mine."

"Just like any fae's wings," I said. "They're all the same shape."

Her sad eyes shifted to me. "It doesn't bother you at all?"

It did, and it didn't. How could I explain to her the two parts of me, Rational Clem considering how she'd killed dozens (maybe hundreds) of once-mages, and the Spitfire glad for it?

I couldn't even explain the divide to myself. For a few years now I'd thought I had coalesced into one person, that my anger didn't bear a life of its own like some separate, eternal entity.

I had been wrong.

"It bothers me," I said. *Part of me.* "But we have no choice."

She eyed me like she was coming to some internal decision. Then, with a sigh, she averted her attention to the passing flora. "And now this."

"And now this," I said, trying to match her tone—and maybe failing. The truth was, I was glad for *this.*

During the meeting, it had been decided: the world was too dangerous for the guardians to rush out after newly kidnapped humans and fae. Not with the Shade's creatures on the offensive against us, now in the air as well as on the ground.

We would have to change. Because now, after centuries, the world had changed. The Shade's powers were growing like a wave about to crest, and soon, Umbra suspected, the full wrath of her powers would tumble over the earth like it had five hundred years ago.

We were still guardians, but Umbra had given us a new priority. We had to be careful, covert.

We would be infiltrating Edinburgh. Working against the Mages' Council and Tristan Rathmore.

"When I was little, my parents used to tell me stories about the illustrious Mages' Council." Eva dragged her fingers through her hair. "Now it's just another thing that's been corrupted by the Shade."

I yanked a leaf off a tree as we passed by. "Umbra said if she runs the council, she runs Edinburgh. But the formalists hate witches."

"Clever of her, isn't it?" Eva said. "The average citizen would never suspect the Shade owns Tristan Rathmore."

Clever was one word for it. Diabolical, another. And deeply problematic, a third and fourth. From everything I knew, the city was ruled by iron and rigidity. I still sometimes dreamed about that prison cell they'd dropped into Farina North's yard—one meant to transport me back to their city.

Apparently they had lots of prisoners. The formalists had thrown dozens of "traitorous" mages in their crypts, ones they claimed would commit treason, would attempt to overthrow the Mages' Council—which was precisely the kind of mage Maeve Umbra was looking for.

We needed allies. And it was our job to bring them here.

"Eva," I said. "That night you got drunk, you said Edinburgh is anti-magic."

"That's right. Very few are competent with it except those on the Mages' Council, so they can keep their power to themselves. And the officers we saw in Aidan's grandmother's home that one day? They're trained to fight magic."

"How?" I asked.

"Remember those nightsticks they carried?"

I nodded.

"Those can absorb our elements, neutralize them."

"Wonderful," I said.

"I don't understand how you talked Umbra into letting you go on these missions into the heart of formalist territory," Eva said. "What did you even say to her?"

"I told her I needed to go." I had pulled Umbra aside after she'd given us our new directive. We'd talked for only thirty seconds, which was probably what had confounded Eva.

She shot me a skeptical eye. "That's all?"

There was much more to it than that. Umbra and I had hashed things out in the moment I'd ridden up to her on Noir, when I'd insisted on joining the others in Acapulco. I'd told her I was ready, and I was.

But during those thirty seconds in the guardians tree, I'd said something else to her, too. "*I have to find my sister and Callum.*"

And Umbra had given me a look of infinite pity—and understanding. She'd nodded. "You'll go, then, whether I wish it or not. So go with my blessing, but do not think this will be the end of your training to use the leylines."

Eva deserved to know why, too. She was my best friend. But I couldn't even bring myself to say my sister's name. So instead I said, "I have to find my mom, my sister, and the blade. And him," I whispered to her. "And this is my best chance."

She stopped, staring at me. "Who's him?"

I stopped with her. Stared back. Didn't speak.

Then her eyes widened, lips parting into an O. "You're totally in love with Callum Rathmore."

I shook my head. "Don't make me hex you."

She linked her arm in mine, matching my step as she leaned close. "You're the bravest witch I've ever met."

"Aren't I the only witch you've met?"

"Yes." She winked over at me. "Is your enshrouding magic ready, then?"

"My enshrouding magic is good enough."

"That doesn't sound like the same thing to me."

"Really? Because 'good enough' and 'ready' sound like exactly the same thing to me." I paused, sighing through my annoyance. It wasn't at Eva; it was at Umbra. "Our lovely headmistress is unrealistic. She wants me to be bombproof. The woman keeps asking me devastating questions during training, digging into my head."

"Ah. And you lose the magic when she does that."

"Yes. But it won't matter," I said. "Nobody's going to know I'm there with you in the first place."

Eva went silent for a time as we walked. Then, finally, she said, "What does Umbra ask you about?"

My throat stoppered like a cork had been shoved down it, and I still found her name too hard to say. Like saying it would jinx me, ruin everything. Like she was a ghost who could never become real again.

"The past," I said, hoarse. "She asks me about the past."

***

The guardians' horn had been retired—for now. Umbra had told us she would have our first mission ready for us in a few weeks, that it would involve rescuing prisoners, and that she had someone out gathering intelligence for her.

She didn't say who.

But in the weeks that followed, I noticed Professor Milonakis wasn't in the library circulation room. And I didn't see her anywhere else on the grounds, either. Normally she taught at least two classes and otherwise kept a hawk's eye on every student—and every book—coming in and out of her library.

Aidan was still taking books one or two at a time out of the Room of the Ancients and then sequestering them out of the library in his satchel, and no one was there to stop him.

Near the end of the week, I leaned across our favorite library table toward Aidan. "Do you think Umbra sent Milonakis out to gather intelligence?"

He, of course, had been briefed by Eva and me on all the guardians' doings. His eyes flicked up to meet mine overtop his glasses. "Come on. *Milonakis?*"

Even Loki, who slept on the table, cracked an eye at me. "Seriously?"

I nodded toward the circulation room. "She's had Saoirse subbing in the circulation room all week. Not that you seem to mind, North."

Aidan's neck reddened. He and Saoirse had been a thing since last year, but he wasn't much for kissing and telling. Which made teasing him all the more satisfying.

"Besides," I said, "what else has Milonakis got to do? Really."

He sighed, readjusted his glasses. "So first Milonakis is out in Edinburgh doing thrilling spy work for Umbra, and now she's too dull to have any sort of life outside the library. Which is it?"

"It's both," I said. "That's exactly why she's spying."

"It's not Milonakis," he said. "She's too..."

"Straight-laced? Hard-nosed? Bitchy?"

"Yes to the first two, no to the third." He gestured around to the other students doing some early morning studying. "Also, you know cursing's not allowed here. You're going to get me banned from the library by association, and then who will help you poke your nose into all the things you aren't supposed to know?"

"Still you," I said. "Saoirse will just sneak you in."

He groaned. Set his pencil to the map laid out before us, his eraser atop a building on the Royal Mile. "This is the prison Umbra will likely be sending the guardians to. It's directly underneath the Mages' Council building, underground."

I stared at the layout. This was the map of the city Umbra had given me during that two-hour meeting last week; all of us had received identical, conjured copies of it. Between then and our mission, she wanted us to memorize the buildings, the streets, the intersections, the points of power.

"Loki," I said, "are you paying attention?"

Loki opened one eye. "I've already memorized it all."

I sat back. "The whole city?"

"Yes, the whole city. I'm much older than you, remember? I visited several times before it went to hell."

Literally, I thought.

"Also," Loki added, "I've got a mind like a steel trap. I'm the perfect infiltrator."

I scratched under his chin, which lifted for me to get a better angle. "But you're totally susceptible to fingernails."

"We all have our weaknesses," Loki murmured.

Meanwhile, Aidan ignored us, all business. "There's another part of the city we haven't looked at for the blade." His pencil shifted to another section of the map, also on the Royal Mile. "The vaults under South Bridge."

I refocused. "Why are you looking there? I don't see any closes."

Aidan tapped the map. "I read about these vaults in *A Mages' History of Scotland*. They've been around since the city's founding. Certain to be full of mystery and treasure."

"Unless the treasure's an orichalcum blade, I'll pass."

Saoirse, now a second-year, appeared at our table with a stack of books in her arms. She passed one down to Aidan, who half-stood to kiss her on the cheek. "This is the one you wanted, isn't it?" she said through a smile.

"Just the one." His hand went to her elbow. "You reshelving those? I can carry them for you."

"I'm good, Aide." Her eyes flitted over our map, then to me. "Hello, Ms. Cole."

I hid my grin. "Call me that again and I will retroactively fail you." I winked up at her. "How's your bareback riding?"

"It's coming along." She straightened with her stack of books. "The quartermistress is teaching me to ride barrels."

Barrels. Only the most advanced students made it that far.

Her eyes drifted over our table. "You studying old Edinburgh?"

"She's Scottish," Aidan said to me.

I shot him a *No kidding* look. "We're looking for a specific close," I said carefully. "An old one where a magical item might be buried."

"Have you tried Mary King's Close?" she said at once.

The tourist trap. Aidan and I had ruled that one out instantly; thousands of people were funneled through it each week. It was a real money-maker for Edinburgh, and thoroughly trodden and excavated.

Aidan and I exchanged a glance, both of us trying to keep our faces serious. "I think that one's too touristed," Aidan said softly. "I doubt they could keep anything hidden down there."

Saoirse shrugged. "Afraid that was my best guess. Good luck Clem, Aide."

When Saoirse had climbed to the third floor, Aidan sat back down, and I just set my elbows on the table, fingers steepled, grinning at him.

A wariness came over him. "Don't."

My eyes flicked to Loki, then back to Aidan, and my smile grew.

"Oh, just say it," Loki said.

Aidan got flustered, sensing Loki had spoken, and knowing whatever he'd said wasn't to his benefit. "Let's just get back to work."

"Okay." I sat back, picking up a biscuit from the plate of them, snapping into it. "No problem, Aide."

His hands went over his face as he groaned, and from the third floor, Saoirse's face appeared over the balcony. "Everything all right?"

"Fine." I waved my biscuit up at her. "Aide's brain is just getting to be too big for his skull. It aches sometimes, you know?"

CHAPTER FIFTEEN

The end of September came and went, the days began to cool, and Umbra still hadn't given us our mission. When I asked, she simply said, "It's not yet time."

I itched to cross through the veil, to be in Edinburgh. But Eva and Aidan told me to be patient, strategic, and they were right.

Still didn't stop the itching.

Life at the academy achieved a humming pace. Weekday mornings Aidan and I met in the library, and sometimes we had nothing to talk about except life. We had run out of ideas for how to dig into Umbra's mysterious past, and we'd studied the maps of Edinburgh to exhaustion.

I still didn't know which close the blade could be in. We'd narrowed the options down to... forty.

Forty closes.

And each one had dozens or hundreds of nooks, crannies, secrets.

We met anyway, because it was our tradition to sit at the table on the second floor and eat cookies and drink tea. And it gave me a chance to keep an eye out for Milonakis, who still hadn't returned.

After the library and breakfast, I taught my bareback riding classes, one and then the next, until the sun began to beat down. In the strangest quirk of my life, the first-years had collectively decided they loved me. Or maybe it was Loki they loved. He often showed up to our classes, sitting on a fence post as though he were watching us. Really I knew he just liked the angle of the sun at that time of day.

I usually took a quick lunch with Eva, sometimes Liara, sometimes Aidan, too, and then I struck off to the meadow. There, I trained with Umbra for three or four hours a day, depending on when I exhausted myself or she needed a nap. Apparently even headmistresses need naps.

We worked on the enshroudment, but also on tapping into the leyline running through the grounds. Feeling its power, and using it as a conduit to other places.

And after all that, I was left to myself. To my thoughts and my itching, and it was in that state I convinced Saoirse to let me take *The Witching World* from the Room of the Ancients.

She should have known better. But I also wasn't about to disabuse her of the idea that letting the witch take the witching book out of the library was a good thing.

I hadn't cracked this tome since my first year, when Aidan had to pull it from my clutches. It had sent me into an obsessive depression, and as soon as I touched it again, I remembered why.

Raven Murkwood's book held some strange, latent power. But this time, I had power, too.

It was strange, sitting at the edge of the meadow in the sunlight, and knowing I held a book the Shade herself had held. She had written in this very one—the original version, according to the first page, and maybe the only one still in existence.

Funny that it would end up at Shadow's End Academy.

When I began to read it again, I was surprised. Before I'd known Raven Murkwood was the Shade, I had read her book like an instruction manual, trying to glean everything I could from it. I hadn't thought beyond the acquisition of power.

Now, I heard her voice in her words. I felt her character.

Raven Murkwood seemed ambitious, curious, sharp. Even witty.

I wanted to find evil in what I was reading, but she didn't seem evil.

If Eva or Aidan or maybe even Liara had read with me, they would probably have agreed.

This was a young woman, maybe in her twenties. Fire hadn't corrupted her yet, because she hadn't discovered how to harness it. She'd been an air witch when she wrote *The Witching World.*

She wanted to know about the world and what lay in it, especially during the 1500s, when, living in Scotland, she'd been surrounded by suspicion about what she was.

People hadn't liked witches even before she'd become the Shade. In her chapter on how witches travel, she'd written, *Early on a witch must discover her means of succor, for she will likely be pursued, perhaps persecuted, and always distrusted for what she is, and most of all, what she's capable of.*

I read for clues as to how she became the first fire witch. Before, I hadn't cared so much about the origins of her magic—I'd just wanted to know how to harness it.

In just about every chapter, I encountered one mention or another of her partner, Catriona. Catriona had accompanied her through the fae portal to one of their courts, and there they had taught Murkwood a rare fae magic, words she could imbue into the air to stop a man where he stood, to get into his head.

Hexes. The fae had taught her the origins of what would become the art of hexes.

Catriona, an air mage herself, had taught Murkwood about many things: conjuration, tangible manipulations, points of power. Things she should have learned the beginnings of in a magical academy like this one, but hadn't.

Which meant Murkwood had been an outcast, deprived in some way. Maybe she'd lost her family. I couldn't tell.

But it became clear to me that she and Catriona had known each other since they were very young, maybe even children, and it was because of that early affection that Murkwood had trusted Catriona, and Catriona had trusted her.

They'd had a bond.

I flipped back to the beginning of the book, found a dedication written in almost incomprehensible old script. I leaned closer, staring at it for a time, scrutinizing each letter until I could decipher each one.

And, finally, I understood it.

Catriona, for as long as you live, Murkwood had written, *I'm eternal.*

I sat up straight, squinting into the empty meadow, the book splayed open in my lap. Parts of me had fallen asleep in the grass, and the sun had moved from one spot in the sky to another entirely.

I felt like I'd been transported and suddenly returned.

"Raven Murkwood," I said as though the woman sat beside me, "you loved her, didn't you?"

In early October, Umbra sat across from me, my magic swirling between us, enshrouding me. We were near the boggan's cave, the dark shadow of it only a few feet from where we sat.

Not the most scenic place. But definitely distressing enough to test me.

"Headmistress," I said into the silence.

Her eyes fluttered open. "What is it, child?"

"It's Milonakis you sent to Edinburgh, isn't it?"

"Hm." One eyebrow rose. "And what makes you think that?"

"The library's her fiefdom, and she hasn't been in it for weeks."

Umbra laughed, a pretty, rare sound. "Her fiefdom?" She wiped at one moist eye. "I suppose it is. We do get set in our ways as the decades go by. I shall have to tell her that."

I half tilted my head with an expectant look. "When she gets back from Edinburgh, you mean?"

Umbra sent a sudden blast of lightning into the skein of my magical shroud, nearly piercing a hole in it. But the fire held. She gave a soft nod of approval. "Can't catch you off guard any longer."

"You're dodging my question."

She gave a great sigh. "And what difference does it make to you whom I've sent? Get to what you want, girl."

"What I want"—I paused, then barreled on—"is to find Callum Rathmore."

"Yes, yes. You've told me this. And certainly you want to find him and rescue him from his imprisonment, but I know that's not all with you."

She was right. It wasn't all.

"I spent a summer training you," she went on, tapping the side of her nose. "Every day. Hours. Don't think I can't read you, child. It's one of my few talents."

The magic went on swirling around me, though now I did have to divide my concentration. I was nearing a difficult subject, which of course was exactly what Umbra wanted. "Back on the tundra, Rathmore told me something. He said I would find my sister in the city."

Umbra sat up straight, hands on her crossed legs. "Did he now? And I suppose in finding him, you hope he'll lead you to her."

"Wherever she is," I murmured.

"And," Umbra went on, "you hope Milonakis will have information on either or both of them when she returns."

"So it *is* Milonakis."

Her eyes slid into an elegant, annoyed roll. "Of course it is. Nance Milonakis is one of my most trusted professors, and quite good at sticking her nose in places it doesn't belong."

I snorted, and Umbra's face warmed. "She's been gone a long time," I said. "Are you worried?"

"No. Not one bit. She and I have been in contact, and she'll return sooner than you think. So why don't we continue our training *inside* the boggan's cave?"

"Have you heard anything from her about my sister?" I said, quieter, unmoving. "About Tamzin?"

"Believe me, child," Umbra said. "If I had, I would have told you that very moment. Tamzin Cole disappeared almost a decade ago now, though that doesn't mean Callum Rathmore is wrong about her. If he's seen her, then that simply means your sister has become someone else."

My jaw hardened at the thought of it. No more Tamzin Cole. Who was she now, then? "You know I'll have to look for them both," I said. "When I go there, to Edinburgh."

She patted her hands on her lap. "If you've told me once, you've told me twice. Isn't that the way with you, Clementine Cole?"

I squinted at her. Then, "You just called me a dog with a bone. But you said it so elegantly, I can't even be offended."

She half-smiled. "I know you will do what you must, as I've said to you before. I would prefer it if you were to stay here until you're ready, and I would prefer it if you would be cautious and prudent in all things —as I would all my students—but trying to change any one of you would be like trying to enclose the wind in my fingers."

"That's funny," I said. "Seeing as how that's actually possible."

"A poor analogy." She paused, growing more intense. "You believe he's been imprisoned by his father, don't you?"

I nodded. "He's too powerful not to be."

"Wise girl, and boy. Callum Rathmore is indeed one of the most powerful fire mages alive—which is why I hired the young man—and would need a particular kind of imprisonment."

"Like what?" I asked.

She rubbed a thoughtful hand over her mouth. "I'm not sure what Tristan Rathmore would need to do to keep his son from running back to you."

I squeezed my eyes shut. "Why does it always have to be so hard? And by hard, I mean impossible."

"Because, child." When I opened my eyes, Umbra was standing up and dusting herself off. "Things must be impossible before they are possible. Otherwise we'd be very fat and lazy mages indeed."

"Do you have any idea what this impregnable place would be?" I asked.

"Gods no." She reached out a hand to help me up. "If I did, I would have told you."

"So you're leaving it to the twenty-one-year-olds to figure out."

She patted the dirt off my cloak. "It's often the young who make the impossible possible."

CHAPTER SIXTEEN

Nance Milonakis returned in the dead of night. I woke to a commotion outside, slipped out of bed, and stepped out onto the landing in time to see her being rushed inside Umbra's office.

It was four in the morning, and it didn't look like Milonakis was walking on her own. Two people helped her along, one of whom was Umbra, and the other I didn't catch a glimpse of. Their voices were intense whispers, urgent.

I grabbed my cloak and started down the steps toward the clearing. By the time my bare feet touched grass, they were already inside. The double doors of Umbra's office closed behind them, and I was left in silence.

For a half-second I contemplated not following, and then I shut that right down. What good was being a lying, cheating, cursing fire witch if I didn't slip into places I wasn't supposed to?

When I got to the doors they'd passed through and opened one six inches, the hollowed-out anteroom to Umbra's office was empty of people—and a floor. As in, part of the floor was gone.

I stood at the doorway, staring at a staircase that descended into the ground around the edge of the room, following the circular shape of the tree's trunk. These steps took the same path as the steps up to her office—which meant this was one continuous staircase. I'd just never known the part beneath the earth existed.

Below, a golden light emanated up. Calling to me.

Umbra had secrets on secrets.

Whatever had happened to Milonakis in Edinburgh, I wanted—needed—to know. The itching had only gotten more intense, and now it was a feral drive that started me down the stairs.

The steps began as dirt and, partway down, became cold, narrow stone, the ground rising to my right, my hands trailing along the hard walls. As I left the anteroom, I followed the stairs down and down, feet tapping around and around, until I couldn't see the blue light from the wisps any longer.

At the base of the stairs I found myself at the start of a hallway with magically lit torches set at intervals along it. The walls and ceiling were made of carved stone, probably crafted by an earth mage.

Down here, it smelled of earthworms and dirt and a strange scent I didn't know, but it stuck in my nose and throat like cat pee.

And it *felt* old. Centuries-old.

Several closed doors peppered the hallway, which ended in an intersection some thirty feet from where I stood. And somewhere, voices echoed.

I approached the first door, stood close to it and heard nothing, saw no light under it. There wasn't a doorknob on it but a very old-fashioned latch, and when I tried it, the door wouldn't move a bit.

A voice cried out from down the hallway, jolting me stiff. Milonakis.

"Nance," a muffled voice said from not far off, agitated. Umbra's. "Nance, please."

I turned, spotted shadows near the intersection of the hallway. When I came closer, leaning around the edge, the shadows came clear, as did a brighter light. They were in a room around the corner, the door partway open. The hallways off this intersection went on into darkness. The torches hadn't been lit here, and I didn't know what lay beyond them.

I came to the partly open door, caught a glimpse of Umbra's back to me and the edge of a bed. Fae wings fluttered past the opening, and

I backed up as I heard Nurse Neverwink say, "Valerian. It's the only thing that'll calm her."

So Milonakis was sick, but Umbra hadn't brought her to the infirmary. She'd called Neverwink down here, to this place—whatever it was—where she had a bed and, I guessed, whatever it was she needed to treat this particular illness.

On the bed, I spotted Milonakis's boot, the toe of it up in the air. She moaned words I didn't know, her voice thick and worried. She sounded like she was speaking to someone who wasn't even here.

A glass jar clinked, and through the doorway I could see Umbra rummaging through shelves lining the far wall, her fingers moving over jars. "Ah," she said. "Here it is." She turned with a jar in hand, uncorking it, disappearing from view.

I ventured closer to get one good look at them all. And when I did, I wished I hadn't.

Milonakis grasped at Neverwink's arms, her face partly in shadow, but I could make out that her mouth was open as wide as it would go, her eyes unseeing but also frantic. It was the kind of undignified sight I knew Milonakis would never want a student to witness.

Hell, no one would want people seeing them like that.

I was about to step away when Neverwink said, "You're back, Nance. You're at the academy."

Finally, Milonakis said something I understood. "Let me be! I'll never be free of them. I can see them now if I shut my eyes."

Umbra took over Neverwink's duties, handing her the jar of valerian and sitting by Milonakis, keeping her from sitting up. Meanwhile, Neverwink plucked the valerian root out, set it into a mortar and pestle on the nearby table, and began grinding.

"Nance," Umbra said. "Listen to me: they cannot leave the vaults of Edinburgh. They cannot follow you."

The vaults of Edinburgh. Aidan had mentioned those weeks back during one of our research sessions.

Milonakis grabbed at Umbra's arm, staring at her. "The children. The children are as stuck as the rest, for hundreds of years they've been stuck there." And with a guttural grunt and wrench of the arm, she pushed Umbra aside, managed to climb out of the bed with force and speed I'd never expected from Professor Milonakis.

And just like that, she was up and moving—and found herself staring face-to-face with me in the doorway.

Umbra rose, Neverwink turned, and I was fully exposed.

But so was Nance Milonakis.

Her eyes had caught the light, and they gazed at me with a strange, milky whiteness. The pupils and the irises had lost most of their color, and I wasn't sure how much she could even see.

But she did see me.

Her finger rose, and she pointed at me. "The children are trapped down there."

And then Umbra and Neverwink were on her, urging her back into the bed, and the moment they'd gotten her horizontal, Umbra stepped away, took two steps toward the door, glaring at me.

"I'm sorry." I nodded at Milonakis. "What's wrong with—"

"Go back the way you came," Umbra ground out, hand on the door, "and if you do not, I will know. If you ever return to this place, I will expel you from the academy."

She shut the door, closing me from the room, sending up dust and dirt and leaving me in silence.

I stood there for a second, eyes still on the door, Nance Milonakis's face—her milky, half-unseeing eyes—floating in my vision.

The children, she'd said. They're trapped down there for hundreds of years.

I had no idea what she meant.

When I turned away, I found myself gazing down a hallway into blackness, where I was sure more of the academy's secrets lay. The scent of cat pee was stronger that way.

I started walking, turned back down the hallway I'd come by, and passed the closed doors, which I felt half-certain I could have burned down in seconds.

Not tonight, but someday. My gut held the certain knowledge I'd be back here, and I would find out why this place existed.

For now, I needed to know what valerian was, and why Milonakis had gone crazy.

"It's an herb," Eva said simply, healing tomes spread around her on the library table. "It's used as a sedative."

I blinked down at the book in front of her, back up at her. "Neverwink said it was the only thing that would help Milonakis."

"Maybe it was. It's quite potent."

A first-year library assistant passed along the floor below us, reshelving books. It was well into the next evening, and Milonakis hadn't returned to her duties. In fact, I hadn't seen her at all. Or Umbra. Maybe they were still in that underground room.

The existence of which I had, of course, told Eva all about.

Now she leaned past the books, speaking low and confidential. "What do you suppose that place is, anyway?"

"Part of her office, I guess. An ancient part." I shook my head, teeth on my bottom lip. "How old did you say this academy is?"

"Not clear. You know, the records don't really go past the Battle of the Ages, when just about everything got destroyed, and the school's been around at least that long."

Five hundred years. Those hallways *felt* five hundred years old.

Footsteps sounded up the stairs, and Aidan said on approach, "All right. I canceled a date with Saoirse to be here, so make it good."

I turned in my seat. Since we were very nearly alone in the library, I said, "Last night Milonakis got snuck into Umbra's underground lair, where she was raving about trapped children, and her pupils had turned white."

Aidan stopped short. "Is this like a Halloween thing?"

I made a face. "I'm not screwing with you."

From behind me, Eva said, "Witches are supposed to be obsessed with Halloween. Black cats, brooms, peaked hats..."

I glanced over at her. "Not helping my argument, Eva. And you're right about the cat, but that's still a lazy stereotype." I set my arm over the back of the chair, facing Aidan again. "I saw Milonakis down there last night. She's probably still there."

"No she's not." Aidan jerked a thumb toward the circulation room. "She's here."

I straightened up. Glanced at the closed door as though I could spy her through it. "Now you're playing."

He shrugged. "Check for yourself."

I did check. Eva and I both rose, she flying over the balcony and I taking the stairs two at a time, and we both arrived at the door to the circulation room at the same time, but I got my fingers on the handle first, yanking it open. Together, we pushed our way into the room and found a surprised Milonakis staring us down.

And her pupils and irises were very much not white.

"You," she said to me, scanning me up and down behind her glasses, which she hadn't had on last night.

My eyebrows rose, fully clueless as to what she would say—or do—next.

"You checked out *The Witching World* from the Room of the Ancients twenty-nine days ago." She tapped a ledger. "And it's still not returned."

Eva looked at me with surprise, as though the weirdest thing about this encounter was me taking a book out.

"I... I have it back in my dorm." I took a step closer to Milonakis, studying her. "Are you all right?"

Her face hardened. "With you sequestering one of our most precious books away, which you know wasn't supposed to have been taken out of that room in the first place? I'm very much not all right, Clementine Cole."

My head tilted as I stepped closer again. "How are the children?"

Her eyes narrowed. "You're changing the subject."

"Are they still trapped?" I pointed toward the ground. "You know, down there."

Milonakis's gaze followed my finger, then rose back to my face. Then over to Eva. She looked cornered, and finally she sighed out, "There are no children. They're not real. Not part of this world. What you heard last night, you shouldn't have. Forget it."

"Oh, sure." I waved a hand through the air. "Seems easy enough to forget I walked barefoot into a centuries-old underground section of the academy and saw you down there going on about the children with your white—"

"Enough," Milonakis cut in, her voice high and sharp. "For gods' sake, enough of that."

Finally, Eva came forward. "You went beneath the city, didn't you?" she whispered. I suspected she meant Edinburgh.

Milonakis's sharp eyes cut over to her. "And nearly lost my way. Tomorrow the headmistress and I will come to you lot with your mission, but I'll say this to you now: Do not venture beneath the cobblestones. Not if you want to keep your heads. Not if you want to keep your lives. If I had the power to forbid you, I would."

"What's down there?" I said.

Milonakis's lips parted, trembled in the vaguest way, and I sensed whatever Neverwink had done to help her last night hadn't fully made its way through her brain and nervous system.

She still bore a twinge of that mania.

"Death," Milonakis whispered. "So much death, years upon years of it."

"What do you mean—" I began, but Milonakis had fully snapped shut, closing herself off with a straightening of the spine and her fingers on her ledger.

"Bring me that book," she said, "or I'll ban you from the library until you do, Clementine Cole."

That was all. She was done talking about anything but her obsession with books and control over this one place at the academy. She was still the same woman as she'd always been.

I left with a promise to return her book to her, and when we returned to the table, we found Aidan poring over the books we'd left open.

He glanced up at us. "Why's this one open to valerian?"

"It's what Neverwink gave Milonakis last night." Eva flew back up, landing on the balcony and then dropping lightly to the second floor. I wasn't jealous, not at all, as I trudged up the stairs. Eva tapped the book's open page. "She was raving, and her eyes had apparently turned white. Neverwink used valerian with healing magic."

Aidan's face paled, and he gazed down at the page with a graveness I didn't even know he was capable of.

"Hey," I said. "What is it?"

His eyes raised to me. "She went under Edinburgh's streets, didn't she?"

I nodded.

"My grandmother did that once, on one of her many research trips." He paused. "She returned weeks later in the same way. The only cure was valerian."

"Cure for what?" Eva said.

His Adam's apple bobbed, eyes flicking between us. "Ghosts."

――――――

CHAPTER SEVENTEEN

――――――

"We thought my grandmother had just gone temporarily mad down there," Aidan said as the three of us walked among the dark trees, following the path circling the central grounds. "My parents took her to all sorts of doctors, and finally we took her to a fae like Neverwink who knew what to do."

"I'm struggling here," I said. "You're saying valerian root cures... what? Ghosts?"

"Ghost-madness," Eva said without a pause, without any skepticism.

"That fae doctor believed my grandmother had been driven a little mad by her exposure to them under the city," Aidan went on. "Of course, we thought she'd just gone a little mad from lack of light and too much isolation."

"Maybe she did," I said.

"I thought so for years." Aidan dragged his fingers through his hair, fully agitated. "But now I'm not so sure."

"Why?" I asked.

"Because my grandmother came back with white eyes," he said, and that was when the three of us stopped walking.

"This isn't a Halloween thing, is it?" I said, half-wanting it to be.

He shook his head.

"When I met your grandmother," I said slowly, "she wasn't exactly..."

"Sane?" Eva offered. Then, "Sorry, Aidan."

"No, you're right." He drew in air through his nose. "She's nutty."

"And I assume," I said, "we met her years after her trip to Edinburgh's lovely underground crypts and vaults and streets."

"Ten years after," he said. "She was never fully the same. Not from how I remember her as a child."

"And you chalked that up to senility?" I guessed.

"Yeah." Guilt laced that single word.

"That explains a lot about how she acted when I met her," I said, and with a big exhale, I didn't know what to say next. So we all started walking again in a sort of aimless daze.

Ghost-madness awaited me under Edinburgh. And there was no chance I wasn't going into the undercity.

The blade waited for me.

Eva sensed the direction of my thoughts because she grasped my arm. "I'll go with you, when you venture under."

"No," I said at once, and I knew as I said it I wouldn't budge on this. "If anyone's going white-eyed and a little insane, it'll be me and me alone."

The next day, the guardians were called to our meeting room as Milonakis had told us we would be. She and the headmistress were already there when I arrived with Loki, and Milonakis remained conspicuously silent as we all sat down.

She sat at the head of the table while Umbra stood, and it was the headmistress who began speaking to us. "After over a month, Nance Milonakis has returned from Edinburgh," she said. "She braved much danger to walk amongst the formalists, whose ranks she left years ago in order to gather information for us."

I stared at Milonakis, who didn't meet my eyes. Her fingers clasped and unclasped atop the table.

Suddenly, much about her made sense. She had once lived in Edinburgh, had been a formalist herself. And maybe still was in some ways, rigid and shrewd as the woman could be.

But she was on our side. That much I knew from the past three years.

Umbra paused, eyes drifting over the group. "She managed to visit the mages' prison underneath the council building, where she found over thirty mages held captive. These are lifelong inmates, never to be released. They are people who have defied the formalists, many of whom do not believe in their ways. They deserve to be free on principle, and some may very well aid us in our efforts against the Shade."

A prison. Where mages were kept. I stared at Umbra like I was a cat and she was an oversized fish; this was my godsdamn mission.

He had to be in that prison.

Umbra stepped to the board, where she'd written out a list of names. "These are all the names of potential sympathizers Nance was able to collect during her time there. Some of these people have been imprisoned upward of a decade."

In a glance, I counted them. Twelve names. None of which were the one I was looking for.

"What about Callum Rathmore?" I said, surprising myself. But once the question was out, I pushed onward. "He'd be sympathetic."

"You mean the celebrity professor who mysteriously disappeared after one year here?" Keene said. "The guy who can't seem to stay in one place for long enough to have a photo taken of him for *Witches & Wizards?*"

I turned what I knew must be venomous eyes on Keene. On the table, Loki's head turned toward him, too. Between the two pairs of green eyes staring him down, Keene's hand ran over his sparsely haired head in a subconscious attempt to comfort himself.

"Yes," I said. "And why do you think he's been featured in magazines? Because he's strong. Stronger than any of us."

"I saw just one floor of the prison," Milonakis's voice cut in, the first time she'd spoken since we'd all arrived. "The first floor is all fae.

If Callum Rathmore is held there, he'd be on a different floor. Or perhaps they hid him somewhere."

"Nonetheless"—Umbra tapped the board—"Nance procured twelve names for us. That's twelve fae whose lives we can reclaim."

And just like that, Callum Rathmore's name had dropped away. Umbra and Milonakis had moved on.

Umbra asked Milonakis to show us a diagram of what she'd seen, and the professor stood, crossed to the whiteboard, and with a flame-lit fingertip, etched out the prison from memory. She even placed names inside various cells.

By the time she was finished, she had created a replica of the first floor of the Edinburgh prison. It was all hard, black edges and perfect spacing and sizing, nothing out of place. Another clue as to why Umbra had chosen Milonakis: she could produce things like this from memory.

But I did notice her fingers at her side held a tremor. She curled them, held them in a fist to keep the tremor away. *Ghost-madness*, I thought.

Umbra pointed to the board. "These are the exact locations of these inmates. Milonakis will render this diagram on parchment, and you will memorize this before you leave for Edinburgh in three days."

Three days. Three days.

The itching intensified.

"Nance," Umbra said. "Tell them what they will face on entry."

Milonakis turned to us, hands folded before her. "The prison has no guards. At least, not of the sentient variety. Centuries ago, a master of enchantments cast a permanent animation on sixteen suits of armor. They patrol the prison night and day, without sleep or rest."

"Permanent?" Liara cut in. "That's impossible. When the mage died, the enchantment should have died with him."

Milonakis glanced at Umbra.

"Should have," Umbra said, "but clearly did not, as Professor Milonakis can attest. It would take a year-long course on the intricacies of enchantment magic for us to understand why. Suffice it to say, they are wardens of the prison to this day."

Milonakis nodded, resumed. "Should they hear or see an intruder, they have been enchanted to cut them down by any means. No escort out, no questioning—simply death by broadsword."

Elijah clapped his hands. "Fantastic. Now I've got to know how you did it, Professor."

"Simple." Milonakis's hand dove into the folds of her robes, pulled out a card. "I presented this."

We all squinted toward the two-by-four-inch card she held out. On it were printed a tiny picture of her face and some identifying information, like a driver's license. "This," she said, "is what every formalist carries. And it is what Liara Youngblood will carry into the prison, flanked by her twin fae guardians."

Elijah and Isaiah grinned at one another. Meanwhile, my eyes shot to Liara, whose face had gone stony.

"Brilliant," Keene said. "Just brilliant."

The other guardians gave approving nods.

"What am I missing?" I said.

"For those unfamiliar," Umbra said, careful to avoid looking directly at me, "twenty years ago, the Youngbloods joined the Mages' Council. Liara's father was one of the founders of the formalist movement."

***

The plan was stupidly simple: Liara Youngblood would enter the prison as a Singaporean ambassador, and she would present doctored papers approving the extradition of twelve mages to Singapore.

And just like that, the guards would stand down. They would open up the cell doors and escort our prisoners out, and before the prison transmitted word of Liara's prisoner extraction to the formalist officials, we would have escaped.

While Liara and the twins were inside the prison, the rest of us would keep watch at various spots outside. Make sure no one else went in or out. The fae would take high-up perches, and the rest of us would run interference from the ground.

But I fixated on one thing: This was why the Youngblood name was so important. That was why Liara so rarely talked about her family's history. While Singapore was no longer a formalist city, it was formalist-aligned when Liara's father served on the council. That was why nobody in Edinburgh would stop her from entering the prison.

Her name was synonymous with the formalists.

"So," I said as we stepped out into daylight. I'd made sure I was right on Liara's heels, and now I moved into her line of sight with the Spitfire roiling inside me. "Your dad founded a movement."

She stopped, and together we moved aside as a few of the others filed out. Umbra and Milonakis had left first, and were now off and away. Only the other guardians remained, most of them trying not to rubberneck as Liara and I squared off.

Loki stood by my side, tail upright. "Hey, Red Hot, try dialing it back a notch or two."

"Fine." My eyes flicked back up to the fae, whose arms were now folded. "My cat would like me to rephrase. For his sake, let's try this again. What the fuck, Liara?"

"Oh, well done," Loki grumbled.

Liara's eyes rolled away. "Your faux-outrage is boring, Cole."

"Okay, let's try real outrage." I stepped into her line of sight again. "You do know the formalists tried to put me in a big metal box, right? They chased me down in cars."

Her unwilling eyes met mine. "That's got nothing to do with me."

"You *are* a formalist."

Now those black eyes narrowed. "Say that again, and I swear I'll slap you."

"You have a driver's license."

"It's not a license, you normal idiot. It's an identification card."

I looked her up and down. "Show me."

She did the same up-and-down. "No."

"*Honey*, Clementine," Loki said to me, threading his way through Liara's legs, tail swishing against her. "Or anything that isn't the rotten-eggs approach."

I swallowed back my retort. In my first year, I'd learned how it would look to argue with my cat. Also, I'd learned I couldn't beat him in an argument. He was almost always right.

I gestured down to him. "Just so you know, my cat's behavior does not represent my feelings toward you."

Liara purposefully avoided reacting to Loki's presence between her feet. "Noted."

Finally, the question I'd wanted to ask since that revelation an hour ago found its way out. "Just tell me one thing: Do the Youngbloods have a seat on the Mages' Council?"

"Yes," she said at once. Eyes steely, challenging me. "What of it?"

"And does that seat belong to you now?"

"Yes," she said again.

"Why aren't you in it?"

Now her arms unfolded, unchecked anger showing. "What a stupid godsdamn question. After everything you've seen over the past three years, you think I'd sit in that tainted chair?"

"I don't know," I said. "You've got one thing in common with them. You both hate witches."

She slapped me. The violence came out of nowhere and disappeared just as quickly, and I was left with a stinging cheek and a roaring of adrenaline, the Spitfire flaring inside me.

It took clenched fists and Loki's claws on my cloak to ground me, to prevent me from losing myself to my own fury.

How dare she. How *dare* she.

"You of all people," she said, low and poisonous, "should know that your birthright doesn't dictate your life's choices."

And then she'd turned away in a wave of dark hair, disappearing around the tree, and I was left with my cheek still tingling and my fists tight and, when I turned around, Eva and Elijah and Isaiah and Keene —all the fae—standing there, unabashedly staring.

"Wow," Isaiah said. "You're braver than I thought, Clementine."

The Spitfire, keening with my shame, receded a little at Isaiah's words.

"Holy hell," Elijah said. "If I'd had time, I would have put money on Youngblood sending lightning right through Cole's heart."

Eva came over, eyes sorrowful. Set her hand to my cheek. "I can take the sting away."

"Don't," I said, and I knew saying so would come off as an attempt to appear tough. But really I wanted to sit with the pain, to feel it, to let it focus me on *what the hell had just happened*.

For the rest of the day and the next one, that slap hurt more than the time Liara had zapped me in combat class during our first year. And by the end of those two days, I had decided:

Not a slap—never a slap—but Liara was a little bit justified in her feelings. And so was I.

CHAPTER EIGHTEEN

The morning of our mission, I sat in the guardians' common room with a map of the prison on my lap. Loki lay stretched on his back by the fire, all four paws extended.

We were leaving at noon, just two hours from now. It would be too strange for Liara to arrive at the prison at night, so my first time in the city would be with the sun at its zenith.

My mind kept wandering; I'd only gotten four hours of sleep last night because I'd been studying maps of the city and prison so late. This would probably be my only chance at the mages' prison. I needed to get it right.

When my eyes drifted to Loki and the fireplace, I snapped them back, fingers smoothing out the edges of the map. When it crinkled, Loki groaned.

"Even if they flipped that place on its head," he murmured, "you could still navigate it. So please let me nap crinkle-free."

He was right, and wrong.

I could navigate the first floor—the one Milonakis had diagrammed for us—but the other two floors? Unknown. Aidan and I couldn't find any maps of the prison, and the closest he'd gotten was a picture of the entrance in a tourists' book, which was captioned: *The mages' prison in Edinburgh, where three floors of inmates are held.*

Three floors. That was all we knew.

Well, for the time being. Soon—in about two hours—that would change.

Loki lapsed again into sleep, and I fell into my study until a voice sounded dreamily far away, and I was brought back into the world by Eva standing above me.

"It's time," she said. "Are you ready?"

I stood, folding the map, and nodded. I had everything I needed on me—including two spare cloaks for the fae we would rescue—and I had my familiar. "I'm always ready."

Eva's amusement was soft, tempered. "You should talk to Liara before we go."

I knelt by Loki, stroking his belly to wake him. "I will. Eventually."

"You should do it now, Clem."

Loki's claws snapped around my hand, catching me like a Venus flytrap. I winced as I turned my face up to Eva. "She slapped me, you know."

"Which was patently wrong." Eva paused. "But don't let her standards determine yours."

I shook my head, extricating my hand from Loki, who was now awake and getting to his feet. "It doesn't need to be now."

"Would certainly help me feel better about what we're walking into if our leaders were on speaking terms," Eva murmured, but she let it go.

Together, Loki and I walked with her out into the clearing, where the others were already gathered around Umbra.

Liara didn't meet my eyes. She was dressed in formalwear I'd never seen before, luxuriant blue-and-red robes with a high collar. Her black hair, normally long or in a ponytail, had been braided intricately around her head.

She looked like Singaporean royalty.

Elijah and Isaiah also had on blue robes, and they looked pleased as punch about it. Their shocks of silver hair had been groomed back, and they flanked Liara, dwarfing her.

The other guardians were dressed simply, like nondescript humans. As was I. Only I wore a cloak, but otherwise we were the same. Instead of our academy uniforms, we wore simple fall clothes—pants, long-sleeved shirts, calf-height boots.

Umbra spied Eva and me, gave a nod. "All right, thumbs to foreheads, everyone. We don't want any of you incommunicado."

We followed her lead, each of us exchanging thumbprints on each guardian's forehead. When Liara and I came to one another, we both had an enforced, steely gaze, as though challenging the other to look away.

Neither of us did.

Afterward, we turned to Umbra. It felt strange to be starting a mission on the ground, on my two feet. I was so used to riding Noir, to having his steadiness and power. I felt half-naked, exposed.

"We're ready," Liara said, her voice deep—a leader's.

Umbra's staff began to glow green, and she said, "When I part the veil, you'll find yourselves atop a leyline running along the outskirts of the city. Liara, Elijah, and Isaiah will pass through three minutes before the rest of you. Once you're through, you'll move to your designated position along the Royal Mile. Understood?"

We understood. We had understood the first time Umbra laid out the plan, but then it had hardly seemed real.

Now, we were at its doorstep. I was about to head into the beating heart of a world where witches were outlaws.

A moment later, Umbra drew her staff through the air, cutting a seam in the veil from six feet up to the ground. When she drew it aside like a curtain, she stepped back, revealing pure, unadulterated darkness.

"Oh." She cleared her throat, allowing the curtain to fall back to place. "That one's corrupted, then."

Elijah snorted, and the rest of us just met eyes. Apparently that wasn't a huge deal.

"Let's try it again," Umbra said. "This time, I'll send you all to a less convenient spot—near Arthur's Seat overlooking the city. It'll be a bit of a walk, but at least the Shade can't corrupt it."

When Umbra parted the veil this time, pulling it aside, an empty, hilly vista appeared, wind blowing in through the other side. There, the sky was streaked with fast-moving clouds, the city peppering the view below.

It was beautiful.

"Well," she said with a gesture of the hand, "off you go. I trust you all most highly, and I know you'll make your luck."

Liara, Elijah, and Isaiah passed through first, disappearing from view. And three minutes later, it was our turn.

The others went through ahead of me, and Loki and I waited to last. When I stepped up to the veil, I raised my hand, enshrouding the two of us in iridescent flame.

Umbra's eyes were intense on me, piercing through my magic. "Do what you must, and return." As though she knew. Not just suspected, but knew I wouldn't do what I'd been told.

I nodded at her, and together, Loki and I stepped through.

On the other side, lush grass and a blowing wind greeted me. The others had already moved off, heading straight for the Royal Mile. They weren't supposed to wait on the enshrouded witch, or even to acknowledge I existed.

To all of Edinburgh, I was invisible. A wraith.

I surveyed Arthur's Seat, the jagged green rise of it, taking my first breaths of Scottish air. A long ways off, tourists—non-mages—trekked toward the edge of the overlook. How could I tell? They were wind-battered and led along by a tour guide. The biggest tell: three of them wore *Scotland* T-shirts.

A small part of me wanted to follow them.

Unlike Eva, who'd visited every country in her childhood, I'd never gotten to properly see the world. Most times I'd been chasing monsters in the dark, or being chased by them.

The thought disappeared in the wind as Loki said, "You want to gawk or get shit done?"

I half-smiled down at him. "Says the cat who, not half an hour ago, was on his back with all four paws reaching for the ceiling."

Together, we began walking down the hill toward the city proper.

His tail weaved through the air as we walked. "That's not true."

"Today, yesterday, or every day you've napped before that?"

As we made our way down, closer and closer to the city, we kept on bickering. I needed this—this facey casualness. This unbothered back-and-forth. It was always how I'd dealt with the most terrifying things in my life: by pretending I wasn't terrified. By making them smaller with humor and smirks and eye rolls.

But when my feet touched the cobblestone of the road, that stopped. Both Loki and I went silent as, not thirty feet away, a fae walked with self-assured swiftness, book in hand, past the road separating one building from another.

The two of us had frozen in place, half-expecting to be spotted. As though the enshrouding magic was like the emperor's clothes—not there at all.

But the fae didn't even slow. She disappeared as quickly as she'd appeared. She had been dressed simply, professionally, in black pants and a forest-green turtleneck, her black hair cropped and slicked to her head. In fact, her hairstyle reminded me of Ora Frostwish's—simple, austere, functional.

A group of adorably young schoolchildren followed a few seconds later, all of them fae, all of them in Scottish school uniforms. Their wings were likely hidden to the human world, they were as iridescent and as beautiful as any fae's to me.

"You think the fae kiddos learn with the regulars here?" I said to Loki.

"Of course not. They're headed toward a magicked primary school around that corner."

My familiar really had studied the maps of Edinburgh. But I still glanced down at him. "How do you know there's a magicked school around the corner?"

He rolled his eyes up to me. "I'm a hundred-year-old European cat, remember? I've been here a few times, back before the city went to the dogs."

My cat was more cosmopolitan than me. Of course he was.

"You think they teach them magic?" I said, remembering what Eva and Umbra had said: this was an anti-magic city.

"If they do," he said, "it's probably just functional stuff, like conjuring food. Makes them useful."

He was probably right.

"Let's go." I started us off, mentally configuring myself to where we were in the city. I had studied the maps so many times, but seeing the place in three dimensions was still disorienting.

We were at the university, which was adjacent to Arthur's Seat. And we weren't far from the Royal Mile, which put us maybe half a mile from the Mages' Council building. It would take us ten minutes to get there, if we didn't encounter trouble.

One by one, I began speaking into the other guardians' heads as we walked, coordinating positions. This was my role as the leader outside the prison: to make sure everyone was in place, ready, watching.

They were all still moving to their places.

For her part, Liara said, *We'll be at the prison entrance in one minute. If all goes to plan, we'll be escorting them out in twenty minutes.*

Twenty minutes. I had twenty minutes.

I walked faster, the city passing me in a beautiful, medieval blur, buildings older than my home country rising simply to my left and right, the roads weaving. At one point I spotted a castle on a hill through the trees, and I could almost forget this place was the epicenter of evil.

Well, aside from Hell.

Edinburgh was sprawling and beautiful, just like in the pictures I'd seen. It wasn't hard or boxy or bereft as I'd expected. For some reason I'd imagined they would have reformed all the buildings, changed everything to fit their rigidity.

Not so.

As if he'd heard my thoughts—or maybe followed my gaze to the castle on the hill—Loki offered, "The tourism keeps the government flush. Nobody wants to visit an ugly city."

Which made the formalists even cleverer, cloaking their home in beauty.

But cold reality came with the first passing police car. It rolled down the street, black as a beetle as we reached the edge of the university, and inside I spotted two formalist officers.

In a flash, I was standing in Farina North's large living room again, staring down two officers with their nightsticks and their dark uniforms. They'd been shameless and fixated on me.

Maeve Umbra had warned us about the security here. You could usually find a police car on every street, and every officer was trained in anti-magic.

A band tightened around my chest as they passed, but the car rolled on by, not slowing.

We were invisible. We were safe—enough.

Loki and I turned down the street, headed toward the Royal Mile —the next cross-street. When we emerged out onto it, grand buildings rising to the left and right of us down the long slope of the road. I tried to keep my heart from galloping and failed.

The Mages' Council building sat highest of them all, dome-topped, the sight of it cinching my gut. *Eva*, I said into the fae's head, *Is everyone in position?*

Yes, came the reply a few seconds later. *We're ready.*

Good. I paused. *I need you to take over for me.*

WHAT?

I didn't answer. Before I could allow my gut to squeeze me into submission, I started toward the Mages' Council building, Loki trotting at my side.

I hoped Eva would forgive me for this.

CHAPTER NINETEEN

We threaded our way past humans and mages and tourists, the crowds thickening on the sidewalks as we got closer. This was supposed to help our mission: all the people, all those bodies were supposed to be our buffers against the formalists' eyes.

Right now, they just made staying unnoticed hellishly difficult.

At one point I bumped into a young blond man, who looked right through me, his eyes narrowing on an innocent person behind me. "Mind yourself," he called, and I slipped past him, moving onto the street.

By now, Liara and the twins would be inside, presenting their papers, asking for the release of the prisoners. Twenty minutes had shrunk to fifteen.

Loki kept by my feet, a shadow. He knew if he moved too far away, the magic wouldn't follow him. Unlike Umbra, the power of my enchantments still limited them to a small radius of about six feet.

Together, we waited as a car passed, then dashed across the road into the cool caress of the dome's shadow.

Clem? Eva's voice said into my head. *What's going on?*

Just got stuck in the crowd, I said. *Nothing's changed, but I need you to take the lead.*

Got it.

It almost hurt how much she trusted me.

Loki and I came to the edge of the building, passed down an ancient, narrow staircase alongside it, the shadows and coolness deepening. At the base of the stairs, I found it: the Via Pizza restaurant. The sun and sky were only a small strip above us, casting a slender light.

I turned away from the restaurant, facing what would be a bare wall if I didn't have the ability to see. But because I did, I immediately saw a door. Tall and iron and furnished with an iron handle and a large placard overtop it that read, in bold lettering, *Prison.*

Eva, who'd shown me how to see, would have been so proud of me.

I did as Liara had done: knocked three times on the door, the sound of bone on iron ringing through the air. After a few seconds, it opened, and a seven-foot suit of armor stood in the doorway.

"Business?" an echoing voice said from inside the armor.

The helmet was fully shut, no face visible beneath. At its hip, a sword almost as long as me gleamed in the daylight. The armor looked so lifelike, so animate, that I stood there for a second, not believing that a person wasn't inside it.

I waited, my breath held. Waiting to be seen and seized or unseen and ignored.

Seeing nothing before it, the helmet shifted left, then right. With mechanical precision, it turned away from the door, allowing it to shut.

This was it.

I slipped through the narrowing opening, Loki brushing past my ankles as he moved with me, and as the door closed with a loud echo, I caught a glimpse of a stairway down before perfect darkness enveloped us.

Right, because suits of armor don't need light.

Loki and I huddled in the corner of the entry, against the cold stone, not six inches from the suit of armor. We were so close I could practically feel the chill off the metal.

A moment later, the armor scraped across the stone, clanking as it moved to stand in the far corner of the entry. Always guarding this spot. Always.

I raised my hand, lit a flame on my fingertips. It extended only three feet, allowing me to see within my enshroudment. That was enough, at least, to spot the top of the staircase.

"Loki," I said. "You good?"

"Do you want pleasantries and tea, or do you want to find Callum?"

"Glad to know you're as much a jerk as ever."

"Back at you."

Together we started down the curving stairs. I had to move slow with my limited sight, taking each step with exact precision. The stone was smooth, the edges of the steps worn with centuries of use.

Slipping would be easy, and falling down the whole staircase would be easier.

We curved down and around, arriving at a landing, where ambient light from an overhead lantern met us, along with a low-ceilinged rectangular room, ten iron-barred cells along the two opposing walls. Between the bars, the air shimmered with different colors of magic.

The place smelled of urine, shit, and dampness. The walls were carved from massive old stones, darkened with age.

We'd arrived on the first floor of the mages' prison.

Liara, Elijah, and Isaiah stood in front of a far cell, flanked by a group of four shackled prisoners they'd already freed. She was conferring with one of the suits of armor, pointing to a sheet of paper and nodding at the cell. "This one," she said, and the armor turned to the cell, inserted a key, and the shimmering magic disappeared.

The armor opened the cell door and disappeared inside to retrieve the fae. This was the fifth prisoner, which left seven more to go.

Time was running short. I needed to find the way down to the second floor.

Two more suits of armor patrolled the space, circling it at even intervals with their impossibly long swords sheathed at their sides. One was passing close to us right now, and the other was at the opposite side of the room.

"Keep close," I said to Loki, and started across the center of the room just after the suit of armor had passed. Across the way, an open doorway beckoned—the only other way out of this room.

We had to stop hard as one of the suits of armor passed in front of us, and then continued forward, arriving at the doorway and finding another winding staircase down.

Like the first, this one didn't have light.

"And this one," Liara was saying as Loki and I started down it, my flame guiding my feet.

The stairs curved around twice, brought me to a deeper, damper level of the prison. Here too I encountered only terrifying darkness, and worse, I could hear two suits of armor clanking their way around the room.

"It's identical to the room above," Loki said. "Ten cells, five on each side."

When I knelt and set my fingers to Loki's fur, a new sheen of flame rippled over him. An enshroudment just for him—a thing I could only share with my familiar, with whom I had a magical bond.

"You check the right side," I said, the flame in my hand my only light. "I'll check the left. Be quick."

"Quicker than you," he murmured as he darted off to the right, disappearing into blackness.

I rose, listening. Neither of the animated suits were nearby, so I started toward the left side of cells. In the first cell, iridescent green magic flowed between the bars. Off the shadows of my flame, I could barely make out a woman on a cot, her face half-hidden by her brown hair.

I moved on, a shard of my own callousness piercing me even as I kept walking.

Time was too short to feel bad now.

In the second cell red-orange magic flowed, and an old man sat slumped on his cot, beard almost to his knees.

Halfway down the block, I had to press myself up against the stone divider between two cells as one of the suits of armor passed by, a good two feet taller than me.

Forever. That was how long they would animate this place, guard these people: forever.

When it had passed, I carried on, taking a second's glance at cells three, four, and five. None of them held a prisoner I knew.

When I arrived at the far side of the room, where another set of dark steps beckoned me down, Loki was already there, waiting for me, appearing in the cone of my flame with a flicking tail and green eyes staring up at me.

"Anything?"

His tail flicked again. "Nothing. Down?"

We had maybe five minutes. Five minutes before the door would open to allow Liara and the fae and the prisoners out—my only opportunity to leave. If I missed it, I didn't know how long we'd be in this place.

Maybe always. Maybe we'd never get out.

But I couldn't take the chance, couldn't skip the third floor. I'd live with it gnawing at me: *What was on that last floor? Could he have been there?*

No—I'd rather die here than not know.

"Down," I said.

The third floor of the prison was the final floor, the dampest, the one most remote from any sense of a sky or a world beyond this one. Loki said it was identical to the first two floors.

Down here, ten desolate cells promised solitude. The endless clanking of armor. Insanity.

Loki and I split up, passing down opposite sides of the room. I passed the first and second cells, and it was when I arrived at the third —with red-orange magic dancing between the bars—that an old, old woman bolted up to a seat on her cot, hair half-wild around her face, and stared at me.

"I see you," she whispered. "I see you. I see you, red-haired girl."

She did. Somehow, she saw me.

I took a step back, one finger rising to my lips even as the two suits of armor stopped. It was a sudden absence of noise, and when I spun, one of them stood ten feet away from me, the other on the opposite side not far from Loki.

I took a step away, then another, keeping my eyes on the suit of armor nearest me like it was a bobcat who'd pounce me if it saw my back.

Instead, the armor approached the old woman's cell. As if engaging some speaking mechanism, it went stiff, the head shifted a degree, and a deep voice—the same one I'd heard from the armor who guarded the prison's entrance—said to her, "What do you see?"

She rocked, eyes shifting to me, then over to Loki. Her eyebrows rose a degree, settled lower as though she'd made a decision. Then, with a stabbing finger, she pointed toward the magical lantern in the center of the ceiling. "I see you. I see you." And with her movement, the lantern came to life, illuminating the space. Her voice went hoarse, then broke into laughter.

The suit of armor remained still. The helmet shifted another degree, and then it resumed its pacing. As did the other across the room.

My chest released, breath leaving me. I stepped out of the armor's way, found myself hesitating in front of the old woman's cell. That woman deserved to be free. She deserved—

The old woman shook her head at me. *There's no way*, she mouthed, flicking her fingers off toward the stairs. *Go.* Her head jerked when I didn't move, and she grew irritated, eyebrows drawing together. *Go, go.*

I went, finding myself in front of the fourth cell. Not this one, either.

The fifth cell was empty.

When I turned to Loki, he'd already crossed toward the stairs. Waiting for me. Which must mean he hadn't found who we were looking for.

I came to him, and I knew pleading must be written on my face, because he said, "We have to go. Now."

No Callum Rathmore.

There was no Callum Rathmore in this prison.

So where the hell was he?

Wild anger filled me even as we started up the stairs. I needed to free these people from this prison. If not today, then someday. My hands went out to the slick stone walls as we ascended and I tried not to slip, but failed a few times. My knee banged stone once, pain surging in me, but I ignored it.

Umbra had told me Callum would be imprisoned. If he wasn't in the mages' prison, where was he?

I felt deceived. Lied to.

"Hurry. Hurry!" Loki's tail disappeared around the final corner of the steps as we came to the second floor.

Liara's voice echoed faintly above. "Thank you. We will..."

The rest of it was lost to the clanging as we arrived at the second floor. The two of us ran through the center of the room, trusting fully in the magic protecting us.

We arrived at the stairs, and Loki told me in a breathless rush the rest of what Liara had said. "They're leaving. They're leaving now."

CHAPTER TWENTY

We took the stairs to the second floor at a reckless leap, Loki bounding and me climbing them two at a time. My heart had enlarged to fill my body, became the current of my rushing blood, the adrenaline coursing through me.

This was fight or flight or both. It was both, because I never felt adrenaline without the urge to fight.

And right now, I was piping hot with anger, anyway. No Callum. No goddamn Callum.

Keep your head, Rational Clem thought. *Keep your head or lose the enshroudment.*

She—*I*—was right. The magic had begun to tingle over my skin, which always preceded losing it. I was getting too hot. Too emotional.

You can punch walls later. You can save him later.

An enforced coolness spread across me. Later—I could save him later.

I knew as we reached the second floor and sprinted across it, cat followed by witch, that I had fully committed myself to finding him. Freeing him. If he wasn't here, then I would look elsewhere. If he wasn't elsewhere, I would look everywhere.

I would burn this world down before I let his own father keep him imprisoned. No—no chains or shackles for him. Not after the power he had brought out of me. Not after he'd swung that sword for me on the tundra and sent me away with the possibility of seeing my sister's face again.

Captivity was unacceptable.

Which meant *my* captivity was unacceptable. I wouldn't—couldn't—be stuck here.

Loki and I hit the staircase to the first floor with almost feral intensity, and my hands sometimes touched the damp steps, my boots sliding as I climbed. Up we went, rounding the steps toward freedom and the blue sky, and as we emerged onto the first floor, I found it empty except for the two patrolling suits of armor.

"They're already up the stairs," Loki said, not stopping, not looking back, a black flash across the stones. He wanted out as much as me.

I followed, still sprinting. When I slipped on the stone and my hands went out, fresh pain spiked up my arms and in my knees.

Loki stopped on a dime, spun toward me. Waiting.

I pressed him on, scrabbling up. "Keep going."

We came to the final stairs, crossing into darkness except for my flame, trusting that we would find what we were looking for when we came around the bend and up to the final threshold.

And we did. Sort of.

The big iron door was open, shadows moving as the last of the prisoners passed into the sunlight. The suit of armor stood guard, holding the door open.

No, not holding it open.

Allowing it to shut. Closing it. Closing off the daylight.

As one, Loki and I ran. He rushed a foot ahead of me, and I followed with a heart ready to burst.

It didn't matter. I'd rather it burst than never see the sun again.

The space narrowed, narrowed, until I had to turn my body sideways to slide through. My right hand had to slide behind my back to avoid my fingers being clipped by the door shutting.

It was that close. That close to never leaving.

But we were out, Liara and the twins leading their group of prisoners past the pizza place, down the alley, along the alternate—less traveled—alley we had planned to escape by. Elijah and Isaiah were already passing out cloaks to the prisoners to hide their shackles and ragged appearances.

We're out, Liara's voice said into my head. *Everyone to the river.*

The river, where we would part the veil and leave.

The others weren't supposed to get too close. They were to keep watch from a distance as we all converged on the river. Liara, the twins, and the prisoners would pass through first. Then the rest of us.

I doubled over for a second, Loki's fur brushing my leg as we two stood outside the prison. We did it. We did it.

We hadn't found him, but we hadn't died in the process, either.

We could keep looking.

Footsteps sounded at the mouth of the alley. When I glanced up, Mishka and Akelan were making their way down toward us.

Where are the others? I said into Mishka's head. *Eva, Keene, Paxton, Maise...*

Coming, came Mishka's reply, her eyes drifting out over the alley as though she was trying to find me.

Any trouble? I asked her.

The formalist police are everywhere, but they seemed mostly preoccupied with the tourists.

Good. There was a substantial shot of getting away with this.

Loki and I followed the prisoners—of whom there were only six. Apparently Liara hadn't been able to get everyone.

Six was better than none.

I'm with you, I said into Liara's head. *Just behind you.*

Stay sharp, she shot back.

What else would I—could I—be in this place? But I swallowed my own snipe; we were leaders. These people's freedom and lives depended on us being leaders.

We continued down alleys, the sky mostly shielded from our view as we passed down the old, narrow streets toward Dean Village. Soon the Dean Bridge came into view, and far beneath it, perpendicular old cobblestone paths winding their way alongside the water, houses and buildings peppering the two sides.

The river was so integrated, it was as though it had been built into the city. As though the city had allowed it to flow through.

And down here, away from the Royal Mile, quiet reigned. As Umbra and Milonakis had predicted, no tourists strayed this way in October.

We came to the bridge, and Liara led the cloaked prisoners down a steep staircase toward the Leith river. Loki and I followed, still enshrouded.

This group was conspicuous, came the thought. But we were close. Too close to fail now, after everything. We were practically *on* the water.

Except, as we came down to the cobblestone path and into the shade of a tall old building, the river lapping next to us, a car stopped on the road overhead. Footsteps, sharp and loud, sounded on the stairs. Two formalist officers with their nightsticks already out.

"Ma'am," one of them called. "Ma'am, stop."

They were speaking to Liara. *Don't stop*, I said to her. *Just keep going.*

But Liara stopped. She turned. *I've got this*, she said.

We were screwed.

Liara thought she could handle this. She thought she could ward the formalists off with her regally high chin and her imperious eyes. "What is it?" she called to the approaching officers.

A man and a woman. He was older, salt-and-pepper temples, weary eyes. She was young, blonde with a tight bun, the two of them in the same black, high-booted uniforms I'd seen years ago in Farina North's living room.

The man swept his nightstick in a circle to indicate the group of prisoners. "We received word from the prison that you're extraditing these mages to Singapore. We'll need to see your orders."

We'd been just a minute too slow. Thirty seconds. If we'd just walked a half-step faster the whole way, we might have avoided them.

Meanwhile, a whole different set of conversations were occurring rapid-fire in my head.

Clem, those officers are trained in anti-magic, Eva was saying from her perch atop a building. She and the other fae had all flown to high spots to observe. Somewhere nearby, I knew Akelan, Mishka, Paxton, and Maise were waiting on us, too. *If it comes to a fight...*

How do you know? I said.

See their nightsticks? They're long, like the ones you saw at Farina North's home. They're designed to absorb magic.

I did see them. They were black, gleaming, as long as my femur.

Liara's got this, I said. *She'll show them the papers and we'll be good.*

Of course, to Liara I was saying: *Eva tells me they're trained in anti-magic. Use those wings and part the goddamn veil with that trigger-happy finger you've got.*

No, she shot back, her eyes never leaving the formalist officers. She snapped her fingers at Elijah, who retrieved the extradition papers and placed them in her hand. *This is a formality.*

A formality my ass. Those nightsticks weren't at their hips—they were in their hands. Liara had misjudged this.

"Who made this request?" Liara approached the officers. "Law dictates Singapore is entitled to any and all fae prisoners."

"Yes, Ms. Youngblood." The male officer received the papers from her. "And law also dictates a senior officer lay eyes on any and all extra-dition orders."

Her eyes narrowed to chill-inducing slits. "Since when?"

"Laws evolve," the other officer said. She was facey, less obsequious. "And they have since your father sat on the council. You'd know that if—"

So they know who she is. Maybe it's common knowledge.

The male officer's hand raised, and she went silent. He surveyed the papers in tense silence, lifting one to study the next. "This is an order from the local council?"

"Yes," Liara said, chin still raised, eyes still somehow gazing down on the officers, who were both taller than her. "Singapore may no longer be formalist-aligned, but the law still applies, does it not?"

"Ms. Youngblood." The officer handed the papers back to her. "Why have you cloaked these prisoners?"

"To give them dignity," she shot back.

"Really?" The other anti-magic officer's head tilted, her shellacked blonde hair gleaming under the sun. "Are you sure you don't mean secrecy?"

"Oh boy," Loki whispered.

This was going south. She should have just parted the veil at the start.

The other officer was still playing Good Cop. Or at least Rule-Abiding Cop. "Ma'am, I'd like to check on this with the council. Would you accompany us to our headquarters? The prisoners will join—"

He didn't get a chance to finish.

"This isn't what I was godsdamn promised," one of the fae bellowed, shrugging off his cloak. An afro of green hair emerged, wild with years spent underground, his eyes equally manic. "You formalists can suck my fae stones." He took to the air, wrists still shackled, and we had a half-second of stillness as his words processed.

A half-second as the word "promised" sank in, damning us. A half-second where Liara met eyes with the officers, her ruse exposed, and where Loki and I glanced at one another, and in that glance we knew what we had to do.

Then the nightsticks came up, the extradition papers went flying. Liara's hands rose from her cloak, lightning crackling on her fingertips, but her wings were hidden under her robes. She took a step back, lightning shooting out, but not before the female officer's nightstick came down atop her. The lightning was absorbed into the weapon, and though the nightstick crackled with lightning from grip to tip, it didn't slow in its arc.

The weapon nearly caught Liara in the shoulder, whiffing past her as she leaned away. She was slowed by her robes, her movements less precise. Which was why she didn't notice the second officer's nightstick as it came down on her temple, knocking her to the cobblestones with an otherwise soundless thud.

Just like that. It had all happened in a second.

Get the prisoners through the veil, I said into the other guardians' heads. *Now.*

But Clem— Eva began.

I've got this.

I started forward, both hands erupting into flame. When I emerged from my enshroudment, it was with a jet of fire rushing directly at the two officers, red-hot and pulsing with fury.

That was my fae he'd hit. We may have been in a bitch fight, but nobody screwed with *my fae.*

The male officer's nightstick swept in an arc just before the fire poured over them, and I stared as the fire was drawn into the weapon like a moth to light. What had been an intense, three-foot-wide jet of flame narrowed away into the black weapon, coating it.

"Well," Loki said by my side, "that's not good."

A second later, the man held his flaming nightstick out before him, his hard, challenging eyes on me.

Meanwhile, the female officer leaned into her shoulder, fingers on a radio. She was speaking in jargon, but I got the gist: Backup. They needed backup, because they were being attacked.

By a witch, I added in my head, taking a wide stance as I allowed the Spitfire to rise in me. *You're being attacked by a witch.*

CHAPTER TWENTY-ONE

I had to give the others enough time to get through the veil, and I had to get Liara. That was my purpose. I was their leader, and I would be the last one through that veil, even if I had to drag the fae with me.

She was, after all, unconscious on the ground. She must have knocked her head a second time when she'd fallen.

The two anti-magic officers stood close to one another, nightsticks raised, each flaring with its own magic: the woman's with Liara's lightning, and the man's with my flames.

They both had their eyes on me. Ready.

Liara lay at the man's feet. I had to get close enough to grab her and get out. That would have been the tricky part—if I wasn't a witch.

The woman's eyes lowered to the cat at my side. Back up to me. "It's the witch," she whispered. "Red hair. Black cat."

So they finally noticed.

The man's face went wide-open. "No."

"The witch," the woman said into her shoulder radio, her voice taking on a higher pitch, her cadence speeding up. "The witch is here on the water."

It doesn't matter now what she says, the Spitfire whispered, delighted. *You won't be around long enough for them to touch you.*

I smiled. "Unfortunately for you both, you're a hundred percent right." I swept my hand low, embers of flame dropping away and falling onto Loki's fur. It ignited at once. "Loki," I said. "Go."

At once, my familiar blazed with flame as he raced forward, leaping at the male officer with a scream so fierce and shrill it might have been a banshee there by the river.

Nah, just my cat.

The man lashed out with his nightstick, warding Loki from digging his claws in and latching onto his chest.

But that wasn't Loki's plan, anyway.

His small form sailed below the nightstick's arc and past the officer. He lashed out with his claws as he passed, catching the officer's forearm before he landed behind the two of them.

Meanwhile, I stepped forward, throwing a wave of flame with my left arm. Then another with my right arm, as if the ocean had caught fire, one after another after another.

The female officer deflected each of my waves, swinging with her nightstick, while the male officer had half-turned to ward off the hellcat.

In the course of the fighting, she took a step toward the water. So did he. And in the process, they moved away from Liara.

Clem, came Elijah's voice in my head. *The prisoners are through.*

And the other guardians? I asked.

The humans are making for Arthur's Seat, he said. *The fae are waiting on you.*

Sirens sounded on the bridge, vehicles coming to hard stops, doors slamming. The officers' backup had arrived. *Tell them to go through.*

But what about you? Elijah asked.

I ignored him. Loki and I were facing down the two officers from either side, backing them toward the water. He leapt, screamed, clawed, and I enveloped them with more flame than their sad little sticks could handle.

It was intoxicating, knowing how outgunned they were.

Clem, Eva's worried voice sounded in my mind. *They're coming. Lots more.*

Footsteps sounded down the bridge staircase—more formalist officers. Over a dozen of them.

Some part of me recognized this was bad. Another part wanted to drive these two bastards into the river.

And then Eva appeared in front of me, her gray eyes intense. She dashed my flame aside with her air, hands going to my shoulders. "Everyone else is through. We need to get Liara and get out of here. Now."

Liara. Get Liara, Rational Clem said into my fire-addled head.

Liara. She was still down.

I squeezed my eyes shut for a moment, fingers curling to fists to quell the flames. Then focused past Eva on the officers sprinting down the cobblestone path toward us.

We needed to leave.

I flicked my attention to the two officers near the water. *"Pairilis síoraí,"* I whispered, staring at one and then the next as I repeated the words.

Like that, they went still. Immobile.

Anti-magic my ass.

"Loki"—I spun toward Liara, ducking down to haul one of her arms over my shoulder as Eva grabbed the other—"let's go."

For all her gravitas, Liara was astonishingly light. She couldn't weigh more than a hundred pounds with those fine fae bones. Her head slumped as Eva and I lifted her, carried her down the path and toward the water.

"The veil," Eva said, breathless.

"I've got it."

If Liara had shown me one thing in the past year we'd spent together as guardians, it was how to part the veil in a rush. It wouldn't be pretty or clean, but it had to be.

We hit the water's edge, and my finger was already moving through the air, drawing down, down, doing my best to close out the noise behind us, to focus on Umbra and her glowing staff.

All that mattered was this.

I knelt to finish the cut, and then, "Go. Just go."

Eva swept the veil aside, and I caught a glimpse of trees and light— the academy—before Loki dashed through, and we threw ourselves after him, two fae and a human tumbling to the soft ground on the other side.

I rolled onto my back, lifting my head to stare back at the space we'd just passed through as the veil swept to place. I spotted the man's face, his nightstick, and then it was just a seam in the space before me, and then nothing at all.

No more Edinburgh. Just the academy.

Beside me, Liara lay still. Eva also rolled onto her back, slight chest moving fast, her eyes on the canopy above us.

We lay there in silence, just breathing hard, until the sound of Maeve Umbra's staff touching the earth echoed behind me, and then her head appeared upside-down over us, her long curtain of white hair shadowing her face.

"Well," she said, eyes settling on me, "it seems you've gotten into trouble again."

Trouble. Wherever I went, trouble followed—or I brought trouble.

In this case, the trouble I'd brought had saved Liara, which was what Eva told the headmistress as she stared disapprovingly down at us. Her lavender head had risen from the ground, eyes shooting to me, then up to Umbra. "Clem gave them way more trouble than they gave us."

Thank you, Whitewillow.

"I'll be very curious to know what Clem did this time," Umbra said, straightening.

I forced myself up onto my elbows, surveying around us. "Is everyone here?"

"Everyone's here." Isaiah appeared from my periphery. He knelt beside the still-unconscious Liara, moving her hair from her face. "She looks in a bad way."

"She needs Neverwink," I said, finding a regular seat in the grass.

Isaiah nodded, gently lifted Liara, carrying her out of sight.

Umbra observed our interaction a moment before her name was called from across the clearing. When she turned, Milonakis was calling for her, standing with the huddle of shackled fae. "Head-mistress," she called. "Could you lend us your magic to break these shackles?"

Umbra glanced back at us, gave a long nod. "Trouble or no, you brought five lives to safety today. I hope your pride in yourselves equals mine."

And with that, she turned with a sweep of robes and was gone.

I reached out for Loki, my hand settling onto his back as his tail rose high into the air. "She meant you, too, you know."

"You sure she didn't mean *all* me?" His green eyes flashed on me as he turned a circle to be petted again.

"I can't believe you did that." Eva came to a seat, letting out a long breath. Her eyes drifted up to the sun, and she let out a small laugh. "Gods, I'm about to be late for Neverwink's class."

I kept on petting Loki. "Tell her you have a note from your guardian co-leader explaining your lateness."

A smile appeared, then disappeared. She leaned closer. "Clem, what were you doing in that prison?"

My eyebrows rose like I didn't know what she was talking about.

"Those officers said there was an incident at the prison," she said. "It was you. I know it."

I shrugged, patting grass off my clothes. "I guess so."

Her chin lowered. "Why?"

The jag of frustration and pain returned, the memory and knowl-edge of one fact: Callum Rathmore wasn't in that prison. He wasn't there. My promise came back with it, the acknowledgement I'd made to myself while sprinting through the prison that I would not stop looking for him.

Eva must have seen it in my eyes, because they widened. "Did you sneak in?"

Loki snorted. "Did she ever."

I half-shrugged, gaze sliding away from her. When I got to my feet, she was up, too. "Why?" she said. "And why didn't you tell me?"

She had placed herself in front of me, forcing acknowledgment of her presence. Her questions. So I fixed my attention on her and told her the truth. "I wasn't there for the mission, Eva. And I didn't think you'd approve of that."

"Why were you there?" she whispered.

Why was it so hard to say his name? *Because you failed*, came the small voice. *Because he's not here with you now.*

My face lowered, unable to say it without Loki in view. "I was looking for him."

She stepped confidentially close. "Rathmore?"

I gave one nod.

"But you didn't find him."

I shook my head.

"Oh, Clem." Her arms wrapped around me, warm and slender. "You romantic idiot. You should have told me."

I'd known she would understand, but I had kept it from her anyway. I'd kept it from everyone but Loki, as though by revealing what I wanted, I was making myself vulnerable. Open to attack.

When she stepped away, she looked upset. "Did you check the whole prison?"

"All three stymy levels."

"So if Rathmore's not there, then where is he?"

Evanora Whitewillow, once again being the friend I'd never knew I needed.

"God, I don't know," I said in a rush. "But he must be locked up, according to Umbra. I just don't even know where that would be."

Eva came around, arm across my back, clasping my shoulder. We started walking with Loki alongside us. "You'll figure it out like you do all things. First we're going to shower, and then we're going to eat. And drink. And probably take a long nap."

"Cutting class?" I asked.

She laughed. "Don't tell Neverwink."

On the way, we passed the group of rescued fae with Milonakis. One of them, an old man with a bald head, met eyes with me. His were an incredible blue in his pale, drawn face, and they warmed on me. An acknowledgment.

Later, I would find out his name was Cornelius Norwood. He was one of the most powerful earth mages alive, and he had disappeared fifteen years ago after he'd spoken out against the formalist consolidation of power in Edinburgh.

And now he stood barefoot on grass, free.

In the end, we'd rescued five mages from the prison beneath Edinburgh. One had flown off, still shackled—which we'd all laughed about later in the guardians' common room ("suck my stones" would become Elijah and Isaiah's new favorite catchphrase), after everything was said and done and Liara had been to the infirmary and found *not* to have a concussion after she'd taken the blow from the nightstick and then hit her head on the cobblestones.

Umbra had escorted the freed fae to various faculty members' homes, giving them each a place to sleep and stay and recuperate. Among the other fae we'd rescued were two dissidents who'd fought against the formalist government, a tangible manipulations savant, and a professor from the University of Edinburgh who had specialized in magical history.

All five of them agreed to join us at the academy.

CHAPTER TWENTY-TWO

The next day, Umbra spread her robes around her as we sat on the cliff's edge, our legs hanging over. This was the only part of the academy grounds that met up with real geographic peril, not far from where I'd first met Callum Rathmore.

"So," she said, gazing out over the late-fall landscape, "you snuck into the prison, caused a kerfuffle with the guards, Liara was hurt, and we lost one of the fae."

"Yes, yes, yes, and we didn't technically lose the fae. Not in the mortal sense. He just flew off talking about sucking—"

She raised a hand. "I know. The fae twins made sure of it."

Even while I knew I was in some trouble, and even while I did my best to keep the enshroudment alive around me, I wondered if Umbra ever thought of those things. If she'd ever loved someone in that way.

She had a daughter.

"I needed to find him," I said.

"Oh, I understand well." Her eyes caught mine at the corners, her mouth in a slight upturn. "We always have reasons for what we think we need. Excuses for the mayhem we create in attempting to get it."

"It wasn't mayhem..."

Her face turned skeptical.

"Fine," I said. "It was a little bit of mayhem. Just tell me my punishment."

"Your punishment"—a slender thread of humor wove through the gravity of her voice—"is not for me to deliver. We punish ourselves worst of all for our own mistakes, if we care even a little."

I sat in silence, my own eyes traveling across the sunlit hills.

"I think you would like to speak to Liara," she murmured, "about everything that has happened. But you feel guilt, and maybe an ever-present shame interwoven, too."

She got it. How did she get it?

"And so," she went on, "since you arrived back you've avoided the fae, probably didn't sleep well last night. Maybe you even had a moment in the bathroom mirror, staring at your own—"

"Okay." I lifted my hand as a white flag. "I get it. You're either spying on me or spying on me."

"Like you did the evening you followed Nance, Nurse Neverwink, and me into my underground chambers?" She watched me with the sagest *gotcha* face.

I tugged at my uniform's collar, then found sudden interest in the pleats of my skirt. "So different."

She laughed. "I'm not spying on you. But I've lived long enough to know what a drop of empathy will produce when we've wronged someone else."

My magic simmered around us; it had been keeping the two of us warm for the past fifteen minutes. Today, after the insanity of yesterday, Umbra had decided this would be the perfect afternoon for me to begin enshrouding not just myself or my familiar, but other people, too.

"I'm going back there," I said, raising my face to her. "I'm going back to Edinburgh."

She shrugged. "Of course you are. You're the only guardian who can skip around the city in your skivvies, singing your country's national anthem without the slightest concern. You think I'd just keep your power locked away here?"

"You tried to. At first."

She waved a dismissive hand. "I wanted to see your grit, child. Your assertiveness, your perseverance in the face of authority. No wallflower will save this world." She paused, angling her head toward me. "And what I taught you while you were here was important. More important than you may think."

At this, something tensed, snapped in my chest; the familiar feeling of reaching my limit. My magic faltered around Umbra, the red-orange sheen of it drying up and leaving her out in the wind.

"Twenty minutes," she said, pulling her robes tighter around her. "A fine first effort."

When Umbra began to stand, I stared up at her. "So, your baby daddy."

Her eyebrows rose. She blinked twice, lost for words.

"Did you love him?" I said. "Your daughter's dad."

"Oh." She gave a thoughtful shake of the head, as though finding those memories. "It was long ago. After so much time, it's hard to identify exactly what the feeling was."

"How long ago?" I pressed.

Her fingers played over the grip of her staff. "Feels like centuries to me."

I stood with her, the wind blowing my skirt back toward the headmistress. "Headmistress, how old are you?"

We began walking, and she leaned toward me, her elbow finding my side. "Impolite. But some days I feel about five hundred years old."

I laughed. "Sometimes I do, too."

She went silent, staff tapping over the ground as we walked, her eyes lowered. Then, in a clipped, serious voice, she said, "Time grows short."

I eyed her. Was she feeling that ancient? "Short?"

"The Shade has grown in power even since this summer. I can feel it; all but a few of the leylines are no longer safe to travel by."

"So we'll take the scenic routes."

Her eyes narrowed on me. "Only you would so flippantly analogize leylines to highways."

I shrugged. "I guess more people need to be daring with their analogies."

She gave a sigh as we continued on, her pace increasing. "You must go back to Edinburgh, and soon. The more intimately you know the city, the more information you gather, the better prepared you will be to retrieve the final piece of the Shade's weapon when the time comes. Wherever the damned thing may lie."

So she fully believed in the prophecy, too. I wasn't exactly sure when that had happened, but it was clear now she had crossed a threshold in her mind.

"Good. Great. When do I go?"

"As soon as you've gotten the proper feel for sharing your enshroudment. Someone must go with you for what I have in mind."

"And what do you have in mind?"

Her jaw hardened, eyes ahead, as though Edinburgh lay before us, the Royal Mile stretching long instead of the forest. "You will enter the Mages' Council building, and you will put those eavesdropping skills to better use than on me and Nance Milonakis."

"I didn't—"

We had arrived in the central grounds, and she stopped, turned to me. "You did, and it's a waste of both our time discussing it." She turned toward her office, turned back toward me. "Don't go to Liara. Wait for her to come to you. She will."

And then she left me there in the clearing, my hair blown back. I had been Maeve Umbra'd.

⁂

After the prison rescue, Liara, Elijah, and Isaiah couldn't show their pretty faces in Edinburgh. They were wanted, all three of them, and would replace the rescued fae in those prison cells if they were ever caught.

I couldn't show my face, either, but I had one thing they didn't: enshroudment. Which meant I could still move freely through the city.

And I would. Oh, would I.

Tristan Rathmore led the Mages' Council, and we knew the Shade owned him. We needed to know what he told the council, to know their plans in the midst of the corruption spreading across the world.

Much of the Shade's power in the world stemmed from Edinburgh. And it grew every day. The more powerful she grew, the narrower my chances of killing her.

My second opportunity came in November, when Umbra gave us our next mission based on the intelligence she'd gotten from one of our rescued fae, a former professor at the University of Edinburgh. A security tunnel ran from the university to the Mages' Council building, created long ago in case of outside threat, and forgotten—abandoned—when the formalists took over.

The formalists had been the inside threat the city's government hadn't expected.

The fae professor showed us the tunnel's location on a map, explained that it emerged into an unused space behind the walls of the building. From there, a secret door led into the building's offices and corridors.

"And once you're inside," she said with a gleam in her eyes I hadn't seen the day she'd been rescued, "well, who knows what you'll hear?"

And because of my power, it came to me to get inside. Me and Loki.

I would have gone anyway. I'd have insisted on going. If there was a chance I'd learn the truth of what Tristan Rathmore had done with his son, I'd take it.

We'd learned from another of the fae prisoners, a native of Edinburgh, that the council met on the last Thursday of every month. That meant I would be headed into the frigid city at the end of November.

The other guardians—minus Liara, Elijah, and Isaiah—would watch outside the building as the council members came and left, keeping me apprised of everything I couldn't see.

After that meeting, when I'd volunteered myself so easily to sneak into the tunnel and spy on the council, was when Liara finally decided to warm to me.

I'd seen it in her eyes for weeks. She'd wanted to talk to me, but the thawing came that day in November when the first snowfall arrived.

She'd pulled her cloak on, nodded me away from the others as we came into the flurries. Our boots crunched over the earth as we walked together through the academy grounds, and she said, "So you snuck into the prison."

It wasn't a question. And I knew it would be pointless playing dumb.

"It was me," I said. No one knew but her and Eva—at least as far as I understood. "I snuck in after you. Hidden."

"I know," she said, low and level. "I've known since the day it happened. Since you told me I needed to get out of there."

I squeezed my eyes shut. "And you've been hating me even more?"

"At first, absolutely. But over the years, I've come to learn one important thing about you."

My eyes opened, the blistering white of the snow all around me again. "And what's that?"

"When you do reckless things, you have good reasons for doing them." She stopped, turned to me. "And that's more than I can say for myself."

A sudden jag of emotion hit me. I hadn't expected that empathy from Liara, of all people. I stopped with her, raised an uncomfortable brow, unsure how to handle this moment.

"I'm sorry, Clementine," she said. "For slapping you."

That was maybe the first time I'd heard an apology from her lips.

"Liara—"

"I should not have slapped you," she ground out, like a child repeating a phrase she'd been told to say. I could see how hard this was for her. Then, in a rush, she said, "I really shouldn't have. It wasn't okay."

"No, it wasn't," I said, low. "But neither was what I did in the prison. Lying to you. To everyone."

"And then you made up for it"—she flicked the edge of my cloak—"like you always do. You make it so hard to loathe you."

I didn't know what to say. I settled on: "That's my goal. Invoking slightly less than loathing."

She walked on, shaking her cloak off, a drizzle of snow falling to the ground. "If you had slapped me, I don't know if I would have helped if it was you who'd been beaten with a nightstick and lay unconscious on the ground."

"You would have," I said, and in the silence that followed, I wanted to tell her I'd experienced worse, much worse, than a slap. But she probably knew. She had, too. "You would, Liara."

Then, because neither of us knew what to do with compliments, she said, "Umbra asked me to go into Edinburgh with you."

"With me?" I echoed.

Her eyes drifted up and down me. "Yeah. Inside your enshroudment."

I sucked in air. "That was bold of her." I'd only been studying the enshroudment of others for a month.

"Are you saying you can't do it?"

I scoffed. "In front of Liara Youngblood? Never." I glanced over at her. "Why does she want me to bring you, anyway?"

Liara shrugged. "I know all the council members' names, the names of their wives, their assistants, their pets. You know, just part of growing up with a powerful formalist dad."

That made sense. A lot of it.

I also suspected Umbra had another reason for sending Liara with me: to stress-test me the way she'd been doing since the summer. It was effective, if not an absolute pita.

"And what did you say to Umbra when she asked?" I said.

"I told her it was up to you." She turned to me, snow dotting her black hair. Her eyes were wide and wet with the cold, or maybe real feeling. "I just want you to know, I don't hate witches," she said. "Not all of them, anyway."

CHAPTER TWENTY-THREE

On the third Thursday of November, Liara and I moved through the city side by side, almost but not quite touching. Loki jogged between us, tail upright, the three of us enshrouded from the world.

Ever since the day of her apology, I'd kicked my own ass to be able to enshroud another person the way I was doing for Liara now.

"So this is what your magic is like," Liara said as she weaved her way around a young guy who would have walked straight into her. "Feels like being encased in jello."

I glanced at her as we turned a corner, now just a few blocks from the campus. "You know what that feels like?"

"Please." She returned to my side, still not touching but close enough not to strain my enshroudment. "Everyone who's not a prude knows what it feels like to be encased in jello."

"Well"—my attention drifted to a man playing bagpipes in the middle of the campus—"now you're just screwing with me."

Liara's hand reached out, redirected my attention. "I know the kilts are distracting, but the council convenes in thirty minutes."

Loki struck out a few feet ahead of us, leading the way. "Twenty-nine minutes."

When we came to the right building, we had to idle by the doors for a few minutes, waiting for someone to come in or out. At this time of day, with students everywhere, it would be conspicuous for the door to simply... open.

We got our chance soon enough. A group of students passed out as a class ended, and we were able to slide inside the building as they allowed the doors to swing shut behind them.

I'd never been in a university this old. It even smelled old and austere in here, the hallway wainscoting a beautiful old oak, the doors to the classrooms the same.

And the oldest building on campus held a secret.

We started off, passing down the hallway and taking our first left to a dead-end stairwell with a half-height door placed beneath it I never would have noticed if I hadn't been looking.

"Ah," Loki said, trotting up to stand beside it as though waiting for his servants to do the honors. "A familiar-sized door. Finally."

Liara ducked, tried the latch. The door jiggled, but didn't give. She glanced back up at me. "What do you think—a little spritz of lightning?"

I shrugged. "Sure." Then leaned back, waiting for the sound of footsteps to pass. One student came down the stairs, continued on toward the main hall. When they were out of sight, I nodded at Liara.

She lifted her finger and a blue flash appeared, disappearing with a crackle into the door's keyhole. The door flung itself open, the latch coming half-dislodged from the wood itself.

Inside, darkness awaited.

Loki disappeared straight in, upright tail brushing the doorframe. Liara followed at a crouch, and I came last of all, pulling the door shut behind me. Inside, I found myself in a tight space with her, the ceiling too low to stand properly.

"I spotted stairs," Liara said. "Can we get some flame?"

I dropped the enshroudment around us and ignited a large flame in my hand. The staircase came illuminated—gray, monochrome steps down into the darkness. The walls and ceiling were the same, low and tight and stifling.

My hand went out, bracing myself against the wall as I started down after Liara, who'd followed Loki. "Am I missing something, or were the Scottish a hell of a lot smaller thirty years ago?"

"It wasn't meant for adults," Liara said with her familiar petulant impatience. "The tunnel was designed to ferry children who lived nearby."

"And cats," Loki said.

My hand went up to gauge the ceiling and avoid running into it as we passed down the straight steps. "Isn't it generally best for adults to accompany children into dark, spooky tunnels?"

"Who's spooked?" Liara's voice lilted now. "Are you, Clementine?"

"Yeah," I said. "And I'm woman enough to admit it."

Her faint laugh bounced off the close walls as she reached the end of the stairs, her boots tapping on the cement. "You should be. Beyond this tunnel lay the crypts of Edinburgh. Skeletons, ghosts..."

"Not ghosts again," I said.

She glanced back at me as she walked ahead, her dark eyes gleaming. "Again? That's a story if I've ever heard one."

I told her about Milonakis's return to the academy. About the things she'd said of her time under the city. How her eyes had turned white and milky. About Aidan's grandmother, who'd experienced the same thing and never been the same afterward.

"So Milonakis and Farina North both saw them," Liara said when I'd finished. "They wouldn't be the first."

I stopped. "You believe they saw ghosts?"

She disappeared from the halo of my flame, and I continued on after her. "Of course I do," she said. "Because they're real. My father used to tell me stories about his trips to Edinburgh, the times he visited the undercity."

The undercity. That was the first time I'd heard that word, as though an entire bustling population existed under the ground.

It creeped me out. Especially down here.

"What about the white eyes?" I said.

"Nasty, huh? He always told me it's an overexposure thing. If you've seen too much of them, it's like staring at the sun too long, or into a camera's flashbulb. It's only cured with valerian."

To this point I had never considered the real possibility of ghosts, or ever meeting them. All my life I'd been agnostic about the paranormal, but then again, I was a witch. I had a familiar. I was walking through a tunnel under Edinburgh with a girl who had wings on her back.

Why not ghosts?

"Did your father see them?" I asked.

"Once or twice," she said. "He thought he saw children in glimpses. Enough to believe ghosts existed for the rest of his life."

I winced. Children had died down below the city, too; of course they had.

Liara came to a stop, and I nearly ran into her. "What's up?" I said.

She looked back at me. "We're here." Her finger went out, pointing. Before us rose an identical staircase to the first one.

We had arrived at the Mages' Council building.

***

Umbra had explicitly warned us about two things before this mission:

One, we had to evade every councilor's and assistant's notice.

Two, if we didn't, the whole building could be locked down tight. It was also outfitted with anti-magic security measures. With the press of a button, my fire and Liara's lightning would be nullified no matter where we were in the building.

"Easy enough," I'd said.

Now I wasn't so sure.

When we arrived at the top of the staircase, a strange assortment of old, dusty furniture greeted us. We picked our way through it to stand on the landing, and Liara and I met eyes, flanked by overstuffed armchairs and rolled-up rugs. "Storage room?" I said.

"Storage room."

"That's one way of asserting your dominance over fear. Plug up the escape route with old furniture." I extended my flame toward the walls, searching for the exit the professor had told us about. I found at half-height: another door, this one not locked but blocked from the other side.

When I pushed against it, it wanted to give, but I sensed I was pushing against something bigger behind it.

"Open the door an inch," Loki said, "and I can slip through."

I smiled at him. "An inch?"

He stared back, unblinking. "I'm a cat. I could do a half-inch in a pinch."

Liara stood over us, arms folded, waiting for our apparently one-sided conversation to be over. When it was, I said up to her, "We're shoving it open. This is going to take some back. Come on, Youngblood."

She got down beside me, sinking into the enshroudment I spread over the three of us. As we began pushing, I said, "So, would you still pick this over Mages' Council royalty?"

"Every day of the week," she grunted, turning to push back-first, her boots digging into the ground.

Eventually, a shaft of light eased into the space. Not much, but enough that Loki said, "Good. I'll check it out."

He stuck his head through, wriggling to get the rest of him through the crack. He had to contort his body, his hips turning sideways, but he eventually popped through, the black tip of his tail disappearing with a flick.

We waited in silence, and I had a slim view of the room beyond this one. I couldn't make out anything but oatmeal-colored walls.

Finally, Loki's head popped back in. "It's a bookcase against the door. This is someone's office."

"Office?" I whispered.

"It's fine—we're alone. Come on, girls, get on with it. We've only got eight minutes."

My attention flicked to a waiting Liara. "My cat's giving us instructions. Says it's an office, we're alone, and we're deeply failing him by struggling so much to push this bookcase out of the way."

She snorted. "Guess we have no choice but to show him."

"Guess we don't."

Two minutes later, we'd pressed the bookcase out far enough to be able to slide our way out into the office with similar contortions. When I'd made it out, I slumped on a floral rug.

Immediately, Loki's face hovered above me, close enough that I could smell his cat breath. "Four minutes."

Liara was already up, staring around the room. "This is one of the councilors' offices." She approached the desk, glancing over it. "Councilor Delarosa. My dad always said he was a real bastard."

I got to my feet. "Let's go. We've got four minutes before they convene."

We crossed to the door, setting our ears against it.

Loki looked up at me and sighed. "Just send me through as a scout already."

I turned the knob, opened the door just an inch. When Loki poked his head out, he only swiveled it once before he ducked back in. "Hallway's clear. Except for the scent of arrogance and bureaucracy."

I grinned, and Liara said, "What?"

"I just... The hallway's clear." When I pushed the door open, we came into a wide, elegant hallway with portraits hung at intervals and tall, beautiful windows facing back at us at the far end.

"These are portraits of former councilors," Liara said as we passed down the hall. "They're everywhere in this building. The Mages' Council has been around since the Battle of the Ages."

Five hundred years.

My gaze swept over all those faces. There must have been twenty just in this hall, and a few of the councilors wore antiquated bouffant-style hairdos. I could practically see the centuries in portraiture.

When we reached the corner, we peeked around as though we weren't enshrouded. A young woman passed out of an office carrying an official-looking clipboard, her style very much overdressed summer intern in a suit and pumps.

"She's an assistant, headed toward the council room," Liara said. "Come on."

We followed at a distance, taking a right at the next turnoff. The next hallway was considerably busier, with four or five young people who all looked similarly intern-ish, waiting around with clipboards and folders outside a pair of grand wooden doors. One nodded as a much older man in green-and-red patterned robes spoke in a low voice, his long, slender beard touching his chest every time his lips parted.

This hallway was a strange mixture of old and new, of centuries-old traditional robes and modern officewear. Just like the formalist officers I'd encountered, with their old-style beliefs about witches and their nightsticks and radios.

And amongst them I spotted a familiar blue bob: Ora Frostwish. She was completely consumed by her phone, only the pert tip of her nose showing, but I recognized that long neck and those elegant wings.

I wished I had torn one of those wings, at least a little.

The three of us pressed ourselves to the wall, and my chin jutted toward the man with the man in the patterned robes. "That's a councilor, isn't it?" I whispered, though I didn't need to.

"Councilor Delarosa," Liara whispered back. "The bastard."

"I knew that skinny beard was suspicious." I jerked my chin at him. "He's our best chance of getting in through the doors."

She nodded. "The assistants wait out here. It's councilors only inside the room, and he's the last one in."

So we waited. The meeting would convene in just a minute or two, but apparently Councilor Delarosa wasn't keen on timeliness so much as the sound of his own dictation to his assistant, whose pen scribbled away.

Finally, Loki's tail flicked against me, as though he knew my eyes had unfocused. "This is it."

I nudged Liara, and as the councilor pulled open one of the doors, we weaved our way past the assistants toward him. I managed to slide through along with Loki in the councilor's wake, but Liara had to dodge one of the assistants, who paced. She reached out by instinct and grabbed the door, holding it open a moment to slip inside.

I stared at her, wide-eyed, as it banged closed behind us like a gavel. Then at the massive domed room surrounded by bookcases, the enormous horseshoe table in the center with twelve councilors seated around it.

None of them had so much as looked in Councilor Delarosa's direction, much less the doors. They were much more consumed by leaning over to chat to each other than anything else.

In the highest-backed chair at the highest point of the horseshoe sat Tristan Rathmore. He was flanked by a slender young woman with a deep purple veil over her face, her hands clasped before her. She wore black on black, her boots tall, her stance wide. Powerful.

"Is that Rathmore's assistant?" I pointed at her.

As I did, I caught the vaguest hint of her eyes shifting toward us beneath the veil. But she didn't otherwise move. Her eyes just remained fixed on the spot where we stood for a second, two, then moved off.

Liara leaned toward me. "When I said only councilors were allowed in this room, I forgot about the head councilor's bodyguard."

A young woman for a bodyguard. She was either wildly powerful or a pretty showpiece. Maybe both. Either way, I didn't want to find out.

CHAPTER TWENTY-FOUR

Councilor Delarosa took his seat, the chattering dropped away, and Liara, Loki, and I moved along the edge of the room, backing up against one of the bookcases.

Here we were, surrounded by the formalists' most powerful, and none of them even knew. It was a strange, heady thing, that Umbra believed I could keep us safe with my power.

Maybe that was why I could do it. Because she believed.

"Fine of you to join, Councilor Delarosa," Rathmore said from the head of the table. Beneath his robes, he had the powerful build of a man who had chased Maeve Umbra and me down a train platform in platemail. His jaw was still defined, his gray hair well-combed to his head.

"Of course, Head Councilor," Delarosa said with a little too much backhandedness.

Rathmore's eyes sharpened on him for a cut-glass moment of severity. If he'd looked at me that way, I doubted I could have kept up the enshroudment. The man was that mean with his eyes.

He was, after all, a half-demon.

"We'll begin, councilors." His hands came to steeple under his chin, elbows on the polished table. "Who brings urgent news?"

"I do," said a woman, her body stout under her robes, her chestnut hair woven tight at the back of her head.

"Councilor Sangrey," Rathmore said. "Please, tell us."

Liara leaned toward me to whisper, "She's head of magical security."

The purple-veiled bodyguard's head shifted again, her veil shifting as I glimpsed her staring in our direction.

I set my hand to Liara's arm. Nodded at the bodyguard. Before Liara could speak, I set my thumb to her forehead.

Without word, Liara did the same to me.

She can't possibly see us, Liara said, half in question.

Umbra told me the enshroudment was complete, I said. *There shouldn't be a way*.

And yet the young bodyguard's eyes remained on us. She wavered in place, as though tempted to move. But decided against it, her focus returning to the councilors.

"In light of the escaped fae," Sangrey said, "we've transferred the remaining prisoners to Falaichte."

My attention sharpened on the discussion. Falaichte—that wasn't the name of the prison below this building.

What's Falaichte? I hissed at Liara.

Her eyes narrowed. *I wish I knew.*

Rathmore gave a nod. "Excellent. How many have been transferred?"

"All but three."

"See that any future prisoners are transferred there until the culmination."

As Sangrey nodded, a male councilor—the youngest of them, with a long neck and prominent Adam's apple—raised a thin finger. "And what word of the culmination?"

Rathmore lifted a hand. "Patience, Councilor. You know our protocol." He paused, eyes traveling like a hunting hawk's. "Councilor Whitarrow, surely you have something to report on the state of the leylines."

That's the head of intelligence, Liara said into my head.

So chief spy.

Basically.

"Surely." Whitarrow, a tall man in his fifties with an easy, charmed way of sitting, swept a hand out. "The report isn't good, Head Councilor. Every leyline we've surveyed has been corrupted."

If that wasn't good news to the council, then the council was either in the dark about who Tristan Rathmore actually was, or they knew something we didn't about the leylines.

"All of them?" Rathmore said.

"All we're aware of, yes. As you know, some remain outside our purview."

Rathmore nodded. "And what of the escaped prisoners?"

"No word, I'm afraid. Our belief still remains that they're being held by Maeve Umbra, or have been brainwashed into joining her."

Held. Brainwashed. Of course they would think that, though it still hurt—in an oddly protective, nobody-talks-bad-about-my-mom-but-me way—to hear it about Maeve Umbra.

Rathmore's jaw moved. "And what were her intentions, Councilor? Surely not just a prison break."

"I believe now, as I always did," Whitarrow began, "that Maeve Umbra serves the Shade. That she will do everything she can to thwart our efforts here, including the recruitment of the imprisoned fae, as she works toward the culmination."

None of the other councilors disagreed; a few nodded.

So they believed Maeve Umbra intended to revive the Shade. Which meant the council thought they were working *against* the Shade. And it was then I realized: the Shade was universally hated like some evil icon of history. It was unacceptable to support her no matter who you were, or what you believed.

Which meant that for Tristan Rathmore, this was all theater.

The culmination, I said. *They keep repeating that. Have you heard of it?*

Liara shook her head.

"And so," Rathmore said, "you believe Umbra will continue to work against us here in Edinburgh?"

"Such are her ways," Whitarrow said.

"Which is why I've briefed the city's security," Sangrey said.

"They're aware of the faces working for her, the fae and the witch, and on alert for magic."

Rathmore raised a hand toward his bodyguard, who leaned down toward him. He whispered something to her, and she nodded. Her lips moved, and Rathmore set a hand to her arm before returning his attention to the meeting.

"Fine, Councilor," he said. "Continue your vigilance until Whitarrow's forces have found her and brought her to justice. We cannot allow her to succeed, here or anywhere, for she will deliver any victories to the Shade's feet, and upon the culmination, our battle will be terrible. I bring urgent news, Councilors, about this very thing."

All eyes were on Rathmore, who sat under so many gazes with perfect composure. I didn't sense he relished this, but he was used to this sort of thing. He was the kind of man who had been raised to rule, in whom someone had instilled a deep, unbreakable belief that he was a man others would look to.

Rathmore set a finger to the table, leaning forward, eyes traveling around the council. "At this pace, the Shade will rise within one year."

Liara and I met eyes, and hers were as wide as I'd ever seen them.

One year. *One year.*

Silence ensued, during which a few of the councilors leaned toward one another in whispers. Finally, Whitarrow—obviously the least afraid of the bunch—swept his hand out once more in that peacemaking gesture. "You've predicted it several times in the past, Head Councilor. Why is this time different?"

"I've witnessed the growth of the Shade's power, Whitarrow," Rathmore said easily, with silky confidence. "My father studied her, as did his father, and his. Never in five hundred years have the Shade's tendrils found their way to the leylines. The pale simulacrum of her power never lasted. Remember: this is why the formalists came to be, Councilors."

I had a gross, creeping feeling I knew what "the culmination" was.

But I didn't want to know. My mind wanted to reject it but couldn't, so I was having a hard time focusing on anything but the feeling.

"It shouldn't be possible," one of the councilors said—her first time speaking. "The exile was—"

"It is possible, and has always been, Councilor," Rathmore cut in with the smoothness of a knife. "One year. We must prepare for the second Battle of the Ages."

The feeling cemented.

In the same moment, Liara leaned toward me and said, "The culmination is when the Shade destroys everything, makes herself—"

Footsteps sounded at the far end of the room. Rathmore's bodyguard was in motion, her hands still clasped behind her back, all her attention directly on the spot where we stood.

The meeting went on, but Rathmore's eyes were on his bodyguard. Which meant this was atypical.

And she was headed directly for us.

I set my hand to Liara's arm. *Move.*

Together, we edged our way toward the doors as the bodyguard approached, Loki's tail feathering along my leg as he kept in step with me.

Rathmore's bodyguard stopped in the exact spot where we'd been standing, and which we now stood only two feet from. She stared at the bookcase, her eyes rising and dropping as though trying to perceive.

My breath came fast, my adrenaline up, as I recognized that she had *heard* us. When we'd spoken, she'd heard us. I didn't know how, but she had. And the closer she got, the weaker my magic became, like the simple fact of her nearness repelled it.

And with that realization, my enshroudment began to wane.

Liara, I said, *we need to leave.*

Except the doors were closed. We were supposed to wait until the meeting was over, when the councilors would leave and we could slide out behind them.

We couldn't just open the doors. Not without giving ourselves away.

Rathmore's bodyguard was still staring at the spot where we'd stood, but she seemed confused, uncertain. She began feeling along the wall, stepping in our direction, eyes traveling. Pressing my magic away as she did.

"Clem," Loki whispered, and as soon as I lowered my eyes to him, I knew he felt it, too. The urgency.

I also knew what he meant to do. He sensed the trouble we were in, and he was creeping under one of the councilor's chairs.

I shook my head at him. *Not like this*, I mouthed. But Loki had already turned away from me, and bursting from my enshroudment in a flash of black, he darted between the legs of a councilor and out into the center of the meeting room with a feral yowl, all his fur up, tail low.

Everyone's attention strayed to him, councilors standing.

"Now who let a bloody cat in?" one of the councilors asked.

"Corner it," another said, and soon feet were shuffling, the whole council moving to capture the darting cat. For the most powerful mages in Edinburgh, they were slow, ungainly, their hands closing over Loki's shadow as he slipped beyond them.

Even Rathmore's bodyguard had turned, focused completely on the cat.

This was our chance. Our best chance. Nobody was paying attention to the doors.

I grabbed Liara's arm and grabbed the doorknob. I pulled it open, and in the same moment Liara slid through ahead of me and into the hallway.

That was when Rathmore's voice cut through the mess of councilors like hot metal. "It's the witch's cat," he bellowed. "It's her familiar, which means the witch is here. Forget the cat—it's a distraction."

A wild white heat surged through me, adrenaline and fear, and with my enshroudment still wavering but intact, I glanced back for Loki, hoping he'd heard the door open.

He appeared from the throng with fishlike ease, slipping between legs and under the table and threading his way through the chairs to dash past my feet and through the doorway.

I didn't wait. The moment he was out, so was I, allowing the door to fall shut behind me and finding a waiting Liara standing apart from the group of confused assistants, who were all staring at the door that had opened to reveal the room full of yelling councilors.

But no one had come out except a cat.

Thank god Ora Frostwish had disappeared to somewhere else in the building, or else she would have spied Loki right away.

Rathmore knows, I said into Liara's head as Loki and I took off at a run down the hallway, back the way we'd come. *He knows I'm here. Let's get the hell out of here.*

Liara didn't answer; she just started running. Just as we hit the hall-way's junction and turned the corner, a strange, low sound echoed through the building, like a muted buzzing, followed by a wave of heaviness in the air.

And just like that, my enshroudment disappeared.

This was what Umbra had warned us about: the anti-magic security measures.

Liara grabbed my arm, stopping me from passing down the hallway of portraits. "We can't go back the way we came. The building's locked down, which means Delarosa's office door will be locked."

Footsteps sounded from behind us—lots of them—so with one exchanged glance, she and I did the only thing we could do: we followed the only other hallway available to us.

We passed doors and more portraits, and at the end was a great stained-glass window with a series of busts beneath it, and the closer we got to it, the more a single word repeated in my mind: *No, no, no, no.*

Because, from what I remembered of the building's map, this seemed a lot like one of those dead-end hallways. And when we arrived at the busts, Loki and Liara and I stopped hard.

This *was* the dead goddamn end of it.

CHAPTER TWENTY-FIVE

Liara turned in a circle, kicked at one of the bust pedestals with her boot. "We're trapped," she whisper-hissed as the bust rocked in the wake of her sole before settling.

"We're fine." I stepped back to the wall and the ornate window, eyes darting. "Get behind one of these pedestals. They won't see us."

Liara stared at me like I wasn't in my right mind, but she said nothing as she dropped down behind a pedestal.

I lowered behind one on the opposite side of the hallway with Loki beside me, and as three security guards with nightsticks at their hips strode by with nothing but a glance in down the length of our hallway, I began to think it might carry us through.

As long as I didn't see Rathmore's bodyguard again.

More footsteps neared. They were running. But if we crouched very still...

A fresh crop of people rushed by, including a few of the councilors. When I peeked out, spotted Rathmore's head and his long-legged stride, every part of me went still, and even Loki pressed soft and warm against my leg.

But Rathmore, too, passed on. Followed by his bodyguard, her purple veil appearing for a heady second and then disappearing—

And then reappearing.

She had backtracked, stopping at the dead center of the hallway and staring down the length of it toward where we stood. She went stock still as though she was waiting for something. Or listening.

What the hell is she doing? Liara mouthed over at me.

I shook my head. She hadn't noticed us—she was just looking for clues.

Rathmore's bodyguard started toward us, her bootsteps nearing. Her pace wasn't quick, but it was confident, as though she was following an invisible trail.

If she comes one step closer... Liara mouthed.

The bodyguard came to a halt a second later, just as Liara's finger rose to point at her. And then I heard the bodyguard.

She knew.

Somehow, she knew.

We had to get out of here.

I pointed toward the window, then nodded back at the bodyguard. I hoped Liara would get the message.

And she did.

Liara rose and started forward. "You need to go back the way you came."

The bodyguard didn't answer. She moved with snakelike grace, her hand slid over the grip of the weapon at her hip. For the first time I noticed she sported one of those nightsticks, but this one was different than what the formalist officers wore. This one was longer, thinner, with silver etchings down the side.

I didn't see the outcome; I turned toward the window, reaching up and pulling myself onto the sill. But as soon as I thrust my shoulder against it, I knew my body weight wasn't gonna do the trick. The glass didn't even tremor.

Behind me, something shattered.

"We've got a problem," Liara called back.

When I glanced over my shoulder, one of the busts was broken on the floor by the bodyguard, clearly thrown by Liara and easily dodged. The two of them fell into a vicious hand-and-foot combat, throwing punches, kicks, each of them blocking the other. Except Liara had no weapon, and the bodyguard had her nightstick in one hand.

That thing could easily shatter Liara's bones.

I dropped off the sill. Before me stood a bust of an old, smiling man, his eyes crinkling with a life well-lived. So he probably wouldn't mind what I was about to do. Maybe he'd even laugh from wherever he was.

If there was a Hell, there had to be a Heaven, right?

I grabbed both sides of his marble face, hauling him up off the pedestal. "Loki," I said, "when you hear the glass, climb up my cloak and hold on tight."

Then I threw the bust right through the center of the stained-glass window. The thing was so interconnected that the bust didn't just create a single hole; half of it shattered away all at once.

I climbed onto the pedestal, feeling the weight of Loki leaping onto my cloak and clawing his way up. My boot went out, and I kicked out the remaining glass, which clattered in beautiful shards on the street below.

It would be a long drop—ten, twelve feet—but it wouldn't kill me. I hoped I'd get a little fae help.

"Liara," I said over my shoulder, "time to go."

I stepped onto the ledge, and in the moment I angled forward, Liara yelled out, her voice echoing through the hall. "Stop," she called. "I can't make it to you."

Even if I'd wanted to, I couldn't stop now. I was already falling toward the alley, my teeth gritted for impact. For a moment I was in freefall, the ground rising toward me, and I turned my face aside so my nose and teeth wouldn't take the worst part of the impact.

But that didn't happen. Hands grabbed my arms, pulling up, slowing my fall.

When I hit the ground, it was jarring; I dropped to one knee amidst the glass and nearly had to roll onto the shoulder Loki wasn't on, but it wasn't a bone-snapping impact.

Liara landed over me, huffing. "I told you I couldn't make it to you in time."

"So you thought." I took a second to reorient myself as Loki hopped to the street. "Wish you flew that fast all the time."

She rolled her eyes, extended a hand. "Let's go."

When I took it, I couldn't help but glance up at the shattered window. For some reason I'd expected to see Rathmore's bodyguard staring down at us, but there was no one.

We escaped the city in my enshroudment, keeping to little-used alleys until we climbed up Arthur's Seat. We didn't speak until we passed through the veil to the leyline outside the academy, and then, finally, we allowed our shoulders to slump.

The walk back was slow. We didn't rush. We'd gotten everything Umbra wanted and more.

The culmination. The hunt for Maeve Umbra. Falaichte—whatever that was.

As we passed through Umbra's enchantment and onto the academy grounds, where it was still midday, I felt Liara's attention on me. When my eyes focused on her, she pointed at my hand. "You're bleeding."

I lifted my arm, found a cut on my palm I hadn't even remembered receiving. "From the glass." Now that she'd pointed it out, it began to sting.

She shook her head. "That was the stupidest thing you've ever done."

"You've only known her a couple years," Loki said as he trotted between us. "You missed the bulk of her adolescent idiocy."

Liara's eyes flicked between Loki and me. "Was your cat just meowing, or...?"

"Yep," I said at once. "Just meowing, like cats do. Anyway, if you're referring to the window-shattering maneuver, it seemed to work out all right for us."

"I'm not," she shot back. "I'm referring to *jumping through* the window."

"Oh, that?" I shrugged. "You caught me before I died."

"But I might not have."

"But you did." I raised my bloody hand in goodbye as we reached the center of the grounds. "Can you debrief Umbra? I have somewhere to be."

She stopped, dismay on her face. "'Somewhere' better not be the dining hall."

"We've all gotta eat, Youngblood."

I knew that would piss her off. I also didn't have time to care.

When I turned away, Loki followed close by my feet. He knew where I was headed; it was the obvious choice after everything we'd heard and seen in that room. "What did she smell like?" I said down to him.

Loki paused, as though he was recollecting the scent. He knew I was referring to the bodyguard. "It's hard to recall. I didn't get a great whiff of her."

"Was it a regular human smell, or did she have magic?"

"She definitely had magic."

I knew it. Only magic could repulse my enshroudment like she'd done in the council room. "So she's a mage. An anti-magic mage."

"But she carried a nightstick," he said. "Like the rest of them."

That was a mystery.

We had arrived at the library. When we passed through the circulation room, I nodded at Milonakis, who nodded back at me. We'd developed a certain unspoken way with each other after the ghost incident. We got along. Well, as long as I wasn't breaking her strict code of rules.

She cleared her throat, and I stopped. Milonakis pointed at my hand. "You're bloody."

I nodded. "I won't drip on your floor."

She reached into the desk, pulled out a first-aid kit like a properly empathetic human, which made me suspicious. "Have you just returned from Edinburgh?" she asked.

I nodded again, approaching the desk as she opened up the kit, pulled out an antibiotic ointment and a Band-Aid. I had never encountered this Milonakis. "I shattered a window. An old, stained-glass one. Probably worth more to the city than capturing the fire witch."

Milonakis's eyes widened, then she extended her open palm for me to place my hand in. As she dabbed at the cut, she said, "So you made it inside the council room. You and Ms. Youngblood."

"We did."

Loki hopped up on the circulation desk, overseeing the treatment. "I was crucial, but she'll never tell you that."

I jerked my free thumb at Loki. "It's very important to my familiar that you know he helped."

Milonakis studied him above her spectacles, as if deciding whether or not to kick him off her desk. In the end, she went back to treating the cut. "You did more than I ever managed." She dabbed on the ointment, and I kept my eyes on her, wondering. She probably knew the name of every book in this library, and the contents of at least half of them.

How had I never thought to come to her?

"Professor," I said. "Have you ever heard of Falaichte?"

Her eyebrows rose, and she went still. Then her eyes lifted to me. "Yes. Why?"

"In the meeting, the councilors spoke of transferring prisoners to Falaichte."

Her face lightened, a half-smile appearing. "Now you've gone too far."

"Too far?"

"You're pulling my old, atrophied leg."

"Professor," I said, "any other time you'd be right. But not this time."

She went stiff, the smile vanishing like smoke. Her eyebrows drew together, and she placed the Band-Aid on my hand so harshly I thought she might reopen the cut. "You've taken this little ribbing too far, Ms. Cole." Before I could ask her anything else, she pushed out her chair and walked from the circulation room into the library proper. As the door began to swing closed behind her, she popped her head back through. "Wait there."

"Okay," I said, hands raising as though I'd been apprehended. "We're waiting."

She was gone five minutes. When she returned, it was with a book that could only have been from the Room of the Ancients. And I wasn't about to tell her she was breaking her own rules; not today.

She thudded it on the desk beside me, close enough that we were touching, and began flipping old, yellowed pages before I could even read the title. When she got to what she was looking for, her hand went to my shoulder, urging me in front of the book.

"Look," she said. "Read here."

I stared down at it. "It's not in English."

"Oh, for gods' sake." She pressed me aside, her finger traveling beneath a line of words as she summarized. "Falaichte Prison is part of an old Scottish folktale, which you've no doubt encountered to have recited the name to me. It isn't real."

"And why not?" I said.

Milonakis removed her spectacles, stabbed the page with one perilously pointed finger. "Because, Clementine Cole, the prison has no entrance and no exit."

CHAPTER TWENTY-SIX

The next day, it snowed. And in the evening, Eva and I sat on the edge of the meadow with a fire I'd lit in my palm hovering between us, watching a battle between the first-years and, well, everyone else. Even a few professors.

None of them knew what we knew about the Shade. And it was a strange comfort, to hear them laughing and screaming.

Eva rocked on the log beneath us. "Clem, that was us last year. In Novi Sad, remember?" I knew what she was doing: trying to bring me a little peace of mind, to rope me into the present with winter happiness and joy and make me stop fixating on the prison with no entrances or exits.

"Yeah," I said, "except we were drunk. These people don't have an excuse."

"Anyway, Milonakis is right," she said. "Falaichte isn't real."

"So was magic"—I twirled flame around my fingertip—"until I discovered it was."

"All right," she said, "so where is it, then?"

"That's the question, isn't it?" I closed my fist around the flame, extinguishing it. "It's out there. I just need to find out where."

She eyed me. "You're awfully stoic for someone who just found out the Shade is arriving within the year."

I kept my face on the battle, the flying snow, people's faces lit by the moon. It was hard to explain why I had gotten used to the idea so quickly. It didn't feel like as much of a surprise as it had to Liara, or to Eva, or to Aidan.

Maybe because I'd been watching all along. Or maybe because, for a decade now, I'd expected the worst from the world. This wasn't the other shoe dropping—it was a steel-toed boot hitting the ground, and it finally felt like I could exhale.

The worst was confirmed. And now I knew exactly how long I had to kick that witch's ass.

One year. I had one year—if that.

I turned to my best friend. "That's because she's not arriving, Eva. I'm going to stop her before she does."

Her head tilted. "And what did Umbra have to say about it?"

"According to Liara, Umbra's face took on a 'grave, serious look when she found out, and she started drinking her tea faster.'"

"Is that all?"

"You have to understand," Eva said. "When have you ever seen Umbra *not* savor her tea?"

"Point taken."

Eva nodded, not even smiling. Which finally brought home what I'd suspected: this was a faster timeline than Umbra had expected.

"Eva," I said, my eyes still on the flung snowballs, "I think things are going to move faster now."

She clasped her mittened hands in her lap. "Yeah, Clem. I think they are." Her face lifted toward the sky. "Come on. If we're late to meet this mystery person, Umbra will turn us into newts."

We stood, began walking toward the guardians' tree, where I knew Loki had been sleeping in front of the fire for hours. "Can she do that?" I asked.

Eva smiled over at me. "Why do you think there are so very many newts in the world?"

I knew she was joking, but I did walk faster. "Nobody's change-you-into-a-newt-for-lateness important."

Eva let out a chuff but said nothing more.

And when we arrived at the meeting room with the other guardians, I understood why: standing with her back to the circular table where we all sat was none other than her mother, Nissa Whitewillow. She and Umbra were in close discussion as we gathered at the table.

As we sat, I shot Eva a glance—had she known her mother was coming?—but she only had eyes for Nissa.

When we'd all gathered and Loki hopped on the table, Umbra gestured for Nissa to turn. She did so with a sway of gauzy wings, eyes surveying the assembled guardians. She smiled at Eva and Loki and me for a moment before her attention moved past us.

"Academy guardians," Umbra said, stepping up with one hand on Nissa's shoulder, "allow me to introduce your visitor, who went to great trouble to visit the academy today. Your work in Edinburgh has attracted the attention of Europe's Guardians' Council, and they've sent Nissa Whitewillow, one of their most trusted and esteemed agents, to meet with you."

It was my second time hearing of a Guardians' Council. The first time had been from Eva, but it hadn't quite seemed real. Not until now.

Nissa unclasped her hands from behind her back. "I was told you all rescued six fae from their prison, but I didn't fully believe it until I met one of them in Maeve's office earlier today. But then, even more surprising, you were able to infiltrate a Mages' Council meeting and gather information that has allowed the Guardians' Council to make strategic decisions about their stance on the formalists." She paused. "You all have done immense work. Important work."

She let out a breath through her nose, eyes lowering. "The world's guardians now believe that Tristan Rathmore does not work in the interest of the city he lords over, nor does he intend to stop the Shade. Quite the opposite—he somehow plans to free her from her imprisonment. And so it is our position that we must intervene."

"Intervene how?" Liara asked.

Nissa nodded at Liara. "We will focus our efforts on stopping, slowing, and otherwise ending the Mages' Council's stranglehold on Edinburgh. We intend to prevent a second Battle of the Ages by whatever means possible. And to accomplish that, my husband and I would like to coordinate with the guardians at Shadow's End Academy."

My eyebrows rose, and Liara and I looked at one another. That had sounded like an offer—like we had a choice in the matter.

"Students," Umbra said, "this is an honor, but it also brings a measure of risk unlike any I've asked of the academy's guardians in decades past. The work you would do with guardians like the Whitewillow could result in your capture, imprisonment, or worse, but it may also save us from the Shade's reign. And nothing, I can assure you, would be worse than her as empress of this world. I leave the choice to you."

Silence followed as a question rose in my mind, then slipped out my mouth.

"How will this be any more dangerous than what we've already done?" I asked. "You know we've broken into a prison and into a Mages' Council meeting. I'm sure Umbra told you about Liara and me jumping out a third-story window."

Nissa's eyes fixed on me, and they held the same warmth I'd seen when I'd first met her in Vienna years ago. "Yes, she did, and I'm stunned and grateful for the sacrifices you made. All of you. What the Guardians' Council intends to do will pose the greatest risk we've taken on in a very, very long time." She drew in a breath. "We plan to capture Tristan Rathmore."

Capture him? Capture Lucian the prince, the half-demon.

I sat back, seeing him again on the train platform. The man had felt like a statue—immovable, terrible, all-powerful.

It had never occurred to me that he could be captured.

As my eyes flicked up to Eva, I was struck by a sudden and intense realization: this was Nissa, her mother. She was asking this of her own daughter, which could only mean one thing. The shadow the Shade would cast over the world must be that much greater than asking Eva to sneak into Edinburgh to coordinate the capture of a half-demon.

This mission was the lesser danger.

A band tightened around my chest, but only a moment had elapsed before Nissa Whitewillow's hands went up, palms out to us. "Decisions like this are never to be made lightly. We'll give you a week to decide—Maeve knows how to reach us."

When I stood from the table and turned, Nissa had already stepped onto the balcony and dropped off the side, her wings expanding.

I came to the head of the staircase, hands on the bannister, and stared down after her as she glided down to the hearth room.

"Clem?" Liara called from the table. Eva was watching me, too, with a certain look in her eye. Like she had known this was what her mother would propose.

"I'll be back in a bit," I said, and started down the staircase, following Nissa Whitewillow. I needed to talk to her about Tristan Rathmore.

I circled three times, came to the bottom as she passed through the doorway out into the sunlight with her cloak pulled off the hook by the door. I grabbed mine, too. "Nissa," I called after her.

She stopped, pulling her cloak on, and smiled at me. "Clementine."

"First"—I came to a halt in front of her, gesturing with a thumb over my shoulder—"how did you get into the guardians' tree?"

Her head tilted a degree. "Once an academy guardian, always an academy guardian."

Oh. Right.

"Walk me to the headmistress's office?" she said. "I have a long trip ahead of me, and I'd much rather delay it for a little while with the sight of your face."

I fell into step alongside her, the two of us crunching through the snow. "Where are you headed after this?"

When she glanced over at me, she said it all with her eyes: it was a secret, and she was sorry. She shrugged. "I'll be with my husband, at least."

"Florian."

"That's right." She paused, pointed at my boots. "How are those serving you in the new school year?"

It had been so long since anyone had treated me this way: like a mother would her child, concerned over little things. I smiled. "They're great boots. Thank you for them."

She raised her hand, set it on my shoulder. "It's the least I could do, Clementine. You're my daughter's favorite person here."

"Am I?"

"Of course. When we talk, she always tells me what you're up to. You inspire her."

I eyed Nissa, wondering how much Eva was actually telling her about what I was up to. If she knew about the prophecy and what had happened to Eva on the Siberian tundra, she might feel differently.

And then I realized I was just deflecting from the compliment she had given me. I said, "She inspires me, too. She's a good person, you know, your daughter."

Better than me.

"She is. She always has been good." We walked a little farther, passing between trees, and Nissa said, "You followed me out here with a purpose in your step. Tell me, Clementine."

I stopped. "Tristan Rathmore."

She drew in cold air, her eyes finding the canopy before she stopped and turned to me. "Yes."

"He's Lucian the prince. He's the Shade's lieutenant."

She nodded. "Yes."

I spread my hands. "Why doesn't the Guardians' Council go after him? Why us?"

A pained softness crossed Nissa's face, and she brought a hand out of her cloak, ran it over my curls. "That's a very good question, and one you deserve an answer to. All of you." She hesitated. "I'm afraid all I can tell you is that it must be us. It must be us, or it will be no one."

I didn't understand. How could I? She wouldn't tell me the answer. But as we stood apart from one another and I studied the rise in her eyebrows at the center, those two lines of anxiety forming between them, I thought I might have some idea.

"Are you desperate?" I whispered.

Her eyes closed, and she seemed to wince. "The Guardians' Council is not what it once was" was all she said.

"Aren't you worried about her being involved in this?" I asked. "Eva?"

"Of course. But what can I say to stop her, Clementine? She's grown. She makes her choices."

Fair enough. I doubted there was anything I could say to stop Eva, either.

"And do you believe we can capture him? Rathmore?" I said.

Her head shook, eyes opening. "I believe capturing him is our best hope of interceding. I believe with you and the others, we have a chance."

It wasn't clear to me whether she did believe. I saw uncertainty in her face—and, too, a grim resolve.

So that's where she stood: she and the Guardians' Council needed this maybe more than we were capable of pulling it off. Which meant Nissa Whitewillow was desperate.

When I returned to the guardians' circular table a half hour later, no one had moved. The others were in low conversation while Loki sat atop the table grooming his head, one paw swiping over his ear over and over.

As I sat back down, silence slowly fell. After thirty seconds, I realized the others were waiting on Liara and me—the leaders. This was our job, our role. So I straightened. "Nice to be offered an easy job for once."

Elijah barked a laugh, crossing his arms over his chest and leaning back. Isaiah took on the same posture, though I doubted they realized they were mirroring each other. "And here we thought being guardians would land us girls," Elijah said.

Loki paused in his grooming. "So nineties."

"'Girls?'" Beside Elijah, Mishka swirled a finger in the air and a small plate of baklava appeared before her. She lifted one piece, took an aggressive bite as she stared icicles at him. "Do tell me more about 'girls.'"

"He meant women." Isaiah patted him on the back. "Strong, capable women."

Maise rolled her eyes.

"What is this, a guardians' meeting or a lecture on feminism?" Keene said.

Groans resounded, even from Loki.

"What?" Keene said, totally baffled. "It was a legitimate question."

I just stared at the ceiling. Now I knew why the Guardians' Council hadn't called on us before: we were a bunch of college kids. And the last thing I'd ever expected was to be more mature than somebody else in the room. "Any other thoughts about the *mission?*" I finally asked.

"Why is Tristan Rathmore helping the Shade?" Akelan asked. "Why would he even want a second Battle of the Ages? It makes no sense."

I set my hands on the table. They didn't know. Only Umbra, Aidan, and Eva had learned what I was about to reveal. This would be rough on them, but they needed the truth to make a real decision.

"So," I said, "there's probably something you all ought to know about Tristan Rathmore."

All eyes shifted to me—except for Loki's, who went on grooming. He, of course, took everything the way a cat would: silently, like an unconcerned little sociopath.

"Tristan Rathmore," I said, "is also Lucian the prince."

My eyes shifted to the others, waiting for them to be shocked, outraged, to fall from their chairs. Instead, I only got narrowed eyes and furrowed brows. Only one person reacted the way I'd expected: Liara. The look in her eyes when I said that name—Lucian the prince —was murderous.

"Who's Lucian the prince?" Keene finally asked.

"Ugh, idiots," Liara said. "Didn't any of you pay attention in primary school?"

"Sometimes," Isaiah offered.

"Lucian the prince is the Shade's lieutenant," she said, her voice still laced with disgust. "He's a demon and immortal like her. Wildly powerful and strong."

Something in the way she described him struck me as firsthand knowledge. Had she encountered Lucian the prince before the Mages' Council meeting?

"Ho-ly shit," Isaiah said.

"He's a half-demon," I said. "And he's not immortal. It's a lineage from father to son."

Liara turned to me. "For five hundred years?"

I nodded.

"That's a lot of Y chromosomes," Maise breathed.

Liara sat back, arms folding. "And Callum? He's to become the new prince?"

"He gave up his namesake," Mishka said. "Don't you read *Witches & Wizards?*"

Maise shook her head. "I can't believe my professor was a half-demon. And that half-demons are hot."

"How do you think the Rathmores managed five hundred years of continuing their line?" Elijah asked, and Isaiah jabbed him with an elbow.

Mishka glared at the twin so long, even I shivered.

"So," I said, "that's what Nissa is asking of us. She wants us to capture the Shade's lieutenant."

Keene ran a hand over his hair. "I can't even decide what I want for breakfast in the mornings."

Maise groaned. "How did you become a guardian?"

"Sometimes I wonder," Keene whispered. "Sometimes I really wonder."

"We don't all have to volunteer," Liara said. "Those of us who want to go can go. The rest of us can stay here and pretend like the world isn't about to ignite."

"Way to lay on the pressure," I whispered to her.

She shrugged. "Don't pretend like you'd expect anything less from me."

Of course, she was right. The world was about to catch fire, and the glances I'd exchanged with Eva and Liara the moment Nissa had left had told me all I needed to know: the three of us were in. We were unequivocally in.

But now that the others had learned Tristan Rathmore wasn't

totally human, that he was in fact the servant of a woman bound to Hell, they took their time. And I couldn't blame them; it had taken me months to come to terms with the prophecy that had been laid at my feet.

They had far less time.

"Well," I began, planning to offer people a chance to stand, to stretch, to stare at the sky, but I was interrupted.

Loki had paused in his grooming, lowered his paw. "Well, I know what I want."

"You do?" I stared at him. "Does it involve dairy?"

His eyes shifted around to me. "I want to capture the asshole. And yes, I also want some milk. Now."

With a snap of my fingers, I conjured a shallow bowl of warm milk —something I'd learned from Eva this year. As he began lapping, I gestured to him. "So my familiar is apparently the most decisive one here. He wants to take Rathmore down."

"Damn," Akelan said. "The Bengal's putting us all to shame."

I patted Loki. "It's what he does best."

After a cat had been the first to accept the mission, we didn't need to take a break for people to deliberate. They all fell into agreement in ones and twos, and within a half hour, we had our answer for Nissa and the Guardians' Council.

We were going to capture a half-demon.

CHAPTER TWENTY-SEVEN

After we told Umbra of our intentions, she'd relayed them to the Guardians' Council, who in turn relayed to her that preparations were being put into place, and the mission should happen in the spring.

"But that's months," I said to Umbra in her office on the first day of winter break. "It'll be an entirely different season."

Across her desk, Umbra lowered her reading glasses to meet eyes. "Tell me, Clementine: have you ever captured a demon?"

Not unless you count Callum Rathmore... a cheeky little voice said.

But what came out was, "It can't possibly take months to prepare."

She sighed, removed her glasses entirely. Two fingers touched the bridge of her nose. "Shall I relay that to the Guardians' Council for you? I've no doubt they'd take your message to heart."

"Fine." I dropped into the chair across from her. "Tell me what I can do in the meantime."

"You can be a student." She tapped the open book before her. "Reading. Studying. Growing in your knowledge and subsequent power."

"And Edinburgh? Our missions?"

"You seek the thief's blade. That's your true desire, isn't it?"

No point in lying. "It's one of them."

"And Mr. Rathmore told you it was hidden in one of the closes, you said?"

I nodded. "It would save me a lot of time scouring an ancient Scottish city if you had any idea which of them I should focus on."

Her hands spread. "I want to help you, Clementine. I do. But I'm afraid I've never heard of this blade being buried in a close. Have you tried, oh, what do they call it? The one they send all the tourists through..."

"Mary King's Close?" I said, deadpan.

She pointed a finger. "That's the one."

"No," I said dully. "I haven't tried it. Headmistress, have you heard of any other closes in the city?"

Her eyes flicked away, searching her memory. "A few, but I have no leads for you." Then they returned to me. "Clementine, if this prophecy is true and the weapon you carry will bring about the Shade's end, then you *will* find it. A real prophecy cannot help but come true."

I hadn't ever thought of it that way. As though I had no free will. My arms crossed. "Maybe I'll just sit here in this chair. Will the blade magically come to me?"

She rubbed at her fingers, smoothing wrinkles. "You're not one who could sit in a chair for more than ten minutes without being chained to it."

I stood, hating that she was right—about prophecies and me in chairs.

"If you must venture into the closes during your upcoming missions," she said, "then that is what you must do. Don't compromise the guardians' missions or risk your capture. I trust in the power of your enshroudment." She paused. "I have only one request."

"What is it?"

"Promise me you will not ever enter the vaults."

The vaults. Aidan had mentioned them, and Milonakis had warned me about them. "You mean the ones under the South Bridge?"

"Yes. You saw the effects of them on Nance Milonakis on the night you entered a place you shouldn't have."

"The milky eyes? The insanity?"

Her lips folded. "Temporary on both counts, but yes. I could not see one of my own students suffer such things."

"Aidan said it was ghost-madness. Was it ghosts?"

"If you never enter, you'll never need to know." She gestured for me to stand. "Excuse me, but I have a meeting."

Umbra had always made a point of never forbidding me to do anything, and now here she was specifically asking me not to enter the vaults. Which made me wonder: Was she testing me again?

I didn't move. "And the guardians' missions?"

"Will go on when classes resume," Umbra said, returning her glasses to her face. "Be patient in the interim, child, and do your best to live your life as it exists before your nose."

As I came out of Umbra's office and stepped into the winter morning, I wondered if she'd lived so long she had lost any sense of urgency she should properly feel. If the Shade returned, it would mean a second Battle of the Ages. It would mean—

"Cole!" An arm fell over my shoulders, pulling me close to a large fae body. Elijah or Isaiah—I couldn't tell which. "Quit scowling and come with me. Isaiah and I have a bet going on."

"And that's got something to do with me?" I asked as he began walking me bodily down the path toward the meadow.

"Absolutely it does. You're a fire witch."

"Does this bet involve a stake and burning a particular someone alive?"

He snorted. "Always so cynical."

"And I'm not just a tiny bit justified? You know, being the last witch and all."

He flicked a hand like he was swatting a bug. "Listen, you have to win. I've got good money on this."

"I don't even know what I—" I stopped as we came into the meadow to laughter, cheers, practically half the student body standing alongside and clapping as three students raced through the knee-deep snow, decimating it as they went along.

One was a fire mage, flame shooting out of both hands ahead of him as he ran. The second was a fae who blew the snow aside with a wall of wind rushing ahead of her. The third was an earth mage who simply tore the earth up in his path, shaking the snow off.

Or, at least, that's what they would have been doing if they weren't absolute shit. Mostly they stumbled, fell, climbed back up and shot out magic in bursts.

"That's the first-years," Elijah or Isaiah said, laughter breaking into his words. "They really suck, huh?"

"What the hell are they trying to do?"

"Race," he said. "They're trying to race, Clementine."

I rolled my eyes, turned my face up to Elijah. "If you're about to ask me to take part in this..."

"Too late." He nodded toward a group of fourth-years near the end of the crowd. "I already signed you up. That's your competition."

I punched him in the arm, which he didn't seem to notice. "Why didn't you sign yourself up?"

He shrugged, walking me toward the group. "Because, Clementine, nobody would bet money on me."

"Come on. You're a fifth-year guardian."

"And everybody would bet on you," he went on as though I hadn't spoken. "Because you're not just a witch. You're a fire witch. You're the last one of all. That makes you spooky *and* badass."

I stopped, and he turned to face me, his back to the crowd. "Is this because I've stopped eating my meals in the dining hall?"

"It absolutely is," he said. "And because you wear that scowl like it's your favorite shirt. And because all I ever see you doing is sitting hunched over a book in the library or practicing with Umbra or staring into space like you're trying to solve differential math."

I paused. Then, "I scowl all the time?"

His head tilted. "We have a secret nickname for you. Grimace."

"Oh god," I said. "You and your twin?"

"And all of House Whisper."

"Oh," I said. "God. It's so dumb yet effective."

"Yeah."

I nodded, began removing my winter gloves one finger at a time. "All right. Step aside, I have a reputation to uphold."

After the race through the meadow, in which I proved to the academy exactly why witches had been systematically killed throughout history —pure, green-eyed jealousy on everyone else's part—I began, slowly and then all at once, to unwind.

The twins were right. Umbra was right. Damn, were they right.

For the next month, I put aside the books, the obsessive training, the late nights spent staring at the ceiling in bed. I allowed myself to be. To wake up late, wander to the dining hall for cereal, to accept Red the fae's not-so-subtle offer to try "the good stuff" in the woods one afternoon.

"Man," I said, gazing through lidded eyes into the canopy and passing him the blunt, "so that's why they call it the Contemplator's Copse."

He burst into laughter, then coughing. And then I did, too.

Sometimes I tried and failed not to think about the blade, the Rathmores, the Shade. Sometimes I succeeded. It was strange from this vantage to be so single-minded; my whole life from the age of thirteen onward had been a top spinning haphazardly, always threatening to fall off its point. I had never been motivated in school or anything, really.

But since arriving at Shadow's End, I could see my life and purpose through a space the size of a pinhole. It was that simple and that complex.

"Wow," Red said, passing me the joint, "that's one epic analogy, Cole. Why was I so scared of you our first year?"

"You were scared of me?" I glanced over as I took a draw. "But you shared your book with me in Milonakis's class."

"Yeah, *because* I was scared of you."

"Oh." I nodded slowly, eyes returning to the canopy. "Are you still scared of me?"

"Nah. Not when you're like this."

"Aren't I always like this?"

"Nah," he said, and wouldn't say more on the subject. And because

I was so lazy and high, I didn't push it. But the conversation didn't leave my brain, either.

And what had been a week of absolute relaxation shifted into something else. I hated my brain.

"Eva," I said over my bowl of fruity loops in the dining hall the next day, "am I scary?"

She squinted at me. "A little bit, when you stare at me with those bloodshot eyes."

I made a face. "I'm gazing lovingly. When we're on missions, am I scary?"

"Clem..."

"You cannot offend me." I took a bite of cereal and said around it, "But you can betray our immortal friendship bond if you don't tell me the truth."

"Sometimes, maybe."

"Like when?"

"Like when you nearly hurt Maise in Acapulco."

"Oh." My eyes lowered to the safe, non-threatening fruity loops floating in their milk. "Any other times?"

"On that lake in Siberia," she said, her voice lowering. "When you burst into flames."

My eyebrows rose as my gaze flicked up to her. "Anything else?"

She stopped cutting her omelet. "Why are you asking me this?"

I dragged the spoon along the bottom of the bowl to hear its off-key noise. "I scared myself when I nearly hurt Aidan a few summers ago." I paused. "And there were times before the academy. Back when I was in the group home."

Eva tilted her head to meet my eyes. "Your mom and sister disappeared, Clem. You were orphaned. You've been hurt."

But she still thinks I'm scary.

The doors to the dining hall flew open in a burst of flurries, and Torsten and a few other earth mages strutted in, yelling about their New Year's Eve party. And Eva and I both turned that way, forgot about our conversation. As I did, I pushed back down all the things I was thinking about the Spitfire, about how I scared myself, about who or what I was.

I pushed it down. I laughed with Eva and pushed it all down.

If it wasn't the Shade, the Backbiter, the Rathmores, then it would be Torsten's party. If it wasn't Torsten's party—which I stumbled out of at four in the morning on the first day of the new year—then it was the blackout that would follow. It was the hangover of the next morning, which I nursed all throughout the day.

And it was near the end of winter break, when reality would return, I realized the top had never stopped spinning. *I* had never stopped. I had always been the spinning top at the academy, too, weaving uncertainly, making large circles, fixating on whatever could distract me from myself.

"I'm the top," I said to Eva in our dorm the night before classes would start again.

She didn't look up from her stitching. She had worked on tangibly manipulating her whatever-it-was every day this winter break, and it had the appearance now of a large olive-green blanket. "Are you high again?"

"No. Maybe." I squinted, trying to recall when I'd last seen Red. "No."

Her needle and thread kept moving. "So what does that mean, 'you're the top?'"

I twirled my finger in the air. "My whole life, I'm the thing that does this." Twirl-twirl. "And do you know what spun tops eventually do?"

She paused in her stitching, sighed as she met my eyes. "You're not the top."

"Eva, when you deny my reality, I don't feel validated."

She glared at the psychology book on my desk, then at me. "And how do you know your reality is real when you're reading psych books while high?"

I set a hand to my chest. "I'm just trying to understand the inner workings of my mind, okay?" Then cringed a little; my voice sounded like fourteen-year-old Clem.

"Maybe you should focus on the inner workings of someone else's mind for a change." The needle glinted as she resumed. When I stood, looking more affronted than I felt, and put on my boots and cloak, she said, "Clem."

"What?" I said as I made for the door.

"You're not the top."

I closed the door and stepped into the cold night, staring across the clearing. Down below, someone was leaving the library.

But the library was closed.

And then, with glee, my mind shifted over to the next distraction. Away from the top, away from myself and who or what I was.

I came down the steps, intercepted him before he could escape with his secrets. And when I lit a flame in my hand, I said, "Aidan?" Then my eyes lowered to the stack of books under his arm.

He sighed, stopped. "Hey."

My head tilted. "How'd you get into the library?"

"Saoirse."

"Huh. Boyfriend perks." I stepped closer, examining the books. "Those look old."

He shifted them away from the light. "That's because they are."

I moved unashamedly closer. "Really old. Like Room-of-the-Ancients old."

"Gods, you are the worst." He pushed past me, heading toward his dorm. "I'm doing this for you, you know," he whisper-hissed back at me as he disappeared into the darkness muttering about ingratitude.

I watched him go. Maybe Eva was right: if I'd been focusing on the inner workings of someone else's mind, I might have figured out what my two friends had been up to since the school year began.

As it was, I still had no idea.

CHAPTER TWENTY-EIGHT

After winter break, the guardians began running more missions. Lots of them. And I sank back into them like a hot tub on a freezing day. Forget the top, the angst, the two nights I'd locked myself away in our dorm's bathroom while my chest got tight and I couldn't get enough air and saw stars until the panic passed.

Forget all that. The fire witch was back, baby.

At one point I asked Umbra why she was allowing me to go on so many missions, given I was a wanted witch. And she told me, in a moment of rare and vulnerable honesty, that the academy's guardians couldn't succeed without me. She—they—needed me.

I let that be enough.

In the new year, the Guardians' Council began working with us. Umbra fed them what information we'd already gathered, and they often coordinated with us when we went to Edinburgh.

I never actually saw one of them after Nissa came to us that winter morning—everything was done through Umbra—but she would give instructions before our missions. Things like: *Enter through this door, which will be left open*, or, *Arrive to this cafe at three o'clock, where you'll find a council member's coat hanging on the rack*.

Our goal was learning Rathmore's schedule. His plans. When he'd be most vulnerable, and from there, choosing the right moment to capture him.

It didn't matter anymore that Liara and I had been seen in Edinburgh; our work mattered more. She wore a good disguise, and I enshrouded myself every time I entered the city. I was there to do my job, but I was also there for another reason: to gather intelligence about the blade. About where I'd find it.

On our missions, we had the winter to our advantage. Jackets, hoods, people's faces angled down to fend off the wind and cold. As December drew on to Christmas, Umbra began more regularly to siphon us into two teams:

Infiltration, and sabotage.

The fae and I excelled at infiltration. They could find their way to rooftops, stare into windows, keep tabs on people's movement. And though I couldn't fly, I could go unseen like I had to enter the Mages' Council building. And so with their direction, I followed council members and their staff to meetings all over the city.

It was in this way we found out where Rathmore's spymaster was sending his scouts to look for Maeve Umbra. They had entirely the wrong countries: Austria, Poland, even Russia. And it was in this way we discovered that Rathmore frequently returned to his home in Inverness, at least once a month.

And then there was sabotage. The humans—Maise, Akelan, Mishka, Paxton—were good at that. They'd slip into a crowd of tourists and start a street fight on the same road a councilor's car was passing down, forcing them to be late or miss their engagements. They once even managed to send the Mages' Council building into lockdown again, ruining the council's meeting.

The goal was disarray in all the right places. It was inefficiency. It was slowing down the formalists' engine where it counted.

As it turned out, Rathmore was rarely vulnerable. And learning his schedule and plans wasn't nearly as simple as I'd thought. If he didn't have that veiled bodyguard at his side, then it was another—sometimes two or three.

And so we had to be patient. While we were being patient, we had to be careful. The formalists weren't idiots; they knew the Guardians' Council was interfering, and probably the academy, too.

So they increased security. Tightened ranks. Changed up their schedules. And Rathmore began taking more trips to Inverness to get away from the headache. Which was perfect.

Every time Loki and I entered Edinburgh—which must have been at least two dozen occasions by March—we made a little progress in my search for the blade. We entered almost every close on the map Aidan and I had marked off last fall, that hint at top of mind every time: *where power and pleasure cross.* We didn't encounter ghosts. We didn't encounter power. And we definitely didn't encounter pleasure.

Maybe I was just part of a prophecy, destined to find it. That certainly hadn't left my mind since Umbra had said it. *So could I find it just a little bit faster, please?*

The underground closes were creepy, dark, damp. They were tight and sometimes they were completely blocked off, so I had to use a little fire magic to create an entrance both of us could climb through. In three months, I pressed, crawled, and groaned my way into every nook, every room, every alley I could find. More often than not I ended up covered in spiderwebs and dirt and smelling strange, but the weapon never glowed green when I held it out before me. It remained inert, dull.

I began to wonder if maybe I didn't need the blade, if capturing Rathmore was the answer to our Shade problems. I might have been fantasizing, but after so much searching, I could hardly tell the difference.

I just *wanted* to be done. Nabbing Rathmore felt like less of a task than finding the cross between power and pleasure.

So by the time mid-March came and Eva struck gold by crouching on a window ledge outside the window of Rathmore's assistant's flat— the fae was on the phone, talking about his boss being in Inverness for the whole weekend—one thing had become clear:

That weekend in Inverness was our best chance at capturing Tristan Rathmore.

Nissa Whitewillow returned to the academy for the second time on a Friday in late March, and this time she brought her husband, Florian. Eva had never told me as much, but it became clear to me when they told us the Guardians' Council had assigned the two of them as co-leaders that Nissa and Florian Whitewillow were among the highest-ranking guardians in Europe.

At least, they were the most trusted, and as we all congregated in the guardians' meeting room, I quickly realized they were probably the most capable, too.

Together, the academy guardians and the Whitewillows planned out our course of action, the two of them nodding as we explained our specialties—infiltration or sabotage—and what each of us were capable of. My enshroudment, Keene's uncanny abilities with electronics (which was news to me), Liara's lightning, Loki's nose. And within an hour, they had drawn up roles, positioning, timing, contingency plans. Florian had scouted the Inverness home, had drawn up a layout for us on the board. He pointed to Rathmore's bedroom on the second floor. "But this is where he should be."

I was, once again, a chaser. Well, minus Noir. With my enshroudment, I had free rein to keep tabs on everything and everyone, and I needed to stay close to it all. "We'll need you," Nissa said, "to keep us abreast at all times. And to make the call on contingencies."

"But what if she's seen?" Mishka said. "What if she drops the enshroudment?"

"I won't drop the enshroudment," I said.

"Are you certain?" Nissa asked.

There was only one question I had left to answer to complete my enshroudment training with Umbra, and it had nothing to do with Tristan Rathmore. I nodded. "I'm certain."

It was during this all-day meeting that the question at the back of my mind was finally answered: Why was the Guardians' Council working with the academy, anyway? Surely they had better options.

Turned out, we weren't just college kids. Umbra's academy had a history of turning out the most capable mages on the continent, if not the world. Guardians were regularly recruited on leaving the academy. And not just recruited—sought after. Even so, it was still a shock when

Nissa looked up at the group of us when we'd finished planning out our mission and said, "We couldn't do this without you. Thank you."

It wasn't just that we were good. The world's guardians were stretched thin, and had been for a few decades. It didn't help that so many mages had been lost to kidnappings, abductions.

So we weren't just the most capable mages. We were what was left of those determined to beat back the Shade. Most of the world's mages lived with their heads down, trying to avoid what was coming. And, as I learned for the first time, mages were only a tiny fraction of the world's population. "Maybe one percent left," Nissa said offhandedly. Which, with seven billion people, meant only seventy-eight million mages still roamed the Earth.

Which seemed like a lot, but that wasn't even a third of the population of my home country.

"And before the kidnappings?" I'd cut in.

"More," Nissa said. "A lot more."

I also wondered whether it would be better for Eva to stay behind on this one. If her mother or father got into trouble in Inverness, she might do something irrational. And I wouldn't even blame her.

But Eva had been adamant, her eyes narrowed to slits as they shifted between her mother, father, and me. "Don't even start on that. I'm the least irrational person of this bunch, I'm a fantastic healer, and I'm also a godsdamn good set of eyes. You need me, and I'm going."

She wasn't wrong. So we didn't argue further. But I did see her walking the grounds with her parents that evening, and the three of them eating together at the dining hall, like it might be a last walk, a last meal.

Stop thinking that way, Clem, I instructed myself. But commands had never worked on me, and they didn't now, either.

CHAPTER TWENTY-NINE

e left in the night, just after the witching hour. It was the time when we hoped Rathmore would be deepest asleep, groggy and armorless when we yanked him out of bed.

As Eva and Loki and I passed through Umbra's part in the veil and stepped onto the still-dark Inverness city street with my enshroudment around the three of us, I said to her, "How you doing, sister?"

"Sister?"

"It's an expression. But it doesn't have to be."

She glanced at me, her severe expression softening as my enshroudment flickered around her. The two of us had already started walking down the street toward Rathmore's home, just as we had years ago. But back then, we had been a team of two.

Now, we were the first set of eyes.

"I'm good," she said. "I'm ready."

I nodded as we came to Haugh Road. She turned the corner of a building, tossed me her cloak as she did. Her wings came revealed, beautiful and gauzy under the moonlight, and in a moment, she'd flicked away and up to the rooftop.

"Smell anything, Loki?" I said down to him.

His nose rose, eyes half-closing as he scented the air. "Nothing except bread and fish."

I got the fish part—Inverness was right on a body of water. But bread? Then I followed Loki's eyes and glanced left. We were standing next to a bakery.

"Helpful as always, oh cat of mine."

What do you see up there? I said into Eva's head.

Nada, she said at once. *No movement at all.*

Good. I stepped away from the alley and toward the still-open part in the veil, the academy's grounds visible on the other side. I said into Nissa Whitewillow's head, *We're clear.*

Seconds later, Eva's parents stepped through and into my enshroudment. In the intervening months I'd learned how to enshroud two other people and Loki, but that was as far as I could stretch the magic for now.

So that was how many I ferried at a time. First the Whitewillows, who also took to the rooftops, and then the other academy fae. Last of all were the human guardians—Maise and Mishka and Akelan and Paxton—whom I brought to the start of their route they'd take through yards and past darkened fences all the way to Rathmore's home.

It was only when we were all in position and converging on Rathmore's house that I really understood how well Nissa and Florian had planned this all out. Though we'd split into groups, we kept in communication the whole way. And we all arrived outside his grand old home at the same time.

It was perfection.

So given my luck, the rest of the night was bound to be hell.

First, Loki slipped between the gates of Rathmore's yard, moving like a slip against the high, overgrown brick wall around the perimeter until he reached the farthest corner of the yard, where he had a vantage of the backside of the house.

I moved in my enshroudment along the wall, standing on the opposite side from Loki. From where I stood, I could hardly glimpse the second story over the greenery. After a minute, he leapt up, landing with silent grace amidst the leaves.

"See anything?" I whispered up to him.

"Nothing," he said. "All the blinds and curtains are drawn."

"On every window?"

"On every window."

That was no surprise; after all the missions we'd conducted in Edinburgh, the man would at least draw his curtains at night. Or even for the simple reason that he was, and long had been, Lucian the prince, a half-demon.

But drawn curtains were a small price to pay for all the progress we had made over the past few months sabotaging the formalists' work in Edinburgh.

I nodded. Then, to Nissa, *No movement.*

We'll head in, she said. *Keep on your toes.*

My eyes lifted as I glimpsed movement above me. In this dark, cloudy night, it was hard to make out the fae dressed all in black, but sometimes their wings caught a streetlamp just right.

One, two, three, four, five passed over, landed on the roof of the house. Nissa, Florian, Elijah, Isaiah, Liara—all the fae except for Eva and Keene, who had moved from rooftop to rooftop to arrive at the peaks of Rathmore's neighbors' homes, where they would be our eyes. And, of course, Eva was our medic if things went sideways. She was the only one with healing magic anywhere close to Neverwink's prowess.

The faintest footsteps sounded in the darkness behind me. Akelan, whose form I recognized. He was the only non-fae who'd be coming this close to the house; the others—Maise, Mishka, and Paxton—waited at their nearby spots for the moment we would bring Rathmore out into the night.

I dropped my enshroudment for a few seconds to show Akelan where I was standing, and he nodded. Then I wrapped it back around me and said to him, *Show me what you got, earth mage.*

His hands went out, channeling. A second later, the earth shifted beneath me until a square of it gently, gently dislodged itself from the ground. I rose two, three, four feet until I was high enough to climb onto the top of the wall next to Loki. From there, I dropped down into Rathmore's yard.

I'm in, I said to Nissa.

Good. We're in place.

I moved quickly toward the window to the living room. No one would see me—I was invisible and silent, after all—but a lifetime of being the redhead meant I still snuck around like I used to.

When I arrived at the side door to the kitchen, I stood at the edge of it with one extended finger and the tiniest flame. With aching care, I drew a smoldering circle in the glass large enough for a fae to stick their hand through. The cut was so buttery smooth, so precise, that when I said up to Keene, *Ready for you*, and he flew down to my side, it only took the tiniest pull of air magic for the circle of glass to drop into his hand.

Inside the house, I couldn't hear a thing. No footsteps, no snoring, no TV—nothing. It was dead silent. So I stepped aside. *Do your thing.*

One thing Florian had discovered while scouting Rathmore's Inverness home: you couldn't even open a window without setting off his alarm system. With Keene's savvy, we'd decided the best way forward was to disable it entirely.

Keene twirled a hand, and though I couldn't properly see it in the night, I knew air magic flowed around it. His hand entered the hole in the glass, though only up to the wrist. *I've found the alarm system*, he said to me, by which he meant his air magic proxy-hand had found it. *Typical dross technology. Disabling it is stupidly simple. All I have to do is—*

I tuned the rest out. God knew I would never find time in my life to learn how to disable Scottish alarm systems. Mostly, I listened for sounds inside the house. Or outside.

He had two bodyguards in there, somewhere. We were counting on them being asleep.

Keene's hand slipped out from the hole, and he said, *Got it. The house is disarmed.*

Well, that had been completely soundless. So far, so good. I relayed as much to Nissa, and she said, *Stand alongside the house and drop your enshroudment. We'll bring you up.*

As Keene flew off to a nearby rooftop to keep watch, I pressed myself up against the side of the house, and for a second I clung to the enshroudment—my safety—before I slowly allowed it to drop away, exposing me to the world. It was chillier than I had realized, and breezier.

A second later, two fae dropped down in front of me. Nissa and Florian.

Ready? he said.

I raised my arms. *Let's do it.*

Together, they picked me up and flew me to the rooftop, setting me gently—and directly—above Tristan Rathmore's bedroom.

I met eyes with the five fae, then turned toward Eva, who still crouched at the peak of the next-door rooftop.

No movement, she said.

Let's not waste any time, Nissa said, and I nodded.

I wrapped the enshroudment around me once more and dropped to my knees as Florian grabbed and held the back of my shirt, lowering me along the edge of the rooftop until I was half-dangling over one of the windows of Rathmore's bedroom.

When I drew a hole with my fingertip in the glass, cutting it away with a soldering iron's heat and precision, this time it was Nissa who appeared in the glass's reflection, tugging the glass away with her air magic until she caught it in her hand.

Then it was just a matter of reaching inside and flicking the window's lock, and we would have access to the bedroom of the last man I ever wanted to see in his pajamas.

I pressed the window up, and it slid with silent certainty like a modern window in a well-kept house. Rathmore would have been better served by something old and creaky, but as Florian dropped me down onto the sill, where I gently lifted the blinds and ducked my head inside, past the curtains, I understood the reason for the window's quiet hinges.

Admist the nighttime grays and blacks of Rathmore's bedroom, I saw luxury. Modernity. A big-ass bed whose four posters speared toward the cupola ceiling, and in the center of it, the half-demon himself. All alone. If he'd been snoring, I would have been thrilled;

when I saw the Shade, I could have taunted her about her half-demon's sleep apnea.

His mouth *was* open, though silent, his arms spread wide as though he'd never had to make space for anyone.

For a second, my mind flicked to why he was alone. And then I remembered: this was Callum's father. His mother had died decades ago, and his father had never remarried. I wondered if she had ever slept in this bed. I wondered if she had ever known what her husband was.

And then the thought passed, and I moved forward. It took so much care to avoid flicking the blinds that a minute must have passed before I'd finally gotten my feet on the carpet and stood there against the wall, properly taking in the smells of the place.

Mahogany, pipe smoke, a tangy spice I didn't recognize.

Beside me stood an armoire taller than I was, and beneath the far window, an armchair and a small table. I spotted the door to the ensuite bathroom and another to the closet, and finally, the largest of them—the one to the hallway—was shut.

A closed door makes for an easy abduction.

My eyes passed over Rathmore once more, and I was about to pull aside the curtains and lift the blinds for the others when I backtracked, fixating on something massive on the wall above his bed. It was shrouded in darkness, so I stepped closer, squinting. Then closer, until finally my eyes and the angle allowed me to view it with the tiniest gleam of streetlight through the blinds.

It shone silver.

I stopped, straightening, staring down the length of it from one end to the other.

That was a broadsword. Some five feet long, just under a foot wide, exactly like the one I'd first seen Callum holding that night so long ago, before I'd known who the man in armor was, or Lucian the prince, or even the Rathmores.

Uh, Nissa, I said. *There's a real, real big sword on the wall about two feet above the half-demon's head.*

Florian mentioned it to me when he scouted the house, she said at once. *If this goes right, it won't matter.*

Well, she was optimistic.

I backed away until I was touching the wall again—my safety, my home base. Then I tore my eyes off the sword, began moving aside the curtains. When I pulled up the blinds, I did so gently, inch by inch, until the window was fully exposed to the night.

This was it.

Ready, I said, and stepped back.

The five fae dropped in with more fluid grace than my cat, their bodies angling so perfectly through the window and dropping with such soundless ease onto the carpet that they seemed almost like specters, like dreams. First Nissa, then Florian, then Liara, and finally Elijah and Isaiah, who carried Mishka up to the window's ledge.

Mishka stepped down from the sill with soft, slow carefulness as the fae spread out around Rathmore's bed.

We would need to time this perfectly.

Nissa nodded at Mishka, who remained standing by the open window. Her hands went up before her, lifting with the palms facing up, and outside the window a globe of water the size of a basketball congealed from the moisture in the air. As her hands moved, she shaped it until it had the consistency and looseness of taffy, and then she gestured it in through the window, where she split it into two equal parts that hovered before her.

My fingertips lit with flame as I stood at the corner of Rathmore's bed, and across from me, Liara was ready with her lightning. The other fae took up position at intervals between us.

We had three elements present. Nissa and Florian had insisted that would be enough.

Nissa's slender fingers went up in the darkness, and my chest held, waiting for her signal. When they lowered, she was already sweeping air in a circular motion so fluid, so fast, I could barely see her hands. And it converged around Tristan Rathmore's head, sucking out all oxygen, starving him of air.

Mishka shot the water at Rathmore's hands, where it enveloped them like fat mittens, covering his fingers and palms and wrists. Then freezing, hardening—cutting off his fire magic.

Liara's lightning sizzled from her hands down to the half-demon, forming a flickering ropetie that pinned his arms to his body.

By now the man's eyes had opened. He'd half-started from the bed, but that was when Liara's lightning had pressed him back down. And though he'd lifted his hands at the elbow, they were useless and fat with the earthen shackles.

I reluctantly waited, kept hidden from view, fire tickling my fingers. Someone, Nissa had argued, had to provide the element of surprise in case things got bad. "And who better than the feisty, capable fire witch?" she'd said with a wink.

Elijah, Isaiah, Nissa said now. *Lift him.*

Nissa's magic continued swirling around Rathmore's head, cutting off his oxygen; we had to get him out of the house before he passed out from lack of air.

Elijah and Isaiah stepped forward at either side of the bed, each grabbing Rathmore by an arm. And it was only when they were near him like that I fully grasped that this man was *Lucian the prince*. Even in his mid-fifties, he was musclebound, enormous.

The sheer size of Tristan Rathmore, half-demon, put the twins to shame when he stood upright.

Still, they managed to drag him off the bed and to his feet, where he stood at least half a foot taller than them. Rathmore refused to open his mouth, though his nostrils widened as his eyes passed over the others. When they fell on Nissa, they darkened. Then the tiniest, self-satisfied smile tugged at the corner of his mouth.

The man would pass out from lack of oxygen in two minutes, but he was smiling.

That was when I knew for certain we'd vastly underestimated him.

Eva, I said to the fae outside, *I've got a feeling something bad's about to happen.*

CHAPTER THIRTY

Elijah and Isaiah had begun walking Rathmore around the bed when I said into Nissa's head: *This isn't going to go like we'd planned.*

She registered what I'd said with a twitch of the muscle in her jaw; I saw it in a band of light from the window. That was all she had time to do.

With a bang, the shards of ice around Rathmore's hands shattered, bits of ice flying everywhere. Beneath them, flames surged.

I ducked in time to avoid the ice; others weren't so quick. I heard a familiar fae yell, and caught a glimpse of Eva on the windowsill, something glimmering and unnatural in her chest, and then she dropped from sight onto the carpet. When I looked up, glinting shards stuck in the walls, and I definitely saw one lodged in one of the twins' shoulders.

Rathmore's hands rose, yanking at the lightning ropetie, pulling it away from his body like a garden snake. He held it in one flaming hand and, with one swing, shot it out at Liara, who caught it just before it hit her in the face.

"Secure him," Nissa rasped, still channeling the suffocating magic around Rathmore's head. It was the first time I'd heard her voice tonight. "Whatever you need to do."

Florian's hands flew out, and a pointed rush of air shot at Rathmore's chest.

The half-demon swept it aside with his flames as his hands went out to Elijah and Isaiah's arms. He yanked the two of them forward, flipped them to the ground in a move so confident, so effortless, it didn't seem real.

But it was.

Then he stepped onto the bed, rising high over us, and gripped the broadsword, yanking it singing from its place on the wall. When he set both hands to it and lifted it high over Nissa, the flames from his hands licked down it like they were eating the metal. The whole room was illuminated with the flames.

Maybe ten seconds had elapsed since Rathmore had first set eyes on Nissa and smiled. And he was smiling when he brought the blade down singing.

Florian thrust Nissa out of the way, using his wings to pull himself back against the wall practically the moment he did so. Nissa's concentration was broken, the air magic dissipating around Rathmore's head as the sword cleaved through the space where she'd been, the end of it coming to rest deep in the plush carpet.

"So many rats," Rathmore bellowed, the sword rising once more as his eyes surveyed. "So much stink."

From somewhere I couldn't see, Eva moaned. She was hurt—badly. And Isaiah and Elijah still hadn't gotten back up.

This was worse than I could have imagined. He was *unbelievably* powerful—maybe even more than Umbra.

I couldn't think about it now. I had one job, and my mind snapped to it.

We had conceived of eight contingency plans, and I knew without a moment's thought it was time for the very last one: get the hell out of here.

Footsteps sounded on the staircase outside the bedroom. Hard, heavy, intense. Rathmore's bodyguards.

Everyone, I said into the other guardians' heads, *the mission's a fail. Get out of this room immediately and head back.*

Rathmore was already stepping off the bed with the supreme sureness of a lieutenant, a leader, the sword swinging toward Florian, who leapt onto the end table and shot out a tendril of air at Rathmore's wrists—maybe to bind them or to twist them. Either way, the magic disappeared as soon as it touched his flames.

The broadsword shattered a lamp as it chased Florian, whose wings carried him high in a burst of motion. He was fast—almost as fast as Rathmore, who took his momentum around, swinging the sword down toward Nissa.

She scooted backward, scrabbling over the carpet to find her feet. And she would have, but not in time. I reached out, grabbing her arm and yanking her back.

Her hands went out, circling once more in the air, but Rathmore's flames swept up his body, rising from him like a bonfire, ignoring all the other magic we threw at him.

The man had truly become a demon.

Liara grabbed hold of one of the twins and Mishka, helping them up. She shot lightning toward the other window—which we had never opened—and it burst in the same moment the bedroom door flew open.

Two formalist bodyguards with nightsticks stood on the other side. Both of them young men, both of them already evaluating the chaos.

Get yourselves out, I said to Liara.

But Eva— was all she had time to say before one of the bodyguards was on her, the nightstick swinging. She and the twin danced backward, lightning and air shooting out toward him.

Eva. She had flown to the window because of what I'd said to her. She still hadn't risen, which meant it was high time I became the element of surprise.

What's happening? Maise's panicked voice said into my head, but I didn't have time even to think an answer.

The other bodyguard had begun stalking around the bed toward Rathmore and the Whitewillows, who were doing everything they could to dodge the demon's attacks. I understood by now they were providing a distraction to ensure the rest of us got out.

But that could only last so long against someone like Tristan Rathmore. I knew that now.

I came forward, kicking the bodyguard's hand with full force. The enshroudment dropped as I did so, and his eyes flashed on me, full of shock as the nightstick fell to the carpet.

I didn't let him get a second look. My boot rose once more, higher, my hips swiveled, and I kicked him onto the bed. I followed that with flames, setting the man's clothes on fire.

That ought to keep him a while.

When I came around the far side of the bed, I found Eva. She lay only partially conscious with a shard of Mishka's ice sticking out of the center of her chest, her fingers set around it like she'd meant to yank it out but hadn't found time to before the blood loss had overcome her.

I knelt by her, pulling her arm up and over my shoulders, rising. *We're getting out*, I said into her head, though I got no acknowledgement if she'd heard me.

When I rose, Rathmore's voice rang through the bedroom. "Witch," he called, but it wasn't the word that made my heart ice over. It was the way he'd said it: with a little thrill, like all of this was a game. "I knew you'd be here. You can't resist a little violence, can you?"

I didn't acknowledge him, didn't even take my eyes off the far window, through which Liara helped the twins and Mishka to escape.

Behind me, I smelled burning cotton. Heard the yells of the bodyguard I'd set on fire.

Ahead of me, the bodyguard who'd been fighting Liara was just now reorienting himself to the battle between Rathmore and the Whitewillows.

I only had one goal: Get Eva out.

Before he could get his bearings, I stretched my arm toward him, palm out, and sent so much fire in his direction, I couldn't even see him anymore. That is, until he leapt out of the way, crashing into the armoire with a groan.

Good enough for me.

I pulled Eva forward, but her feet dragged. Fortunately she was light, and then Liara and Elijah's faces appeared at the window, wings moving. They reached out, and I helped Eva into their arms.

The moment they'd pulled her through the window, Nissa and Florian both called out into my mind: *Clementine!*

I spun around, instinctively ducking as I did. Rathmore had managed to wade his way past the Whitewillows, and the flaming sword now arced low above my head, its heat billowing over me, making the air shimmer as the tip carved into the wall of the bedroom, eating through paint and wood and stone.

And above me stood the demon. He was pleased as punch.

"Fight me, you bastard," Nissa yelled, a whip of air lashing out toward him, the grip of it in her hand. It broke on the back of Rathmore's head, to zero effect.

The man didn't react at all.

"Show me," he said down to me, one hand reaching for my neck. "Show me your power, witch. Or die."

My face went hard, lips tightening in preparation to spit something back at him like old Clem would have done, but my body was already in motion. I couldn't let him touch me. If he touched me, he'd be able to find me anywhere in the world.

I evaded his fingers, leaning back as my hands found the windowsill behind me. *Liara*, I said, *catch me.*

Not again, came her groan.

"*Pairilis síoraí*," I whispered at Rathmore, and before I could see its effect, I threw myself with a yell out the window.

Strong hands caught me halfway down, and with one swing, Liara and one of the twins leveraged me over the brick wall. They dropped me on the other side of the wall, where Loki hopped down to meet me in the alley. And where Liara and Keene were kneeling over Eva, who lay on her back.

"Get her out of here," I said. "Get her to Neverwink, both of you."

Liara glanced up at me. Instead of arguing, she just nodded. That was how severe Eva's injury was. "Let's go," she said to Keene.

The two of them braced Eva at either side, and then they took off into the night to the point of power we'd agreed on as our evacuation point—the River Ness.

"Clem?" Akelan said, emerging from the shadows behind me.

I glanced at him, nodding. "Don't worry about me. Find the others and get out of here."

Without a word, Akelan broke into a jog down the alley toward where Maise and Paxton were posted. When he'd disappeared around the corner, a bang sounded from the second story of Rathmore's home.

I turned, staring as flames shot out both windows. Nissa and Florian flew from one of the windows ahead of them, spinning in the air to slow themselves to a hover.

Are you all right? Nissa said down to me. I could almost hear the grief and anxiety in her voice—no doubt due to Eva—but she smoothed it over with a guardian's officiousness.

I'm fine, I said. *You?*

Florian and I have some burns, but we can fly. Head toward the river— we'll follow.

What a nightmare of a mission.

I was about to wrap my enshroudment around me when a voice cut through the air, so commanding I felt frozen to the spot.

"*Witch!*" Rathmore bellowed, his tone almost as unignorable as Ora Frostwish's when she'd hexed me. His frame appeared in the window facing over the alley. "Don't run from me."

Nissa flew over my head. *Go.*

I spent a moment staring, transfixed, up at Rathmore, whose eyes narrowed on mine as the flames rose in the room behind him. He didn't even care that his own bedroom—his own bodyguards—were on fire. He only cared about fighting me.

Below me, Loki pressed against my leg. "Clem."

That snapped me out of it. I turned, starting down the alley the way Akelan had gone when I heard a thud from Rathmore's yard.

What was that? I said to Nissa.

Nothing good. She remained overhead, gazing back. *Rathmore's out of his cage.*

The enshroudment's fire danced from my hands up my arms—and then a form vaulted over the brick wall and landed in front of me at a crouch.

His sword flamed, lighting up the alley. And he stared at me with dire intent. "*Lèirsinn*," he whispered, and I could see the magic leaving his mouth, dispersing into the air. It was black—black as his eyes.

Air magic? I had time to think before the fire spread from him to the entire earth, even right under my feet. It was everywhere—white-hot flames on the asphalt, the grass, the overgrown wall.

"Loki!" I yelled, but when I sought him out, he had disappeared from his spot by my feet. He was simply gone, and everything beneath me was on fire. The flames hissed as they licked at my boots, but they didn't burn me.

Rathmore straightened with an almost leisurely slowness, his black armor gleaming, the fire casting dancing shadows across it. "It was you I saw on the platform with Maeve," he said. "That red hair. It's unmistakable."

"How did you know she was on that train?" The question surprised me; I didn't realize it had been rolling around in my mind until this moment, when I couldn't stop it from escaping.

"Once touched, a demon always knows where to find his prey." He started forward, armor clinking, the sword held low and to the side. "And Maeve and I, we clashed long before you."

CHAPTER THIRTY-ONE

I needed the enshroudment. But it wasn't there.

For the first time since I'd begun to learn Umbra's enchantment magic, the enshroudment simply wouldn't respond to my impulse. No fire up my arms or around my body—just Rathmore's fire, everywhere. Even along the brick wall, up the sides of his house, like he'd set a match to the whole world.

It was impossible. But I could see it happening.

Lèirsinn. The word echoed in my mind, unfamiliar but not totally foreign. When Tristan Rathmore had spoken it, everything had changed. But I didn't know why. Or how.

I tried to turn—hell, to lift my feet—but they were soldered to the ground. I couldn't even take a step away from him.

A low rumble sounded. Rathmore's chuckle through his helmet. "Show me your power," he said again, "or die."

I couldn't use the enchantment. When I tried, I couldn't even light a flame on my fingers. Loki was gone, and my feet were useless weights.

But the Spitfire was still there.

It called to me. It wanted part of this, and it wanted the Backbiter's power in its hand.

Of course—I still had the Backbiter. When my hand reached into my cloak, I found its coolness there, its solidity. My chest tightened, but not with anxiety—with the Spitfire's anticipation.

I had *something* to fight the demon with.

When I lifted it out, the chain dropped to the ground, the flames hissing where it touched them.

Rathmore's eyes dropped to the chain, followed its length up to my hand. His eyes darkened with pleasure through the visor of his helmet, and he nodded once. "So Ora wasn't mistaken. Here you are with Murkwood's weapon. Let's see what you've learned."

His sword lifted, and he surged forward, yelling.

With the Backbiter in hand, I gave myself over to the Spitfire's will. And the moment I did, my feet worked again. I leapt into a somersault, slashing out with the weapon as I did.

The chain connected with Rathmore's legs, and he finished his slash with a clang against the asphalt, the fire blown aside as the street crumbled. The chain had no effect, and he barked a laugh. "A witch who doesn't know the first thing about her weapon. Again!"

The Spitfire growled, and I was in agreement.

I found my feet, got in a low, wide stance as he turned toward me. When I saw him angling the sword in a sidelong arc from the left, I dashed under it, slashing out once more with the chain. This time it connected with the chest piece of his armor, but it didn't make a ding.

His chest piece. The thought came to mind: *How—and when—did he change into armor?* There hadn't been time.

But I didn't have a moment to allow it to process, because he was swinging again, still on the approach.

I danced backward, evading the sword, swinging my body and the Backbiter. Once I had to meet his broadsword with the rod held vertical, and to my surprise, the Backbiter held against his force, the two weapons kissing before his momentum threw me back again.

Even as we fought, my brain still processed three things: Loki's disappearance. The armor. The strange word Rathmore had spoken. There was something to all of them.

The Spitfire fought on, lashing and hissing and evading, the Backbiter singing out as the broadsword sliced toward me again and again.

My body moved with feline grace as, deep inside, Rational Clem processed.

One question kept coming back to me: *Where the hell is Loki?*

And then it hit me: Loki would never abandon me like that.

The other pieces fell into place as soon as that piece of logic clicked. If Loki would never abandon me, and he had disappeared, then there was no explanation for the instantaneous fire stretching as far as I could see. There was no explanation for why I couldn't use my enchantment magic or move my feet.

And the clincher: Rathmore hadn't had time to change into armor.

This wasn't real. None of it was real.

Tristan Rathmore was fucking with me.

It is real, the Spitfire countered with a hiss, covetous of this fight. *You feel the heat, the wind off his swings.*

No, Rational Clem said. *This world isn't my world.*

The battle went on inside me even as it went on outside me, the Spitfire and Rational Clem arguing with one another until, in a moment of supreme will, I took over. I gained control of my limbs, and I forced my body to be still.

This would be the test. The real test of things.

My hands lowered. I dropped the weapon, straightening as I did. Staring into his dark eyes.

They were just like his son's.

When Rathmore swung at me with his sword, he meant to take off my head at the neck. I kept my eyes open, forcing them to remain on his.

The moment the sword touched skin, that world fell away.

I was in the alley, and the world wasn't burning. Loki still pressed against my leg, and he was saying, "Clem! Wake up. Goddamnit."

I jolted, fixing on Tristan Rathmore. He still stood where he'd landed when he'd vaulted over the wall.

"You hexed me," I whispered.

Finally, I understood: *Lèirsinn*. He'd whispered it like Frostwish had taught me to whisper hexes. It had sounded unfamiliar because it wasn't a word I knew, but it was a language I had heard before—had spoken before. It was Faerish.

He'd hexed me.

I didn't know how, but Tristan Rathmore had hexed me.

His chin lowered, lips parting, but before he could speak again—could hex me again—I'd wrapped the enshroudment around me and Loki. And then we were sprinting down the alley, away, far away from Rathmore, whose voice chased me into the night.

"Run as Maeve taught you. And don't you dare return, witch, until you learn to use the powers you've been gifted."

CHAPTER THIRTY-TWO

When Nissa's voice came into my head, I was halfway to the river. She kept asking me what had happened, why I had gone stock still—apparently she had witnessed it from on high—but I only asked: *The others?*

They're through, she said.

Which meant I could leave. I could get out of this place.

I didn't say a word until we were also through the veil, back on the academy grounds with Umbra. Safe—home. Away from the demon.

The last time I'd been this shaken up was the night my mother and sister disappeared, ten years ago.

By the time I was ready to say anything, Nissa and Florian had been consumed by their worry for Eva. They'd flown past me toward the infirmary, where Eva had been taken by Liara and Keene.

I didn't know where the other guardians were, except that they had made it through.

"How long did I stand there?" I croaked, keeping my eyes ahead as Loki and I made for the infirmary. "In front of Rathmore."

"A few seconds."

Seconds. Just seconds. It had felt like minutes, at least. And in a fight like that, a few minutes was exhausting. Minutes were like hours when you were battling for your life.

Loki's tail feathered against me. "Clem, this is going to sound insane…"

"He hexed me," I said. "I know he did."

"Okay, apparently not so insane."

"But I don't know *how* he hexed me." I ran a hand over my face as we passed through Umbra's enchantment and onto the academy grounds. "The man's a fire mage. Just like Callum."

Loki went silent as we closed in on Neverwink's infirmary, where the guardians had gathered with Umbra. Nissa and Florian weren't among them; I figured they were inside with their daughter.

I broke into the group. "Eva?" I said to everyone.

Liara turned to me, her eyes sadder and softer than I'd ever seen them.

"She's being treated as we speak," Umbra said. "Her wound is grievous."

I started toward the door, but Umbra put a hand out. "Not now, child. Your presence will only distract Nurse Neverwink. She has a delicate and long business ahead of her."

I squeezed my eyes shut, and the tears that came out were as much of frustration as anything. "This was a mistake," I whispered. "We were so goddamn arrogant."

To think we could take Tristan Rathmore. Lucian the prince. He'd flicked us off like flies, toyed with the Whitewillows, with me. Put Eva in the infirmary.

And he'd smiled while doing it.

I wasn't able to think, to do anything, until I could see Eva. And I was allowed to do so until late the next night, when stillness settled over the grounds. Nissa and Florian hadn't reappeared until dusk the day following our failed mission, which was in itself an indicator of how serious Eva's injury had been.

But when they left, holding each other, they looked exhausted. Drained. But not in grief.

I met them in the clearing. "Can I see her?" I said.

"She's asleep," Nissa said. "But I'm sure she'd be happy for your presence nonetheless."

Guilt was written all over her face. And a hard part of me felt she deserved that, to feel what she'd led us into. What had come about as a result of her mission.

But we had agreed to it. It was our mission, too.

I only nodded, moved past them. When I came into the infirmary and to Eva's bedside, her eyes were closed and bandages had been wrapped around her chest, which moved in a shallow way.

She opened her eyes, looked at me, smiled. "Hey."

I came to a seat on the bed beside her. "I didn't expect you to be awake."

"I've been sleeping for two days. Awake is the only thing I can be right now."

I took her hand, lifting it between both of mine and setting it in my lap. "The mission failed."

"I know." She nodded toward the entrance, where her parents were. "It was the first thing I asked on waking up."

"I'm sorry, Eva."

"It isn't your fault, Clementine."

"It kinda is, though." I rubbed her fingers. "What happened to you, at least."

"No." She pressed her head into the pillow, eyes finding the ceiling. "Clem, I've fallen behind you."

"What?"

"All these years, you've never stopped working, training, obsessing over growing into this power—"

"Okay," I said. "Now you're making me sound a little unhinged."

She smiled. "This powerful, badass witch," she finished. "And I don't want anyone rescuing me. Not like that. Not again. I'm going to do better."

"You're doing just fine, Eva."

She squeezed my hand. "Mama said something strange happened to you. That you and Rathmore faced off."

"Yeah." I blew out my cheeks, then let my breath loose slowly. "Rathmore hexed me that night. The man hexed me."

Her head half-lifted. "How?"

"Can't say. And it was a hex Frostwish never taught me."

"What happened?"

"He said a word, and suddenly the whole world was on fire, and I couldn't move, and he was in armor, and—"

"The word. What was it?"

I paused. "Started with an L." Squeezed my eyes shut. "Leir-something."

"*Lèirsinn?*"

"Yeah," I said. "That was it."

"It's Old Faerish," she said. "The word means 'vision.' He put you under the visions hex, Clementine."

Another hex. Another set of problems.

"Bastard."

"Agreed."

So how are you going to make him pay? a voice in my head asked.

I turned to fully face Eva on the bed, still gripping her hand. "That night made it clear to me what I have to do, Eva."

Her eyebrows lifted, and she waited for me to go on.

"The only way to defeat Rathmore—much less the Shade—is to become stronger. And the best way I know how to do that is to complete the weapon."

She nodded. "You need the blade. Do you know where it is?"

I shook my head, eyes drifting to her hand in my lap. "I've checked every close but one."

"Which one?"

I half-smiled, closed my eyes. "The one I have to pay to take a tour of."

CHAPTER THIRTY-THREE

Mary King's Close was a tourist trap.

Two days later, I came into the gift shop with an enshrouded Loki by my side. A stand of postcards waited to be spun, each of them offering a little glimpse into Edinburgh's dark underside. On one of them, someone had Photoshopped a ghostly family—mom, dad, and two kids—standing in their home, deep down at the bottom of the close, flanked by a pile of real stuffed animals. Apparently tourists loved leaving toys for the ghost-kids.

If the blade was buried beneath this place, I'd eat my own cloak. But I was almost out of options.

"Here for the tour?" a man's voice said from my left.

I set the postcard down. "When's the soonest you have available?"

He was old, well-groomed and probably retired, and set his thumbs in the pockets of his old-fashioned jacket. "You're in luck. The next one's gathering up now, and we've got a spot with your name on it."

"My name?" I started toward the ticket counter. "I can't very well not go then, can I?"

He swept his hand for me to do my thing.

When I'd bought my ticket, Loki nodded toward the other half of the gift shop, where a cafe offered overpriced drinks and sandwiches.

"You sure you don't want high tea before we head into the scary, spooky dungeon?"

"Oh, bite me."

A woman at a nearby table met my eyes over her teacup, eyebrows rising.

I only smiled, gave a little wave. I couldn't even use the excuse of talking to my cat this time.

When the appointed hour came, we followed stairs down to a waiting area below the gift shop and stood with a group of twelve other people, half of them couples from other countries, a few of them families with young kids. When our retired tour guide arrived, he opened a regular old door—one of two set into the alcove beneath the gift shop.

Inside, a dim-lit hallway awaited, the floor angled ever so gently downward. He passed through, gesturing for us to follow. "Step inside, travelers, and journey into the past."

I let the others go ahead of Loki and me, the two of us bringing up the tail of our group. And not just because I was here for non-touristy reasons or because I was a wanted witch. In fact, I realized as the door closed behind me that I'd been doing this for ten years: keeping my back safe, ensuring I could keep an eye on everybody else.

Strange, the little things we do and don't realize why until the day we're under the streets of a foreign, dangerous city, and then it comes to us with total clarity.

Our footsteps echoed on the ramp as we went down, down, arriving in a chilly room with projections of people in old-style clothing describing their lives in Mary King's Close, and beside them, placards to read.

People milled around the room while our guide stood in front of a door at the far end. When a few minutes had passed, he set his hand on the knob, describing it as the true entrance to the world beneath the city. This wasn't just an alley, he told us. It was a world around the street, people's homes that we'd be passing through. "Some of what we'll encounter down here," he said, "was built—and occupied—over four hundred years ago."

He opened the door, and we passed through, me last of all. And to my left, the wall ended to reveal the long cobblestone alley sloping down, deeper into the earth for at least a hundred feet, lights and small windows and viewing spots set at intervals into the walls. The ceiling was cast in darkness, but I knew that once upon a time, it had been open to the sky. A narrow, precious view past buildings to the natural world.

I set my hand on the railing and stopped, allowing the others to pass on into the next room. When I took the weapon out of my cloak, I kept the chain tight to it, avoiding the echoing clinking. There, standing at the head of the close, I held it in my hand before me.

"Come on," I whispered, "light up like a Christmas tree and make everyone happy today."

"Wouldn't that be nice," Loki murmured, sounding distinctly skeptical.

No dice. It remained obstinately the same, no matter which way I angled myself. It had been a faint hope; even if the blade was hidden here, it wouldn't be right at the entrance.

We would have to go deeper into the close.

So I stepped away from the railing and followed the group, Loki trotting alongside. I arrived in a low-ceilinged, tight room that our guide described as the eating room of a house—it contained only a table and chairs, a ceiling light, the projection of a woman standing in the corner, preparing a meal for her family.

The people who'd lived down here, he said, were poor. They subsisted, but as we passed to the next room, then the next, and arrived in a room with bunk beds pressed into all corners of the room and figures with beaklike masks leaning over them, I knew they often didn't subsist.

"Here," our guide said, "we've created a replica of what a sick room might have looked like during the Black Plague. When the plague came, many of the close's residents died down here. Some were walled in to prevent the disease's spread."

If ghosts did exist, they would absolutely be here.

I crossed to one of the figures in his long jacket and his mask and found him caring for a lifelike replica of a child, a little boy with lesions on his face and his eyes shut. He couldn't have been more than seven or eight, barely conscious of the world and his place in it.

For nineteen years I'd lived in a world where I was just as fragile as the boy. In that world, breathing in the wrong air could have ended my life. And I'd never felt grateful for the fact that my life hadn't ended because of sickness. I'd taken it for granted as much as I now took Nurse Neverwink instantly healing two broken arms.

We wound our way through more homes, moving lower and deeper into the earth, for the next half hour. The last room we came to was the deepest in the close, a home with the original wood still laid into the floor and the walls. It was dark, support beams cutting through the already-tight space, and in one queerly lit corner lay a huge pile of old, dusty stuffed animals.

"This," our guide said, "is where people like to leave toys for the children of the close."

And, creepy as it was, I knew this spot was where we needed to stay.

As the rest of the group made their way out of the old home at the bottom of the close, I backed toward a corner not far from the toys. When all eyes were off me, I enshrouded myself, disappearing in a moment.

My best hope was that our guide was old enough—and tired enough—that he would forget about the quiet redhead who'd stuck to the back of the group. Or if he remembered me, he'd assume I stayed long and got caught up in the next tour.

They were, after all, only a few rooms behind us. The tours were staggered close together, feet constantly moving through the spaces of the close. Loki quickly curled up and fell asleep in a tiny enshrouded ball at my feet. For my part, I waited. And waited, keeping vigilant, ready to move us if someone stepped into our space.

But no one did. It was funny how much alike people were: I watched ten groups pass through in three hours, and most adults followed the same path through the old home—basically a circle, eyeing the toys last of all. The kids, on the other hand, beelined to the toys. From there, they zig-zagged, their attention moving effortlessly from spot to spot, whatever their eyes caught on.

At ten-thirty, the last group finally came through. And fifteen minutes after they left, the lights went out. Darkness consumed the space instantly, and it was so all-consuming I felt a moment of absolute terror before I could ignite a flame in my palm.

I was a witch, but I was still a human.

The world came back into flickering, dancing view, but with new shadows. The eyes of the teddy bears in the pile gleamed in the light, which wasn't at all wildly creepy. Above me, I heard soft, intermittent creaks, which my rational mind convinced me were just the sounds of all the wood and earth and stone slightly shifting, settling after a day of people moving through.

When I glanced down at Loki, he was still asleep.

It was only here, in this suffocating darkness under the city, I realized how crucial he was. Without him, I wasn't sure if I could have done this—staying down here alone in the dark until the witching hour.

I allowed the enshroudment to drop, and the stress of keeping it going fell away. Finally, after three hours, I could just be.

I reached into my cloak, pulling out the weapon for a second time since I'd arrived. I was already ribbing Saoirse in my mind, planning how I'd tease her when I got back to the academy. As I held the weapon out before me, it didn't glow. Not even a little.

But something else did. There, just at the edge of my cone of light, a pair of eyes appeared and then disappeared as the flame wavered. And a moment later, the faintest sigh.

A jolt passed through my body, every nerve coming alive. Here in the deep darkness, I felt as primal as I ever got, fully Neolithic cave-woman. "Loki," I whispered, "wake up."

His tail brushed against me, a single flick he often gave right when he woke. "Is it time to go yet?" he said, unconcerned and sleepy.

"No," I said in my smallest voice. "Tell me what you see past my light."

A pause. Then, fully awake, he said, low and gentle, "You won't like it, Clem."

"Tell me."

Before he could respond, footsteps sounded from the darkness. Tap-tap-tap, moving fast, and a little girl raced up to me, her red hair short and unkempt, her cheeks dirty. She wore an unfitted brown dress and patched-together foot coverings and her green eyes were blazing with interest.

But the most notable part of all: I could partially see through her.

Her finger went out, pointing. "Is that your cat?" she said, the Scottish brogue thick in her voice.

I stared, lowering my weapon, then found my voice somewhere beneath the rushing blood and my thumping heart. "Yes."

Ghost. This child was a ghost.

One part of my brain acknowledged this as fact, but another felt like I'd entered a dream. It was as surreal as the day I'd found out magic existed. My world had just been turned on its side again, and I had to keep my back against the wall as a reminder something solid and firm still existed.

The girl's tiny teeth appeared as she grinned, clapped her hands. "I've never seen a black cat. Oh, Wil, this miss brought a cat!"

More footsteps in the darkness. I swung my flame just as two more faces appeared, a boy and a girl about the same age, except these ones were in what looked like bedclothes.

The boy had lesions on his face, just like the one I'd seen in the sick room. He said, "Now come on, Jonet, you're pulling our—"

Loki let out a gentle, friendly meow, rising from the ground and crossing into my light.

All the children let out peals of delighted laughter, the red-haired girl jumping away, her hands clasped tight to her chest as though she were as uncertain as she was excited.

"Nobody ever brought a cat," the other girl said. "Wil, go get the others. They'll want a look."

"Others?" I echoed, but the boy had already disappeared, feet clapping over the wooden planks.

A minute later, six children of varying ages and heights were in the room with me, all of them gathered at a respectful, uncertain distance, their attention fully fixed on Loki. However long they'd been down here, it was obvious they hadn't seen a non-human in a very, very long time.

It was clear what they wanted. And so I said, "He loves to play."

The first girl glanced up at me. "Aye?"

In answer, Loki came forward, tail upright, and gave a trill. This delighted the children all over again, who soon began to run through the room, Loki following and hopping and meowing like a young cat. And it was in watching them play that I knew whatever Milonakis had seen beneath Edinburgh, it wasn't these ghosts. They wouldn't harm me or turn my eyes milky or make me go mad.

They weren't what I'd been looking for, but I had once been just like them: lost, trapped, afraid. Why else would they be down here?

CHAPTER THIRTY-FOUR

Within the hour, I had learned all six of their names. Two were siblings who had died of the plague, three had been lost to regular childhood illnesses, and one boy—Thom, who often stood off to the side with folded arms, a straight back, and severe eyes—wouldn't tell me what had happened to him. It was clear he didn't trust me.

I showed the others my favorite games as a little girl: paddy cake, thumb wrestling, rock-paper-scissors. They were fascinated, especially when I told them about television and my favorite '80s shows: *Rainbow Brite*, *My Little Pony* (the group home I lived in played a *lot* of '80s stuff on the TV). The children only half-believed television existed, but they were completely absorbed by my descriptions of the characters.

From time to time they got up, wandered, playing with each other. And it was during one of those lulls I said to Jonet, the girl, "Why is it only you children down here? Aren't there any adults?"

"Oh no," she said. "They can't escape through the crack."

"The crack?"

Jonet gestured for me to follow and led me over to the pile of stuffed children's toys. She pointed at the pile and gave me a single nod. "The crack."

I held the fire in my palm out to the wall, illuminating it. All I could see was the old wood of the structure, and past the boards, glimpses of the earth. I examined the whole area closely and found nothing.

I came to the slow, sinking realization I would need to dig through the toys. "May I?" I said to Jonet.

She nodded.

When I dropped to my knees, I began setting them aside one at a time—carefully, because these weren't my toys. They were dusty, the teddy bears' fur long dampened and flat, and got worse the deeper I went.

When I finally lifted an antique doll from the pile, I froze. I had reached the floor of the old house, and in the space where the doll had lain, the floor glowed with a strange black light.

Jonet pointed. "The crack."

"Loki," I whispered.

When he approached, he stopped by my side, tail flowing against me.

"You see that?" I said to him.

"I see it."

My eyes narrowed in thought. Whatever I was looking at felt so familiar, I knew Umbra would be disappointed in me for not knowing what glowed in the earth like—

I sat back, breathing out. "A leyline runs under here."

"It used to be prettier," Jonet said, standing close to us. "A different color."

"What color?" I said.

She set a finger to her chin, eyes lifting. "Oh, like gold."

I pressed aside more toys, uncovering more of the leyline. All of it glowed black. Loki and I exchanged a look. We both knew the reason the color had changed. The leyline glowed black because it was corrupted.

Jonet laughed, watching me. "You can't get through the crack. You're too big."

I straightened. "Can you get through it?"

"No." Her face dropped. "Only my head. Daiud and Elspeth found their way through a long time ago, and no matter how much I called for them, they never returned."

From the far end of the room, Loki gave a playful meow. He'd already been pulled back into frolicking with three of the other children. It'd been years since I'd seen him like this, not since we were in the foster system and he would sometimes entertain the new, young kids who were uncertain and afraid. But he seemed to get along even better with ghost children than real children.

I wondered if it was because he felt sorrier for them. At least the real kids had a chance of being fostered, adopted, living a life.

These children were stuck in the dark for eternity.

"It's a trap," a boy's voice called. When I turned, I found the cross-armed militaristic boy staring back at me from across the room. He'd barely moved, only keeping his eye on his crew the whole while. "Those ones above keep us stuck down here in the trap."

I crossed to him, kneeling. "Are grown people in the trap, too?"

"Aye." He gestured in a wide circle. "In the vaults they go around and around, confused. Some spots have a real pretty glow to them, what draws them in"—he nodded toward the pile of toys—"and that spot was one before it turned colors. It has a little crack for a few of the wee ones to get out."

"And what happens when they get out?"

His chin jerked up. "They can rest."

When I glanced over my shoulder, I didn't see any spots for the ghosts to move through. But I didn't doubt he was right; I just couldn't see what the ghosts could. And while I didn't understand what the children meant about cracks and traps, I knew one person back at the academy who would stop at nothing to find out.

I smiled at Thom. "Do you protect this group?"

He shrugged, his arms still crossed. "I'll tell you if you show me the thing you held."

"The thing I held?"

He pointed at my cloak. "It had a long dangly bit."

"Oh." I hesitated, then reached back. Why shouldn't I show it to him? It wasn't as though it would make any difference. When I brought it out, his eyes went wide when the chain clinked on the floor. "This," I said, "is called the Backbiter."

He crouched, studying it. "I seen it."

My limbs chilled. "You have?"

"The great witch carried it, rode down the street when she took the city. Except it had a real sharp, curved blade on the end." His semi-transparent finger went out to the chain.

This boy. This boy had lived before the Battle of the Ages. He had seen the Shade, and apparently she had taken Edinburgh.

His eyes lifted to me, his arms resting on his knees. Suddenly all the rigidness had gone out of him, and he was just a child. A child who was studying my face. Finally, he gave a nod. "You're worthy."

"Worthy?" I whispered.

"Do you know how many people have come here in the last five hundred years?" he asked. "Not one ever bothered to play with us. They treated us like dirt. And here you brought a cat."

"Well I—" I began.

He raised a hand, rocked in his crouch. "We go other places, you know. I've been all through the trap, and I seen what you're looking for. The sharp part. It's hidden so well you'd never find it if you didn't know just where to look."

I was afraid to move, to breathe, to speak. He might blow away in the exhalation.

"The vaults," he said. "That's where you'll find it. But I'll tell you, lately it's got a lady who stands over it every night."

"A lady?" I echoed.

"One hour, every night," he said. "If anyone or anything goes near it, she scares 'em off."

"What is she like?"

"I don't really know." He rubbed his chin. "She wears a piece of cloth on her face all the time. I stay away from her, but sometimes she yells at the others when they get near her. She's..."

He went on, but my mind had drifted. I knew. I knew at once who guarded the blade.

Tristan Rathmore's bodyguard.

When the close's lights turned on in the morning, Loki and I snuck our way out, following the first group of the day as they skidded their way down the cobblestones of the alley itself toward the exit.

He and I hadn't slept; the children didn't, so we didn't, and though I should have felt as hungover as Loki, I was wide-eyed and wired as we returned to the academy.

I knew two things:

First, that Callum Rathmore had never meant for me to find the blade in Mary King's Close. He had wanted me to find the *children*, and somehow he'd known that they would tell me where it really was. Maybe he'd sensed I would like them and they would like me, and maybe he'd known that the kids would warn me about what I would face in the vaults. Because after what Thom had told me, I knew I couldn't walk into those vaults without being ready.

Second, that I would have to fight. Rathmore's bodyguard waited for me during the witching hour, for the night when I would come to steal the blade. And that night was coming soon.

But what I didn't know was what kept me awake. What was this trap? Thom had talked about how the ghosts—adults and children alike—would gather at the glowing spots, and those spots were all over the trap. I knew now those must be where the leylines passed through the closes and vaults.

When I got back to the academy grounds, I knelt beside Loki. "You did good last night."

He blinked bleary eyes at me. "I was a cat."

"Yeah," I said, "you were."

The base of his tail shook. "Don't go getting sentimental on me now."

"Never." I straightened. "Hate you so much. Now go sleep."

He hesitated. "You're going to pester someone, aren't you? You have that crazy-eyed look."

"Don't go getting motherly on me now."

"You do you, booboo," he murmured as he wandered back toward the dorm where Eva had probably just woken up.

The grass was still wet with dew when I crossed through the clearing toward the faculty homes. I climbed one set of steps with energy I didn't know I had, stood on the landing knocking and calling out her name.

She was up. She had to be: if Nance Milonakis wasn't up at this hour, my whole concept of the world was wrong.

When she opened her door, her bedhead was immense. Her eyes looked half their size without her spectacles on. She squinted. "Clementine Cole."

She was *just barely* up.

"Professor," I said, "I'm a believer."

Her eyebrows knitted. "In what?"

I set a hand on the doorframe. "Ghosts."

"Oh." She opened the door wider, a silent invitation for me to enter, as though that one simple word was all that needed to be said. Her body slumped. "Come in, then."

Inside, I sat on Milonakis's floral sofa. It had little give, like it had barely been sat on. Around me, her place felt unexpectedly tight, disorderly, books set in piles, a few dishes left out. Like it had once been clean but she hadn't been able to bother lately.

On the far wall, a framed set of black-ink calligraphic letters shone behind glass, totally unreadable. I pointed. "What's that?"

Milonakis had been removing books and blankets from her armchair. She glanced in that direction. "It's Old Faerish."

"You know it?"

The look she gave me was scalding. But she only said, "I painted it. Any mage worth her earth knows Old Faerish." She sat in the armchair across from me, smoothing her robes and adorning her spectacles. "I'd offer you something to drink, but I can tell by the look in your eyes you're much keener on ghosts. So go on, then."

I sat forward. "The trap beneath Edinburgh. What do you know about it?"

Uncertainty entered her eyes. "How did you hear of such a thing?"

"There are children. Ghosts who live beneath the city. They're all stuck down there."

One hand rose to her chest. "You entered the undercity?"

"If you'd call Mary King's Close the 'undercity.'"

"Oh gods. And you only saw children, you say?"

"Should I have seen something else?"

She adjusted her glasses. "I suppose they keep to the touristed spots for safety."

"Professor," I said. "What do you know about a trap?"

Her eyes had unfocused, now returned to me. "The formal name is not a 'trap,' Clementine, because a trap has an entrance. What those children describe has no entrance and no exit. It is, in the truest definition, a labyrinth—inescapable."

"But the Boundless Labyrinth Umbra sent us into had an entrance and an exit..."

Milonakis waved an irritated hand. "It's not called the Boundless *labyrinth*. It's a common mistranslation I can't even get Maeve to heed. The two words—"maze" and "labyrinth"—are similar in Old Faerish, but they are distinct. It's a *maze* Umbra sends the students into for the third guardian trial."

I closed my mouth. It was clear if I said less, Milonakis would say more.

"The Shade constructed the ghosts' labyrinth in the fifteenth century," she went on, smoothing her robes. "She wanted to consolidate her hold over Edinburgh, and even in her wake, the labyrinth remained."

"Why would the labyrinth have helped her consolidate power?"

Milonakis craned forward. "For the same reason she drags mages down to Hell, Clementine. A soul possesses power."

I still didn't understand. "But how does trapping them give her power?" And then, in the seconds of pointed silence that followed, I sat back. "A few of the ghosts talked about glowing spots. And when I knelt down to one, I saw a leyline. It was corrupted."

For the first time, Milonakis gave me an approving nod. "Those spots are where two leylines *cross.* You're not as dense as I'd long thought."

"But why can I see the ghosts and not the labyrinth?"

"I spoke too soon about your density." She plucked a pen from her coffee table. "Paper. Hand it to me." She gestured for a notebook on the end table.

When I passed it to her, she flipped to the first empty page and began drawing. "The Shade was quite a smart witch, you know, wildly studious and pioneering. She understood that in the moments just after death, a soul still exists in our world. She first tested this concept with will-o-wisps, not long after she left university."

"Women could go to university then?" I broke in.

Her eyes flicked up to me, annoyed and pitying. "Girl, we *created* the concept. A shame the world you came from is so obsessed with the supremacy of the penis. But that's neither here nor there." She didn't see my delighted shock as she went on drawing. "When a powerful, treasonous mage was executed, the Shade convinced the Mages' Council to allow her to cast an enchantment on the body just before the moment of death. She would bring a will-o-wisp to act as a vessel for the soul, and the enchantment would entrap the soul as it left the body."

Disgust filled me. "And she transferred those souls inside the wisps." And now I knew: those voices I'd heard from the wisps floating in Umbra's antechamber were the voices of trapped souls. Trapped mages.

Milonakis hardly noticed; her eyes were on the paper. "Exactly. But it proved quite arduous to entrap each soul individually, so she determined that a permanent enchantment over a large space would effect the same thing, but over time, passively. It was quite brilliant, actually."

When she lifted the paper to me, she had drawn the labyrinth in broad sketches, including the places where leylines crossed. "You see" —she tapped the paper with her pen—"Edinburgh has the greatest concentration of leylines in the world. They cross a number of times throughout the city, and the trapped souls are naturally drawn to those points."

An invisible enchantment, a labyrinth beneath the city. It was as genius as it was thoughtlessly evil.

"But"—Milonakis lowered the notebook to her lap—"after her

death, the labyrinth went unused for hundreds of years. Forgotten by many. It was only with the formalists' takeover that things changed."

"Those pretty spots," I said. "Those places where the ghosts gather. They're powerful, aren't they?"

"Quite." Her eyes drifted, taking on a faraway light. "If you knew where to stand, your fireball could become an inferno."

CHAPTER THIRTY-FIVE

I left Milonakis's home with her drawing in hand. On it was a map of Edinburgh's soul labyrinth with the leyline crossings and the South Bridge underground vaults, where I would find both the thief's blade and much more than that, too.

Ghosts. Except these ones wouldn't be children, and they wouldn't be gentle.

What had led Milonakis to enter the underground in the first place?

"The labyrinth," she'd said. "It's the key to the formalists' stranglehold on the city. And I suspect it's where the Shade intends to throne herself when she returns to the world."

Milonakis had sought a way to destroy the labyrinth. In the process, she'd gone a little nuts. And her eyes had turned white.

When she handed me the map, it was begrudgingly. I'd practically had to force her hand; she didn't want any student going anywhere near that place, no matter how crucial its destruction was to thwarting the Shade.

She didn't know about the blade. She didn't know I had to enter the vaults, which seemed to me like a good primer for Hell, anyway.

"Umbra's a master of enchantments," I said as I accepted the paper. "Does she know about the labyrinth?"

"She was the one who told me about it, years ago."

I paused. "And she never tried to destroy the thing herself?"

Milonakis leaned close to me, eyes traveling between mine. "Do you really not see it?"

I leaned back a degree. "See what?"

"I would die for Maeve, but she lives under a bubble. She doesn't leave it except to see her family."

"Who also live under their own bubble," I added, beginning to see it now.

Milonakis nodded. "In your world, she'd be called an agoraphobe."

Agoraphobe. I had learned that term as a teenager, back when I took a psychology class in high school. It tended to happen to people whom the world had hurt. They became afraid, mistrustful.

And why not? Tristan Rathmore—Lucian the prince—had sent creatures to chase us down a train platform. He had his spymaster looking for Umbra. I didn't know what else had happened to her before that, but I found myself, to my own surprise, justifying the way she lived her life.

"I get it," I said, folding the map. "I'll see what I can do."

Her hand snaked out, fingers wrapping around my wrist. "You need valerian. A bottle of it, or else you'll lose more than your mind down there."

According to Milonakis, Neverwink didn't keep valerian in the infirmary; it was too obscure. But I knew exactly where to find some.

It was the one place Umbra had forbidden me from going.

When I came back to my dorm, Eva had just returned from breakfast and Loki slept sprawled on my bed. She was packing her satchel for class, and she spun when the door opened. Her bright eyes narrowed with concern. "Clem. You didn't come back last night, and you look—"

"Awful, I know. Eva, I'm leaving tomorrow night for Edinburgh."

Her mouth opened, then closed as she studied me. She said, "You need my help with something. I can see it written on you."

I set a hand on her shoulder. "This is why you're my best friend."

She folded her arms, fighting down a smile. "The more you try to butter me up, the more I know I'm not going to like it."

"Valerian," I said. "Do you know how to prepare it?"

"Sure. After that day in the library, I asked Fernwhirl all about its properties and uses. But its preparation depends on what you need it for. What *do* you need it for?"

"Ghosts," I said. "I need it for ghosts."

"Oh," she said. "Gods."

"If they exist, I'll need their favor, too." I unclasped my cloak, slung it on the floor across the room. "So if I bring you some valerian tonight, you'll help me prepare it?"

She stood still, even her wings unmoving. "You've figured out where the thief's blade is, haven't you?"

I kicked off my shoes. "More or less."

"Where?"

"The Edinburgh vaults."

"But I thought it was in a close. Rathmore said—"

I pulled my hair down, raked my fingers through the curls. "It's a long story, but he was right. I did need to go into a close."

"Oh," she said, clearly not understanding. And then, from nowhere, she said, "I'll go with you. To the vaults."

I turned around, and my annoyance melted into softness when I saw her wide-open face. She didn't fully understand, but she would go anyway. A pang of guilt pierced the fog of my sleepiness; Eva cared so much, even though I'd let her in on so little over the past year.

I would rectify that. I didn't know when, but I would.

For now, sleep. I sighed onto my bed. "If I die down there, or go insane, then I give you permission to come after me. Preferably with Aidan and Liara in tow. But otherwise... no."

"And why not?"

I slipped under the covers with all my clothes still on from the day before, my eyelids leaded weights. My body automatically curled around Loki. "Because if we both die, no one will be around to save the kids."

"What kids?" her voice said, distant now as I dropped away into sleep.

Eva would have loved them, the ghost children. Once I told her about them, she would never stop trying to help them. To free them. And if I didn't succeed in destroying the labyrinth, she would be relentless. She would be their advocate.

I didn't answer her, but I did dream about them down there in Mary King's Close. Playing with Loki, laughing, the little soldier boy standing guard the whole while.

They were among hundreds of souls trapped in a labyrinth with no entrances and no exits.

No entrances and no exits.

In sleep, my brain slid two puzzle pieces together, slotting them with a click. It gave me the answer to the question that had been scalding the insides of my head since I'd left that prison:

Where was Callum Rathmore?

He was inside the Shade's labyrinth. And the Shade's labyrinth was Falaichte.

By the next morning, I knew what I had to do. And I knew when I had to do it.

The early spring air brought a bite as my first-years mounted their horses in the ring outside the stables. Each of them did so with ease, swinging up on their first try.

"We're having a test today," I announced. "Get your groans out."

They did so from atop their horses, some of whom stomped and flicked their tails as though in communion.

"I do have good news." I began walking around the inner circle. "You've already passed the first part of the test: mounting from a standstill. Now you're going to mount at a trot."

Hesitation filled the air. They didn't dismount like they should have.

My hands went out. "Well? The sun's only going to burn brighter the longer we're out here."

"But," said one of the guys, "we've only just begun to learn mounting at a walk."

"Yeah," I said. "A month ago."

More silence. More hesitation.

"None of us will pass if it's at a trot," one of the girls finally said, her voice carrying the smallest quaver. She wasn't one to complain, or to speak much at all. She fell a lot, and she usually did exactly what I told her to.

I stopped, couldn't help my smile. They were challenging me. And in that way, I knew how Callum Rathmore had felt back when he'd been my teacher. Sometimes it wasn't about learning the mechanics. Those you could figure out on your own time, just by practicing.

Back in high school, I'd always been too withdrawn to speak up. The only times I'd challenged anyone were when I felt threatened. Uncertain. Afraid. I'd pretended I didn't care about school—about anything at all—but I did. I really, really did.

I forced my smile away. "So you're telling me the test is too advanced?"

"Yes," a third student said. "At a walk, maybe. But not at a trot."

"So"—I clasped my hands behind my back—"you're all telling me you refuse to do it?"

They didn't answer. That wasn't a line they were willing to cross in words, but they were doing so with their silence.

I let out a long breath, my eyes traveling over each of them. It was time to be Sincere Clem. Teacher Clem. "I'm proud of you for knowing that, and for saying it. Mounting at a trot would probably have sent a few of you to the infirmary, and you would have a very unhappy Nurse Neverwink on your hands."

A few looked skeptical. The others were just confused.

"Unfortunately," I said, "today will be our last class. This was your final test, and you've all aced it."

"We didn't even do anything," the first guy blurted.

"You did exactly what was best for you," I said. "You can learn to mount at a trot later. You don't need me—you just need you and the horse and some bruises. Trust me: there'll be a lot of bruises."

"But why is it our last class?" a girl said. "It's only April."

"I have to go away for a while. And besides, my work's done here. Anything beyond today and I'd just get sick of your eager little faces." I twirled a finger at them. "Now, I want you all to mount at the speed you can go. But if you haven't got dirt on your ass by the end of class, you're not doing it right."

I slipped away before the hour was over. None of them noticed; they just kept on practicing. End-of-the-year hugs weren't my thing, anyway.

When I came to the meadow, I was surprised to find Umbra already under our favorite tree. Her eyes were closed, her legs crossed, and she had a peace I'd rarely seen.

The grass betrayed me, and her eyes opened as I came near. "Clementine. You're early."

"So are you." I unclipped my cloak, spread it like a blanket before I sat down. "Were you praying to the gods?"

"The twelve gods?" One side of her mouth quirked. "There are so very many. I wouldn't know which to start with."

"Do you believe they exist?" It was Quartermistress Farrow who'd first mentioned them to me; she was an avid believer. How else, she'd said, could you explain how humans could use magic?

"I don't believe or disbelieve." Umbra's hands folded in her lap. "I have no evidence for their existence."

"That sounds like you disbelieve."

"Let's say I'm open to the possibility. Life has surprised me so many times before."

I exhaled a soft laugh, the whole film reel of the night I met Maeve Umbra running through my brain in a second and a half.

Then I straightened my back. "I'm ready for the last test."

She did the same. "Do you feel ready?"

"No," I said, relieved she'd asked. "But I don't have a choice. I know where the blade is, and I know I have to get it. I have to go tonight."

She nodded, slow and empathetic. "That is the way of things, isn't it? We don't just simply become ready. We do what we must, and we are ready when we must be."

"Yeah." She was absolutely right, and I appreciated that she'd said it, but my queasy stomach forced me to add, "I guess."

I knew what the test would be. I knew I didn't want it.

All the same, I needed it.

"All right." She adjusted herself to face me directly, and I did the same. "We'll begin."

With a snap of my fingers, the enshroudment spread up my body, enclosing me in a second.

"Tell me," Umbra said in a low, unignorable voice, "what happened the night your mother and sister disappeared."

CHAPTER THIRTY-SIX

Half an hour later, I stood up drenched, sweat running down my spine, dotting my hairline. My vision wavered, and my hand went out to a tree trunk.

I was spent.

"I'll admit this," Umbra said, soft and fatigued. Her forehead was beaded, too. "I wasn't sure you could do it."

I wasn't sure, either. My gaze steadied over the meadow, and I let out a long breath. "That's the thing about being ready, isn't it?"

She gave a sharp, amused exhale from her seat on the grass. "Keep quoting my wisdom at me and I'll reconsider passing you."

"As if you had a choice." My fingers dug into the tree's bark. I had held the enshroudment through it all, and I didn't need Umbra's approval to see what was obvious: no emotion could thwart my concentration.

Even the story of the worst day of my life.

"You're right," Umbra said. "I don't have a choice. You're simply marvelous."

In the silence that followed, I didn't know what to say. The head-mistress had never spoon-fed me honey like that. So I bent, gathering up my cloak, and met eyes with her. "I guess that's it until next year."

When I turned away, she called my name—but not "Clem" or "child." She said, "Clementine."

I turned back around, found her eyes wet and large. I suspected if I had been anyone else—someone softer—she would have been reaching her hand out for me. But as it was, she kept them in her lap.

"I'm sorry," she whispered, "for what happened to your mother and sister."

"You and every counselor the state ever mandated for me."

Her fingers went out, touching the grass between us. A request for me to sit back down.

I didn't know why I sat. Maybe she'd trained me well enough over the years to think of her requests as commands, as periods instead of question marks. It definitely wasn't because she was the only person who now knew the truth of that night.

When I was seated, her head tilted, observing me like my features were new to her and also delightful. Finally, she said, "I wish I could teach you more."

"You can," I said. "Unless you don't think I'll be coming back from Edinburgh."

"Life has taught me that every time you see a person, you should treat it as the gift it is." She smoothed a wrinkle in the lap of her robes. "I'm sorry, Clementine, for the times I haven't treated you as you deserved."

At once, the memory of her cornering me in her antechamber, admonishing me, rushed back. I pressed it aside. "It doesn't matter now. All that matters is Edinburgh."

"Right. Of course." She set the heel of her palm to one eye, rubbed. Maybe she really didn't think I would survive this. "And you're prepared?"

"No." I shrugged. "But we do what we have to when we have to do it."

She nodded, eyes on the ground between us. She inhaled, then her eyes lifted to mine, full of intent. "I hope you know, I've come to think of you like my own daughter."

A band I hadn't known existed tightened around my chest,

shrinking my air. And a strange old feeling rose in me; for as much as I wanted it, it made me uncomfortable. But not like it used to.

I swallowed. And in a motion that surprised me even as it happened, my hand went out into the space between us, palm up. Offering.

Umbra's eyebrows lifted, her eyes shifting between my own and my hand. And then, with slow, steady grace, she placed her hand in mine, the mottled fingers clasping. "I do have one last thing to tell you before you go," she said.

"My skirt's rolled up too high?"

Her eyes flashed, the briefest smile appearing. "It is, but you're incorrigible on that front. Clementine, the moonstone around your neck—I sense it will matter more than you know. Remember, it was your mother's gift to you."

My hand went to it automatically, thumb rubbing over the smooth stone. Whether because of Umbra's words or because of the memory of my mom, I wasn't sure, but the band released its hold on my chest. "How?"

"It's just a feeling." She squeezed my hand. "Come back from Edinburgh and find me. We'll have tea and biscuits."

When she let my hand go, I stared at her as she rose. There was a finality about this conversation, as though she knew something I didn't. "You still haven't taught me everything you know," I said, rising. "That was your promise."

She swept her cloak around her, clasping it with a wink. "Haven't I?"

I threw out a hand to indicate the grounds around us. "I can't throw an enchantment over miles."

"Oh, that." She flicked a hand as we began walking. "That's like asking me to teach you to bake a cake when you've already mastered muffins."

When we arrived at the steps to her home, she was Headmistress Umbra again, that strange combination of gravity and flippancy. And it was only as she turned away without so much as a hug that I realized she and I had something in common I'd never had the wherewithal to see.

Vulnerability was hard for her, too.

I rubbed my fingers together. For as much as it had taken for me to offer my hand, it had probably taken her as much to accept the offer.

"Headmistress," I called out, "if you think of me like your daughter, does that mean I can invite myself up for sandwiches and tea?"

She glanced back with a half-smile. "Absolutely not. This is prime naptime for old ladies."

I watched as she ascended the steps to her house, the wisp of her cloak disappearing around the tree's great trunk. And it came to me all at once.

That old feeling I'd experienced when Umbra had told me she thought of me like her daughter—it was how I'd used to feel when my own mother told me she loved me.

Back then, it hadn't been uncomfortable.

When I stepped into Umbra's empty antechamber a few minutes later, my eyes rose—as they always did—to the wisps hovering near the ceiling.

For the first time, I knew exactly what they were. Trapped souls from the fifteenth century, the Shade's experiments. For whatever reason, Umbra was their guardian. Their caretaker. And now I knew why and how they had whispered to me.

But as their words returned to mind, I still didn't understand why they had once called this "the ancient place." Or why they believed I was returning to a spot I had never stood before.

Though now that I knew about what lay under my feet, I had a feeling I was closer to the answer than ever.

It occurred to me as I began pacing the edge of the room, approaching the sun painted into the floor, that I had grown comfortable with my life being a snarl of mysteries. After seven years spent not knowing whether I'd keep on being an orphan or adopted into someone's family, I guess I'd been prepared for it. I had long ago learned how to live with uncertainty. To bit by bit pull away the snarl until the truth was revealed.

When I set my toe to the center of the sun, the spot depressed, and out slid the stairs up to Umbra's office. An old secret.

But—as I kept walking the edge of the room, approaching the far side—I wondered if it was connected to a new secret.

I followed the story of the Battle of the Ages to the far side, day shifting to night in the tale at my feet. And directly opposite the round, blazing sun sat a round, silver moon. When I came to it, I remembered this part: the final standoff with the witch in the forest, where the great mage and a legion of fae allies defeated the Shade. Condemned her to Hell.

It had been nighttime then. And as my toe extended toward the moon, pressing it down, I had a sense of which hour of the night it had occurred. That ghostly, horrific hour when I wasn't supposed to show my face. When I had once been kidnapped. When the Shade gained some foothold in the world.

The witching hour.

As the moon depressed in a perfect circle, sliding stone sounded around the edge of the room. When I glanced over my shoulder, a section of the floor had disappeared, and whatever lay down there was wide open to me.

I approached the head of the stone staircase with a flame already lit in my palm, staring down into blackness. No magical torches were lit now. Nobody was there at all.

I began my descent, my shoes and breath the only noise, until I passed out of the light of the antechamber and into the darkness and one of the magical torches whooshed to life on the wall. Its color, like all of Umbra's magical lighting, was odd—an iridescent yellow-white, like the very center of a flame.

The torch's cone of light revealed the base of the stairs, where the hallway began. And when I reached the bottom, another torch came on, heralding my way deeper in.

I only had to walk to the end of the hallway. I only had to make a left at the junction and then open the first door on my left, where I had seen Umbra and Neverwink bring Milonakis. Where I had seen Umbra lift a jar off a shelf and use a mortar and pestle to grind up the valerian.

I just needed that jar.

But along the way, I passed three doors. The striations of the old wood came into the strange white light as the torches lit, and I stared at them as I walked slowly past, still holding my own flame in my hand —the same hand that itched to extinguish the flame and reach for one of the latches.

Umbra thought of me like a daughter. She didn't want me down here, and for the first time since I'd met her years ago, I had begun to trust she had a good reason for that.

She cared about me. About my well-being.

So I let my hand itch. I kept walking, ignoring the doors as old Clementine never would have done, until I reached the junction. When I turned left, I found the correct door—cracked open—and caught a glimpse of the shelves of jars inside.

I pressed the door open, found the bed where Milonakis had lain now empty. Everything was still and orderly. On the far shelf I found the jar with the violet herb inside it, and I slipped it from the shelf and into the secret pocket of my cloak in one smooth motion.

An old memory came back: M&M's. Back in the system, M&M's were a currency. We'd trade them like coins, and in the cafeteria of our home, the staff always kept bags of them. At thirteen, I got so good at sneaking into the kitchen at night, at swiping the bags, that it became almost like a dream when I did it. I knew how to walk on my toes, how to set my fingers on the bags in just such a way that they crinkled the least, and how to soundlessly slide them into my pockets.

Back then, I was rich. Rich in chocolate and whatever else I wanted, which was mostly information—which staff had beef with each other, who had slept with whom, what so-and-so's file said. And I used that information when I needed it.

Once, when I was caught by one of the male night staff, I hadn't outright said I knew he'd slept with the pretty blonde—and very married—counselor for the twelve-to-fifteen-year-olds, but I'd hinted at it. Prodded. Poked in just the right place to where he'd gotten so afraid that, for the next two years he spent working there, he always looked the other way when we crossed paths at night.

I was a queen of that place. All because I was a thief, and I was good at it.

When I came back out into the hallway, the memory had already slipped away, but the feeling hadn't. And maybe it was that feeling that drew my eyes down the part of the junction I hadn't gone before.

Over there, in the darkness, I felt a pull. And because it had been so easy to get the valerian and that false confidence still sang in me, I approached the darkness.

Just to look. Just for a minute.

CHAPTER THIRTY-SEVEN

When I passed the T of the junction, a torch flamed to life on the far side of the hallway. The darkness shifted into simple reality: more doors, just like the others. But at the farthest end of the hallway, a dark-wood door with a different sort of latch stared back at me.

That was what I'd been called to.

When I came to it, the thing seemed much larger than it had appeared back at the head of the hallway. It was over seven feet high, and the wood *smelled* different. Almost like gasoline: sweet, addictive, chemical. Toxic.

My hand went up to the latch. Pulled gently at it. To my surprise, it had a give, and that was when I paused.

If I wanted to open this door, I could.

Did I want to?

I stood in vibrating stillness, debating with myself. Umbra wouldn't want this. She'd already have kicked me out. But the old thief in me—the girl desperate for knowledge, to be a queen—wanted this so badly.

I hated not knowing. Not knowing ate away at me at night, in the shower, in the moments when I couldn't find something or someone to distract me.

Just open it, a seething voice said, annoyed with my indecision.

With a start, I realized the Spitfire had entered this discussion. It wasn't Umbra at all who was stopping me—it was Rational Clem. And it wasn't the thief who was goading me—it was the Spitfire.

Rational Clem against the Spitfire. An age-old battle.

The longer my fingers stayed on the latch, the more tempting it became to give it a push, the weaker my will to do the right thing. But I couldn't just make myself let go. Walk away. I couldn't do it.

The Spitfire won out. It always did in moments like this.

When I pushed the door open, it creaked like an old, wailing woman, ushering me into more darkness. I couldn't see a thing. Nothing.

One step forward made me jump; two torches flared to life on opposing walls, bringing the whole room into relief. It wasn't a very large room, but a tree grew up directly through the center of it. The roots extended into the walls, into the ceiling, and they emanated that gasoline smell.

A tree within a tree. Because, after all, Umbra's office was built into a massive tree.

If I wanted to go farther into the room, I'd have to duck around the roots. To climb over them. To really work at it—and that was exactly what I did. Because I needed to see what lay on the opposite side of this massive tree with a room built around it, with torches set into the walls.

It was here for a reason. And that reason was a mystery.

When I came to the first root blocking my way, it stretched from the tree's base toward the far wall. Something like dirt and stray hairs spread along its length, and I knew enough about the nature of trees to understand that they had an extensive root system with something like hairs or strands designed to suck up nutrients from the ground.

That wasn't so creepy. It was that the pale, almost see-through hairs off the roots swayed in the non-breeze, almost like they were conscious. They were everywhere, on every root, reaching out.

I stepped high over the first root, avoiding touching it. The next one—ropier and fat, the smell more potent—I had to duck under. And beyond that there was a cluster of them blocking my way, and I couldn't avoid touching at least one.

Be a big girl, Clem. It's just nature.

But nature had never smelled like this.

I crouched, my fingers touching the floor, and made my way through. My free hand went out to lift a root, and I found it heavy and damp, like a clump of hair in the shower. The threads on it reacted to my touch, straightening like they'd been shocked, then veering toward me.

Disgust broiled in my stomach, and I swung under the root, pulled my fingers away. I couldn't help rubbing them together as I moved on; my fingertips were coated in something sticky or abrasive that I wanted to wash off, but couldn't. I knew if I held them to my nose, I'd smell that gasoline perfume. And I knew instinctively that I should smell it as little as possible.

Some part of me sensed this was a mistake. I ignored it and kept on, pressing roots aside as I made my way around the room. If I didn't reach the end of the mystery, it would itch at me.

When I had gotten far enough to see the other side of the root system, I slowly rose, keeping my head tilted to avoid bumping into a higher-slung root. There, in front of me, they wove into an intricate braid, forming the center of the tree-within-a-tree.

It wasn't made of bark like it should be. And it didn't smell like it should—earthy—but like the heart of that sweet chemical smell.

Those roots enclosed something.

Deep in the center, I could swear I caught a glimpse of a feathery orange-red in the torchlight. A flash of unusual color that didn't belong.

Here, now, I was the M&M thief, the queen of knowledge. She'd completely overtaken me with the Spitfire's help, and nothing could stop my hand from lifting.

I stepped closer. Then closer, the smell intoxicating and over-whelming and making me lightheaded, too. I squinted, leaning closer. My fingers went out, touching the roots' heart, pressing them aside.

Red hair. Pale skin.

A scream rose in my throat, didn't escape before it got stoppered off at the top. Everything closed up: my voice, my eyes, my fingers jerking away, curled into a tight, safe fist.

But nothing helped. The sight was seared into my eyes. The feel was on my fingertips. The smell was in my throat.

A person was trapped inside there. Dead and preserved with her green eyes shut. I knew they were green. I knew exactly what shade—emerald with darker rims—because they were my eyes.

The person I had uncovered was me.

———

When I came into my dorm, Eva and Aidan spun. They held a book between them and had clearly been arguing about it. Beside them, Eva's desk was laid out with various tools and instruments for preparing the valerian.

"Tell him," Eva began before really seeing me, "exactly what you saw Umbra do with the mortar and..." She trailed off.

"Clem?" Aidan said, turning fully toward me.

I stood in the open doorway, sticky fingers clutching the frame as though for balance. My breath came fast, my heart out of time with it. And then, with a start, I turned, yanked the door shut. Locked it.

Even as they said my name, I kept my face to the door. Set my forehead against it with my eyes shut.

Now wasn't the time. It wasn't the time for this.

I sucked air in through my nose, let it out between my lips. Again and again, until I was ready to turn back. When I did, I found the two of them standing less than a foot away.

I swallowed, reached into my cloak and fished out the jar of valerian for Eva. "Will this do?"

She accepted it; her eyes never left me. "It's more than enough for one dose."

"Then make more than one dose. Give me all you can make."

She didn't move. "Why?"

The urge to snap at her broiled up my throat, but I kept it down with a twitch of the muscle near my nose. Instead, I said, "I might need it." I knew my voice brooked no argument. "As soon as you can. Please."

Eva nodded, took the jar to the desk. She sat down, referred to the book as she began her work.

The two of them knew everything I had learned about the under-city, the ghosts, what I might find when I went to retrieve the thief's blade. What they didn't know was that I believed Callum might be down there. In the light of day, him being inside the soul labyrinth seemed almost ridiculous, far-fetched, a hope instead of a potential reality.

Aidan remained standing before me. "Did you see Umbra when you went under her office?"

"No." Without anything to hold, my fingers curled into fists, their tension a natural reflection of the fact that *everything* else in my body was taut as a wire.

I wished I had seen Umbra down there. Then I would have been able to ask her the one question I hadn't stopped asking since I'd rushed—tripped—stumbled—out of that room.

What the fuck?

That had been me in that clutch of roots, if a few years younger. Maybe me at eighteen. But fully preserved in death, her freckled skin as pale and unbroken as mine was now.

Even the thought of it now made me nauseous. And I couldn't feel nauseous—not tonight. Not with what I had to do. After. When I came back, then I could think about it. I could scream and cry and force Umbra to tell me what the hell she'd done.

Because I knew it was Umbra who'd done it. *That* was why she'd forbidden me from going down there. Whatever had happened between those roots and my doppelgänger, Maeve Umbra had been responsible.

I couldn't decide if I trusted her or despised her more for ever having trusted her. Nothing could justify what I'd seen.

"Clem." Eva's voice drew me to the surface, and I realized something was scraping against the door. "Open it."

When I unlocked the door and cracked it open, Loki's face

appeared. Then the rest of him, his green eyes traveling as he surveyed us all. "What a morose crowd." He hopped onto my bed, began bathing himself with his pink tongue.

Aidan hadn't stopped watching me, and I forced myself to meet his eyes, setting my jaw. Willing him to leave me alone.

I had nothing to say. The world felt like the overturned snow globe he'd described years ago, back when the academy and magic changed my whole life.

Now, it had changed again.

Aidan shrugged, finally got the message. He crossed to Eva, stood over her, pointing and giving short directions as they both resumed bickering about the recipe. Eva fell into an angry grinding with the mortar and pestle, and I sat down next to Loki on my bed and watched, waited.

Loki knew something was wrong; it was why he leaned against me, butting me with his head, forcing me to pet him.

I had to admit: it worked. He was a cat, after all, and he was my cat, which made me doubly susceptible to his lures. So I rubbed at his ears, just like he liked, and I said, "You don't have to come. I know you're afraid of the dark."

His eyes closed as I found the right spot by his left ear. "Funny how I'm the only thing that'll stand between you and the darkness if that valerian wears off. But sure, I can stay here and nap if you'd prefer."

"Bluff called," I whispered, moving to his other ear. "We're leaving as soon as these two herbalists are done with their masterwork."

"I heard that," Eva deadpanned, never looking up from her grinding.

"Not like that," Aidan said, lifting the book. "You see, it's got to be finer. Much finer."

She groaned, passed it to him. "You win. Grind away with your strong, manly hands."

And Aidan did.

I spent the next half hour getting ready. I showered, braided my hair so tight to my head not a single curl escaped, and after pulling on jeans and a long-sleeved Henley, I put on the calf-height, lace-up boots Eva's mother had gotten me a few winters ago.

When I came out of the bathroom, Aidan glanced up from leaning over the desk, where Eva was pouring out a purple liquid into a vial. His eyebrows rose above his glasses as he discovered my ass-kicking boots. "So, it's going to be a fight."

I crossed to my bed, picked up my cloak. "When isn't it?"

CHAPTER THIRTY-EIGHT

Just after two in the morning, Loki and I left the academy with Eva's promise that she would keep a watch out in the woods for when I returned. She'd pressed the two vials into my hands and said she wouldn't sleep until I was back in case I needed her.

Loki and I arrived at the top of Arthur's Seat not long after, where even in April it was cloak-clutchingly cold. We came down enshrouded, the wind held off by my enchantment, and made our way through the half-dead city. Only drunks or young people were out at this time, and as we moved through the streets, they sometimes made themselves known with yells and whoops and glass shattering.

If I hadn't become a witch, that'd probably have been me on a night like tonight. Happy for as long as I wasn't sober.

We came to the bridge on Milonakis's map, and I stood at the head of a staircase leading down toward Blair Street and the vaults below. Loki started down, paused, looked back at me. "Cold feet?"

"You know me better than that." Even though he was half-right and I would never admit it. My own pride made me start forward down the stairs, and at the base of the stairs and across a short walkway we came to the gated entrance to the vaults. A chain and padlock blocked our way.

Loki slipped through the bars as I gripped the padlock in my hand, sending a surge of heat and flame over the metal until the inner mechanisms melted, and the lock came free with a simple jerk of the hand.

I removed the chain, pressed the gate open to find Loki's green eyes staring up at me from a few steps down. More stairs—always stairs. Above him, an unlit wall sconce promised daytime ghost tours of this place.

If only the tour guides and tourists knew how right they were.

"See any ghosts yet?" I said to Loki.

His green eyes shifted, disappeared for a moment. Then appeared again. "Tons of them. Hundreds. No, thousands—"

"Thanks, smartass." I pulled the vial of valerian from my cloak, uncorked it with my thumb. In one swig, I upturned it and drank the whole thing, which tasted sweet and viscous. And it only gave me somewhere between a half hour and an hour of protection from ghost-madness. "Let's do this."

As we started down, I slid the Backbiter from the pocket in my cloak, allowing the chain to dangle as I illuminated the stone walls and steps with flame in my left hand. Thom had told me the blade was guarded every night. I had no reason to believe it wouldn't be tonight.

Soon the scent of dampness and decay filled my nose, along with humidity. I didn't want to know what was damp, and I most definitely didn't want to know what was decaying. My lips parted, and I stopped breathing through my nose after that.

I followed Milonakis's map in my mind, orienting myself when we reached the bottom of the stairs and arrived in the vaults proper. If she was right about this labyrinth, then there were two spots inside the vaults where the souls would gather, each of them at separate ends. And those were spots I needed to avoid if I wanted to keep the ghost sightings to a minimum.

In an ideal world, the blade wouldn't be hidden anywhere near one of those spots. But let's be real: this was my world. And if someone was going to hide a piece of one of the most powerful weapons in the world, they'd do it in a place so dangerous, no one would want to go near it.

So, when I'd gotten my bearings, I started toward what I'd dubbed in my head Soul Trap #1, the weapon out before me. It hadn't illuminated yet, but the radius was only about thirty feet, and we had lots of vault to cover.

Loki kept close to me, gently brushing against me every so often to let me know he was there. As we walked, we passed open stone doorways into darkness, which could have been storage rooms, taverns, brothels, even homes to the homeless. One room could have been all of those things at different times.

Someday, for shits and giggles, I'd come back and pay for the tour.

"Stop," Loki whispered.

I went still, staring into the darkness ahead. I couldn't make out a thing beyond the cone of my flames. "What is it?"

"A man." My spine went cold as Loki paused. "He's coming toward us. Get against the wall."

I moved with Loki, the two of us pressing ourselves up against the cold stone as footsteps sounded from down the hall. And the sound of something dragging.

Then, a man's voice, gravelly and deep and angry. "Fecking hen thinks she'll have one over me. I'll hollow out her skull and stick my..." His words disappeared beneath the rushing blood in my ears as his face appeared in the light of my flames, lips twisted in fury as he stopped, yanked something along behind him, took another two steps, kept yanking.

My eyes lowered.

A body. It was the body of a middle-aged woman, her eyes open, blood trickling from her mouth.

The flame wavered as my hand wavered, and Loki's centering voice said from beside me, "Ghosts, Clem. They're just ghosts."

I couldn't stop staring as the woman's semi-translucent hand slid along the floor not eight inches from where the toe of my boot ended, leaving a small smear of blood behind.

"Can you even kill a ghost?" I whispered down to Loki.

"Either that or she's doing a bang-up job of pretending," he said.

The man and his body disappeared back into the darkness, and I was left standing against the wall, my lungs feeling inadequate for the job.

So this was what Milonakis had seen. This was what had driven her a little insane.

"They can't see us," Loki said. "Not in the enshroudment."

"I know," I breathed. And I didn't say what I wanted to say: *If it's going to be a fight, we won't have the enshroudment.* My words to Aidan in the dorm room came back to me, unbidden and unwanted: *"When isn't it?"*

I shut my eyes for a second. The valerian; I had the valerian in me, and a second vial in my cloak.

Keep moving, Clem, the rational voice in my head said. I forced myself to turn back into the hallway, to start my feet moving. *You're not nearly done yet.*

As Loki and I walked, the ghosts multiplied. We passed a woman leaning against the curved entryway to a room beyond, one foot hiked up along the stone, her hands clasped behind her to press her chest out. She kept repeating a phrase I didn't know—it sounded like, "One'll do you?"—and tilting her head from one side to the other, hair falling over her face.

Beyond her, the sounds of coins clinked from somewhere nearby, men shuffling, laughing, one of them singing somewhere.

"They're living out illusions," Loki said as someone shouted ahead, and what sounded like a table scraped and upturned. "Illusions of their lives."

I kept the flame and the weapon up before me, eyes darting. "And what joyful lives."

We came to the end of the hallway, turned left to an open doorway, and then...

Growling. Low, wary growling.

I remained in stasis directly outside the room. "Loki, tell me what species that is."

"Human," he said with the vaguest tremor in his voice. "Definitely human."

In my experience, humans only growled for two reasons: they were very sick, or very horny. Neither of which I wanted.

Soul Trap #1 was on the other side of this room. I had to go through this room to get to it.

But I didn't move. And the growling didn't stop.

I just needed to build up—

"I'll go ahead," Loki offered, and before I could object, he slipped past my peripheral vision and into the darkness ahead.

Without him beside me, touching me, or at least goading me, the darkness weighed in. Pressing, pressing, like fingers feathering over my skin. No, that was just goosebumps. That was a shiver going up my arms.

Ahead, the growling lurched to a stop, then started again with renewed anger. Hotter. Louder.

"Loki?" I whispered.

Silence. I was about to call his name again when his green eyes opened up in my vision, as perfect and unmarred as ever. "Follow me. Whatever you do, keep the flame steady."

"What does that mean?"

He didn't answer, which was worse than if he had. More answers meant less unknown. Less unknown meant my mind couldn't imagine the worst. Which meant whatever was in this room was the worst I could imagine.

The green eyes disappeared as he turned, his tail flicking as he passed into the void of darkness. I followed, and he reappeared, trotting ahead of me. I kept my eyes precisely on him, watching my cat, doing my best to drown out the growling that reverberated in my head, in my chest.

The worst, the worst, the worst.

I'd always hated the dark. Now, since I'd become a witch, I had justifiable reasons. I'd been kidnapped in the darkness. Ghosts lurked there. The Shade probably did, too.

At one point the growling was loudest, directly left of me—maybe two or three feet away. And though I knew they were ghosts and they couldn't attack me the way a living person could, my body didn't.

The flame danced, the chain tinkling as my hands shook with a rare, cold adrenaline. This wasn't fight—it was all flight. It was knowing the supernatural was beyond my understanding, beyond my world, and that I couldn't control it.

I knew if I lost my shit and ran, I'd probably knock myself out on one of these walls. Tomorrow, one of the tour groups would find me bleeding and concussed. That didn't sound so bad. But when they saw my white, milky eyes? When they saw the madness in them? Not ideal.

I had exactly two doses of valerian and as much time as they afforded me to do what I had to do.

You're safe in the enshroudment. So quit holding your breath and follow the cat, Rational Clem snapped.

Safe. I was safe.

I sucked in air, kept staring at Loki, and within ten steps, the growling was behind us. Another arched doorway appeared, and as it did, the weapon took on a new shade in my hand.

A faint, unmistakable green.

We were near the blade. Within thirty feet of it.

"This is it, Loki." I passed through the doorway, eyes on the Backbiter in my hand. "This is—"

"Clem!" he yelled.

My eyes lifted as a shadow darted into the cone of flame. It materialized as tread on a shoe, and in the instant I realized it was a black boot, it had already connected with my chest.

The kick was powerful, precise. It got me in the solar plexus, and I slammed against the edge of the stone doorway. I caught a second glimpse of the boot rising, twisting as it approached my head, and then my face was knocked to the side. First the boot rattled my brain, and then the stone rattled back.

My body went limp. And then true darkness fell over me.

CHAPTER THIRTY-NINE

When I woke, it was to throbbing. My head, my lip, the sounds of two people breathing hard and fast. My eyes opened and I saw an ancient ceiling above me, the stones dark gray in a dim, dim light.

Not my light. Not my flame.

The breathing quickened, became louder. Somewhere nearby, two people were having a much better time than me.

Nearby, a young woman's voice—ringing and only vaguely Scottish-accented—demanded: "Get up, witch."

I knew that voice—somehow, somewhere. Apparently it knew me, too.

Witch. That was me. Though my head swam and I had trouble focusing on one thought, I knew I was the witch. And I knew I was being told to stand.

Oh. I'm not standing.

I lay on cold stone, my limbs at awkward angles. My eyes rolled toward the voice, but I couldn't see anyone. Just more ceiling. My breath came shallow, like I couldn't get enough air.

Glasses clinked against one another, and a woman giggled high and sharp. Three, four voices had joined together in a faint, drunk chorus of some song I didn't know.

Where was I?

My mind searched, hurting all the while, trying to understand everything I heard around me, and finally settled on one thing: Loki. I was with Loki.

Wasn't I?

"Ora knew you'd hide behind your magic," the voice said.

I knew that voice. I knew it.

And then her words came to me: Ora. Ora Frostwish. This was dangerous. I had to fight.

Get up, Clem. Get up now.

I gritted my teeth, my lips pulling and stinging where the bottom one had split, and forced myself up to an elbow. My breath came a little slower, a little deeper, and the ache in my solar plexus reminded me I'd been kicked. In the gut.

Then, with that clue delivered, it all unraveled.

Loki yelling my name. The boot appearing from the darkness, kicking me in the chest and then the head. My head hitting the stone, and now I did have a concussion after all.

I was in the vaults. I was surrounded by ghosts.

The screwing couple crescendoed, the man's breathing turning almost pained as he came. And though I couldn't see them, there was a hell of a lot to see.

Around me, a long, large room was lit by just two candles at the far end. They were half-melted and as real as the young woman standing with her feet apart, blonde hair in a bun, the veil over half her face, the hem of her cloak floating just at the lip of her black boots.

Rathmore's bodyguard.

To her left, the trio of singing men swayed around a table, and I could partly see through them and the table to the bare wall. I could see through the young women pacing through the room in their reveal-ing, haggard dresses, their hair long and bountiful. Through the seated or standing men leering at them with crossed arms or their hands on their knees. Through the man who'd cornered a girl and stood over her, one unwanted finger tracing the length of her face to her chin.

They'd drive me crazy, if I let them.

So my eyes traveled, seeking, seeking. The only real things in the room were Rathmore's bodyguard and the candles she'd lit.

Where was Loki?

"If you're too weak to get up," her voice came a third time, "I could always kill you where you lie."

My gaze sharpened on her, and suddenly it was easy to rise to a seat. It was something about the way she'd said the word "weak." It was all her words, but when she'd arrived at that one, it came clear to me.

Her accent was only vaguely Scottish because she wasn't Scottish. Not for long, at least. Not to start.

The way she'd said "weak," I knew. I knew it.

She was American. Like me.

"Now the feet, witch." Her voice had lowered with her chin. "The valerian won't last forever, and I've been waiting far too long to lose you to madness."

Yes. Yes, I knew her. The general thought crystallized, hardening in my center until it felt hard to breathe, my mind racing toward a name, a name that was very important to me. The most important.

When the neurons finally lit along just the right path, my vision blurred. I swiped the moisture away with the back of my hand, keeping her face clear. Unobscured.

I loved that face.

The stinging in my lip had shifted elsewhere—to somewhere in my chest—when my lips parted. The word wouldn't come out, my mouth struggling to configure, my tongue working to shape, until finally, in a stammer:

"Tam?"

The bodyguard's hand went up, gripping the clasp of her cloak at her neck as the brothel-goers broke into a fresh chorus. With a click, the cloak dropped to her feet. She wore black, form-fitted clothes—a long-sleeved shirt and pants. At her hip, a leather belt offered a sheath for her nightstick, which hung in pretty silver etchings almost to her knee.

She started forward. A steady, even walk straight toward me. "I've been waiting for you to call me that." She pressed up her veil, and when her blue eyes came clear, I let out a sob.

It was my sister. Not the ten-year-old; she'd leapt through time, and now here she was at twenty, beautiful and confident and ready to kill me. Her voice had taken on a gravelly quality, as though at one point she'd screamed all the color out and made do with the hoarseness that was left.

"Pick up the weapon," she whispered, and I realized in a haze that the Backbiter lay not a foot away from me, exactly where I'd dropped it. "Pick it up before I get there, or you're already dead."

"Tamzin—"

"*Pick it up.*"

One thing hadn't changed: when my sister was deadly serious, even as a ten-year-old, her voice took on a particular unignorable quality. Like she was making a promise, a vow.

My head throbbed as I pulled my feet under me, set my fingers to the ground. My cheek felt sticky under the fetid air; I'd probably been bleeding. Still, I didn't go for the weapon. I just kept my eyes on her, lifting, lifting as she got closer, her face higher over me. "Please."

Her blue eyes held hatred. I'd never seen her with hatred before. "I've waited so many years to make you beg. But I never expected you to do it at the start."

And with a scrape and a swipe, the nightstick was out of its sheath and arcing toward me. She moved like a snake, almost not at all and then all at once she was striking at me—at the center of my head, like she would split it in two.

Instinct carried me, even through my concussion. I ducked away, shifted my weight left, toward the weapon. My hand went out, missed it by a few inches as I rolled away. As I came up, my world swam and my stomach bottomed out.

"Look at this, then," a man's voice said, breaking off from the illusion of revelry. "Fight between the lassies. Watch it!"

My face darted around, and I found Tamzin swinging sidelong at the back of my head. It was only the ghost's warning that made me brace in time to drop low, both hands on the stone, as the nightstick whiffed through the air above me.

Around us, cheers erupted.

When I reached for the Backbiter, this time my fingers closed around it. "Tamzin," I said, even as the nightstick reversed course, a backhand aiming right for my throat.

She was fast. Maybe faster than me when I wasn't concussed.

I brought the Backbiter up with both hands in time to catch the nightstick, the two weapons perpendicular. When my eyes flashed up to her, she stood over me with a snarl, letting off the pressure with a flick, striking lower.

I dropped the rod to meet the blow meant for my chest, then struck one of my legs out to sweep her.

The nightstick flashed away as she leapt back, and I could finally rise, lowering the Backbiter with both hands still clasping the rod, the chain hanging to the floor. Around us, the men hooted and hollered. The women laughed. Someone said, "Show 'em what for, lass."

Tamzin stood wide-footed, the nightstick long at her side, her whole body tensed and ready for my move. She had the speed, but I had the range. When her eyes flicked to the Backbiter, I knew she was waiting for me to lash out with the chain.

I didn't move. "I know you guard the blade."

"From you," she spat, one hand sliding behind her back. "I knew you'd come for it."

"Because I need it, Tamzin. To—"

"Of course you do." Her hand reappeared, flashing with silver. In a quarter second she'd launched three tiny projectiles at my face, and I had no choice: I couldn't dodge them, couldn't raise the weapon fast enough to block them.

I let the Spitfire respond, and my body erupted in flame. The metal hissed as it met the heat, dropped clinking to the floor in front of me.

Knives. They were tiny, angular knives she'd launched at me.

"There she is," Tamzin whispered. "There's the witch's flame."

I stared at her wavering image. "You say that like you aren't one, too."

Her eyes narrowed for a moment—was that confusion I saw?—before she snarled, launched herself into a series of arcing swipes with her nightstick as she closed the distance between us.

With the Spitfire half in control, my blood was up. I lashed out, shooting fire from one hand and then the other.

In both cases, she raised her nightstick in an elegant motion, sending the fire in a concentric arc up and over her, around her, and the moment before she absorbed it into her weapon, I saw it.

For a split second, the fire formed a sphere around her, enclosing her. She didn't take my magic—she controlled it. Imprisoned it. Neutralized it.

And something told me this was only a drop of her real power.

Then she was on me. As the nightstick descended to slice me from cheek to kidney, I brought the Backbiter up to meet it, and the two weapons clanged against each other. One foot rose automatically, and I front-kicked her in the chest.

She grabbed my foot with her free hand as she staggered back, pulling me with her. The flames should have burned her at once, but they didn't. Wherever she touched, the flames receded. Just like she'd pushed away my enshroudment back in the Mages' Council building.

This had something to do with Ora Frostwish. She could see through my enshroudment. She could repulse my fire. Like she'd been trained to fight me.

She twisted my foot, urging me sidelong. I had no choice but to go with my momentum, dropping the Backbiter as I braced my shoulder to hit the floor. When I did, I reached out, grabbing her ankle and yanking.

She began falling backward, caught herself with one hand and dropped the nightstick. She swept around, regaining her feet, and I rolled away to a crouch.

We turned toward each other, both rising unarmed, and she was on me before I could part my lips to speak. She had a boxer's bounce on her toes, and when her fist came toward my mouth, she swung from her hips.

Tamzin wanted to break my face.

CHAPTER FORTY

Someone had taught my sister to fight like a hellcat.

I ducked right, backing up as Tamzin advanced. She swung again, this time at my ribs, and I protected with my forearms over my core, all my training from my combat classes, my duels with Eva in the meadow coming back to me through the dullness of my concussion.

With the next two swings, I knew Tamzin liked to be on the offensive. She kept coming forward, backing me up, as light on her feet as she was a quick strike. I managed to kick at her shin once, but she raised her foot, deflected it with preternatural quickness.

We fought around the room, trading punches and kicks, ducking, weaving, she always keeping me on the back foot. I couldn't keep my breath and speak at the same time, couldn't reason with her.

I could only defend myself.

The next time she struck out with the nightstick, I angled my body away, kicked sidelong at her wrist. The nightstick fell, rolling away, and she was after it before I could advance on her. Not like I wanted to.

"Tam," I breathed, "I need to talk to you."

Her eyes never left me as she knelt, retrieving her weapon. And the second I was outside the cone of power, she came at me with new ferociousness. "You lost that chance a long time ago."

And then she was on me again.

I tried to evade, but she was vicious in her approach and the swing of her nightstick. It blazed with flames as it whistled through the air in my wake, and then on the backswing it rushed toward the tender bundle of nerves on the side of my thigh. During my first year, Torsten had taught our combat class about the sciatic nerve. "Never let anyone get you in the thigh," he'd said. "Not there, at least."

My lips opened, and the Spitfire pressed words for the paralysis hex out: "*Pairilis síoraí.*"

It was as though I hadn't spoken. The nightstick connected with my thigh in a blistering spike of pain, my own flames eroding away as numbness set in.

As my leg buckled and I dropped to a knee, Tamzin broke into a pitying little laugh. "The paralysis hex? Ora told me you would try it, but I'd never quite believed you would go that far."

Ora Frostwish had trained her in hexes. Or, more specifically, she'd trained Tamzin to resist the very hexes she'd taught me. Because Frostwish knew I would come, and she served the Shade.

So she did train her to fight me.

Which meant my enshroudment, my hexes, and my flames were useless against her.

I used my hands to push myself back, away from her, and as I did, I felt myself cross an invisible, almost palpable barrier, the candlelight on my back. I'd come to the far end of the room, and everything seemed to clear. The concussion dimmed, my sight sharpened, and my muscles buzzed with energy. Foul, potent energy.

And I knew at once: *this* was the leyline crossing. And it was corrupted. This was why the labyrinth had been constructed. The Spitfire knew it, too; inside me, it swept up to twice its size, palpating with power.

It was easy enough to stand. To erupt into fire.

Tamzin saw it. This wasn't part of her plan; it had happened accidentally, in the frenzy of battle. Her eyes narrowed. When her fist came toward my face, I didn't just evade. I swung under it easily and dropped for a roundhouse kick. As I came around, my heel caught her in the cheek.

She staggered back, the back of her hand rising to her cheek, staring at me with blazing eyes as her hand slipped behind her back, and she unleashed another set of those tiny blades at me.

At this range, I could only avoid two of them. The third lodged in my shoulder, and the Spitfire roared inside me as the pain drove home. And when I say "roared," I mean fire erupted so large and loud from my hands, it consumed them in roiling flames.

I won't lie: I was pissed, too. My own sister had kicked me, punched me, stabbed me.

The Spitfire brought my hands together by instinct, all rage focused on the face in front of me, a growing ball of fire forming between them. *More, more*, the Spitfire said, and it was so easy to give in to that desire, to make that fireball into an inferno. To unleash it on her.

She wouldn't have been able to move, to dodge, to avoid this. And I suspect whatever training she'd been given against my fire, it wouldn't apply while I stood here.

And she knew it. For the first time, Tamzin took a step back. Her eyes flashed with something besides anger. Fear. She felt fear.

The Spitfire loved it. Wanted to show her why that fear was justified. *Kill her now*, it hissed. *Before she kills you.*

Because she could—would—kill me. She had already proven that. Every strike had been to maim, and ultimately to kill.

No, Rational Clem said. *Not her. Not like this.*

I stood in place, the fireball growing in my hands, magnificent and huge and capable of sending my sister to outer space. It trembled with the desire to be released, and I could imagine the way this room would light up, every corner of it wild with flame.

But then Tamzin would be dead. She would be dead again, and this time for real.

I met her eyes as Rational Clem and the Spitfire contended in me, her face orange-white behind the fireball.

She had our mother's eyes. And her bravery.

Killing her would be the greatest regret of my life.

I sidestepped away from the power, and as I did, the fireball dissipated, and the fog of my injuries returned. Gravity felt more intense, the whole world now pressing down on me. I fought the urge to double over, to drop to the floor.

She stared at me, stunned. I could see how terrifying I'd been to her.

"Tam. I won't hurt you," I whispered. "I need the blade to kill the Shade. To end her."

My own flames danced along the nightstick as she stood before me. Her shock had begun to fade, replaced again by that mask of hatefulness. "I know."

She knew? She knew. "Why protect it, then?"

"You're a fire witch. You can't encounter power without wanting it. Needing it. You may think you want to kill the Shade—maybe deep down, you think you have a noble heart—but I know you, Clementine. It's all about getting what you want."

With a pang, I realized my sister had finally said my name. And it was then, hearing it from her lips, I saw a flash of the little girl she'd been. Afraid. Needing me.

I knew what she meant. She knew, too.

That night.

The memory of it came back to me, whether I wanted it or not.

You'd think a fire witch's childhood would be full of flames and dire portents.

Mine wasn't.

We grew up in Virginia, across the river from the district. Our mother worked two jobs to keep us fed and clothed: daytime, as a receptionist at a dentist's office. Nighttime, she stocked groceries until after midnight. She was too smart for answering phones and lining cans on a shelf, but I never thought to ask why. I accepted it as kids accept all realities of their life: as final, irrevocable, a fact.

By some miracle, my mother was always present when I needed her —to help, to hug, to soothe. She loved my red curls, always told me they were a gift. She liked to run her fingers through them when I lay my head in her lap. My mother was good. Without her, I would have floated away into some godforsaken ether when child protective services came for me on that awful morning after.

So why, the night it happened, didn't I do what she'd asked?

She asked one thing: after I turned ten, I had to look after Tamzin while our mother worked.

My sister wasn't hard. She liked every food, every game I put in front of her. Mostly she was easy because she loved me, like I was some kind of goddess who'd come to live in Northern Virginia with her. Even when I was twelve and she was ten, she always wanted to be in my room, reading my books, watching me do my homework.

Thinking back on it, she was lonely for Mom. She was starved for her. But that was impossible for me to understand. So mostly I humored her. Sometimes I couldn't stand her. Hell, sometimes I couldn't stand myself. Isn't that kind of a requirement of being a pre-teen girl?

That night was one of those nights. I'd gotten a bad grade on a test, my least favorite food—pot loaf—was in the refrigerator, and Tamzin wanted to put barrettes in my hair while, after dinner, I lay on the couch with the remote out in front of me, pushing the button over and over to find the right show. Mostly I just liked pushing the button.

Finally, when she'd yanked my hair for the third time while trying to brush it out, I flung the remote away. Pulled all the barrettes out and threw them on the floor. I'd said something angry—we never remember the mean things we say, only what's said to us—and stalked out of the living room and into my bedroom. I slammed the door, closed myself in my cocoon of pixelated movie-star printouts pasted to the walls and a mirror over my dresser that, from the age of ten, I examined myself in at least three times an hour.

My sister complained, knocked a few times over the next hour, but I told her to go away. Every time, I told her to go.

Finally, she did. Until, late into the night, I woke up to her frantic knocking. When I looked at the clock, it was after two. That meant Mom was home. But Tamzin had come to *my* door.

"What is it?" I snapped, groggy and still remembering the barrettes.

"Open the door." Her voice was strained, afraid. "Please, Clem, open it."

I didn't open it. I didn't even move. "Go to bed."

"Clem." Her voice was a whisper in the crack. "There's someone else in the house."

That wasn't the first time she'd said that about shadows in her room. Sometimes she said it just as an excuse to climb in bed with me. And though she sounded different this time—almost a little hoarse— all I could remember were the goddamn barrettes. *Go to bed, Tam.*

A pause. "I can't."

And then I was past the memory I had told Maeve Umbra in the meadow to pass her test. With Umbra, I had stopped there—at "I can't"—and then, like a fast-forwarded film reel, I'd woken up the next morning and she and my mom were gone, and a black cat waited for me in the doorway.

I didn't lie to Umbra. I didn't omit anything.

That was all I could remember.

Only here, with twenty-year-old Tamzin standing over me, staring down at me in the vaults, did my brain allow the rest to unlock.

My mom and sister hadn't just disappeared. I hadn't woken up and found them gone.

A sob rose in me, pressing up my throat as the memory unspooled in my mind.

I had sighed, gotten out of the bed to open the door for her. I'd taken two steps when footsteps sounded in the hallway. Not my sister's, and not my mom's.

Big steps. Hard steps. They had to be a man's.

Someone *was* in the house.

I froze as Tamzin shrieked, banging for a half-second on the door and then not at all. As though she'd blipped out of existence. And then I was outside myself, like a ghost watching from a corner of my room as twelve-year-old Clementine dropped to the floor, her eyes searching. Searching for a place to hide.

The bed. Under the bed.

I watched as she slid herself under, disappearing into the shadows. And shrank farther back as the doorknob turned. When the door opened, my eyes shifted to the doorway as a man stood wreathed in shadow.

Tall, so tall. Almost as wide as the door itself. A long sword at his hip, the toe of his metal armor gleaming in the moonlight from the window.

It was him, the reason I hated the dark.

Now, ten years later, I finally knew who he was.

Lucian the prince.

CHAPTER FORTY-ONE

In my memory, he advanced into the room, and I kept watching from the corner as he paced toward the bed. When he stopped, her face—my face, if I'd been able to watch the scene from inside my body—was just a foot away from those spiked sabatons, though I hadn't known the word for them at the time. I'd only known they seemed completely out of place. Wrong. Eerie.

He'd stood there a while as if surveying the room, not otherwise moving. And then, after ten or twenty seconds, he walked back out, disappearing into the hallway.

He should have looked under the bed. Anyone would have looked under the bed, in the closet if they were looking to capture a twelve-year-old girl. And it was obvious that my room belonged to a twelve-year-old girl.

So why didn't he?

Maybe he knew I was there. Maybe he didn't want to take me.

But that made no sense, to take Tamzin and my mother and not me. It made about as much sense as my own blood, my sister, standing over me in the vaults beneath Edinburgh, hating me, wanting to kill me.

"He took you," I whispered, barely able to hold on to my voice. "He took you and Mom that night."

And I hid.

And I hid.

Lucian the prince—Tristan Rathmore—had taken my mother and sister and I hadn't fought. I hadn't chased after them. I hadn't even called the police. I'd just hidden under my bed as his footsteps receded, he passed down the stairs, and out through the front door. I stayed under the bed the whole night in a daze. And it was in the morning I'd finally crept down, found the door wide open and a black cat sitting in the doorway.

They were gone. My family was gone.

How had Tristan Rathmore known where to find us?

It didn't matter now. All that mattered was the toxic fallout, my sister's bitterness filling the air between us.

My eyes met Tamzin's, and her gaze pierced me. *Betrayer*, those baby blues said. *You betrayed us.* She had carried that hurt, that anger, for ten years. She'd molded, used it as fuel, no doubt came to believe I was the evil witch Rathmore and Frostwish told her I was.

And she had become marvelous. Marvelous and terrifying, full of the same fierceness I had, but for different reasons. She was faster than me, struck harder, didn't ever hesitate.

Rathmore took her.

"Of course he did." The nightstick came down, lashed me across the face. I didn't have the right to move, so it was only the Spitfire that protected me. The flames rose to meet the nightstick, but she swept through them like butter. It struck me across the face, temple to chin, and I dropped to the stone. The Backbiter fell from my hand, rolled across the ground.

Her boots moved into my view. "Get up."

I didn't know what stopped me, whether it was my body or my brain. One of her boots swept out of view, connected with my stomach. The Spitfire tried to block it, but I didn't, and I sensed if neither of us had done anything, that would have broken a rib or two.

As it was, it sent all the air out of me in one massive go. "Tam," I said, hollow, "I should have let you in."

"No, you shouldn't have." Her boots tapped across the stone, the flaming end of the nightstick appearing as she passed. She was agitated. "Tristan Rathmore saved me from you. From what you became."

Tristan Rathmore was her savior. He'd raised her, in one sense or another. That was why Callum had known me as *the sister* the first night he'd met me. *Because Tamzin had talked about me.*

"What about Mom?" I whispered.

She scoffed. "Don't you dare talk about her."

"Where is she, Tam?"

Her boots reappeared, and the nightstick came down on my arm in one white-hot slash. "A bit late. You abandoned her." Another slash, this time against my hip. Then somewhere lower, like she was swatting at a disobedient dog. And finally she rolled me over, the Backbiter's chain clinking as she lifted it from the ground and held it above me, breathing hard.

She dropped to her knees, straddling me, the nightstick discarded for the weapon, both hands at far ends of the rod, still glowing green. "This is all that matters to you, isn't it? I can see why."

The green reflected in her eyes, wet with anger and hurt. And I sensed she was debating with herself.

Not whether to take the weapon, but whether to kill me with it.

Warmth trickled into my ear. My blood. I stared up at her through the veil of my hair. "There's nothing I can say to you," I said. "Except this: I never stopped looking for you."

She hissed, her face contorting as though she was trying to hold back, but couldn't quite. "Liar. You've always been a liar."

She knows. She knows you've always lied.

I swallowed the blood in my mouth. Cleared my throat. "Then kill me. I deserve it." And with stinging slowness, I leaned my head back, exposing the length of my neck.

When my eyes caught sight of the upside-down ghosts, I realized they'd been jeering us on this whole time, but I'd stopped hearing them. And I saw something else, too: the outlines of furniture. Of beer glasses. Of the ghostly world that only they saw.

The valerian was wearing off.

"Look at me," Tamzin said from above me. "I want you to look at me."

My eyes drifted back to her, and I saw her as though through fog.

She hovered over me, the Backbiter at the ready, her face wet from her eyes to her chin. At some point she'd gotten a cut at her hairline that bled in a tiny line down her forehead. Her hands shook, the chain clinking as they did, and suddenly a small form flashed into view, landed on my chest, hunching down as though to take the blow.

Loki.

He wouldn't move, his claws digging in, and he growled, low and protective.

A moment later, a familiar voice said: "Stop!" Then his little face appeared beside Tamzin—Thom the soldier boy—but he looked even more real to me than she did. Where before he'd been hazy, semi-transparent, now his face had color, contours. "Don't hurt her."

Loki had gone to get the boy.

Other faces appeared, all the children from Mary King's Close. They gathered around us, plucking at Tamzin's clothing that they couldn't really touch, their voices overlapping each other:

"She's nice."

"Let her go."

"The red-haired miss is funny."

"I want to play with the cat."

Tamzin's eyes went wide, first on the cat and then on the soldier boy and, in a sweep, the other children.

Jonet came forward, hands clasped, eyes on Tamzin. "She said she would get us out of the trap."

In a blink, Tamzin's chin crumpled in the same way it used to when she was overcome with emotion, but now she had learned to fight it. Correct it. Her face took on that fierce mask as her eyes returned to me.

She squeezed the Backbiter, fingers turning white, even as Loki remained warm and solid on my chest, refusing to move. With a snarl, she sat up, flung the weapon across the room. It clanged against the far wall and hit the floor, rolling hollowly until it came to a stop near the candles.

When her eyes found mine again, she pressed them shut. Forced herself to stand, swiping the nightstick up as she did. All the children watched her, faces lifting. "One Rathmore's down here, and the other knows you're here. You have ten minutes before the madness takes you or he does."

"Tam," I whispered, a frenetic sort of wildness pulling at my mind. It was the madness Milonakis had talked about.

She'd already half-turned away. When she paused, it was the first time she'd stopped to listen to me.

"Come with me," I said.

Her head gave the slightest shake, chin lowering. I may have heard her scoff. "Don't you ever come back to Edinburgh, witch. I'll kill you if you do."

And then she was gone again, her bootsteps tapping over the stone as she left.

***

She was gone. Tamzin was gone again, and if this wasn't its own madness, I didn't know what was.

Loki stared into my eyes, still seated above me. He and the ghost children, who all gathered in, gazing down at me.

"She don't look so well," one remarked to another, joshing with an elbow.

"It's that sickness," the other said, her blonde hair so real and matted I could practically reach out and touch the tangles.

"Clem." Loki's claws dug in past my shirt, ten little thorns. "The second vial of valerian."

The second vial. There was another vial.

I began to reach for it, the muscles in my arm protesting the whole way, when I stopped short. "No," I whispered.

"No?" Loki's claws dug harder.

Around me, I could see it—the illusion of the labyrinth, though half of me didn't really believe it was an illusion. Not the tables, the chairs, the faint growling still coming from the other room, the ghosts. Not the mesmerizing, glowing spot in the corner of the room.

My head angled right, toward the end of the room with the two candles. There, glowing like the black sun off an angel's halo, was the place where the leylines crossed.

It was beautiful, shimmering, iridescent in its corruption.

The ghosts congregated around it, drinking, laughing, carousing—but over a dozen of them had gathered right there.

Where power and pleasure meet.

The blade was buried there.

I wouldn't be able to see it all if I took the valerian. More importantly, I wouldn't be able to destroy it.

I struggled to sit up, and as Loki hopped off, he said, "Didn't you hear her? She said Rathmore's coming—"

"I heard. Ten minutes." I reached out, fingers closing around the Backbiter. "So help me."

The kids all backed up, though Thom remained where he stood, eyes severe. "Help you do what?"

My palm slapped the ground, stinging as I shifted weight onto it. "The blade. I can't leave without it."

"The blade," I heard one of the children whisper to another, her voice vibrating with excitement. The echo passed through the children and to the adults, who began to eye me, a lull passing through their drunkenness. "The buried blade," the whispers said.

As I moved toward the far wall, no one made to stop me. In fact, the children sidestepped alongside me, hopping and chirping to each other as though they had been anticipating this. Or maybe it was the Backbiter they were excited by, the increasing glow of it in my hand, the chain clinking across the floor as I arrived at the candles.

When I did, I dropped to my knees, feeling the pull toward the leylines and the earth. The weapon wanted to be with itself, and the urge was like nothing I'd experienced. Not with the key to the rod or the rod to the chain.

This was the last piece slotting into place. Its power was so close, even the Spitfire purred inside me. And it never purred.

I had nine minutes.

What happened next felt automatic, as though I knew what to do.

My hands went to the floor, fingers splayed, the Backbiter pressed between my palm and the old stone.

When I pressed down, the stone didn't feel as solid as the rest. The grout between the stones was crumbled, some of it entirely gone. This part had once been dug up and then reassembled, stones placed back over but not properly repaired.

It would be an easy demolition.

The flames flared to life in an instant, covering my hands and the Backbiter, illuminating the dark room to brilliant proportions. Behind and at either side of me, gasps sounded, their voices as real as Tamzin's had been.

I knew my eyes must be as milky as my face was bloody, as my bottom lip was fat and broken. The madness pulled at the threads of my lucidity, even as the Spitfire urged me to go, go, go.

Nothing could stop me now. I couldn't stop me.

The flames rose high, enveloping my arms and face, casting the whole world in blue-white heat as, with a yell, I gripped the Backbiter with both hands, raised it up high, and drove the flaming weapon into the stone. It sank right through the rock, burning a hole down, down —until it encountered an equally hard substance. Orichalcum.

The Backbiter remained speared into the floor as my hands released it. I sensed Loki coming to stand by my side, watching as I watched my own fingers work. I grabbed at rock, flung it aside, removing the layer of stone until I quickly reached earth.

And then I dug, excavating the Scottish dirt around the weapon, deep and deeper, fast and faster, until, distantly, I realized it wasn't Clementine digging at all.

It was the Spitfire.

The creature inside me had taken over without my consent. At least on the Siberian lake I had given it an invitation to take me over. This time, it had happened without even my awareness, until I was clawing like a feral creature at the dirt and turning my hands brown.

But you did give it consent, Rational Clem said. *It's part of you.*

Of course it was. Of course. It had always been part of me, ever since I could form memory.

And so it was when I finally uncovered a glimpse of green, glowing metal laid flat into the earth that I had forgotten whether it was me or the Spitfire in control, and I had accepted that my fingernails were half broken. I had accepted that Loki hadn't said a word. That the ghosts had gone silent.

I pressed the remaining dirt aside with frantic tenderness, uncovering an outline of the blade. Two feet long, curved like a scythe. Unscratched, totally undiminished by its time under the earth.

When I managed to dislodge it from the ground and lift it up in both hands, I felt the sting of its tip pricking my finger, like a religious rite.

Now that I'd given my blood to it, the blade and I were joined.

CHAPTER FORTY-TWO

When I struggled to my feet with the blade in one hand and the Backbiter in the other, the chain dangling long, I understood at once.

The chain was missing its head. Its lethal face.

I brought the blade toward the chain, and the two hummed with resonance, wanting to be together. And when I joined them, the flames from my hands licking over the metal, they reattached in total silence, seamlessly, as though they had never been apart.

And for the first time in my life—despite the broken bones and my lame leg—the Spitfire was fulfilled. Absolutely and completely, all its burning desire and need brought to a momentary halt as the power hummed in my hand, almost too intense and yet not enough. Not nearly enough.

The madness no longer tugged at my mind, and I knew I didn't need the valerian. Not anymore. That was for weakness, for fear, for uncertainty.

With the Backbiter, I didn't feel any of those things. Not even the pain of my broken bones and cuts and bruises.

I turned with the weapon in my hand, the blade swinging from the chain, its face turned upside down. Loki stood at my feet, the ghost children gathered around me, dozens of ghosts filling the room in an eerie hush.

And it was in that hush I felt it.

It was coming. From far, far away, *something* was coming. I didn't know if it was good or bad, except that I was now tethered to something I could sense anywhere, and it was racing to my location.

For now, the leyline. I turned around, facing the spot where power and pleasure crossed—the two leylines corrupted by the Shade. And as the blade hung long beside me, I understood two things:

Now that I'd touched the thief's blade, reassembled the weapon, I knew it wasn't meant for anything as crude as severing heads from bodies. It was meant for thieving the most crucial thing in the world: magic—*power.* Which meant Aidan was right.

And I knew that Umbra's training in the fall had been for this moment, when I would have the Backbiter in hand and stand before a corrupted leyline which I could see with my own eyes, and know exactly what to do.

"Careful," Loki murmured by my side.

"You'll either get Careful Clem or Quick Clem," I said, "but not both."

I gripped the rod in both hands at my waist, raised the chain end up and swung it once in front of my body, bringing the blade in a vertical arc by my left shoulder and then up and around. When it swept low to the ground, it skimmed the glow off the leylines, drinking in the darkness.

The blackness was swept aside like smoke, and some of it remained with the blade as it came back around. I caught the chain in my grasp, staring at the blade. The dark tendrils swirled around it, and then up the blade, up the chain, braiding their way toward me. Soon they slithered up the rod, and when they reached my fingers, I sucked in air just as the Spitfire did.

This was the Shade's power. It was immense, and it was delicious, smoky and rich. It swirled up into my mouth, between my lips, down my throat, and after that, all pain was gone. This was a drug, and both the Spitfire and I wanted more of it.

I swept the blade like a scythe—once, twice, three more times over the leyline and the darkness, each time drawing in more of her power until it had receded entirely, and the glow that remained was as clear and brilliant as the sun.

Behind me, gasps sounded—the children and the adults.

The leylines had been uncorrupted.

Now the Shade's power was inside me, thrilling through my chest, my veins. And still I wanted more. *The Spitfire* wanted more.

"Clem," Loki said, sharp and insistent. Bringing me back. Reminding me.

When I forced my eyes down to his, I remembered: I was Clementine. And I wasn't down here for this.

"Callum," he said. "Tamzin said Callum is here."

I turned away from the leylines. Around me, the labyrinth was as clear to me as the real world, a strange spiderweb enchantment. I could practically see the magic at work, the mesh of it throughout the room, keeping these souls trapped here.

"Move back," I said, and Loki and the ghosts backed away from me, clearing a space.

I swung the Backbiter, the blade swinging up and shearing the air near the ceiling. As it did, it cleaved a rip in the enchantment, the illusion of the brothel torn away to reveal the dank old vault.

The ghosts' faces lifted, staring wide-eyed, their five-hundred-year prison just revealed for what it was: a goddamn soul trap.

Beside me, Loki whispered, "What'd you just do, Clem?"

The blade whistled to a dangle beside me, the enchantment magic licking over it, seeping into my fingers. This was the Shade's magic, too. "I tore a hole in the labyrinth, Loki." I started forward, angling the Backbiter into another swing, the blade racing through the air on my opposite side. "Come on. We're going to get Callum."

I stalked through the vaults, the blade swinging as I went. I knew I was riding a high on this magic, that soon enough the pain would sear through me, send me to the ground. But for however long it lasted, I would use it.

Thom ran alongside me. "They're escaping. The people are escaping."

"Which people?"

"All the ones stuck down here."

The souls. They were escaping the labyrinth. I took another swipe as we passed into the next room, ripping away another section of magical scaffolding. "Good. You should escape, too."

"But more are coming," he said as though he hadn't heard me. "Jonet told me the big one is coming. She said he's at the staircase by the bridge."

"The big one," I murmured, still in motion.

"He means Rathmore," Loki said from beside me.

The boy nodded. "The big one with the sword."

So Tamzin hadn't been lying: Rathmore was coming for me. And he probably wasn't alone.

"We should go," Loki said. "Now. While we can."

"No." My walk quickened as we entered a fresh hallway. "Not yet. Callum's here."

"Callum?" the boy said.

"As big as the big one," I said. "Long black hair."

"Oh!" Thom's hand rose, finger pointing. "One of the sleepers. He's in that one."

He was pointing to the entrance to one of the vaults at the end of the hallway.

I didn't know what "the sleepers" could possibly mean, but I was used to not knowing anymore. I only knew recognition had entered Thom's voice, and that was good enough for me.

"How long has he been asleep?" I asked.

"Oh, ages. They brought him in here a year ago, and then a woman did magic and his body stayed but the rest of him walked off."

This was familiar, but I couldn't place exactly how. "But he's asleep."

"Aye," Thom said without hesitation. "As long as he's sleeping, his soul can't go to Heaven."

The pain was starting to set in, creeping up my limbs, gnawing at my chest and face. Bones were definitely broken, but my legs and arms still functioned. The blade still swung. I kept moving forward.

Thom danced alongside me, sidestepping. "You're mad, but I like you. So we'll help you."

Before I could ask him what that meant, he raced in the opposite direction, bare feet slapping over the stones. And a few seconds later, his child's voice rang out through the vaults, echoing back to me.

It was accompanied by other children's voices, a cacophony of noise and running feet. A chaos only children could create.

They were buying me time.

Loki and I came to the vault entrance the boy had pointed to, and flames burst along the length of the Backbiter the moment the thought entered my mind that I needed light.

Before us were bodies hanging from shackles along the wall, each of them seated with their heads down and their arms affixed high, legs out before them. They weren't decomposing; they just seemed to be... not there. And as I came forward, lifting faces, I didn't recognize any of them.

Not until I arrived at the far end of the room. There, his shadow dancing in the light off the flames, was the sleeper I'd come for. I knew it was him without even seeing his face.

Callum Rathmore hung from the wall, chains affixed into the stone and glowing cuffs around his wrists. His clothes were damp, soiled. His black hair veiled his head, which dropped toward his chest. One leg was folded under him, the other straight out.

I rushed to him, dropping to my protesting knees, setting the Backbiter down to free up my hands. When I pressed his hair aside, he didn't respond. His head didn't lift, and he seemed dead.

Or asleep. Because when my hand went to his chest, it rose and fell under my fingers.

"Callum?" I said, but I got no response. As though he were in a coma, or wasn't even in his body.

Like the will-o-wisps.

I stared at him, eyes wide, my hand still on his chest.

This was the kind of magic the Shade had used five centuries ago to remove mages' souls from their bodies and place them inside will-o-wisps. Except Callum's soul had been released into Falaichte, the labyrinth, and Callum's body hadn't died.

CHAPTER FORTY-THREE

I stood, the Backbiter in hand, turning a circle. "Callum!" I called out, as though his soul would hear me over the yelling echoing all around, the children's clamoring.

No one came. The only person whose eyes were on me were Loki's.

"Clem," he said, "you're bleeding."

When I looked down, blood slid down the length of my left arm, dripped from my fingertips. I was bleeding from so many places, hurting in so many places, I couldn't even figure out which was the worst of them. But I did know one thing: even through the adrenaline, I was starting to feel lightheaded.

Time was running out. The Shade's power had come and gone so quickly.

But I couldn't leave without him.

Thom's words came back to me: As long as Callum's body was alive, his soul couldn't leave the Earth. Which meant there had to be a way to join his soul with his body again.

I could figure that part out later.

I turned toward Callum's body. My fingers went up to the white, glowing cuff around his wrist, and the cold off it scalded my fingers. I yanked my hand away. I didn't know what kind of magic this was, and I didn't care.

It was cold. And I could always defeat cold.

I raised the Backbiter, gripping the chain in one hand, and called on the Spitfire. Allowed it to take over. The Backbiter raced with fresh, hot flame licking a foot out from the weapon.

"Clem," Loki began, "you can't—"

"You don't know what I can or can't do." With a growl, I swiped the flaming blade through the air. It raced toward the two chains affixed to the wall, sliced through them without any resistance at all. Callum's arms dropped, and he slumped, falling to his side.

"Okay," Loki said. "I guess you can now."

The Spitfire receded, spent already. I had overused it, or maybe I just didn't have the life energy to do much of anything.

The children's voices were getting closer. Which meant Tristan Rathmore was getting closer. And through the blood rushing in my ears, I heard Thom cry out, "He's coming!"

Now I heard it, distantly: clanking. The clanking of metal sabatons on stone.

I grabbed Callum's hands, leaned back, testing how draggable he was.

Not at all. He must have been over two hundred pounds.

When I released him, I fell to a seat, breathing hard, overwhelmed by the pain, the blood loss, the exertion. Stars appeared in my vision, white spots blinking in and out as I squeezed my eyes shut and opened them again.

Loki spun toward the doorway, tail upright and bushy. "Do you see that?"

I squinted at the doorway, where I could have sworn a strangely hued light grew and grew in the empty hallway. "Loki," I whispered, "am I dying, or is that a blue light?"

"It's definitely blue."

In the next moment, the blue glow turned into a flash of white light, blinding my retinas. I threw a bloody hand up over my face—

And then I heard the whispers.

They were voices I had first heard years ago, back before I'd known who they were, whom they belonged to, why they spoke to me.

Years ago, they had called me Shadowend, told me I'd returned to the ancient place. They had protected me. And they had given me a key.

Now, as I lowered my shaking hand and the brightness receded, I saw them: six will-o-wisps. The Shade's creations, bound to her power and to the Backbiter. That was what I'd heard from so far away. Now that the Backbiter was whole again, they were drawn to it.

To its wielder. To me.

They raced in through the doorway and over my head. When my eyes tracked left and then up in an arc, I found them arrayed behind me like a halo. They held their distance from one another, hovering, waiting.

And in my hand, the Backbiter's energy shifted. It still simmered with flame, but now it glowed blue in the wisps' light. When I lifted the weapon, staring at it, the colors were scintillating, perfect.

Its power had changed. Grown. And the wisps were key to that. *They were part of the weapon.*

What do you wish? they whispered to me.

What did I wish? My mind raced, and settled on one word: escape. I wanted simply to escape.

Loki began backing up, his eyes still on the doorway, back arched. The metal clanked louder, nearer.

Then escape, came the wisps' reply. Simple, effortless, unconcerned. But with it came the knowledge in my mind's eye, as though they were showing me exactly what I needed to do.

And it was simple.

My fingers tightened on the Backbiter. "Loki," I whispered, "come here."

He must have heard the tone in my voice, even if it sounded distant to my ears, because he turned and came to my side, pressed against me and still facing the doorway. A low growl escaped him as he faced off against what was coming. Obeying and prepared to die.

I gripped the Backbiter, lifted it with the energy I had left. The wisps rushed toward it, encircling it, their glow growing as they danced around the rod, up the chain, toward the blade.

With gritted teeth and one palm to the ground, I pressed my way to my feet, swaying as I took the rod in both hands, swung the chain with the energy I had left.

The blade, blue with the encircled wisps, flashed through the air, swooped down toward the floor. As it did, it cut a jagged, uneven rift in the veil. It was crooked and crude, but it was enough.

On the other side, I could see the forest outside the academy.

"Go, Loki." I threw the Backbiter through the parting, where it landed—still flaming—on the grass. Loki darted through, stood staring at me from the other side. The wisps left the blade, flew through the parting back into the vaults, where they hovered around my head.

They were mine. Not the weapon's, but mine to command.

Hide us, I thought, or maybe I just wanted it. I just wanted to be hidden.

I slid my hands under Callum's armpits, my blood dripping onto him, and a throbbing head and a yell boring its way up my throat, I pulled. I pulled and pulled and moved him an inch, and then a few inches, my boots sliding over the stone.

The wisps raced through the room, circling, circling, glowing brighter. Their glow growing to encompass the two of us in a shimmering veil of blue-red magic. I could feel them tapping into the magic inside me, using my knowledge to act as an extension of my desires.

They had cast an enshroudment before the doorway, hiding Callum and me. Keeping us safe, even as the horned helmet appeared in the hallway. Even as those eyes—familiar to me now—fixed on the broken chains on the wall, the blood on the floor.

I can't, I thought, but I didn't stop. I couldn't; it was the only way. I kept pulling until he was halfway onto the grass, and then it became easier to slide him over the fallen leaves and needles. And with a final scream and a tug, his bare feet were through the veil as Tristan Rathmore stepped into the room, penetrating the wisps' enshroudment.

His gaze fixed on me and Callum, and he surged forward, striding hard and loud.

I could only stare back and hold onto Callum as the wisps flew through the veil, and it was already reseaming, the hole shrinking. But I could still see Rathmore's face as it got closer. Closer. I could have sworn I saw a shadow pass through the veil ahead of him, but the rest became fuzzy, faraway, remote.

"Witch," he hissed, and then the parting had closed, the vaults disappearing and leaving only dark woods and me clutching Callum, the two of us alone with Loki and the wisps.

He doesn't know where I am, came the desperate, delirious thought. *Even if he can part the veil, he doesn't know where this place is.*

Then came the far-off sound of Eva's voice. "Clem? It's Clementine!"

I dropped to a seat, and then my head found the ground.

The next parts were a waking dream. I was being dragged and then lifted as voices sounded around me. Eva, Aidan, Liara, Loki, and another voice. Jags of pain shot through me, bringing me closer to consciousness. Some time later a needle pricked my arm, coldness seeped into it, and then I was truly asleep.

When I woke, it was still nighttime. Or maybe the day had passed and it was nighttime again. I could hear the nighttime breeze rustling the trees. Around me the smells were the same: cool, Eastern European air, that woodsy spring aerosol.

One thing was different: Loki was sitting on my chest.

My hand went out automatically, came to rest on his head. And as it did, pain shot through my arm. My fingers moved stiffly, and I realized I was bandaged from the shoulder down. My fingers were puffy, like I'd had an infection.

It began to come back. First in dribs and drabs—the blade, the vaults... then Tamzin.

Tamzin.

Callum.

My head lifted, eyes opening. I wasn't outside. I lay in a bed in the infirmary, but the lights were off, and the main door was open to the night. Nurse Neverwink would never leave it open; she was particular about this place being closed off, sanitary.

Around me, I saw the blue glow of the wisps. When my eyes lifted, I found them hovering near the ceiling above my bed, erratic like a group of fireflies. They weren't talking to me now, and they didn't provide enough light to see much past my nose.

"Loki." My voice grated like sandpaper. I reached out for the magical lamp beside the bed, and it flickered to life as my hand neared.

He came illuminated in the half-light, green eyes cracked. "About time."

Before anything else, I found myself searching for it. I couldn't tell whether the impulse inside me was me or the Spitfire, because right now they felt one and the same. My hand ran over the end table, into the shelf below. I half rose, ignoring the pain and Loki, who dropped to a seat on the bed beside me.

"It's by your feet," he said, recognizing my franticness like an enabler would do a junkie.

My eyes shot to the end of the bed, where the Backbiter lay as neatly as it ever had in its reassembled life: the rod perpendicular to my body, the chain laid in a neat pattern with the blade resting at the center like the head of a snake.

I reached out, took hold of it. Once it was in my hand, I could let out a breath. The world felt at least a little right. "Who brought this here?"

"Eva," Loki said, half-lazy, half-unconcerned. "She carried it."

"Did anyone else see it?"

"I don't think you'll care once you step outside."

"What?" And then, my second concern: "Callum. Where is he?"

Loki's head turned. "Behind that curtain."

When I slid my legs out from the covers and onto the cold floor, I realized how long I'd been out. More than a day. Days, at least, because I didn't trust my feet right away. The bandages were on more than just my arm—they were across my head, my chest, elsewhere below.

Neverwink's healing magic should have been enough. I shouldn't have to need bandages.

I had more questions, but first I had to see him.

When I found my balance, I crossed to the curtained bed, the Backbiter's rod and chain bound up in one hand. I pulled the curtain aside and found him there, eyes closed, black hair smoothed away from his face. Someone had brushed it, and he lay asleep with his hands clasped over his chest.

Callum was alive. He was real.

"He's not here," a voice said from behind me.

I jerked around, my eyes lowering. It was Thom, his arms crossed high up, still as ghostlike as ever. "Where did you..."

"I followed you into the woods," he said. "That night, I followed you here."

So he was the shadow. It was him I'd seen pass through the veil with us.

"I destroyed the labyrinth," I whispered. "You can... ascend, Thom."

"Or descend," Loki murmured, still seated on my bed.

I shot him a glare.

"What?" Loki said. "I'm not judging."

Thom shook his head. "Back in the vaults, I vowed I would help you."

"You vowed?" I said.

"Sure. Just like I vowed I would protect the others, and now they're free."

"The other kids, you mean?"

He nodded once.

So the kids were free. They had escaped.

"You did help us," I said. "We only made it because of you."

He jerked his chin at Callum. "He didn't. And he's your family—I can tell."

My eyes drifted between the two of them. I ignored his question. "You said he's not here."

"That's right. But he's somewhere, because his body's sleeping."

I took another step toward Callum, touched his fingers. They were warm. "So you're saying he's alive somewhere."

The boy nodded. "Lost and wandering."

My fingers remained on Callum's hand. "Do you think he's still in Edinburgh?"

"I saw the spirits of those others who were chained wandering the vaults," Thom said. "But not him. Never him. He's somewhere else."

My eyes shut, my fingers tightening on the Backbiter. "I wouldn't even know where to start."

The boy's voice sounded closer. When I looked down, he was standing beside the bed, too. "So I'll find him."

"No," I said. "It's too..."

"Dangerous?" Loki offered. "He's a ghost. He can't get hurt."

Thom sensed what I meant. A smile broke out on his face. "After so long stuck under the earth, you think I'll mind spending some time seeing the sky?"

I didn't know what to say to that. Except, "How will you know where to look?"

"Oh, I heard lots of stories," Thom said. "There's places where we go in the world when we can't pass on."

I turned fully to Thom, dropped to a crouch in front of him, my whole body protesting as I did. "Promise me one thing."

He waited, arms still crossed.

"When you find him, your vow to me will be fulfilled."

"When we bring him back to his own body," the boy said, "and his eyes open. Only when they open."

I sensed this was about more than me or a vow to me. As I studied him, I realized the boy also had black hair. He may have grown tall and broad like Callum one day. But Thom's eyes had closed when he was nine or ten and never reopened.

"Okay," I said. "It's a deal."

CHAPTER FORTY-FOUR

"I'll find him," Thom said. "I swear it."

Before I could respond, he disappeared through the wall of the infirmary, and I remained kneeling, staring after him.

On the bed, Loki said, "Your first deal with the dead."

My eyes tracked to him. "Think it was a mistake?"

"Probably not." He raised his paw instinctively, licked it once. "Even if it was, the consequences couldn't be much worse than the hell you've already been through."

I would have smiled if I wasn't in so much pain. Not just physical, but psychic, emotional—everything hurt. When I stood again and turned back to Callum, I wondered what I would say to Umbra.

Umbra.

My fingers tightened on the weapon. She was keeping... a *thing* under her office. A thing that looked like me. I had managed to put it out of my mind until now.

It was time for the headmistress and I to have a talk.

I approached Callum's bed, stroked his forearm. His face remained as expressionless as ever. "Don't worry," I said. "I've got a nine-year-old ghost on the case of your soul."

"I'm sure that brings him such comfort." Loki leapt to the floor, landing lightly. "Clem, there's something you need to see."

I turned, watching him trot toward the open door of the infirmary, feeling a strange foreboding. When I followed him to the doorway, I stood with my hand on it, looking out into the night. Usually I could hear students' voices, the sounds of people walking or chattering, but nobody was out. I didn't hear anyone.

"Where's Neverwink?" I murmured down to Loki.

"Probably with all the other faculty," he said. "Meeting in Umbra's office."

"At this time of night?"

Before Loki could answer, a voice called out: "Clem!" And then, in a flutter of wings, Eva landed right in front of me, pulling me in with her arms around my neck. "You're awake. Just in time."

"For what?" I said, muffled by her hair.

She leaned back, and even in this light, I saw it written on her face. Something bad had happened.

My eyes drifted past her, and I realized far fewer lights were on around the academy grounds. The place was uncommonly dark.

"Umbra," I said. "Where's Umbra?"

"That's just it, Clem," Eva said. "She's..."

Footsteps sounded off to my left, and Aidan materialized from the darkness. "We don't know where she is."

I eyed the two of them in turn. A smile found its way onto my face, disappeared just as quickly when they didn't return it. "She's holed up in her office again?"

Eva shook her head.

"So she's somewhere else on the grounds."

"Nobody's seen her since the day you left," Aidan said, his voice low and serious. "We don't even think she's at the academy."

"You've searched for her?"

"Everyone has," Eva said. "Even the woods all around. She didn't leave a note, no word, nothing."

That wasn't the Umbra I knew. Hell, Milonakis had just gotten done telling me the woman was an agoraphobe. She didn't leave the grounds unless it was to see her family, and that was once or twice a year.

And not without word.

My fingers rubbed over the doorframe. The infirmary had been left open to the night, which meant even Neverwink wasn't thinking. People were anxious. Afraid. I could hear it in Eva's and Aidan's voices.

"Tristan Rathmore has been hunting for her," I said. "For a long time."

"You think he took her?" Eva said.

"I don't know." My eyes tracked over the grounds beyond Eva, as though Umbra would simply appear, her staff tapping over the path. "Whatever happened, she left suddenly."

"Agreed," Aidan said. "The faculty has spent the past few days trying to figure out what to do. Who to appoint as interim head."

Days. *Days.*

I stared up into the canopy. "And the enchantment over the grounds?"

"It's still there," Eva said.

"So she's not dead," I said.

"Probably not," Loki said by my feet. "But who knows about tomorrow?"

My morbid cat. But he was right—we didn't know what would happen tomorrow. If Umbra had been gone for days without a note or any word, then she was unlikely to return tomorrow. Something had happened.

The Backbiter clinked as I shifted its grip in my hand. The academy had to be protected—and I knew what I had to do to keep the students and faculty here safe.

I had to leave.

After all, I had the weapon. If I was going to destroy the Shade, it wouldn't be from Shadow's End.

I straightened, my hand leaving the doorframe. "It's time for me to go."

My two friends went still, a palpable silence descending between us. And then, in a small voice, Eva said, "You're going...?" Her finger pointed straight down.

I couldn't help a grim smile. "I guess I am. You'd think it would be easy enough to get to Hell."

"But you don't have any idea where to go," Aidan said.

"No clue," I said.

Of course, over the years I had read the fables about the entrances to Hell. The ways into the underworld. But there was no place definitive, no route I could google.

I would figure it out. I had to.

Aidan gave a quick exhale, then nodded. "I'll get my stuff."

Eva glanced over at him. "Don't forget the healing book I asked for."

"Got it," he called back.

I stared between them as Aidan disappeared into the night.

"It sounds like they've been planning this," Loki said, as surprised as I should have been. But I wasn't—not deep down.

"Yeah," I murmured. "It does." My eyes shifted to Eva, and my lips parted to speak.

She raised a finger. "Don't start in on a talk-me-out-of-it speech. I'm sick of being on the sidelines, taking all the licks and not getting in any of the hits, especially after our last blowout of a mission. Besides, I'm the only one who spent all year tangibly manipulating a tent, so unless you want to sleep on the ground every night—and I *know* you're a city girl—I'm coming."

"Ooh," Loki said. "I've missed a good tangibly manipulated tent."

I blinked. "Do you mean that olive-green thing you were working on every free moment?"

"Yes," she said, half-sullen. "I mean 'that olive-green thing.'"

Emotion prickled in my chest, behind my eyes. That was what Eva had been working on all year. And that was why Aidan had been stealing books from the library. They had been preparing. They knew I'd need to leave, and they were preparing to come with me.

A certainty crystallized in my chest after four years. I had been building toward this for four years, and now I finally accepted a new truth of my life:

Evanora Whitewillow and Aidan North would never, never leave me.

I swallowed back my speech, leaned forward, and wrapped my arms around Eva, squeezing her. Not saying anything.

"Don't cry," she murmured, patting my back. "We haven't even gotten to Hell yet."

I laughed, realized I was crying a little. When I leaned back, I wiped my eyes with the backs of my hands. "We need to bring Callum with us."

"Easy enough." Eva turned toward our dorm, preparing to take flight. "We may need the twins to help us get him in the tent, but after that, we fold him up and go."

"Fold him up?" I called after her, but she was already flying back to our dorm.

"Don't worry," Loki said, dropping to a seat beside me. "It's much less gruesome than it sounds."

Two days later, we left Shadow's End at night.

Our first stop was the infirmary, where Callum still lay—soulless, asleep. Nurse Neverwink was asleep in her home above the infirmary, so I'd had to enshroud the three of us as we snuck in and over to Callum's bed. Loki waited outside, sitting on a tree branch, keeping watch.

When the three of us stood around him, staring down at the man who weighed more than two of Eva, I'd lifted my eyes to her. "This can't possibly work."

She removed the tent from her backpack, a bundle of olive-green cloth like any other tent from my old life. When she crossed to the aisle and began setting it up, she said, "Oh ye of little faith."

Aidan and I helped, pulling together the skeleton and clipping it all on. When we'd finished, Eva gestured. "Take a look."

I knelt, pushed aside the flap, and found myself at the entryway to a much larger field medic's tent. Inside, six cots were spread at intervals.

I leaned back out, pointing at the thing. "Don't tell me mages didn't steal this concept from pop culture."

Eva leaned close. "Clementine, my dear, pop culture stole it from *us*." She gestured at the tent. "I know it's simple. But I plan to make it bigger, add some rooms, even a kitchenette—"

"It's insane," I said, rising. "You did all that in a year?"

Eva smiled. "More like eight months."

So she *had* been working on this since the start of the school year. God bless Evanora Whitewillow.

Together, the three of us worked to lift Callum from the bed and dragged-pushed him into the tent on the floor. God, he was heavy; how had I managed to drag him through the veil myself? Even three of us struggled.

When he was inside, Eva stood. "Good enough for now."

I hesitated. "We should get him onto a bed in there, at least."

They assented, helped me lift him onto one of the cots in the corner. His feet hung off the end, and Eva groaned. "Now I have to resize all my furniture plans," she grumbled as she crawled back out.

When the other two had left me alone with Callum, I got on my knees beside his cot, took one of his hands in both of mine. I rubbed my thumb over his knuckles and found they were scarred—each and every one.

But he wasn't here to tell me why, or how they'd become that way.

And I wanted to know. I wanted to know all those little stories.

"You saved me," I said to him. "More than once, you saved me. Now it's my turn to save you."

I kissed his knuckles, and then I left him there on the cot.

When I was outside, Aidan began disassembling the tent. I watched queasily as Eva bunched it all up and handed it to me for safe-keeping. Even if I had crafted one myself, pockets in the veil didn't jibe with my basic instincts: big man doesn't fit in tiny space.

"Don't worry." Eva patted my back, quelling *my* anxiety for once. "He's fine in there."

After the infirmary, we had one thing left to do.

Eva waited, still enshrouded in the clearing, as Aidan and I snuck together to the stables. Each of us took a horse: he chose Siren, and I, of course, chose Noir. It wasn't a difficult heist: no one was around, or had been around the stables for days. Even the quartermistress had only shown up twice a day to care for the animals, but everything else was otherwise silent, still.

Classes had stopped when Umbra disappeared. Everything had stopped.

At least one good thing had come of all this: Professor Goodbarrel had become Interim Headmaster Goodbarrel. He somehow managed to smile at students when he passed them, tried to make the world feel as safe as we all knew it wasn't.

Over the past two days, I'd prepared. Gathered my few belongings. Gotten Eva to heal my wounds, which she found bafflingly resistant to her magic. Helped Aidan figure out exactly what he wanted to say to Saoirse, whom he'd promised he'd come back to. Learned how to command the will-o-wisps.

As it turned out, the wisps would do exactly what I wished. I didn't even have to say it; I only had to think it. If I wished for them to stay in my dorm while I snuck out, they hovered obediently near the ceiling. If they had a tether, I hadn't yet figured out how long it was.

Aidan asked me many times over those two days how I'd gotten back to the academy from the vaults. How I'd parted the veil without a nearby point of power. He'd theorized that I might have been over a leyline, but I knew that wasn't the case; no leylines crossed under the room where Callum had been imprisoned.

I only knew one thing: I couldn't have done it before I'd assembled the Backbiter, and I could do it after. And I'd tried multiple times to part the veil with it over the past forty-eight hours, to no avail.

I was missing something.

Mostly, I tried not to think about Tamzin. About where she was, and how she was, and what she was feeling. I failed, of course. I thought about her in what felt like an endless stream, seeing her face, hearing her voice. Wondering if I would ever see her again.

When I brought Noir out of his stall, he jerked his head, eyes gleaming in the moonlight in the aisle. One foot stamped, and from Siren's stall, Aidan said, "Can't you keep him quiet?"

"Nope." I began leading Noir down the aisle, toward the back paddock. There, I mounted up and turned to wait for him. "Better get used to it, North."

When we arrived in the clearing, I came unenshrouded for a moment, clicking my tongue at Loki. He dropped to the ground and took a running leap to catch the end of my cloak, climbing his way up to my shoulder.

"See anyone?" I asked him.

"Nobody," he said. "Well, maybe a fae."

"Are you sure it wasn't Eva?"

He tsked. "Don't insult me."

Eva approached us. "You're ready?"

Beside me, Aidan nodded. "As I'll ever be."

Noir stamped on the grass, and I patted his neck. "Time to go, then." I started Noir forward, Aidan fell into step with Siren, and Eva took to the air above us.

With a thought, the will-o-wisps appeared from my dorm and came rushing toward me. They could slip through any crack, I'd found. And if there were no cracks, they could pass through any wall. They could travel at incredible speeds—from the academy all the way to Edinburgh in minutes—and best of all, my magic came easier.

And I could enshroud them along with me.

As I was sending the enshroudment over all of us, someone stepped out from the shadows, stood with hands on hips, staring us down.

I sent the wisps over to provide some light, and they illuminated Liara's severe face in blue.

Her eyes lifted. "You going to sic them on me again?"

"What are you doing out here?" I whisper-hissed, the wisps flying back to me.

She came closer, arms folding now. "You don't really expect to leave without me."

"And why's that?"

"Do you even have any idea where to go first?" Her head tilted. "Be honest."

"And you do?" Aidan said from atop Siren.

"I do, actually." Her wings brought her up to a hover, and I glimpsed a satchel over her shoulder, her cloak waving in the breeze.

She had prepared for this, too.

Liara's chin lowered as she stared at me. "There's someone you need to meet, Clementine."

END OF BOOK 4

BOOK 5: *She's a real witch, and even Hell can't hold her.* Clementine's adventure as a fire witch concludes in the fifth and final novel in the Academy of Shadowed Magic series.

Good Witches Don't Die is available to read on Amazon.

FREE SHORT STORY: Liara Youngblood and Lucian the demon prince clash in the prequel story *The Fae and the Demon*.

Join S.W. Clarke's reader newsletter and get *The Fae and the Demon* for FREE only at subscribepage.com/swclarke.

AFTERWORD

Hello friend,

Long ago, I learned the concept of writing what you know. And while it was taught to me as a kind of instruction—you *should* write what you know—it's with this series I came to a realization:

It's not an instruction. It's a prophecy.

Because no matter who my characters are, or where on Earth I put them, I'm always circling (obsessively, endlessly) one concept: Safety. What it means to be safe. To trust. To be good.

Because what I knew early on in life was a lack of safety, a lack of trust in myself and others. It's why I create moonstones. Enchanted bubbles. Enshroudments.

Maybe you know what I mean. It's why certain books—movies—music speak to us, why we keep revisiting the same concepts throughout our lives.

They are *what we know*, and if you've struggled with feeling safe, with feeling trust, then maybe you've felt the deep and strangely comforting/discomforting dichotomy of experiencing what we know in other people's art.

For those of you who have struggled—or are struggling—like Clementine: I see you. I see you.

As promised, here's the soundtrack to *Good Witches Don't Steal*: https://open.spotify.com/playlist/6QaIf4JXeNWeOECzyIGJCB?si= 626c4571e2504917.

Until next time—

Shavonne

ABOUT THE AUTHOR

S.W. Clarke is a fantasy romance and urban fantasy author. She lives in a magical tree (well, we all have dreams, don't we?) with her partner and two identical, unrelated cats. She writes to inhabit the lives of the smartest, bravest women her brain can conjure.

Want to be notified of her latest releases? Join her newsletter!

facebook.com/authorswclarke

instagram.com/authorswclarke